HOLLYWOOD SECRET

BOOK I OF THE DISCREET DUET

NICOLE FRENCH

This is a work of fiction. Names, characters, organizations, places, events, and incidents are either products of the author's imagination or rendered fictitiously. Any resemblance to real people or events is purely coincidental.

ISBN: 978-1-950663-18-7

www.nicolefrenchromance.com

To my mom, who loved the lake,

and

Patricia and Danielle, who loved Will more than anyone.

PROLOGUE

May 7, 2014
The New York Times

Fitz Baker, Actor, Missing After Boating Accident off Maine Coast

Fitzwilliam "Fitz" Baker, whose standout performance in last year's "The Dwelling" earned him an Oscar nomination, disappeared off the coast of Maine last weekend. His catamaran was found wrecked off a particularly treacherous channel, and Mr. Baker's body has not been recovered after an extensive search. He would have been 25 in June.

After more than a week of looking, the Maine Coast Guard finally called off the search. Emilio Adams, the detective assigned to the case, stated, "At this time we have no reason to suspect foul play. It appears to be a boating trip gone bad. We have no choice but to presume Mr. Baker dead."

Mr. Baker grew up outside of Stamford, Connecticut, where he was discovered as a young talent in a local mall during an open call for child auditions. His early work in commercials led him to a part in the popular sitcom, "Bailey's Life," playing the child prodigy, Nick Bailey. The show was canceled in its fifth season after Mr. Baker's mother, Tricia Owens-Baker, could not come to an agreement with the network about his contract renewal.

Mr. Baker, however, had already started moving on to consistent film roles and had his first breakout performance in the high school comedy, "Drama Camp," at the age of 17. From there he began appearing in more serious roles, demonstrating his range in such films as the Boston legal drama, "City on a Hill," and the Revolutionary War epic, "State of Liberty."

But it was his last film, directed by legendary director Corbyn Creighton, that earned Mr. Baker his first major critical recognition with Golden Globe and SAG awards for Best Actor in a Drama, as well as a Best Actor Oscar nomination. After Mr. Baker's performance as a recovering alcoholic and AIDS victim in "The Dwelling," Creighton called him "this generation's Brad Pitt" for the combination of humor, wit, and magnetism he brought to the screen. Creighton said yesterday that, "a light in the darkness of the world has been extinguished. Fitz will be dearly missed."

But it wasn't all bright lights and awards for the charismatic young actor. Mr. Baker had acknowledged publicly that he suffered from debilitating anxiety attacks, which often prevented him from taking part in major press events unless under the influence of some kind of substance. After suffering a near-fatal attack from an obsessive fan in 2011, Mr. Baker had become quite reclusive, traveling only with a large security entourage and generally keeping to his 25-acre compound in Vermont when not traveling for his job.

In an interview with *The New York Times* last month, he admitted that he was trying, for the first time in his life, to cope with the effects of his anxiety without medication, drugs, or alcohol. Mr. Baker stated, "I don't want to live my life in a haze. For better or for worse, I need to face my life with my eyes wide open."

Exactly four weeks later, his boat was found in pieces on the rocky Maine channel.

"It just makes no sense," Tricia Owens-Baker, his mother, said in tears after the search was called off yesterday. "He was an expert sailor and swam like Michael Phelps. There is just no way he drowned out there. I don't believe it."

"We'll never stop looking for our son," added Michael Baker, his father. "Never."

I would not wish the burning blaze
Of fame around a restless world,
The thunder and the storm of praise
In crowded tumults heard and hurled.

— John Clare, "Idle Fame"

CHAPTER ONE

Dust flew into the air, a dry, hot flurry. I turned at the familiar fork in the road and the car kicked up even more.

Hot. Hellfire and damnation, *hot*. My skin was "glowing" if you were polite, which at the moment I was not, so really I was sweating like a pig. I'd been driving for three days at a breakneck speed from New York with a busted taillight and a broken air conditioner, but none of that had been an issue until I'd crossed the Idaho border into the city limits of my hometown: sleepy Newman Lake. And of course—*of course*—the last five minutes would be the worst. Because that was just the kind of luck I was having. That was just the kind of life I was having.

I rolled down my window, eager to let in some of the breeze off the lake where I grew up. I squinted at the sun-dappled surface, reveled in the low rustle of the cattails and shoulder-high tules, inhaled the brackish scent of lily pads abloom with massive white flowers. I wasn't sure I could call it home anymore, since I hadn't set foot anywhere near the West Coast in about six years, when I'd last visited home and given my mother an ultimatum: get sober or get a new daughter. But at the tail end of my trek and four years that would ruin anyone's resolve, Newman Lake was the only refuge I had. Funny how ultimatums lose their potency when you're equal parts broke and broken.

My humble Passat hatchback was packed with every belonging I had to take or couldn't sell before leaving the city. My life was in that car, in more ways than one.

Clothes.

Books.

Guitars.

They were all locked away in their cases and had been for a while. Three weeks, exactly, since I last played, which was the longest I'd ever gone without tickling the strings since I'd picked up my first guitar at age seven. The old Yamaha was a birthday present Mama had found at a yard sale, and it was still one of the best guitars I'd ever had, sound-wise. Playing it used to make me feel like I was flying, but now just the idea was like dead weight.

Sometimes I could still hear my name blaring over the loudspeakers of the club. Maggie Sharp. Once a promising singer/songwriter, or so said my manager, Calliope Jackson, when she would announce me before my gigs. To A&R reps. Really, anyone who would listen. Now I was just *that* girl.

The one who screwed up her chance.

The one who ran off stage.

The one who ruined her entire career, all her dreams…over a man.

Flower…

The word drifted through my mind, his voice slithering between memories like the snake he was. Theo del Conte. I could still hear the pet names he used, feel the tender touch that gradually turned wicked. I turned a corner, past the ramshackle Barrett house with its yard full of daisies. Fear knotted in my stomach, though I knew Theo couldn't find me here. I punched the gas, urging the bald tires to squeal on the pavement, blocking out the low thrum of his voice. Three more turns and I'd be safe at last. In a place where I could lick my wounds in peace. And, of course, in shame.

The truth was, coming back to Newman Lake was the last thing I ever thought I'd be doing. Ten years ago, if you had asked me where I thought I'd be at twenty-six, I would have said making music with the greats and hopefully on tour. Nobody plans on failing. Coming home to take care of an alcoholic mother. Figuring out what the hell to do with your life when all your dreams are nothing but a faint vapor.

At the top of the last winding curve, I turned onto the familiar gravel road that led down to three parking spots terraced into the side of a steep hill. Those were new—must have been put in when Mama got the idea to start the bed and breakfast a few years back. That was during her Alan phase. Mama had a phase for every man she was with, and they were good until they weren't anymore. That was usually when I would get a phone call begging me to come home for a visit. Phone calls that were laced with gin; messages I'd guiltily erase before I heard all of them. Before they turned from pleading to nasty.

Everything about the old place looked the same. The tall pine trees scaling down the rocky hillside to the water, the thatches of nettles and wildflowers blooming from the crevices of massive boulders. The chicken coop just above the main house, the two small outer cottages surveying the rest of the property, and a sleeping shack perched on the point below. It was too big, really, for a single woman in her early fifties to maintain, the remnants of her grandfather's dream of opening a grand resort with his prospecting money. The resort had gone bust in a matter of years, but the dream remained, along with the estate, passed down through the next two generations until landing in my mother's lap.

I parked my car next to Mama's old Pathfinder and inhaled a deep breath of the warm lake air, enjoying the familiar scent of pine trees, freshly turned dirt, and smoke from a barbecue somewhere. The occasional hum of a boat punctuated the soothing chime of waves while the chickens clucked from their roosts. I'd moved out eight years ago, and it had been six since I'd last visited. Six years since I told my mother she had to sober up before I'd ever return.

Just one more way I turned out to be a liar.

I grabbed my purse and a couple of duffel bags, then locked the car before starting down to the house. Seventy-three stairs. I only knew because I used to run them daily, up and down ten times every morning except during the winter. Track and swim were easy to practice when I was in high school, harder to maintain when I left. You can pretty much run anywhere, though I found myself doing it less and less often the longer I lived in New York. I hadn't swum anywhere in that concrete menagerie.

But home didn't hit me—didn't *really* hit me—until I wound around the small concrete path at the bottom of the stairs and saw the small yellow house where I grew up. The deck looked the same, with two weathered Adirondack chairs facing the lake that shimmered through the willow tree boughs. There was a small terra cotta chimney in one corner, a gas barbecue in the other, and a variety of planters, all bursting with bright blooms and green foliage. Emmylou Harris crooned from the speakers mounted above the sliding glass doors, open except for the screen. Mama used to wonder why I ever wanted to be a musician. She never realized it was her record collection that inspired me in the first place.

The scent of roasting chicken wafted through the screen door. Well, then. At six o'clock at night, she was sober enough to cook. I took it as a good sign.

"Mama?" I called, dropping my bags.

"Back here!"

I walked around to the back of the house, where I found my mother, Eloise Sharp, struggling to move a huge plastic rain barrel under a drainpipe.

"Ouch!" she yelped, as she heaved again unsuccessfully and broke a nail in the process. "Dag nabbit!" She spotted me just as she stuck the wounded digit into her mouth. Nevertheless, her face lit up, and her hands flew to her hips. "Well, who's come to visit? Is that my daughter I see there?"

I nodded, unaccountably flushed. "Hi, Mama."

This was Ellie Sharp's magic. She always had the power to make everyone she talked to feel like the center of the universe. Even if you hadn't seen her in six years. Even if the last time she saw you, she was crying in a heap on the ground while you walked away, nursing a slapped cheek.

"You just wait there, baby," she said before she replaced her glove, squatted back down, and shoved her whole body against the barrel. "Mama's gotta finish her chore, and then I'm gonna give you the biggest hug and kiss you've ever seen."

With a great grunt, she pushed again. The rain barrel stayed put.

"Mama, why don't I help you with that?" I asked, starting toward her.

She waved a hand at me. "I can do it, Maggie Mae. Just give us a second." She took a deep breath and stared down at the barrel with immense hatred. "I'll admit, this is the kind of thing that makes me wish I still had a man around. Say what you want about Alan, but he did help me take care of the place, the goddamn bastard."

I blinked. That was new. My whole life Mama called herself a church-going woman. Despite her more unsavory habits, she always said things like "heck" and "dag nabbit," but now apparently had a mouth like a sailor.

As if the mild profanity inspired her, Mama gave one last almighty push and managed to reposition the barrel correctly under the spout. She swiped a handkerchief across her forehead under the fringe of carefully dyed brown bangs. The bones of her wrist pressed knobby through the skin. We were both thinner than we should have been.

With a sigh of relief, she weaved her way back to the deck.

"Let me look at you, baby girl," she said as she shucked her gloves onto a bench and turned to face me.

She was a tall woman, with thin legs her best friend, Barb, always said looked like a stork's. Her worn gardening pants that looked like they were probably Alan's or some other lover's hung loose on her hips. She reached out to take my hands, holding my arms open like a bird's wingspan. Her familiar touch, which I hadn't felt in so long, was electric.

"You're too thin, Margaret," she noted as she perused my spare frame. "I think you need a cookie. Or four."

I pulled my arms back and held them around my ribs. I was several inches shorter than her, but we had the same delicate bone structure. She used to say I must have gotten my insides from her and my outsides—the skin that was tanner than not, the deep brown eyes, the unruly dark hair—from my father. Hard to say, considering I had no idea who the man actually was. But yeah, a few pounds gained or lost showed more on me than it did on her.

"You're one to talk," I retorted. "You must have lost, what, twenty pounds? Thirty since…everything?"

"And we weren't exactly big women before, were we?" she agreed with a sad nod as she sat down in one of the chairs. "Well, that's what having dirty, lying, good-for-nothing shitbags around does to you, don't it? Sucks the life right out of you."

I sank into the chair beside her. I didn't know the whole story about what had happened with Alan—one never really did with Ellie Sharp. I'd never met the man, only heard the stories at first of how he'd wooed her, taken her to expensive dinners and on expensive trips, and slowly convinced her to share just about everything she had with him before he'd up and left. Everything but the house. I didn't know if Alan was as bad a guy as Mama made him out to be. Maybe he just got tired of living with a drunk. Or maybe he was something worse.

I closed my eyes, breathing in the warm, familiar air of the lake. Mama wasn't wrong. I did feel like the life had been sucked out of me. I felt like a shell of myself, and had for years now.

Mama looked at me sadly. She didn't know the whole story that had happened with Theo, but she knew enough. Had heard my choked sobs over the phone. Had shared a few hushed phone calls with Calliope.

"I hate that you know what this feels like, but I'm glad you're here." She reached out and patted my hand. "You're safe now, honey. We both are. Just have to keep tellin' ourselves that until we can believe it."

Suddenly, I felt exhausted. The fatigue of the long car ride, the frantic goodbye to the friends who shoved wads of ones and fives in my pocket to help me get here, the fear at every gas station and rest stop that Theo would show up with some new threat, even if he was still in jail for what he did. But really, it was the loss that weighed me down the most. The loss, the complete and utter loss, of everything I had built since striking out on my own. The music—*my* music—was gone.

All of it came crashing down at once. A lone tear dripped down my cheek, quickly followed by more. It had been so, so long since I truly felt safe.

"That showcase-thing was just a few weeks ago, wasn't it?" Mama asked, still gripping my hand.

I sniffed back a few tears, recovering quickly. We'd never been huggers, Mama and I. *Talk it out,* she'd always say. *Get it out, and let it go.*

"Yeah," I sniffled. "It was."

"And he showed up, did he? That's what finally sent you home?"

I shook my head. "N-no. I just thought he did."

She already knew the story. I'd told it to her on Saturday when Calliope, my manager, and I were packing everything I owned. Four years prior, I'd met Theodore del Conte, son of Max del Conte, CEO of Del Conte Entertainment, which owned one of the biggest independent labels in the world. We met at one of my shows—my biggest show to date, actually, where I'd had the luck to sub as an opening act for a major artist. Theo had been there with his father and began tracking me. We met a few months later, and he quickly consumed my life. He accompanied me on the short tour, then whisked me back to New York. In less than two months, I went from being just another starving artist in the city to being Theo del Conte's girl, from sharing a two-bedroom apartment with three other women to living in his loft in Soho. I would have done anything for him. And he knew it.

Things were good for a while. But then they turned bad quickly and lasted much longer. It had started with a shove here, a grab there, and then progressed to much, much more. So much that when I did finally manage my escape, I had enough documented evidence to press charges. It took me close to a year in court and a completely depleted savings account, but I won. Theo was behind bars. But that didn't stop me from seeing him everywhere I went. Or forgetting so much of who or what I had been before him.

The showcase was supposed to be my grand reentry into the scene. I still had some notoriety as Theo's ex-girl. People came to see me the same way they would come to see a car wreck, but Calliope said it didn't matter. They were there. Theo was not. There was no one left to threaten me. Ruin me.

Until, of course, I did that myself.

"Just as I was about to start, I saw him," I said to Mama. "I was already a mess. I fell on my way to the club—tripped on the sidewalk. Nerves. My wrist was already hurting, and it reminded me of one of those times when he—you know. And then, Mama, I know he's in jail. I know he's locked up. But I swear, I saw his face, and, Mama...God...y-you know?"

I focused on breathing through the stutter that had emerged over the last four years. I couldn't cry. There was no crying in this house. When I was little that was a sure way to get a smack on the ear. So I sucked in air and hissed it out. Mama just nodded and murmured her agreement. She knew. Of course she knew.

"I—I just froze," I whispered. "My hand slipped. I screwed up. The biggest night of my career, and I messed it up because I was scared. And now…it's over."

"Maggie, come now," Mama put in. "It was one show. I'm sure with time you could get somethin' else together. Call the men back, have them come watch you again."

"No, Mama," I replied lamely. "You don't get another chance like that."

It was supposed to be a night about celebrating the fact that I had moved on from the man who had torn me down, bit by bit, for years. But instead, I'd had to watch all of my dreams tumble down around me too.

Mama tapped a fingernail on the wood armrest. "Hmmm. Well, we'll see."

I gave her a grim smile, and she tilted her head to the side, as if checking me over for something she'd missed.

"People come around," she said kindly. "You did."

I didn't want to tell her that I wouldn't have come unless I'd had no other choice. That I had wanted to keep my promise—hold her to sobriety or stay out of her life. But principles are luxuries for people with money, like valet parking or fancy French cheese. I didn't have time for them anymore. I just needed to be home.

"Oh, honey, come on. Let's get you settled. You look like you need a nice long sleep, and then you'll want to see the lake. Barb and Jimmy are coming with the boat for a cocktail cruise, and we'll have just the thing to brighten you up."

I leaned my head back in the chair and stared up at the sky. Mama chattered on, but all I could think about was that she was doing the same thing she always did: solving her problems with friends. Parties. Drink. But instead of fighting it, trying to talk her out of it like I used to, I was far too tired to care.

CHAPTER TWO

Chicken shit really, really stinks. It was one of the things I'd managed to block out in the last six years, but now that I was ankle-deep in the stuff, the memories of just how much I'd always hated mucking out the coop were vividly clear.

"Shit!" I yelped as a big glop of it fell down the top of my boot. "Oh, gross!"

In return, I received a loud cluck from the ringleader of the brood, which sounded suspiciously like laughter.

"Oh, shut it, Glinda," I snapped at the busty bird, named for the rosy tips of her mostly white feathers that made her look like she was wearing a bubblegum-pink gown. That, combined with the jaunty pink comb crowning her head, recalled the good witch from *The Wizard of Oz*.

Unlike her namesake, however, Glinda was most certainly a force of evil. Having done her very best to thwart every attempt to clean up the coop, she'd burrowed into the dirt and shit at the bottom of the building. I had to lock her in the area normally reserved for new chicks while I shoveled the last of the mess into the compost barrel. A few more scoops, and I was done.

It was the fourth large chore, along with cleaning the gutters, fixing some of the Adirondack chairs, and straightening the wood pile, that I'd done on the property that day. Mom wasted no time putting me to work once I asked what needed to be done while she left for her morning appointments at the salon. Unlike me, she hadn't totally given up on her dreams, and the reality was, she needed to make some money now that she didn't have her boyfriend's income to live on. So it was back to cutting hair for her while I stayed home, knee-deep in chicken crap.

It wasn't really the restful sanctuary I had hoped for, but even if the work was hard, it was familiar. At the end, I could see exactly what I'd achieved.

I tossed the last shovelful into the composter, then spread fresh hay at the perimeter of the outdoor caged area and inside the coop. After I freed Glinda to chase the other birds, I headed back down the hill to put away the shovel and cool off in the lake.

Down on the main dock, I stripped off my sweaty work clothes until I was just in my sports bra and underwear, then tugged my dark brown hair from its ponytail and dove into the water. It was warm again for the beginning of June—more like July or even August. "Global warming, even if some of these yahoos out here don't believe it," Mama said with a snort the night before. Global warming or not, the water felt perfect as I swam out to the floating dock by the five mile per hour marker. Both our docks were floating a little crooked—they had waterlogged buoys that need to be replaced. Also on the list.

I took a few laps between them, then climbed onto the floating one and lay on the warm wood slats, gazing up at scattered white clouds.

The lake was quiet. The water was fairly still, even in late afternoon, with only a few boats here and there rippling over its surface. Come the weekend, people from Spokane and Coeur d'Alene would bring their boats and jet skis, which would echo everywhere and cause larger waves from their wakes to crash against each shore. But just then, I could close my eyes and listen to the sound of an occasional fish jump and the distant cry of the osprey nesting in the hills.

"Maggie Mae!"

And, apparently, my mother, back from work already.

I tipped my head back toward the main dock, where Mama waved and held up the basket of eggs I had just brought down from the coop.

"Can you take the eggs to the store?" she called over the water. "And get some baking stuff too while you're at it? I'm all out."

I lay back down and sighed up at the clouds. No rest for the weary.

"Margaret!"

"I'm coming!" I yelled back, then rolled off the dock and into the water to start my next task.

NEWMAN LAKE BOASTED one teeny store located at the far end of a small marina where vacationers could store their boats. It was about a mile from the house—an easy walk this time of day, especially when the weather was starting to cool for the evening.

"Well, look at what the cat dragged in!" Cathy, one of the owners, greeted me from behind the counter that stored both fishing bait and ice cream sandwiches.

"Hiya, Cathy," I said as I leaned over the counter to accept a hug.

Cathy was maybe ten years older than me, and started living at the lake full time when her father died and left her the store. Since she had gotten a divorce just before that, it was strangely good timing, despite the loss. I might not have been back for six years, but that didn't stop Mama from giving me all the gossip.

"Look at you, honey," Cathy said as she combed a few fingers through my hair. "You finally figured out what to do with this hair of yours. It looks lovely."

I patted self-consciously at the long, mostly straight waves drying down my back. My natural hair, which was curly to the point of unmanageable, had earned me a lot of crap over the years. Despite the fact that my mother was a hairdresser, my hair had been the bane of both our existences through most of my adolescence. It wasn't until I moved to New York, met Calliope, and let her escort me to a hair salon uptown that I finally learned how to take care of it the right way. To get ready for my showcase, I had sprung for a keratin treatment a few weeks ago, but it was already starting to wash out a bit, and in a few weeks, I'd be back to ignoring my hairbrush and using Moroccan oil treatments.

It took me that long too, to really understand myself as a woman of color in the first place. My whole life, people would ask me what I was. Where I was from. But if my hair was straightened or I had on the right makeup, sometimes they wouldn't. On the outside, I looked a lot like my mom in the face. We had the same light skin, though mine had more than a touch of brown in it, the same deep brown eyes, though mine were a little darker, the same button nose and full lips, though mine were just a little more pronounced. But where her hair was a light brown that verged on blonde and was manageably wavy, mine was a darker brown mass of curls. I didn't look white, and I didn't look black or Hispanic, or whatever was responsible for half my genes. I just looked…different.

She didn't say it, but other people did. Illegitimate. Bastard. I was born out of countless one-night stands, out of hundreds of careless nights. The only thing either of us knew for sure was that my father wasn't white, though that didn't narrow it down much. And everyone around us made sure I knew it.

These were the things Mama never knew. It was hard enough helping my mother recover from her hangovers without complaining about the way kids at school called me Simba because of the way my corkscrew curls stuck out around my face. And I definitely didn't tell her about the times some of them, even with their parents not five feet away, called me the n-word. Wetback. Chink. Whatever seemed to occur to them that day —they were never very original.

No. I definitely didn't tell her about that. But it was one of the main reasons why Newman Lake, even if it was where I grew up, never quite felt like home. And Cathy's touch, though it was intended to be kind, only reminded me of that.

"Lemme guess," Cathy said. "Ellie's out of baking soda again. I swear, I'm going to gain another twenty pounds with all the cookies she brings by the house."

I nodded. Mom did have a habit of baking, especially when she got a little tipsy. It was a bittersweet thing. When I was a kid, I'd wake up in the middle of the night to the smell of chocolate chip cookies. I'd be excited, because what kid doesn't like cookies, but dread it at the same time, because I knew I'd find her passed out on the couch. I wouldn't be able to sleep until I knew she was done and the house wasn't going to burn down.

I also ate a lot of burned cookies.

"I've got some eggs for you too," I confirmed. "Mama said you've got a bunch of buyers these days."

Cathy eagerly took the carton from me. "Yes, ma'am. All these young couples out from Seattle for the summer. Would you believe they'll buy a carton of eggs for six whole dollars? I swear, you put organic on anything, people will pay double for it."

I chuckled. She had no idea. Cathy's eyes would have probably fallen out of her head if she saw what some of the grocery stores in New York charged for "premium" produce.

"Hey, Cath, what's this?" I picked up a neon-pink flyer from the stack sitting on a clipboard next to the cash register.

"Oh, that's for the new triathlon event the inn is starting this year. Don and Linda Forster are trying to bring in some more tourists, I guess. Their boy—you remember Lucas, don't you, hon?—got the bug for marketing last year."

I nodded back and turned away to avoid her knowing look. Of course I remembered Lucas. Lucas was my first boyfriend. The one who took my virginity in my room one lonely night while Mama was at the bar. For so long, Lucas was the one who kept me safe. When we were in high school, he was the type of guy people wanted to be around—a pickup truck driving, football-playing golden boy, and so when I was with him, people wouldn't call me names. I stopped being the one "colored girl" in our class and became Lucas Forster's girlfriend. It traded one limited identity for another, but the latter was far preferable.

And then I got my scholarship to NYU and left him and Newman Lake behind. I hadn't meant to break his heart, but deep down, I think I always knew I would. Because as much as Lucas Forster had been in love with me, it hadn't been enough to keep me here. Now he was just one more person I hadn't seen in six years. We hadn't even spoken once since I left.

Like my thoughts called a ghost from its grave, the bell over the store door jingled, and the man himself walked in.

Lucas looked the same as he ever did. A little more filled out, sure. Maybe a little softer, with a slight belly that pressed at the bottom of his t-shirt. But he still had the same smattering of brown stubble over his rounded jaw. Still the same old Mariners cap perched on the crown of his head. Still the same big shoulders that would shelter me from a world that was less than kind.

When he caught sight of me, he stopped in front of the beer case, jaw dropped.

"Holy…Maggie, is that you?"

I smiled shyly and gave an awkward wave. "Hey, Luke. Yeah, I'm home for a little while."

"Dang…wow." His eyes roved over me openly, like he was checking for cracks. He pushed off his cap, revealing a severely receding hairline, then quickly put it back on. "You look good. I, um, like your hair like that."

I fingered the half-dried waves again. I didn't know why, but it made me feel weird to hear him say that. Lucas's sisters both had pin-straight hair, and they were always flat-ironing mine when I would come over. Back then, Lucas would tell me I looked beautiful no matter what. Of course, that was usually when I was sitting on top of him in the bed of his pickup. It's hard to take compliments seriously when the guy is trying to sneak a hand down your jeans.

"Thanks," I said. "It's temporary. How, um, how are you?"

"Good. Good." He reached into the case and pulled out a six-pack of Bud. "Just, you know, getting ready to take over the inn, doing some contracting on the side. Dad's retiring next year, so he and Mom are stepping back."

I nodded. "That's great." It was pretty much what I would have expected. Don and Linda owned the Forster Inn, the single lodging accommodation on Newman Lake—a big, five-bedroom house that had been converted to a bed and breakfast years ago, plus a camping "resort" that basically just allowed people to park their campers or pitch a tent on their five acres of lakeside property at the north end.

Lucas removed his cap again to rub his forehead, revealing just how far back that hairline went now. It wasn't unexpected—his dad was totally bald, and Lucas was already losing hair when we were in high school.

"You thinking of doing it?" He pointed at the flyer in my hand. "Kick everyone's ass again, like the old days?"

I looked down at the paper. *Compete in the first annual Newman Lake Triathlon this Fourth of July!* It was only about a month away.

Once upon a time, I had been a decent athlete. Good enough to get myself a few scholarship offers to state schools, all of which I had turned down when I'd gained acceptance at NYU. "Like a workhorse," my coaches had said. It wasn't until I left Spokane that the undertones of that particular term, directed at someone who looked like me, would really sink in.

I shrugged. "I doubt it. I'm not much of a swimmer anymore. And I haven't been on a bike in years. I'd probably fall over during the transitions."

Lucas looked me over frankly. "You look pretty fit to me."

Cathy hummed, barely masking her grin at the comment. She was leaned over the counter, chin propped on her hands while she watched us like her favorite soap opera.

I blushed. "Um, thanks."

"I just, uh, I just mean that you used to like it, didn't you? Racing?"

His fumbling once again returned me to those heady days in the back of his truck. Lucas, always caring and tender with me, but always so unsure. Though we had been together for close to two years, and were one of those couples people assumed would "end up together," whatever that meant, there had always been that hint of uncertainty when he approached my character. Every statement ended with a question. I had been left to provide the answers.

Still looking at the flyer, I nodded. "Yeah," I said softly. "I did."

It was the truth. If music had been one constant in my life, sports had been the other. I had given up the latter when I moved to New York to pursue the former. But now that part of my life was over. Maybe it was time to return to rediscover something else that made me tick.

I looked up at Lucas. "All right, sure. Count me in."

Lucas grinned. "Awesome. Just put your name over there on the sign-up, and I'll be in touch."

"Already on it!" Cathy called out from the register, scribbling my name and Mama's number in the appropriate columns.

I turned back to Lucas with a sheepish smile. "Sounds good."

"So, your mom, how's she doing? We heard about Alan leaving and everything..."

Inwardly, I grimaced. The gossip of this place was something else I never missed. Didn't matter how hard you tried—everyone always knew your business. While Mama has yet to reveal the whole story, I could guess what probably happened. Clothes tossed out the window. Shouts that echoed over the water. Shit-talking on a cocktail cruise. She and the Forsters didn't exactly run in the same circles, but they still attended the same church. And it was a small town. A very, very small town.

"She's all right," I said. "We're trying to get the property cleaned up so she can move forward with the B and B licensing. There's a lot to do, though. The work that Alan did was pretty shoddy to begin with, and he walked off with a lot of their savings."

Lucas frowned sympathetically, but he didn't seem surprised. "Sorry to hear that. I'll come by and see if there is anything I can help with."

"No, that's okay," I replied quickly. "You don't have to do that. Especially since we'll be your competitor and everything."

In response, all I got was a lopsided smile that told me neither he nor anyone else on the lake really believed that Ellie Sharp would be able to run a bed and breakfast. And really, they were probably right. But it didn't make me any less irritated.

"I'll stop by," Lucas said again, though this time his smile was warmer.

I blinked, but saw no sign of ulterior motive. It was just Lucas, as kind and straightforward as always. Maybe I really had been in New York for too long.

Slowly, I smiled back. "Okay, then. I'll, um, tell Mama you're coming."

Lucas tipped his hat at me, then paid for his beer and waved to Cathy on his way out. Cathy and I both watched until the bell over the door rang after him.

I turned to Cathy, who was examining me with far too much enthusiasm. I sighed. "How much do I owe you, Cath?"

She pushed off the counter, opened a small laminated binder, and ran a finger down the price list on the first page. "Six fifty minus four for the eggs—that's your cut—is two fifty." She pulled out a calculator to finish the math. "With tax, that's two seventy-two for the sugar and soda."

I dug out three dollars from my wallet and set them on the counter. "Keep the change."

CHAPTER THREE

"It all needs a lot of work, Mama. I don't know how else to say it."

I plopped into one of the chairs on the front lawn and handed Mama a bottle of water, hoping to temper the rum and Coke she was already nursing after work today. I took a long drink from my own bottle and used the bottom of my stained t-shirt to wipe sweat off my brow. Before sweeping and collecting dried pine needles around the cottages, I finished reviewing the list of Mama's maintenance requests and had made a list of my own. If she was serious about turning this place into a B&B, there was so, so much to be done. But for some reason, the looks on Cathy's and Lucas's faces just made me that much more determined to help her do it.

The water bottle toppled over on the grass while Mama took a long sip of her drink. She grimaced and shook her head, her bangs bouncing slightly. "Don't sugarcoat it, Maggie Mae. Lay it on me now."

I sighed. Over the last few days, I'd been combing through all of the requirements needed to get this business off the ground, and Lucas had come by earlier to walk around the property with me, doing an informal inspection. Mama's pet project had morphed into my crusade.

"You and Alan did some nice cosmetic stuff on the property with the paint and the landscaping. But the two outer cottages need new plumbing since last winter's freeze, and they both look like they have some pretty bad flood damage from the spring flooding that will probably require us to replace the drywall completely. All three houses need new roofs, but maybe we can get away with some patching. I don't know. On top of that, if you want to get licensed, there are a bunch of things that have to be done to the stairs, to the electric and heating systems, all in order to get the place up to code."

I looked to Mama, who sipped nervously on her cocktail. I knew what she was thinking. Repairs meant money, and money was what neither of us had at the moment.

"This is beyond me, Mama," I admitted. "I can paint and clean. Some minor landscaping, help with the livestock. But these are major infrastructural problems. You need someone who can help you with this stuff now, even if we don't try for the B&B thing."

"And with what money am I supposed to do that, Margaret?" she bit out. She stared angrily out at the lake, refusing to meet my imploring gaze.

"Mom," I said gently. "We'll figure it out."

I didn't know what else to say. She didn't move, likely hearing the uncertainty in my voice. I reached out and touched her arm gently, causing her to look down at my fingers on her freckled forearm. When she finally looked back up, her eyes shone angrily with a fine gloss of tears. Tears and drink. Always drink.

I removed my hand.

"That goddamn bastard," she muttered fiercely. "Left me in this mess. We sunk everything into this place, Maggie. *Everything*. I've got nothing left. Do you understand that?"

I didn't have to answer. I'd seen the state of her finances. She had liquidated her entire 401k in order to finance the remodel on the property, all wasted through Alan's bad investment schemes and debt maneuvering. Just before he left, Mama filed bankruptcy. This property was all she had left, and only because it was her home.

She looked back at the lake, taking deep breaths. She slid the sunglasses resting on her head down over her eyes, masking her emotions while she drained the rest of her glass. I stood up, sensing her need to be alone. You couldn't talk to her when she was like this, though

I'd almost certainly be picking her up off the couch in another few hours.

"I'm going to go for a run," I said. "I'll take a quick look in the storage shack to see if there is anything worth selling on my way up to the road." It was a feeble attempt to make things right, but I already knew I'd be calling Lucas tomorrow. So much for independence.

"There's not," Mama snapped. "But you take your time. Take the whole evening if you need. Honestly, Maggie, I just want to be alone without you bothering me for once."

I tried not to let her words hurt, though the sharpness in her voice reminded me of why I left in the first place. And just how much worse it could get.

"I'll look anyway," I said quietly. Then I patted her on the shoulder and left.

IT TURNED out that Mama was right—all that was left in storage were boxes of yard sale knickknacks, my childhood paraphernalia, and a few pieces of miscellaneous furniture and other odds and ends. Certainly nothing of monetary value.

But if I was being honest, that wasn't what I was looking for anyway. I found those things right away: a bag of the gear I once used to swim laps across the lake in the early morning, and my old bike, resting in the back next to a pump. Nothing was too out of shape. The swimmer's buoys just needed to be pumped up, and the bike, though definitely in need of a tune-up, still seemed rideable. Thinking vaguely of the triathlon flyer, I decided a ride sounded better than a run. I used to cycle the hilly twenty-eight miles around the lake on a regular basis. If I could still do it now, maybe doing a triathlon wasn't so far-fetched. And I couldn't ask for a better distraction.

After pumping up the tires, I wheeled the bike up to the road. Some cloud cover had finally settled across the skies after almost a week of sweat-inducing sunshine. I turned left down the backside of the hill, basking in the peace of the lake and a sense of freedom I hadn't felt in years.

Come back soon, Flower.

It was what he always said anytime I left him. For a walk. A run. A gig. A job. In the time we lived together, I had stopped running or doing anything outside completely, locked instead in his lavish apartment. I was lucky if I found an hour a week to myself, let alone an afternoon to do what I wanted. He so intensely resented anything outside of our life together that gradually, I gave up almost everything that mattered to me to make him happy. Everything except music, and for that most of all, he had punished me. A slap here. A shout there. And eventually, so much worse. Still I had taken it, having been convinced for most of my life that I was never enough.

I coasted down the hill, feeling that knot in my stomach release just a bit more, continuing even when I started to pedal uphill and felt a long unfamiliar burn in my thighs. *Go!* I thought fiercely. This was my time. I didn't want to waste it.

For most of the ride, I did all right. I had to stop around mile eight to walk the bike up one nasty hill, but from there, I rode another ten, huffing and puffing up the smaller hills in order to fly down again, the comforting smell of dry pine needles and briny lake water filling my nose as I went.

Unfortunately, it was in the middle of one long coast with my eyes partially shut that I missed a massive pothole. It pitched me off my bike and down another steep hillside. I rolled about twenty feet through the soft, needle-covered forest floor until I hit the base of a large pine tree with a thump that made me see stars.

I lay there for a second and focused on breathing in and out with the wind. Could I move my fingers and toes? The answer was yes—okay, I wasn't dead or paralyzed. I sucked in another large breath and sat up slowly, feeling the side of my head that had smacked the dirt and gravel. There was only a slight scrape, although I'd definitely have a bump there later. I didn't *think* I had a concussion. And shockingly, I didn't appear to have any other major scrapes and bruises—just an unholy amount of pine needles and dirt clinging to my bike shorts and shirt.

I looked up the hill to where my bike lay innocuously on its side.

"You little shit," I denounced it.

There was nothing to do but get up and ride home. All nine-plus miles there. But when I tried to push myself up, a shooting pain lanced through my right ankle, and immediately, I yowled and fell right back on my ass, sliding a few more feet down the hill.

"Fuck!" I cried, clasping the offended body part. "Shit! You fucker!" I yelled at the bike, now more than a little annoyed with it.

Slowly, I managed to pull myself up onto one leg next to a tree. I looked down the hill, hoping to find a house or a cabin or *someplace* to find help. I didn't know many people on this side of the lake, although there had been rumors of a clan of skinheads since I was a kid (not that I've ever seen any). Even though neighboring Idaho supposedly had a fairly large white power community, I'd always thought there were more likely meth labs than Neo-Nazis. Still, considering my skin was a few shades darker than most folks around here, and I had the notoriety of being Ellie Sharp's bastard kid, I wasn't interested in taking my chances.

"Great," I muttered. "Now I'm going to be whacked by Walter White."

"There are worse ways to go."

At the sudden deep, male voice behind me, I screamed and jumped onto my bad leg, falling again and rolling another three feet down the hill. I scrambled back up, ignoring the pinches around my ankle and calf, then grabbed another tree trunk, looked up, and froze. There he was: a real, live yeti.

Well, not quite. Upon closer inspection, it was a man, but only just. He was tall—at least six feet, more likely six-two or six-three. Dressed in grungy cargo pants and a t-shirt that looked like it had more holes than fabric, his tan, sinewy limbs filled out hole-ridden cotton better than it deserved, revealing muscles that looked more like the product of natural hard work than hours spent in a gym.

His hair was a wild riot of dark blond that, when combined with a severely unkempt beard that extended well past his collar, made him strongly resemble a lion. And yet, even in the midst of this wild man's ferocious appearance, a pair of equally wild green eyes looked just the slightest bit familiar. Did I know him from somewhere? Maybe an old high school classmate, or someone who used to hang around Lucas's crowd from before. I squinted, trying to place him.

His mouth, wide and full, twitched. He tilted his head, and something in me clicked, like a lock that had just been picked.

Gorgeous.

The word echoed through my head before I could even think consciously.

Wait, *what*?

The man shuffled down the hill, then reached out a hand. Slowly, I took it, though I gasped at the warmth of his grip, apparent even in the early evening sunshine. His hand was broad, practically a paw, and slightly calloused across his palm and fingertips. This was someone who spent his days using his body, not sitting indoors.

He jerked at the contact too, like he'd been shocked. His squeeze tightened, and I allowed him to guide me toward the road.

"I—uh—thanks," I stuttered, hopping toward him on one foot and nearly losing my balance again.

He didn't answer, just cast a look over at my hobbling form, pulled my hand around his neck, and slung an arm around my waist before lifting me completely off the ground, effectively carrying me the rest of the way up the hill. I might have protested more if I hadn't been one hundred percent entranced by the solid wall of *man* pressed against me, feeling intoxicatingly...good. Because *God,* did he smell good.

Like rain. That's what it was. Soap, of course, and a bit of sweat—he had clearly been in the middle of some kind of workout when he'd seen me fall down the hill. But through all of that was a fresh, vibrant scent, the kind I used to crave when I was stuck in the city for weeks at a time. The kind that would make me run up to the roof of my building when summer thunderstorms hit Manhattan, or make me stop on the side of the road when I'd cross the unlikely bay or river driving between gigs. He smelled like water. Briny. A little sweet. Unbelievably fresh and potent.

It wasn't until he set me down next to the fairly unkempt dirt road that I realized we weren't just stuck in the woods. We were obviously on someone's property—*his* property, if the narrow driveway, the beat-up Toyota pickup, and the battered wood cabin were any indicators.

"There," he said, stepping a solid three feet away, almost as if he couldn't stand to be next to me. He wrinkled his nose. It only then occurred to me that after an eighteen-mile bike ride, I probably reeked. Fantastic. Mountain man was all delectable fresh water, and I probably smelled like a shoe.

"You all right now?" he asked. "Those pine needles are slick."

I had to physically fight the urge not to step back toward him to answer. What the hell was wrong with me?

"Um, y-yeah," I managed, unable to cover my stammer. "I'm f-fine."

His gaze dragged over me. In the sunlight, his green eyes were clearly flecked with gold. We stared at each other, letting the sounds of the wind in the trees and the cry of the osprey fill the space between us. My heart thumped. A vein in the man's temple twitched.

"So, um, thank you…" I ventured, waiting for him to fill in his name. I extended a hand, telling myself it was the polite thing to do, not because I wanted to touch him again.

But the man only stared at it, then shoved a hand into his wild hair and looked back up at me like I'd just offered him a handful of stinging nettles.

"Do you need a ride home?" he asked abruptly.

"I, uh, it's okay, I can just—" I took a step backward, and immediately, my ankle buckled. Shit. I could stand on it, but the idea of riding nine miles home sounded like pure torture.

Goldilocks (as he had become the second he refused to tell me his name) glared at my ankle like it had personally offended him. I glared back. He blinked.

"Let me grab my keys," he grumbled and jogged down the hill into the house, returning a few moments later. "Come on," he said, and before I could reply, squatted down and scooped me into his arms, dangling my feet over one elbow.

Damn. That smell. It really was even better up close.

"Here." Goldilocks dumped me unceremoniously into the passenger seat of his burnt-orange pickup, then dusted off his hands, like he was trying to get rid of all traces of me.

He paused, one hand on the door while he watched me situate myself. When I looked up, his penetrating green gaze practically bore through me.

"What?" I asked, suddenly picking at my hair. God, I probably still had pine needles everywhere. We were quite a pair. Yeti-locks and the pine needle bear. Awesome.

The stranger jerked, as if pulled out of a trance, then folded his mouth into a thin, tight line. "Nothing," he snapped and shut the door in my face.

I sat awkwardly as he walked around the car, got in, and started it up. The windows were down and the old engine was loud, but that did nothing to distract from the immediacy of his scent crowding me in the small cab. Rainwater, yeah. And something else, something sweet. Caramel? Chocolate?

I wasn't ready to think about just why I was so interested.

"Um, that's my bike on the road," I pointed out as he backed past the old Schwinn lying in a heap by the potholes.

Goldilocks rolled his lips together, cast his eyes upward like he was searching for patience, and stopped the car to throw the bike in the back.

"Your tires look like shit," he remarked once he got back in and started driving. "No wonder you crashed. They are completely bald."

"They were fine until I hit that pothole up there. The bigger problem is probably that I had my eyes shut."

At that, his full mouth twitched again. This time it was definitely noticeable.

"You were riding with your eyes shut?"

I blushed. "Only for a second. Don't you ever get that feeling when you're just kind of caught up in how good something feels? I was coasting, and the wind was blowing, and it just felt *awesome*." I sighed, and giggled to myself. "Well, until I toppled down the hill and busted my ankle. But before that I felt…free."

"Free," he repeated quietly. The thrum of his voice filled the car, and almost matched the engine.

We passed more than half the drive around the lake without saying anything beyond me giving directions and him grunting in response. Either the radio didn't work, or the guy wasn't feeling music. But I wasn't the kind of person who could sit easily in silence.

"So, um, I haven't seen you around. Have you lived on the lake long?"

He darted a side-eyed green look at me. "A few years."

I ventured a smile. Okay, he was talking. "Where were you from originally?"

Another suspicious glance. Jesus, the guy could seriously break glass with his intensity. "Connecticut."

"Connecticut, really? You're a long way from home. What brought you all the way to Newman Lake?"

He worried his jaw for a minute, and a gust of wind through the window caused his beard to wave slightly. I didn't even like facial hair on men—it obscured the face, not to mention made it scratchy when you kissed—but this guy, those eyes. I swear, I could barely see anything past them.

"I just wanted a change of pace," he said finally, gripping the steering wheel so hard his knuckles turned white.

I nodded. "I get that. That's why I'm back myself, I suppose. I was actually living in New York for the last eight years, believe it or not. But I grew up here, so this is home, I guess. I'm Maggie, by the way. You, um, you actually look kind of familiar. Are you sure we haven't met before, maybe back in the cit—"

"We don't need to do that," he cut in abruptly.

I recoiled against the force of his voice. "Don't need to do what? Turn left here, by the way."

His eyes remained steadfast on the road as he turned onto West Newman Lake Road. "The whole getting to know you thing. 'What's your name, where're you from, blah, blah, blah.' I don't give a shit who you are, and that's all you need to know about me. I'm taking you home because it was the quickest way to get you the hell off my property."

Then he finally did look at me again, and his expression sliced like a knife. Everything about him seemed etched by a razor: the long line of his nose, the chiseled edges of his muscles, the angles of his bent knees and elbows. There was nothing soft about this man. He was sharp. Feral.

I flinched. I couldn't help it. His eyes flickered over me with something I might have confused with concern if I didn't already know what a dick he was.

"Hey," he started. "Ah—Maggie. I—"

"It's fine," I said, hating how small my voice had become. I crossed my arms and wrapped my hands over my shoulders, hugging myself. I had already lived with someone who treated me like shit. I wasn't interested in putting up with it from complete strangers, ride home or not. "You can pull over at the sign right there."

"It's all right, I'll just drive you down to the—"

"It's *fine,*" I said again. "Just pull over."

He opened his mouth like he wanted to say something more, then sighed and did as I asked. I hopped out while he pulled my bike down from the bed. I took it and wheeled it to the curb, limping on one foot. The pain was already better, but I'd be exclusively swimming for at least a week if I still wanted to compete next month.

"You all right?"

When I turned around, Goldilocks was back in the driver's seat, his door still open as he watched my progress. One long, muscled leg balanced on the ground. I parked the bike, then hopped back over to him as defiantly as I could.

"I'm the hell off your property now," I told him evenly. "So we don't have to do this. Thanks for the ride."

Before he could reply, draw me back in with those hypnotic green eyes and that scent that made me forget where I was, I shut the car door in the stranger's face. Eager to return to the house that, for all its faults, never left me feeling as disoriented and confused as I'd been for the past twenty minutes.

CHAPTER FOUR

Where are you, Flower?

Just four innocuous words, but they might as well have been bombs dropped through the clear morning light. I sat up in my bed, the old double mattress and creaky metal frame I had moved to a sleeping shack on the edge of the property. The shack, originally constructed as a shelter for ice fishermen in the thirties, had a sink, but no running water, and would heat up like a sauna by mid-July. But it was a quiet space of my own and allowed me to get a good night's sleep when Mama stumbled in a 2 a.m., like she had the last three nights. People used to joke, even at church, that my mother was a bigger party animal than her teenage daughter. They had no idea.

It was a few minutes after five in the morning, and the lake was relatively silent. If I went outside, I might see deer in the garden, or maybe a family of wild turkeys scuttling around the property. Bass fishermen were the only people up at this hour, floating around the lake's glassy perimeter.

I looked back at my phone. The screen still glowed with the message, sent from an unknown number. No. This couldn't be him. Theo was in jail for what he'd done. He was supposed to be serving a full six months

—a drop in the bucket, as far as I was concerned, but still something. Long enough that he was supposed to forget about me. Let me go. Move on with his life and let me try to recover mine.

It could be from a friend, one of the many members of his entourage. The kind of idiotic yes-men that only very rich people travel with. It wouldn't have been the first time he'd gotten one of them to mess with me.

I breathed. That was all this was. A message sent through a visitor's phone, a cheap prank meant to rile me up. But he wasn't a danger to me anymore. I was safe here. As safe as I could be, anyway.

I dialed the first number I could think of, eager to erase the nasty gag. Calliope picked up on the second ring.

"You bitch."

I exhaled and flopped back onto my pillow to stare at the open rafters. "Hey, Cal. You awake?"

"I am now, damn you. How's the sticks? Bored yet?"

I chuckled. "Not at all. You'd be surprised how much there is to do. I get to strip wallpaper off two bathrooms today. Top that."

"Well, I *would be* sleeping until ten if it wasn't for you."

"Shut up. You wake up at six every morning to go to the gym."

"Weekdays, darling. Weekdays."

I smiled. She was giving me a hard time, but if I knew my former manager, she'd been up for hours going to a daybreak SoulCycle session, making phone calls, and basically running half of New York. Calliope was the hardest-working woman on the eastern seaboard and had been since we first met in college. After getting her start doing music A&R right out of NYU, she was picked up by a much bigger firm just last year. Two pretty big clients followed her, and I was supposed to be her third… until I fucked it all up. Our professional relationship was over, but she was still my best friend.

"So what's up?" Calliope asked. "I know you didn't call to give me the goods on your mom's remodeling. Is Eloise behaving herself?"

I thought back to last night, when Mama had gotten back around two thirty and parked the car sideways in her spot. The tires had slid against the gravel, causing a minor avalanche of gravel to shower the chicken coop and my shack, waking us all up. I'd gone up, straightened out the car so our neighbors could get by, and then put her to bed.

"She's…fine," I said. "Today. You know her. She's pretty functional most of the time. Honestly, it's the driving I worry about most."

"Dude. She needs to get hooked up with Uber."

"Dude yourself," I retorted. "This is an unincorporated community forty-five minutes from the nearest city, not the five boroughs. We don't have Uber, and taxis only exist if you're willing to wait an hour or more. We have our own cars and the trucks of weird men at Curly's."

"Is there really a bar named Curly's?" Calliope asked. "Just the name of that place sounds like I'd get hepatitis from a water glass."

I snorted, rubbing my hand on my face. "Don't knock it 'til you try it. I had my first gigs at Curly's. They have a killer karaoke night, you know."

"Is that where I'm losing your talent to? A fucking sing-a-long bar with wannabe cowboys?"

I sighed and rolled over. Even though she had helped me pack my car, Calliope made no secret of the fact that she thought I was making a mistake in leaving. She had wanted me to stay with her instead, go back to waitressing, save money, and keep trying to get my singing career off the ground.

But in the end, she hadn't argued because she knew the truth too. She knew exactly what kind of power Theo's family had in New York. Even if I wanted to come back, it would be that much harder with one of the biggest entertainment names bearing a personal grudge against me.

"He texted me this morning," I said. "Or a lackey, maybe."

The line went very quiet.

"Ah, shit," muttered Calliope. "What did Psycho say?"

"He asked me where I was," I said. "And he called me 'Flower.'"

Calliope groaned. "That name was always creepy as fuck. It made him sound like a pedophile."

I cringed—not because Theo was much older than me, but because Callie was right. Once, I had loved it. His attention. His obsession. I was his flower, he said, meant to make his life more beautiful, in every possible way.

I shuddered and closed my eyes, though I knew the refuge of darkness would only be temporary. It had been more than a year since our explosive ending, and three months since the verdict that had landed him in jail, but his face still haunted me whether I was asleep or awake. It winked, cajoled, sneered, threatened. I was beginning to accept that Theo was simply a ghost who would follow me around my whole life, for better or for worse.

Ironic, really. After all, marriage, the one thing he wanted, was never something I could give him no matter how many times as he demanded it. His proposals were orders, not requests. "Marry me," he'd say, as if I didn't have a choice. But always, always, there was something deep down that told me not to say yes. Maybe I should have. It was the last refusal that became his downfall and mine.

But this time, as I shut out the world, it was a pair of green eyes that flashed unbidden, instead of Theo's dark brown. They'd been appearing all week since I'd crashed on the side of the road. Every time some part of Theo came to mind—the curl of his lip, the arrogant tip of his nose—some feature of that strange, curt man with the wild hair and angry eyes would immediately replace it. For the last seven days, his face was like a fly that wouldn't buzz away, though it seemed to chase away the worst of my fears too.

When my heart rate slowed, I shook away the face. I didn't need to be thinking about him, or any man right now. I needed to figure out how to be normal again. How to be me.

"Just…will you keep tabs on him for me, Cal? I know you two move in a lot of the same circles, and if—I don't know, if he's somehow out, you'll hear about it. Just let me know, okay?"

Text messages I could tolerate. They were easy to delete. But Theo had the resources to find out where my mother lived or send someone to find me. He was lazy by nature, but I also knew not to underestimate him. There was nothing Theo del Conte loved more than nursing a grudge, and incarcerated or not, right now I was probably his number one nemesis.

"Of course," Calliope said. "And in the meantime, tell me about the lake hotties. I am *so* over these metrosexual assholes in the Village. Give me some farm boys to fantasize about. I'll even take a Curly cowboy. Have you run into luscious Lucas?"

I chuckled. "Well, yeah. But sadly, he's not so luscious anymore."

"For real? Oh that's tragic. Let me guess: two babies and a beer gut."

"No babies yet, but the beer gut is making progress. And I'll raise you a bald spot."

Okay, so I was being a little mean. Lucas still looked just fine—like you'd expect an average twenty-seven-year-old with a taste for Bud Light to look. I'd bet money he was on a lot of most eligible bachelor lists within the Newman Lake zip code.

"Don't disappoint me here, babe. There's got to be some hot mountain man who can fuel my fantasies. Give up the goods."

I gulped. I didn't want to think about him. No. I wouldn't.

But there he was again, in the back of my mind. Green eyes scattered with sparks. A lean, muscled chest. That thick mane of wild hair. It wasn't fair. I didn't even know his freaking name.

"Who the *fuck* are you thinking about?" Calliope's sharp voice cut through my quickly clouding thoughts.

I touched my suddenly heated cheeks. Christ, that escalated quickly. "No one," I said. "I didn't say anything."

"Bullshit. Lady, your silence was so deafening it practically split my eardrum. Spill."

I closed my eyes, and the tan, bearded face appeared, framed by a halo of unkempt gold. The breeze outside blew in the fresh scent of the lake water, and just as fast, I felt his arms under my legs and back again. The heat coming off his skin, his hands, his arms.

Shit. What was I doing? The guy—Goldilocks—was a complete and utter asshole.

"There's no one," I repeated again. "This place is just stacked with the same tired dudes who are always here. Pickup trucks and beer guts. That's it."

"Yeah, but I bet those dudes have filled out since high school, huh? Farm boys look good in them t-shirts."

"Callie, what would you know about it? You've barely left Manhattan your entire life."

I could practically hear my friend rolling her big brown eyes. But Calliope knew me better than anyone, which also meant she knew when I wouldn't talk.

"I'll get it out of you eventually," she said. "In the meantime, use whoever he is to write more beautiful songs, all right? This is just a hiatus, kid. It's not forever."

I glanced at my guitars, propped in one corner of the shack. I still hadn't taken them out. I wondered if I ever would.

AFTER I GOT off the phone, I went up to the main house and grabbed some coffee and fruit, careful not to wake Mama while I got ready for a morning swim. It was better to go early, before the boaters came. My ankle still wasn't a hundred percent yet, so I had to be disciplined about the other parts of my training if I still wanted to race by the Fourth, in just over three weeks. Today would be my longest swim—across the lake and back, which was about a mile, the same distance I'd need to do on race day.

When I strode out carrying my swimmer's buoy, I practically ran right into Lucas, who was about to knock on the front door.

"Whoa!" he burst as he steadied the two of us on the threshold of the sliding glass door.

I took a step back, clasping the buoy to my chest. "Hey! What are you doing here so early?"

Lucas looked around and shrugged. "I thought I'd check to see if you had gotten any help with the outer cabins yet. If you haven't, I can get started on some things until you do."

I shook my head. "We haven't, but it's really okay. I'm chipping away at what I can, and eventually I'll find a job so we can pay for it. We're good."

"Look…I wasn't going to say anything." Lucas rubbed the back of his neck. "But I ran into Ellie at the bar last night when I was, um, out. I told her I would come by, see what needs to be done and if I can help at all."

I could just see it. Lucas hanging out at Curly's with his posse, enjoying pitchers of cheap beer and the attention of local girls. Someone would have put Journey or Guns N' Roses on the jukebox, or maybe some Garth Brooks, and then an impromptu dance party would have started in the space between the vinyl booths. And then Mama, with her loud, boisterous self, would wander up to a group of men half her age and make an ass of herself until Lucas, with his polite manner, would guide her back to her friends making all sorts of promises so she'd leave him alone.

Same story. Different time.

"Lucas, you don't have to do this," I said. "Really. She can't pay you, and it's not fair of her to take advantage. I'm here now, and I'm taking care of things, slowly but surely."

"Hey. I told you too that I'd come."

He gave me a look that I was so, *so* tired of seeing. I'd been on the receiving end of people's pity for being Eloise Sharp's daughter my entire life. Poor, sad Maggie. How adorably pathetic that I would actually consider myself competent.

But then that gaze, initially harmless, morphed as it floated over my body. My one-piece swimsuit wasn't anywhere near what you would call revealing, but it definitely showed off a lot more of me than Lucas had seen the other day. He crossed his beefy arms, causing his biceps to stretch the sleeves of his t-shirt. Okay, so maybe I was giving him kind of a bad rap earlier. Soft gut or not, Lucas's arms definitely weren't anything to laugh about.

By the time he met my eyes again, he was blushing, his cheeks two cherry-red circles. I looked away.

"I, um. Right. I'm going to get started, then," Lucas said and turned toward the back of the house.

I stood there for a moment, trying to figure out if I wanted to go after him or not. In the end, I went down the other stairs and jumped into the water feet first, trying to tell myself it was because I was eager to get moving and not because I needed to cool off.

I HADN'T SWUM in years, not since college. Pools took up space, and space was premium in a city like New York. Only the poshest athletic clubs had them, and considering I could never afford even the shittiest gym membership, my exercise regimen in the city had mostly consisted of jogging up and down the river when the weather wasn't terrible.

But my muscles hadn't forgotten the strokes, the even glide, the breathing work of swimming in open water. This early in the day, the lake was still enough that it was basically a pool of its own. I enjoyed the rhythm of the movement, the flicker of fish many feet below me, the alternating patches of cold and warmer water that gave me a slight thrill when I glided through. The feeling was back, the same one I had just before crashing my bike. Things felt natural again, after years of confinement and pressure. Always trying to be something I wasn't.

I closed my eyes. Once again, I was free.

Until I wasn't.

One stroke later, I was viciously jerked back as something tugged me under the translucent green, forcing water into my lungs and up my nose. I popped back up, coughing and sputtering, then twisted around to find the leash of my buoy completely tangled in a bunch of lily pads I had passed without realizing. Dammit. I really needed to shorten the leash.

"Shit!" I exclaimed. I pulled as hard as I could, but the leash wouldn't come loose. I yanked at the stems of the lilies, but none of them broke, too strong and pliant in the late spring water. Fuck. I was seriously stuck here without a pair of scissors in sight. I was going to have to chew through some of the stems, which were looking more and more like tree roots.

I turned in the water, peering around for early morning fishermen. Of course, just when I needed them to be lurking around, they were nowhere to be seen. Of fucking course.

I turned onto my back and stared up at the clouds rushing across the sky. "Fuck," I muttered. Then, I shouted it: "Fuuuuuccccccck!"

"What the fuck is wrong with you?"

I screamed at the sound of the deep voice echoing over the water. I kicked around, sinking for a second, swallowing more lake water before popping back up to find a man jogging out to the end of a long dock about fifty feet away, his hand perched over his brow like a visor as he glared at me.

His hair, just like yesterday, flew around his shoulders in a wild, wavy mess in the morning breeze. He wore nothing but a pair of shorts that sat low on his hips, and even from this far I could clearly see the square, cut edges of his deeply tanned chest and abs, and the two diagonal lines of muscle that followed his narrow hips and disappeared under his waistband. Jesus *Christ.* My imagination hadn't done him any justice whatsoever. Even tangled up in a mess of lily pads and tule stems, frustrated to holy hell, I couldn't ignore a sight like that.

"I'm—I got stuck," I managed to call out. "Do you—can you bring me some scissors or something? My leash is tangled, and I can't break the stems."

Goldilocks shook his head and muttered something to himself that sounded like, "Oh, for fuck's sake," though it was hard to make it out from fifty feet away.

"What was that?" I asked, feeling more desperate and pathetic by the second.

"Hold on," he called out, his deep voice skipping ominously over the water. "I'll be right there."

CHAPTER FIVE

Twenty minutes, one canoe, a pair of garden shears, and one very disgruntled mountain man later, I was sitting in an Adirondack chair on the deck of Goldilocks's old cabin, enjoying his elevated lake view from behind a camouflage of pine trees halfway up the hill. I had lived here my whole life, taken countless cruises in our boat around the lake's perimeter, but I had never known this place existed. That's how well it blended into the forest.

I leaned back in the chair, catching my breath and spying my house directly across the water, while my yeti man tried to repair my knotted leash. I couldn't swim safely back across the lake without a buoy, and I had a feeling he wasn't interested in driving me home again. I looked up at the sky. The sun was rising higher, and several more boats and jet skis were already buzzing around. It was possible swimming wouldn't be an option anyway.

"So, are you stalking me or something?" Goldilocks asked while he sawed at the lily pad stalks with a camping knife.

I jerked my head back at him. "What?"

He shrugged, keeping his eyes trained on his task. "Twice in a week when usually I can go three times that without seeing anyone. I did tell you I wanted you off my property, didn't I? If you wanted to meet me that badly, there are better ways to do it than trespassing."

I recoiled into my chair. "Someone certainly thinks a lot of himself."

Okay. So maybe it wasn't the smartest thing in the world to be goading a man who not only had come to my rescue, but who also seemed to have a relatively short temper. But I couldn't help it. I didn't even know this guy, but I resented the hell out of him. I resented him for being kind of a dick the first time we met. I resented him for not having enough manners to even shake my hand. And I *really* resented him for getting inside my head all week, and now having *that* kind of body, the kind I probably wouldn't stop thinking about for another month.

Goldilocks ground his teeth. "You should be more careful. If you're not a stalker—and jury's still out on that one—then you're obviously accident-prone. What were you doing this time, *swimming* with your eyes closed? You'd think you would have learned your lesson."

"Listen, Gold—" I stopped, took a deep breath. But it was no use. "Do you think you could at least tell me your name if you're going to lecture me? Otherwise, I'm going to keep calling you Goldilocks in my head, and that basically makes me one of the three bears. I'm not sure I'm cool with that, since *you're* the one being a dick."

The man froze with an expression halfway between irritated and shocked. But his eyes practically sparkled in the sunlight, and his lips pressed together into a crooked line under his beard.

"Goldilocks?" he asked.

I looked pointedly at the wild riot of blond. "If the shoe fits."

He picked a lock off his shoulder and examined it critically. "Huh." He set the buoy and his knife on the ground and stood up. "Hold on."

He disappeared into the house, and when he returned, wore a shirt, just as ratty as the one from the last time I saw him, and had tied his hair into a bun at the crown of his head. I thought I had gotten my fill of man buns from the hipsters in the Village, but this guy...well, let's just say there's something different when a man ties his hair up out of expediency instead of pretension. With his hair pulled away from his face, revealing high cheekbones and the hint of a strong jaw that couldn't totally be masked by his beard, he had gone from feral and somewhat yummy to freaking delectable. Seriously. *What* was wrong with me?

"Better?" he asked as he resumed his task.

I just stared. "Um...yeah. I guess."

Again, there was the hint of a smile. I couldn't help wondering what it looked like when it was all the way there.

"Will," he said quietly, maintaining focus on the mess of stems.

"What?"

He looked up again, and this time, the sparks in his eyes were even more potent. Or maybe that was my heart thumping in response.

"My name," he said a bit louder, "is Will. So no more of that Goldilocks bullshit, all right, Lily pad?"

I scoffed. "Lily pad?"

He glanced at the mess of stalks and leaves dripping on the deck, and this time that hint of smile was even more pronounced. "If the shoe fits," he said and went back to his cleaning.

A breeze rose through the trees, and I rubbed my arms, bracing myself against the chill. Now that I was out of the water and in the shade, I was getting kind of cold. Will looked over at the motion, and his eyes drifted briefly over my chest, which I realized was showing quite clearly just *how* cold I was through the thin Lycra. The path of his gaze didn't stop, falling over my bare legs, suddenly making me feel the very opposite of cold. I wondered if his touch, which I already knew was just as warm, would have the same effect.

This was wrong. Three months ago, I put the final nail in the coffin of a nasty, years-long relationship by sending my ex to jail for what he had done to me. My heart and my soul were currently in tatters. And here I was, flickering like a live fire under the gaze of some weird mountain hermit with a sharp temper, crazy hair, and a beard like Gandalf. What was going on?

Will cleared his throat audibly. "So, the biking, the swimming. Are you training for something, or just messing around?"

I shrugged. "Well, there's that triathlon that the inn is doing on the Fourth. I used to compete in events like that in high school, and it sounded like a good way to get back into shape." *And back to myself,* I wanted to add, but didn't. This stranger didn't need to know more about my issues.

Will examined me for a moment. "What's the inn?"

I looked at him, surprised. "The place down by Muzzy Cove? The Forster Inn, you know? The family has owned it for three generations, I think. It's literally the only place to stay on the entire lake other than vacation rentals."

Will shook his head. "What's Muzzy?"

My frown deepened. "The cove on the northeast leg of the lake. Don't you know the basic geography? When did you move here?"

He shrugged. "It's not on the map. I came about four years ago," he replied. "I just keep to myself."

"It's pretty hard to keep to yourself in a community like this unless you're purposefully avoiding people." I looked out to the lake, which I knew was full of gossips. There's no way that Barb, my mom, the Forsters, or any other number of people out on a cocktail cruise around the lake's perimeter, had missed the fact that a stranger had been living in this old cabin for the last four years.

But then again, it was pretty well hidden. I hadn't even known it was here until today.

Will sawed at a particularly stubborn piece of stem. "When I see boats driving by, I go inside. I don't bother them, and they don't bother me. I moved here to get away from people, not see more of them. I don't really get along with most."

Shocker, I wanted to say. But instead, I just hugged my knees to my chest. "Well, maybe you should. People around here are nice, for the most part. And it's good to have some neighbors who care about you."

He looked at me like he didn't believe me.

"What if your house burns down?" I continued. "What if you need sugar in the morning? No one's an island, much as they might want to be."

Will just stayed quiet, staring fixedly at my leash. His hands stilled, but the one holding the knife grasped it so tightly, his knuckles were white.

"I don't like sugar," he said finally, and then went back to his work more intently than before.

I looked up at the house and back at him. "So, what do you do all day, then? Do you have a job or something? Do you work from home?"

Will looked up sharply. All humor vanished. "Why do you want to know?"

I frowned. "Whoa, buddy. I was just making conversation. Most people ask those kinds of questions when they are getting to know someone, you know?"

His fierce expression didn't waver, but this time, I was ready for it. No flinching. Instead, I sat up straight.

"Okay," I said. "I'll go first. My name is Maggie Sharp. I *used* to be a waitress-slash-musician. I was out in New York for a while trying to break into the industry, but I fail—I just got burned out of being a starving artist. And when my mom's life fell apart, she needed some help getting her shit back together, so I decided to come home and help us *both* recalibrate and figure out our lives." I cocked my head at him. "Okay, your turn, mountain man."

In return, I got a withering glare full of disdain. But this one didn't cut like the others. Instead, it made me giggle.

"Don't make me start calling you Goldilocks again," I warned him.

One side of his face tugged upward into a half smile. Even just that half managed to tug equally at something unnamable in my chest. Damn.

"Okay," he said as he went back to picking at a particularly nasty knot of greenery. "My name is Will...Baker. I used to work in, um, advertising. But after I made some money, I decided to cash out and move someplace where people couldn't fucking bother me anymore." He looked back up, and his eyes danced with mischief. "Clearly that's working out really well for me."

I grinned. That half smile broadened a little more. I stuck out a hand just like I had yesterday, and after looking at it for a moment, he took it in his much larger one.

Yeah. Sparks.

"Nice to meet you, Will Baker of Connecticut," I said. "Thank you for rescuing me, twice now."

His expression flared. "How did you know I was from Connecticut?"

"You told me yesterday, remember?" I tapped my head. "I'm like an elephant. I never forget."

His sudden temper receded, and the half smile returned. Jeez, this guy was hot and cold.

"Ah. Okay. Well, nice to meet you too, Maggie Sharp of Newman Lake. And, um, sorry about yesterday. You caught me by surprise. I don't really do well with surprises."

"I gathered," I said, leaning back in my chair. "So you've really been here for four years and haven't met *anyone*?"

"Nope. Don't want to, either."

"But how is that even possible? I get that you stay off your dock, but I grew up here. People on this lake are nosy. No one ever walked over a casserole or came and knocked on your door?"

Will shrugged. "It's easier than you might think. I have most of my food sent here so I don't have to go shopping. I hike, camp, read, write. My house sits on five acres, way out of sight for most people. It's easy to be here, alone." He looked up. "You think I'm some crazy psycho, don't you?"

I twisted my mouth around uneasily. "Well..."

His shoulders hunched. "It does sound crazy," he murmured to himself, and the sadness in his voice caused any anxiety on my part to melt immediately.

"Hey," I said, reaching to touch his arm gently.

It was just as warm as it had been before, but it still caught me by surprise. Will looked at my hand for a moment, but didn't pull away. When he looked up, his eyes were wide, almost mournful.

"You don't sound crazy," I told him. "Maybe a little lonely, though."

Will blinked. "Ah, well. Yeah. Maybe." With a quick jerk of his knife, he freed the last of the lily pads from the leash. "There you go," he said triumphantly, holding the buoy out to me. "You're free, so to speak." He glanced out to the water, where even more boat traffic now congested the water. The sun was high, and weekenders were making an early start. "I don't think you should swim back, though. You'll get tangled with someone's propeller instead, and that would be a lot harder to fix."

I nodded with a smile. "If you have a phone, I can call my mom to come grab me."

But Will shook his head. "No, that's all right. I'll give you a ride. I should get out more anyway."

AGAIN, we rode in silence. Will notably kept the radio off and the window down. This time, I didn't mind. Although when we drove by the store where Cathy was just unlocking the door for the morning, Will's eyes widened when she raised her hand in greeting, clearly interested in just who was giving me a ride at nine o'clock on a Saturday.

"Who was that?" he asked over the roar of the engine as we sped by the emu farm and started twisting up my hill again.

"Cathy McDonald," I called back. "She took over the store after her dad passed last year. She buys our eggs."

Will's mouth quirked again. "Your eggs?"

I shrugged. "We have chickens. They're kind of assholes, but they're good layers. We gotta make some extra cheddar somehow, right?"

"Right," he murmured.

This time, instead of stopping at the top of the gravel driveway, he turned the truck down it, navigating down the rocky incline until he stopped just above the stairs.

"I assume this is you," he said, nodding in the direction of the house below.

I nodded, opening my door. "Thank you again for the rescue. Again. And the ride…again."

We shared another almost-smile together. One of these days I was going to get him to break and grin completely. It was a new goal, just like the triathlon. And somehow, I wanted this one more.

I stepped out onto the stairs and turned to shut the door, but Will stopped me. "Wait, Maggie."

His words were stunted, like he hadn't done this in a long time. I waited patiently for whatever it was he wanted to say. I suspected that underneath all of his surly bravado, Will really needed a good friend. I understood the feeling, better than he knew. I didn't have that many myself anymore.

"Yeah?" I asked.

"Would you…" His words were measured, yet drifting, like he didn't quite speak the language. "Would you…do you…would you like a partner? To, um, to train with?"

My eyes widened. Whatever I had been expecting, it wasn't that. "*You* want to do the triathlon? You know that means running, and swimming, and biking, all with a large crowd of people. Those weird, two-legged creatures you go out of your way to avoid."

He shook his head, causing a few loose strands of gold to fly around his temples. "No, I'm not going to compete in something like that. But I'd train with you. If—if you want the company."

"Now we're going from 'get the hell off my property' to running buddies?" I teased. "I thought you didn't give a shit who I was, Goldilocks."

I tipped my head, enjoying the flush on Will's cheeks. I didn't know why, but I liked poking the bear, so to speak. He was giving me a peek of his soft underbelly, and I wanted to scratch it. Mmmmmm scratching Will's belly… *Down, girl.*

"Well, I won't if you keep calling me that," he said, though the new spark of friendliness in his eyes said differently. "But you obviously need someone to keep an eye on you. I don't want to worry I'm going to have to run you to the emergency room next."

I scoffed, but didn't argue with him. I told myself it was because I was just being nice, and not because I actually wouldn't mind seeing him running, or swimming, or biking with me. And not because the summer heat would probably mean a high probability that he'd be doing one or all of those things shirtless. With his hair up in a knot. Just…like…that.

"So, bike ride tomorrow?" Will interrupted my daydream. "Or maybe a run?"

I couldn't think of a reason to put him off. So instead, I grinned. Will's smile wasn't full—not yet—but this time both sides of his mouth seemed to broaden a little.

"Meet you in front of the corner store at seven," I confirmed. "I got new tires by the way. So no more sliding on the pine needles."

Will's mouth quirked once more in acknowledgment as I shut the door to his truck.

"See you, Lily pad," he said softly through the open window, and for a moment, I was mesmerized by the last hint of smile in his eyes.

I sucked my lip between my teeth. "See you, Will."

CHAPTER SIX

It was a good thing I hadn't tried to call her, because Mama still wasn't up by the time I came tramping down the stairs instead of from the dock. Lucas was on the other side of the property clearing some debris, so I managed to avoid the third degree about just how I had gotten home. Although part of me was dying to ask if they knew him, another part wanted to keep Will's and my strange morning to myself. And that, I suspected, was also how he wanted to keep it.

So instead, as I got ready for the day, I let my mind drift instead to Will's gentle, yet insistent touch when he swung me up from the dock and even when he carried me the week before. Those deep green eyes, with their guarded earnestness, appeared whenever I blinked. So yeah, maybe I spent some extra time shaving my legs and primping my hair, thinking of our meeting the next morning. Maybe I decided not to think too much about why.

I emerged from the shack to find Lucas behind the house, repairing a bunch of loose shingles. He stopped when he saw me, again performing that quick check over my body that had been a lot more overt when I'd only been wearing a swimsuit. *Sorry, buddy.* There wasn't much to see when I wore a pair of cut-off men's jeans I'd picked up at Goodwill and a loose tank top. After years of binding stage wear that Calliope had carefully picked out to make me look "hot, yet accessible," I was more than happy to tromp around in clothing that was more comfortable than revealing.

"Ah, hey, Mags," Lucas greeted me.

He set down the tools on the ground and stood up to lift his cap up and mop a bit of sweat off his forehead. The movement made his biceps flex and the hem of his t-shirt rose to reveal a flat-ish stomach. Not bad, but I couldn't help comparing him to Will. No Adonis belt in sight here.

"Good swim?" he asked.

I nodded. "Yeah. It was nice. I need to watch out for the lilies, though. I got tangled in them."

Lucas didn't seem to notice the flush in my face at the mention of lily pads. I wasn't sure why it was there anyway.

"Who dropped you off?" he wondered. "I noticed you came back from the stairs."

Huh. Maybe I hadn't been as stealthy as I'd thought. I scanned Lucas's face for any indicators of possessiveness or jealousy, but there was nothing there but plain curiosity.

"Just a new...friend," I replied, taking a seat on one of the tree stumps that served as stools on the grass. "Someone bought a cabin across the way. It's the property next to the Butterfly House."

Lucas frowned as he sat down on the other stump. "The old hunting lodge?"

"Is that what it was? I had never seen it before. It's brown and almost totally blends in with the trees." It was an unusual sight. Most of the houses that circled Newman Lake were painted with fairly vibrant colors that stood out from the pine trees and rocky cliffs. Whites, blues, yellows, reds. The property right next to Will's contained one place that was painted bright pink with red shutters and was aptly called the "Butterfly House" because of its winged eaves.

"That whole hill used to belong to a big lodge back in the twenties," Lucas said. "Most of the lake was split up between something like four hotels. Mom said most of the cabins either burned down or were knocked down when other people bought out the property over the years, but the main lodge is still there. Damn, the place must be decrepit."

I shrugged. "I only saw the outside. It looked like a cabin—kind of old, wood, weather-beaten. I dried off on the deck while the owner fixed my swimming buoy, and then he gave me a ride home."

I couldn't hear it, but there must have been something in my voice that betrayed my earlier thoughts, because at the word owner, Lucas looked up sharply.

"I hope you were careful, Mags," he said. "There are a lot of loons on that side of the lake."

I rolled my eyes. "Aren't we a little old to be getting all Jets and Sharks? It's one body of water, and everybody on it is just as much a hick as everyone else."

Lucas snorted. "I just don't want you to get taken advantage of. I can just imagine what some guy thought of finding you in need of a rescue. I bet he was all too happy to help."

His eyes drifted over me, like he was imagining me again in my bathing suit, and immediately I looked away. It wasn't like Lucas had never seen me naked, but it *had* been a good eight years. It felt weird, somehow, him looking at me like he had a right to what was underneath my shorts and t-shirt.

"You don't have to worry about that," I said emphatically. "That's not really what I'm interested in these days." *Liar*. I shook the thought away.

Lucas nodded. "Ellie mentioned you were coming out of a bad relationship. Hey, I'm sorry to hear that. Sounds like New York is full of jerks, just like everyone says."

I frowned. "*I* wouldn't say that. It's a great city, and I really loved it there in a lot of ways. It was just..."

I shook my head, willing away Theo's face. But there he was. Tall. Handsome. Entirely too well dressed for a man under thirty. Lips smirking arrogantly over his immaculately groomed goatee. Fists curled with promise.

This time, Will didn't chase him away.

I opened my eyes again and studied my nails. "This one guy in particular was not good for me. Or to me. We were together for almost three years, and..." I sighed. I didn't know what Mama had told people —likely, she didn't actually know either. But I wasn't interested in getting into any of the gory details with my ex, no matter how much he was helping out. "Well, I'm here now."

Lucas was quiet for a moment, and then he reached out to touch a few big fingers to the top of my hand. His thumb stroked over my knuckles with nothing but kindness. It felt nice.

"I'm sorry," he said. "I really am."

"Thanks," I replied. "I just...I wonder sometimes. A lot of times, really. What I could have done to prevent it. Sometimes I want to go back two years and tie pre-Theo Maggie to her bedpost."

Lucas looked uneasy as he pulled his hand back and stuck it in his pocket.

"What?" I asked. When he didn't speak, I mimed a kick his way, which made him crack a smile. "*What*?"

"Well, you know..." He drifted off, staring at the grass.

"Lucas, spit it out."

Lucas chewed on his lower lip. "Never mind. It's nothing."

"Don't make me kick your ass, Paul Bunyan."

At the old nickname, Lucas smiled again. "Okay, then, chicken legs. I'd like to see you try."

I mimed a slug at his side, and he parried it away easily, slinging an arm around my shoulder for a second before letting me go. My belly warmed. Some things never changed. Lucas was still Lucas—warm and easy. Our relationship had never been fireworks, but he had always been a good guy. Dependable. Kind.

"Well?" I prodded.

Again, he rubbed the back of his neck. I frowned. I recognized the motion—he used to do it when he had something to say that I wouldn't like.

"I saw some pictures of you," he said. "This was a few years ago, when you were starting to get big, I guess. Ellie brought them to church and was showing them around. She said it was some big show, that you were opening for some big name or another." His gaze softened. "She was really proud of you, Mags. We all were."

I nodded, remembering the night, about four years ago, though it seemed like much longer. I was the opener for a Gillian Keller concert at Irving Plaza—easily the biggest gig I had ever played, including my showcase. The seats in the famous yet intimate venue weren't even a quarter full when I started, but I hadn't cared—I was high on the fact that it was just me and my guitar, playing my songs on one of the most famous stages in New York.

"That was a good night," I mused fondly. "At least until there was some kind of fight later on. I don't know—I left early. But Gillian actually bought one of my songs after she heard it, did you know that? My manager said it was cut from her next album, but still. It was good to know my music was good enough for someone like her."

"That's really great, Mags. It is."

I looked up. He didn't sound that excited. "But…"

Lucas's big shoulders lumbered up and down. "I just remember the photo. You were wearing some blue dress. It was, uh, short."

I knew exactly the one. Sleeveless with an asymmetrical hem, it was one of my favorites because even under the dim stage lights, it made my skin glow. I got a lot of compliments when I wore that dress.

I frowned. "Yeah, it's kind of short. What does that matter?"

Lucas shrugged again, and the movement caused his skin to bunch around his neck, which he then massaged vigorously. "I just think… maybe…" He sighed. "Maybe you were attracting the wrong kind of guys. You looked real pretty and everything, Mags. But some guys—and I'm not saying I'm one of them, or anything—but they see a girl in something like that, and they think she's only good for one thing."

If my mouth were big enough, it would have smacked the ground. Lucas worried his jaw for a second, clearly uncomfortable.

"I'm sorry," I said, trying to recover. "*What*?"

"It was just a surprise," he said quietly, now looking around—at the house, the lake, the grass, anywhere but at me. "Especially considering…"

"Considering *what*, Lucas? Spit it out."

"Considering what kind of stuff your mom gets into down at the bar."

And there it was, the family legacy that had been thrown in my face since I was little—a remnant of my mother's promiscuity. Mine to inherit as soon as I grew old enough to earn a little male attention. Because my mother was widely considered the biggest hussy in the Spokane-Coeur d'Alene area, I was forever doomed to be a nun, lest I follow in her footsteps.

For a long time, I bought into it. As a teenager, I wanted to distance myself as far as I could from Eloise Sharp. While my friends wore tight jeans and short shorts, I kept everything loose and modest. While Mama went on pub crawls, I went to youth group and read the Bible. She went home with a different man every weekend, and I avoided boys like the plague.

And when I finally did have a boyfriend, he was the nicest boy within ten miles. Lucas Forster. A gentle giant. The kind of guy who kept his hand firmly at your waist and nowhere else whenever you kissed. The kind of guy who didn't even *try* to cop a feel until I grabbed his hand and put it on my breast after we had been "going out" for at least four months. When he finally took my virginity, on top of my plaid bedspread, we both cried at the loss of my innocence. It was sweet. Safe.

But, of course, there also wasn't any innocence lost. Because I was never the girl they thought I was, the girl I tried my hardest to be. The second I started driving east, I breathed easier, knowing I didn't have to perform as some weird ethical balancing weight to my mother's deviance anymore. And when I got to New York, it took some time, but eventually I got rid of the frumpy clothes, learned to experiment, swung one way, then the other before I finally settled into a version of myself I felt comfortable with.

Until that person was crushed.

I wasn't a Madonna or a whore. Good girl or bad. Like most women, I was probably somewhere in the middle. But Lucas's words brought back all the fears that had been swishing around inside me since that terrible night where everything went to hell. That maybe it was me. Maybe I had deserved it.

"That is such bullshit," I said, standing up. My stomach growled. I needed food twenty minutes ago.

Lucas got up and followed me around the front of the house. "Come on, Maggie, that's unfair. It's not like I was one of the ones talking trash about you and her back then. How many times did I come with you to pick her up at Curly's, huh? I wouldn't say any of this if I didn't care, and you know that."

I whirled around. Lucas was right on my tail, and almost crashed into me. An uncomfortable silence fell between us, and he toed his boot into the ground while I stared at him. He sighed, and then I did too.

It was true. It had been eight years since Lucas and I had dated, and six since we'd seen each other at all. But back then, when Mama was going through one of the bad times, he was always there. There to help me lug my nearly passed out mother out of strangers' houses. There to pull over so I could help her puke on the side of the road.

He was always there.

"Look," I said kindly, but still guarded.

Lucas looked down at me, brown eyes hopeful.

"I'm not her," I said. *Aren't you*? A little voice echoed inside. I shook my head. *No*. I couldn't start down that road again.

"I didn't say you were—" Lucas started, but I held up a hand.

"And one dress doesn't make me a wh-whore, Luke."

He gulped, and his eyes bugged. "Mags, that's *not* what I said."

"No, but you suggested it. It was a dress, not a vacancy sign, and it's pretty damn tame compared to what I've seen some people wear on stage. Anyway, showing my legs doesn't make me responsible for how men choose to see me or treat me. And that g-goes for you too."

Lucas opened his mouth—to argue or apologize, I wasn't sure which. I also didn't care.

"I need to eat something," I told him, grateful when my stutter faded away. "And then I'm going to replace some of the broken steps on the stairs."

I turned around and started walking back to the house, eager to put the conversation behind me.

"Maggie," called Lucas. "I'm sorry, okay?"

I raised a hand, but didn't turn around.

"We're good," I called out behind me, though I felt anything but. With every passing minute, I was starting to wonder if coming back here had really been the right thing to do.

CHAPTER SEVEN

Lucas left an hour later, but not before leaving me a note on the counter that included an apology and an invite to a bonfire at the inn with some of our old friends from high school the following night. I looked at the Post-it for a lot longer than necessary and thought about tossing it in the garbage, but in the end, I tucked it in my pocket before going back to work. While I wasn't particularly interested in stepping backwards, the idea of cleaning up after my mother for yet another night sounded depressing.

The next morning, I walked up to the house early for my bike ride with Will and found Mama asleep on the couch, a Bloody Mary half-drunk on the side table. The tip of her nose was tinged with the flush of broken blood vessels.

I picked the glass up and wiped away the water ring with my hand. The only time she didn't use coasters on her grandmother's precious furniture was when she was too smashed to think about it. She must have had more than a few admirers last night at Curly's. Her car wasn't even in the driveway when I went to pull my bike out of the topside cabin.

But as they had for the last week, the frustrations and clouds of the day, the year—hell, my life, floated away as I coasted down the hill toward the general store where Will would be waiting. I tried to tell myself I wasn't excited about spending more than a few minutes with him, but it didn't work. For better or for worse I was intrigued by this sad, lonely man who had locked himself away on the hillside. I wanted to learn more.

Except he wasn't there. I waited for thirty minutes by the store, long enough that Cathy came out to check on me carrying a Dixie cup of coffee.

"Hey, hon," she greeted me, holding her hand over her eyes like a visor. "Getting hot out here, isn't it?"

I looked up at the sun shining fingers of light through the trees. "Yeah, it is."

It was only seven thirty, but it was probably close to seventy-five outside. I didn't want to ride in the late morning heat.

"Who are you waiting for?" Cathy asked curiously as she waved to one of the neighbors down the street out watering her plants.

I looked up and down the road, as if Will might appear from around the bend. But he didn't. And I was feeling increasingly pathetic.

Well, screw that. I didn't need a man—even a gorgeous, bearded yeti who somehow made my chest hurt whenever I thought about him. The whole point of coming back here was to get back to myself. A man would only complicate that even more.

"No one," I said before downing the rest of the coffee. "Just taking a break before the rest of my ride." I handed the cup back to Cathy and gave her a warm smile. "Thanks for the coffee, Cath. I'll bring some more eggs for you tomorrow, 'kay?"

Cathy nodded with another bright smile. "Sounds good. Have a good ride!"

I hopped on my bike, determined to put the mishap behind me, and took a left at the fork in the road instead of a right, continuing across the state line to the flat Hauser Lake route instead of the other side of Newman. If I was going to fall off my bike again, there was no way I was going to land anywhere near that hidden cabin in the woods.

I rode a solid twenty miles, enjoying the benefits of the new tires and the equal parts exhaustion and endorphins brought on by intense exercise. It was close to ten by the time I looped back and was winding around the bend toward home. I waved at Cathy as I passed the store, but slowed a little as I saw a caravan of cars coming down the road toward me, led by a familiar, burnt-orange pickup.

The truck rumbled on, slow enough that even here, there were three other cars behind him crawling at its bumper, the drivers clearly annoyed by the snail's pace.

"Hey!" one of them called out his window. "Speed limit's twenty-five here, buddy!"

But instead of speeding up, Will pulled to a stop, right in the middle of the road. My bike coasted slowly toward him, and eventually I put my foot down next to his car.

Our eyes met, and neither of us blinked for what seemed like minutes. There was no stop sign, nothing to require him to do what he was doing. The lake and sunlight flickered behind his green eyes, causing the gold to dance in the otherwise mournful depths. But Will said nothing, and neither did I. I was too tired. Too confused. Too angry.

Will opened his mouth and set his hand in the open window, almost like he was going to jump through it to get to me. A car horn blared from behind him, causing us both to jerk. Will pulled back his hand and rubbed it across his face, then reached down and shifted his truck back into first gear.

And then he kept driving, kicking up dust particles that reflected morning sun in tiny sequins of light. The truck rumbled on like I didn't even exist.

MUCH TO MY EXTREME IRRITATION, I couldn't get those eyes out of my head for the rest of the day. Nothing would do it. Not sweeping all the pine needles off the boulders bordering the edge of the property. Not lugging most of the junk out of the outer cabins and making three trips to the dump. Not swimming another mile that afternoon around the lake's perimeter to the general store and back. Nothing got that stupid, stubborn, silent face out of my mind.

After spending the rest of the day watching me brood while she worked in the yard, Mama had had enough.

"Maggie Mae, I tell you, if you don't wipe that sourpuss off your face, you're gonna get a big ol' bucket of ice water on it instead," Mama threatened from the bathroom that evening, where she was teasing her hair out for dinner at her best friend, Barb's.

I was just relieved that the excuse to go out wasn't trivia night at Curly's or the like. Oh, she'd still drink enough to fall asleep on a couch somewhere, but it would be her friend's house instead of a stranger's, and Barb wouldn't let her drive drunk.

Mama held up a glass of ice water, and I knew she wasn't making an idle threat, despite the teasing grin on her face. When I was in high school, I'd gotten ice water poured on my head more than once for having "attitude." Let me tell you, when it's twenty degrees outside in the middle of winter, wet hair does *not* feel good when you're driving yourself to school.

I stretched my lips into a giant fake smile, and Mama laughed, sipping on her water.

"That's my beautiful baby," she said, turning back to the mirror and her primping. "You doin' anything fun tonight? I saw that note Lucas left you." She winked at me. "He's still sweet on you after all these years. I should thank you for the good deal he's giving me on the drywall for the cottages, not to mention all that free labor. You don't do this much for someone you don't care about."

I pressed my lips together. I really, really hoped that Lucas wasn't doing all this work on our property for cheap just because he wanted to get back together. "I really don't think that's what's going on, Mama. Lucas is just a nice guy."

She laughed again. "No one's suggesting a ring or anything, Maggie. But I bet it would be fun to take another spin on that particular carnival ride again, wouldn't it? He sure has filled out since you were in high school. Bet he's filled out in other places too."

She winked at me, and I scowled.

"Mama. *Ew.* I do not need to hear you talking like that about a man twenty-five years younger than you."

Her laugh chimed around the cabin like church bells. "How is it that my daughter is more of a prude than me?" she wondered as she lined her eyes with dark blue. "We're both grown women here. I know you're no angel, and I'm certainly not. If we can't speak plain about these things, what kind of relationship do we have?"

"A normal one." I said it jokingly, but only halfway.

Her eyes twinkled, and for a moment, I was taken back to those times when, as a child, I had been so in love with my mother. Because it wasn't all hangovers and missed parent-teacher conferences. Ellie Sharp was the life of the party, and when she was willing to put her attention on me, make me feel like her best friend, it had been the best feeling in the world.

But that was when I was old enough to know that just like all her other moods, this one would fade too.

Mama snorted. "Normal's for fools who want to waste their lives staring at the screen, eating Cheetos. You and I ain't never been normal, Maggie Mae. My baby girl was always special, and I've *never* wanted to just settle. Even with you."

I watched as she made her proclamations into the mirror before applying the same pink paint she'd always worn. I used to love this about her. When I was little, I'd sit on that same countertop and listen to her philosophize at me while she lined her lips and rouged her cheeks, telling me all about the greatness that was in us both, no matter what people said. Mama was my hero—a strong, vibrant woman who believed in herself above all others, refusing to bow to the social expectations of a woman in her community. She'd made her life on her own terms, having the fun *she* wanted to have. What did it matter that sometimes our phone got shut off because she mishandled the bills, or that sometimes I missed school because she was too tired to take me? At seven, eight, nine, I didn't care much. We were living our life on our *own* terms, she said. No man, no one else to tell us what to do.

But once I got a little older, I started to recognize the pattern. Weeks would go by and that scent of stale alcohol, always lurking just under her flowery perfume, would grow more and more pungent. I'd miss more school because she'd leave the car at the bar, butter cold bread because at there was nothing else to eat. Then the lights would go off, or maybe we needed to have the septic tank drained. The roof would need to be patched, or her car would break down. And suddenly, there would be a man showing up with her when she toppled down the stairs, and that man would stay weeks, sometimes months.

Until he left. The good ones always did fairly early because no one worth their salt wanted to be involved with a middle-aged alcoholic. The ones who stayed longer did it because they needed her too—those were the ones who stayed to fight. Who threatened her. Yelled at me. And, as I got older, suggested other things that were very inappropriate for her underage daughter.

I never met him, but Alan sounded like one of those. When I called home, he'd shout that he wanted to meet Ellie's beautiful daughter, and when was I coming for a visit? He stayed with Mama long enough to bleed her dry by enabling her worst flaws. And now I was here, trying to help her pick up the pieces while doing the same for myself.

God, we really were a sorry mess.

I slipped a hand into my back pocket, and my fingers brushed the edge of Lucas's Post-it. I pulled it out, comforted by Lucas's frank scrawl. Immediately, I felt bad about the way I had treated him. He was just looking out for me, the way he always had. How many times had he come over in the middle of the night and brought me home with him to sleep on his parents' couch so a stranger wouldn't find his way into my bed in the middle of the night? He knew better than anyone what I was dealing with over here. And he was still trying to help.

At the very least, I owed him an apology. I crumpled up the note and turned to the bathroom.

"How long are you going to be in there?" I asked Mama. "I need to shower. I'm going out after all."

CHAPTER EIGHT

The bonfire was visible from the road when I pulled up in front of the Forsters' old rambling farmhouse off Muzzy Cove that had been serving as an inn for the last fifty years or so. Lucas, his parents, and his younger sister, Katie, lived in a smaller house in the far corner of the property, leaving the inn and the rest of the five acres primarily to the guests. But considering how much time I'd spent in front of the big fire pit that lit up the grassy lawn leading to the lake's edge, the whole place still felt as familiar as a second home.

I stood outside my car for a moment, listening to the laughter echoing from the beach. Doubt piled back in. How would they react, seeing me eight years after I broke their son's heart? What kinds of questions would they ask about why I'd returned? Which ones did I want to answer? My appearance would make a splash. Was that what I wanted right now?

"Maggie? Is that you?"

I swung around to find Linda Forster, Lucas's mother, rounding the corner of the inn with a basket full of linens.

"Hey, Linda," I greeted her warmly, reaching to take the basket from her. I accepted her kiss to my cheek.

"Lucas said you were back in town. We were wondering if you were going to drop by to say hello," she said. "I'm just taking these back to the main house to launder. The kids are all at the pit if you want to join them."

I nodded. I wasn't getting out of this now.

As she walked me toward the lake, Linda chattered about some of the new updates Lucas had done to the inn since starting to take over from his dad.

"You know that Don and I are making the move down to Arizona next year, right?" she asked.

I shook my head. "No, I didn't. I knew you were retiring, but I didn't know about the move. Good for you guys, though."

"We found a little place up north in the desert we like. We'll come back here for the summers when it gets too hot down there, but it was time. We've been squirreling away our pennies since the kids were in diapers." She sighed, looking out at the lake. "We love it here, but it's time to pass the place on to the next generation. Lucas is gonna do well with it. 'Specially if he can find a good partner to help him run it."

She gave me a knowing look, and I kept my gaze squarely ahead of me. Some things never changed. How many times had I heard suggestions of marriage from Linda, Don, half the people around the lake, when Lucas and I were just seventeen? Now I had been home for less than two weeks, Lucas and I weren't even involved, and I was hearing it again.

"Look who the cat dragged in!" Linda announced as we approached the fire pit. She took the basket from me, nodding at the group sitting in camp chairs and overturned logs around the big fire.

All eight or so people stopped their conversations. Lucas, who had previously been engrossed by a very pretty blonde woman on the other side of the fire, jumped up eagerly to give me a hug.

"Hey, Mags, you made it!" He pulled me in and pressed a quick kiss to the top of my head.

I waited, woodenly, until he finished the awkward embrace. It felt overly familiar, considering the context of our last conversation. But then again, that could have been due to the beer on his breath.

I pulled at the hem of my skirt, which, while not super tight or anything, did only come down to mid-thigh. I wrapped my oversized fleece jacket around my torso and looked out to the crowd. "Hey, everyone. Thought I'd come by and say hello."

Their greetings were first cautious, then effusive. John Hawkins, Lucas's best friend, got up to give me a hug before introducing me to his wife, Alex. Katie was also there with her boyfriend, along with a few other people I remembered from high school. Lindsay, the blonde girl Lucas had been chatting up when I arrived, shot nasty glances at me from time to time, but otherwise everyone welcomed me into the circle while Lucas offered me a chair by the fire and a beer.

"Just a water," I said, ignoring the curious looks from the others when I turned down one of the cans of Natural Ice from the cooler.

"Still dry, huh?" Lucas asked as he handed me a bottle of water instead.

I took it and shrugged. "I'm just thirsty." Though I never came out as completely dry or anything in high school, I never drank much either. Lucas knew why, and so did John and Katie. The others didn't press it.

"When did you get back, Maggie?" Katie asked after she'd come around for an awkward hug.

"About ten days ago."

"Where were you?" Lindsay had a voice like a dart as she scooted toward Lucas, who sat down a bit closer to me.

I cleared my throat. "Um, New York."

"Maggie is an amazing musician," Lucas told her. She didn't seem impressed.

"What kind?" Lindsay asked, as she looked me up and down. "Rap? R&B? My mom always said that kind of stuff was basically just medicine for the devil. That's why I like working at Curly's, you know? All they play is country music."

"Oh my God, Lindsay, what planet are you from?" Katie joked, tossing a balled-up napkin across the fire at her. It caught in the flames and quickly burned up.

Lindsay sniffed. "Well, you know, when you really listen to the lyrics, it's true. It's all about sex and drugs. Nothing else."

"Doesn't sound so bad to me," jeered Katie's boyfriend, Scott, followed by a pinch at Katie's waist that made her shriek.

I smiled thinly and took a long swig of my water. "Well, I didn't really perform that kind of stuff. Most of what I did probably sounds like country, maybe folk. Kind of in the middle, like Neko Case or the Avett Brothers."

"Country?" Lindsay gawked. "*You*?" Her gaze traveled up and down my person.

I shrugged. "Why not?"

She looked like she wanted to tell me *exactly* why someone who looked like me shouldn't be singing anything like country music, but instead, Lucas put a hand on her knee and pulled her into a different conversation about the latest superhero movie.

Eventually, the group fell back into a familiar rhythm, and I had to admit there was some comfort in it. We had been doing this since we were kids, gathering around someone's fire, at someone's dock, just shooting the shit and hanging out. The same exact faces, perhaps a bit fuller after almost a decade, were lit golden in the fire. They told the same stories about someone's dog, or the kid who had fallen out of John's truck after that one football game. Even the new ones sounded the same.

"I have an idea, Mags," Lucas said, sometime later. It wasn't until he nudged me in the arm that I realized he was talking to me.

I shook my head. "What's that?"

Lucas stood up. "We got a used guitar for the inn—some of the guests like to play it in the common room. I'll go get it, and you can play for us, like you used to."

I stiffened. "No, no," I said as casually as I could, shaking my head. "I'm out of practice. Not really in the playing mood tonight."

"Come on, Mags. Let's hear that famous songbird voice of yours. Let's see if eight years in the big city was worth it."

It was hard not to hear the bitterness in his voice, and by the way everyone else around the fire fell quiet, they heard it too.

I stared at Lucas for a moment, and he stared at me, his round face suddenly looking heavy, cast with shadow. He wiped his mouth with the back of his hand, but didn't blink.

But I wasn't going to move on this. "Not tonight," I said. I turned to the fire and gave a weak smile to the silent crowd. "Sorry."

"Well, that's a surprise," Lindsay muttered to John. "Isn't that what they all like to do? 'Sports and entertainment'?"

John shook his head, though he couldn't mask an embarrassed smile. "Jesus Christ, Lindsay."

I stiffened. "What did you say?"

Lindsay shrugged and took another long drink from her beer. "Um, pretty sure it was a rapper that said that." She nudged John again. "My brother loves old-school Jay-Z. I am *always* hearing that shit."

"Lindsay, you need to stop talking now," Katie broke in. "Plus, Maggie's not even black, are you, Mags?"

I sighed. I didn't have the patience to do this all over again, reinvent the wheel of my unknown ethnicity, lost even to me. I didn't need to listen to the hush that would come over the group when everyone remembered what a slut my mother was. The knowing looks that would land on me, as if they could see some slutty genetic instincts emerging on command.

"I'm pretty tired," I finally said, standing up. "I think I'm going to go home. Have a good night, everyone."

"Good riddance," Lindsay muttered, but I was already striding back to my car.

"Maggie. Maggie, wait!"

I didn't. It's not like I hadn't heard a thousand comments like Lindsay's over the years, whether in Spokane or New York. But I had forgotten what this was like—how, if I wasn't willing to be someone's token, I was easily dismissed at gatherings like these, previously only protected by the power of dating Lucas Forster. I didn't belong here. I never had, even if it was also the only home I had to come back to.

Lucas grabbed my arm and forced me to turn around to face him. "Maggie, I said *stop*."

I pulled my arm away. "I just need to go home, Lucas. This was a bad idea."

"Come on, don't let one bitchy comment drive you away," Lucas said. "Lindsay's just jealous because she knows you're special."

I shrugged. I didn't feel special. I felt broken and awkward and out of place. "I just want to go."

"Come here." Lucas pulled me into his big body, and despite the scent of cheap beer wafting off him, the solid warmth of him didn't feel awful. I softened slightly.

"*I'm* glad you're back," he murmured as he looked down.

And for a second, I looked back. I saw Lucas, who was mostly kind, supportive, even if he didn't always get it. And for a second, I was comforted by that.

Then he leaned down and pressed a sloppy kiss on my mouth.

"Lucas!"

I turned my head away, but he didn't stop. Instead, he pressed me into the side of my car, his hands running down my sides as he breathed heavily into my neck.

"Fuck, Maggie," he groaned. "I missed you. You feel *so* good."

"Stop! What are you doing?" I shouted.

"*What*?" Lucas spat, his upper lip curling as he slurred slightly. "You wanna tell me you don't feel the connection between us? It's still here, Mags, you know it is."

"*No,* I d-do n-not!!" I sputtered, the stutter returning just enough to make me spout like a tea kettle. "Just yesterday, I was spitting mad at you for calling me a slut!"

"I didn't call you a slut, Maggie," Lucas protested. "I said your *dress* maybe suggested something like it. Honestly, I was just jealous. I didn't like the idea of other guys seeing your pretty legs in something like that. Something like this skirt too, if you want to be real." He looked me over again, and this time, the suggestion in his eyes was clear as they drifted over my bare legs. His mouth quirked with a smile that wasn't nearly as shy as it used to be. "Chicken legs."

But now I didn't find the silly nickname the slightest bit funny. Nothing about this was funny, especially not when Lucas leaned in again with the clear intent to kiss me, whether I wanted it or not. Like somehow I was asking for it.

"Lucas," I said, pressing against his chest.

He didn't move.

"Lucas!"

He stopped.

"Let me make this very, very clear," I said, pushing him back again. This time, he moved. "I am not interested in *anything* like that. Not with you. Not with anyone. If that means you don't want to help Mama and me out on the property, I get it. We'll figure out something else. But you and I cannot be anything more than friends. Do you understand?"

Lucas didn't answer for what seemed like an hour. Finally, he pulled his baseball hat off his head and put it on backwards before exhaling, long and heavy.

"You really have changed," he said, somewhat regretfully. "Yeah, I get it. And you don't have to worry about the work. I'll be there on Monday, bright and early. *I* don't break my promises."

Leaving me to wonder exactly what he meant by that, he turned and loped back to the fire. I got into my car and started to drive, taking a left out of their driveway instead of a right, which would've been the shorter way back to my place. I didn't feel like going back to the empty house just yet, knowing I would brood on the dock or in front of the television, waiting to see if Mama would show up or not. Instead I just drove, a little faster than I should have, asking all the questions out loud that I had wanted to say in the parking lot.

"Promises?" I cried into the darkness. "What *promises*? Did you really think that just because we were high school sweethearts, I fucking *owed* you something? Did you think that I was supposed to promise you my entire fucking *life* just because we said words like love when we were fucking *children*?"

The questions went on, shouted out the window to be lost in the speeding trees. They were questions I couldn't answer, and yet the answers echoed back to me, known, if not spoken. Because this was a place where people had always thought they owned each other in their small lives. Lucas had been good to me once, but had always thought that he owned me too, in his small, kind way. In that way, he was no better than Theo. So that in the end, he could take what he wanted, and most of the time I'd feel like I had to give it to him. Both he and Lucas had wanted me for a life already set up for them. It hadn't mattered that I didn't want those lives myself. And neither man had ever forgiven me for it.

"Will anyone here," I wondered aloud for the thousandth time in my life, "ever just see me for what *I* am? What *I* want to be?"

Just as the question flew past my lips, my car jolted heavily, and the loud flap of deflated rubber jogging on the pavement sounded. There was a screech as I pulled the car to a stop on the side of the dark, deserted road.

"Shit!" I screeched. Some idiot had probably dropped a nail off their truck, and on this dark, unlit road, I had a flat.

With my phone's flashlight turned on, I crawled out of the car and got down to look at the damage. It was bad. Not only was the front driver's side tire totally shredded, but the entire wheel seemed bent off kilter. I guessed that even if I could replace the tire, it wouldn't be drivable. Ten miles from my house, and no ride in sight.

I picked myself up off the ground and glared at the car. And then, I absolutely lost it.

"FUUUUUUUUUUCK!" I screamed, suddenly letting loose at the car with my feet, kicking wildly at the tires and hubcaps. I picked up sticks, pine cones, needles, anything within easy grabbing distance and threw them at my car. "Stupid hunk of junk! What the *fuck*!"

Just as I was picking up a rock to hurl at the hood, no longer caring what kind of dents would come of my assault, the flash of headlights coming down the street broke through my tirade. I froze, suddenly very aware that I was a brown-skinned woman alone at night on the side of a rural road in a county with a less than stellar reputation with people of color. I'd never had anything that terrible happen to me when I was younger besides a few pullovers and some name calling at school, but I'd heard stories of cops harassing black kids in Spokane Valley. And in this day and age, with tensions as high as they were everywhere, I couldn't help but be a little scared.

The car slowed as it approached, but it wasn't until it was almost next to me that I recognized the orange pickup. The fear subsided, but my irritation rose.

Of. Fucking. Course.

Anger and frustration boiled up all over again as the truck pulled over. The window rolled down, and Will's face, etched with sharp annoyance, appeared.

"What the fuck are you doing?" he demanded.

I kicked my foot at the ground, refusing to look up. "What does it *look* like I'm doing?"

Will just glared. "It *looks* like you just happened to break down in front of my property. *Again*. It's two in the fucking morning, Maggie. Don't you think this is a little desperate?"

I flared. "Are you fucking kidding me? You think I deliberately ruined both the tire and axle of my car just to lure you out of your creepy Unabomber cabin at two in the morning? Do I look like I have a death wish? How self-absorbed do you have to be?"

Will leaned out of the cab, examined the maimed tire, and had the decency to appear more contrite. He looked at me, and even through my fury, I had to work to ignore the way his gaze seared over my cheeks, my lips, my neck, even my cleavage. But unlike Lucas's gaze, it didn't feel dirty. This was something else completely.

"What are you even doing out here at this time of night?" I asked, hating that my voice had grown small.

"I went hiking for the day, and I'm just getting back into town. Were you driving drunk?" Will asked bluntly.

I crossed my arms. "Who the hell are you, the police?"

He frowned. "No. I'm just wondering if I need to put on some coffee while I see if I can get your shitty car working again."

I opened my mouth to launch another insult at him, but instead I just shook my head. Beggars couldn't be choosers, and it was either accept this asshole's help or spend the night in the car.

"I don't drink. Water is fine. Or nothing at all."

At that, Will's anger broke, and he looked genuinely surprised. "Really?"

"My mother drinks enough for both of us." I looked away. Tears were rising now, and I was losing the fight against them. Fuck. I just wanted to be…fuck. I really didn't know. And that was the worst part of all of it.

Will examined me for a few more seconds, then sighed. "Get in," he said. "You can come inside while I take a look."

CHAPTER NINE

Will pulled the truck down the long, winding driveway in front of his old wood cabin. In the dark, it looked even creepier than during the day, since unlike most houses, Will's had no porch lights to give some aura of welcome. The whole thing was basically swathed in black. The woods were pretty much opaque at night, and you really couldn't see anything except for the glimmer of moonlight on the lake down below. That, combined with the general decrepit state of the property, with its peeling, faded shingles and sagging roof, made me walk a little closer to Will than I might have otherwise.

He was a shadow in front of me, somehow even taller and more solid in the dark. His hair was tied up on the top of his head, but in the darkness, all that was really visible were the long lines of his silhouette—the breadth of his shoulders, the taper of his waist. And if I hadn't been so close, I might not have been able to smell that clean, fresh scent of his. That wasn't helping me clear my head at all.

He unlocked the door and flipped a switch, which immediately flooded a large, comfortable room with light. We stepped inside, and as the screen door slammed shut behind me, I swallowed my surprise at what lay before me.

First of all, it was big—bigger than you'd imagine a cabin that didn't look like it was more than a thousand square feet. It made sense, of course. If this was a remodeled lodge, it was going to be spacious, but you certainly wouldn't expect it from the outside.

As I looked around, it seemed as if the house had been completely gutted. All of the walls had been removed so that, as I turned around in a circle, parts of a kitchen, living room, and study all flowed seamlessly into one another, more like a loft space than an enclosed cabin. In the front of the wide-open room was a large couch and loveseat set up around a rustic wood coffee table, all facing a picture window that looked through the trees to the lake. Bookshelves lined the opposite wall, framing a large desk in the middle. In between the living area and the kitchen was a dining set—a giant carved table surrounded by ten matching chairs.

"Where do you sleep?" I wondered before I realized I had said it out loud. And just like that, I was imagining Will in a bed, his long, lean frame stretched out atop rumpled linens. Maybe they'd be white, setting off his tanned skin, draped just so across an otherwise unclothed, sculpted middle…

And then, of course, I was blushing. Dammit.

Will raised a brow and pointed to one corner where a set of stairs disappeared down to a lower floor. Wow. This house really was bigger than it looked from the outside.

It was also a lot nicer. As I followed Will farther inside, I noticed that the furniture and decorating, while not particularly flashy, had the quiet elegance that you could only attain with real money. Fabrics that you knew didn't have a thread of polyester in them. Furniture that was obviously solid wood—no particleboard crap for this guy. Whatever "advertising" Will had done before he came out here, he'd obviously cleaned up. This place was nice. Really nice.

"Give me a second, and I'll take a look at your car," Will said as he moved into the kitchen. "I'm going to make some tea."

Was that an offer? Without waiting for my response, Will turned next to the center island and set a kettle to boil on the wide Viking stove. Not knowing what to do, I slid onto one of the bar stools at the island and watched him work.

He was...competent. I wasn't sure how else to say it. Even with tasks so minor, Will moved with the kind of surety a lot of people lacked. Especially men in the kitchen. Especially in this part of the world. All my life, I'd grown up around men and boys who could barely butter toast on their own. I honestly would have been shocked if Lucas or his father had the first idea about how to boil water or make something simple, like boxed pasta.

Will was clearly self-sufficient. At first glance, I would have taken him for someone who at the very least spent his life outdoors, probably working with his hands, and with the smears of dirt and residue of dried sweat that stained his shirt, maybe even homeless. But in close proximity and in the comfort of his home, it was hard to ignore the natural, somewhat animal magnetism and confidence emanating from his body. Transfixed, I watched the lines of muscle moving under his thin t-shirt. He was built like a swimmer, with shoulders that managed to be broad, not bulky, over an otherwise lean torso, and legs that went for days. And yeah, it was hard not to notice the perfectly shaped ass that filled out his carpenter pants indecently well.

Still, between the hair and the clothes, Will seemed to be working really hard to mask his natural looks. I couldn't help wondering why.

He turned around as the thought echoed again and again through my mind, and caught me staring directly at his ass. I flushed. The right side of his mouth quirked under his beard.

"What's on your mind, Lily pad?" he asked as he passed me a mug of tea. "Peppermint all right?"

"Who are you hiding from?" I blurted out.

Will's green eyes darkened, and three rows of worry lines appeared over his brow. He took a sip of his tea, then set it on the counter.

"I'm going to take a look at your car," he said, ignoring my question. "Stay here."

Shit. I opened my mouth to apologize, but before I could, he'd already abandoned his mug on the counter and was gone. So much for making amends.

I studied the big open room again while I waited, sipping my tea. It was really good tea, actually—maybe some of the best I'd ever had. And the rest of the room, as far as I could tell, had the same kind of quality. The sofa and loveseat had that look of soft, supple leather that probably cost a fortune. Every appliance in this kitchen was state of the art, immaculate stainless steel. The counters were a brilliant, polished granite, and the wood floors gleamed. This wasn't just a cabin in the woods. It was a sanctuary.

A sanctuary that was pretty much devoid of life, I also noticed. There wasn't even a plant in here to keep alive, much less a cat or a gerbil or any sign of social connections. No birthday cards pinned to a bulletin board or stuck on the fridge. No family photos on the walls or shelves. There wasn't even a trace of mail left anywhere—magazine subscriptions, bills, nothing. If you were to walk into this house, you would have absolutely no idea who lived here.

The front door opened with a loud squeak and Will strode back in, retying his hair on top of his head. I liked it when he did that—not just because the man could rock a man bun way better than should be legal, but also because it allowed me to see at least some of his face. I wondered when the last time was that he'd shaved. If he'd ever shaved, by the looks of that beard.

Suddenly, I was desperate to know what he looked like underneath it.

"Your axle is toast," he announced. "After we're done here, I'll drive you home. I doubt you'll be able to get AAA out here at this time of night."

I nodded and faced him across the counter, still unsure of what to say. I was still mad at him about this morning. The way he'd stood me up and then treated me like a stranger.

"So what were you up to before you just 'happened' to crash in front of my driveway?" Will asked. His voice was awkward, like he was trying to be nice, but couldn't quite manage it. I knew that sound. That sound was all guilt, couched in a passive-aggressive mask.

I set my mug down on the counter. "I know what you're thinking, and you can get off your egotistical high horse. I'm *not* stalking you."

Will pressed his mouth together and raised a brow in a way that told me he didn't totally believe me.

I scowled. "I'm *not*."

"All right, all right," he said, almost like he wanted to laugh. "So what *were* you up to?"

"I met up with some old friends for a bonfire. *They* actually showed up."

Will's jaw tightened, and he set his mug down. "Okay. Okay, sure. I guess I owe you an apology."

"You *guess*?"

He frowned. "It was just a suggestion to meet up for a ride. I told you, I decided to go hiking around Pend d'Oreille instead. You saw me on my way out, and I didn't get back until just now. I couldn't call you because I don't have your number. Or a phone, for that matter."

I shook my head. "How do you not have a phone?"

Will shrugged, but I could see him withdraw. Jeez, the guy *really* didn't like questions about himself.

"I don't need one," was all he said. "Listen, I'm—I'm sorry, okay? I am. I don't have friends, Maggie, and to be honest, I wasn't really looking for any. I didn't think you would really care."

"You..." I trailed off. The guy was so much more than frustrating. "You are *so* full of shit."

"Come again?"

We stared at each other for a minute over the counter, neither of us blinking. I didn't believe him. Not that he didn't have friends—that much was completely obvious. But he didn't care? There had been moments with Will where I could have sworn he was dying for me to touch him. He had stopped traffic in the middle of the street just to stare at me for a full minute.

The question wasn't if he cared. It was how much. Because the guy certainly wasn't indifferent.

"What happened to you before you came here, Maggie?"

I looked up, surprised. I thought I was the one doing the interrogating here. "What do you mean?"

Will passed his mug back and forth between his big hands for a minute, then took a long drink. "That day we met," he said. "You seemed really freaked out."

"You mean the day you were a complete asshole to the girl with the twisted ankle?"

Will blushed. Full-on, red-faced blushed. It was adorable and made me want to hug him. I wanted to, but I didn't. Will had made it very clear that we weren't friends. That we were nothing.

It would just be a lot easier to believe if he weren't *looking* at me like we were a lot more than nothing.

He chewed on his upper lip for a second. "No, it was something else. The biking, the swimming. You're running from something. I recognize the signs." His green eyes flickered. "Takes one to know one."

Again, that curious energy, an unnamable understanding, flamed between us.

I swallowed and stared at my mug. "I…something happened in New York."

"I figured. What was it?"

I turned the handle of the mug to the right, then to the left. "Bad breakup."

The air between us thickened. Why was I even divulging any of this? Wasn't I trying to get away from the stigma of my mother's behavior? All I needed was for the truth about Theo to get out. It would seal that legacy for good.

But Will just waited for me to think, much more patient than I ever was, until he asked his next question. "What did he do?"

"Why do you think he did anything?" My voice was much sharper than I wanted it to be.

"Lily."

With the casual use of the pet name, the fissures cracked open. It was a reminder that, if only in one small way, this strange, distant man had made me his. We barely knew each other, and yet, clearly there was some kind of connection here, even if it confused both of us. I wasn't Theo's flower anymore. I was a grouchy hermit's lily.

Slowly, before I was even aware of it, a tear fell down my cheek. I sucked in a breath.

"Hey." Will's voice was a low burr, a comfort that slid through my thoughts. "You don't have to tell me if you don't want to," he said. "But if you do, you can trust me, Lil. I promise you that."

"Like I trusted you to meet me for a ride?"

This time he didn't look away. His eyes met mine and didn't waver, and I saw the true remorse I had been looking for since he picked me up, that I had begged for the entire time I was with Theo. Will might have his secrets—that much was clear—but right now, he was an open book.

"I am sorry," he said, his gaze unmoving. His hand squeezed mine. "I am."

I watched him for a few more seconds, but he never blinked, never looked away. The rest of the house faded, until finally, I sighed.

"Forgiven," I said simply. "You've rescued me three times now. I suppose that means we're even. But I think I'll divulge my life's story another time."

"Fair enough." Will's mouth quirked, and more than ever I wanted to know what he looked like when he smiled. Actually, I wanted to know what he looked like period.

"So what's with the Dumbledore look you have going on here?" I said, gesturing up and down.

Will blinked. "Dumbledore?"

"The hair. The beard. You're right out of Hogwarts. I can't decide if you want to murder me or turn me into a toad."

Will snorted. "I was going more for Hagrid." He paused with an uncertainty that was disarmingly adorable. "You think it looks that bad?"

I cocked my head. "Do you care?"

"No." But then he answered again. "At least, I didn't until now." He cleared his throat. "So, your friends. It was a good time?"

I frowned. This was weird. He was trying to take the attention off himself by making stupid small talk. I didn't know Will very well, but I knew that wasn't his style. And it certainly wasn't mine.

"Not really, if you want to know the truth," I said frankly. "I sat around drinking water while they shotgunned Natty Ice like we were still seventeen. Then one of them basically called me a tap-dancing monkey, and another told me that I was a slut for wearing a short dress."

Will's eyes immediately flared. "They said *what*?"

I shrugged. "It wasn't exactly like that. But...yeah. The insinuations were there. It's about par for the course for this area."

"What the..." he sputtered, repeating himself again and again until he finally managed to string together a sentence. "Who was this racist motherfucker who called you a dancing monkey? *To your face*?"

I flushed. It was my fault for bringing it up, but now that I had, I felt embarrassed by it. People said shit like that and didn't really understand how it felt—little comments under which they could claim plausible deniability. I'm sure if I had confronted Lindsay point blank, she would have said she was talking about my age, or people from New York, or literally anything other than my ethnicity.

Because if you did bring it up, you were either told to let it go, like Lucas told me to, or people went crazy, like Will. But there were always going to be Lindsays in the world—ignorant bitches who would never *really* understand how their words cut. Or maybe they did, and they didn't care.

"She was just jealous," I muttered. "Because the guy she liked flirted with me instead."

"This was your ex?"

I looked up. "How did you know?"

Will shrugged. "Lucas Forster. The way you talked about him. It's kind of obvious."

I pressed my lips together before taking a sip of tea. "Well, yeah. He ended up making a move, but I wasn't interested. I just..." I sighed, shoving a hand through my hair while I looked to the side, toward the trees brushing against the windows. Anywhere but the pair of intense green eyes staring holes through me. "I had to leave, but I didn't want to go home. I already feel like I'm moving backward enough, you know? And Lucas...he was the one who mentioned my skirt."

"What did he say?"

I stopped playing with my mug. "Who?"

"Luke Skywalker. What did he say about your skirt?"

I shied, but Will just waited. Seriously, the guy could probably get the Mona Lisa to talk if he stared long enough. It was even more annoying because he kept his own story locked up so tight.

"He saw a picture and suggested that I was somewhat responsible for...certain things...because of clothes I wore." My face was heating up. God, this was mortifying.

"Dumb motherfucker." Will's voice was louder than a grumble, just barely.

I looked up. "Excuse me?"

Will's brow rose. "You heard me."

I shook my head. "Lucas is not dumb. He's actually great, and he's doing a lot for me and my mom. He's allowed to think a certain way if he wants to. He's just looking out for me."

"He's dumb as a fucking post," Will said, "if he thinks for one second that covering up your legs would do a goddamn thing to hide how beautiful you are."

His words echoed around the room, and again through my mind. *Beautiful.* Will thought I was beautiful.

Will thought I was beautiful?

What?

But before I could respond, he cleared his throat, polished off his tea, and stood back up. "Fuck 'em, Lil. You're better off without people who make you feel like less than you are. Fuck them *and* their shitty beer."

I shook my head. "You don't understand—"

"I understand plenty. And I'm telling you, you don't need that kind of bullshit."

"Well, maybe I don't need them *or* you telling me anything!" I burst out, suddenly tired of having anything dictated to me whatsoever.

Theo used to dictate my entire world. Mama spewed advice on my social life. Lucas on my wardrobe. And now Will was standing here telling me to write off people I had known forever. I just wanted *everyone* to keep their stupid opinions to themselves unless I asked for them.

"Lily—"

"*Stop*," I said, pushing away from the counter. "I've had enough. Sure, Lucas pissed me off, and I left, but you don't know him at all. He's a good friend, and he's been there for my mom even when I haven't. Do you know what he's doing right now? Basically *all* the major work on our property for a song because he knows we can't afford it."

"And why do you think he's doing that, Lil?" Will cut in. "Maybe to get under another skirt of yours?"

"No, you asshole! Because that's the way he is! Because real fucking people don't lock themselves away in a cabin and pretend the world doesn't exist! And the good ones actually try to make it better. They see a woman in need, and they stop to help without shouting at her. They *fucking show up*!"

I seethed at him across the counter, but Will didn't move a muscle. No quirk of the mouth. No stress lines over his forehead. No indicator that my outburst made any impact whatsoever.

I pushed off the stool.

"Where are you going?"

"Home."

I marched toward the door, and Will immediately grabbed his keys off the counter and followed.

"Lily pad, wait."

I kept going. "I just want to go home," I said as I reached for the doorknob.

"Maggie."

I paused, still facing at the door. I didn't dare look at him—I didn't know what I'd find swimming in his deep green depths. Anger? Annoyance? Irritation? I felt all of that and more.

Will's hand drifted down, fitting naturally to my waist. His fingers were strong, holding me still. I wasn't moving, but I knew if I tried, he wouldn't let me. His intent vibrated clearly.

"You could stay," he said quietly.

When I turned, he wasn't looking at me. His eyes, instead, were fixed on the spot where his fingers rested over my hip. My shirt had risen a few inches, and his middle and index fingers rested directly against my skin. It was strange—he had touched so much more of me when he had pulled me out of the lake, or when he had picked me up from the road. But this touch, so incidental, so minor, had my heart racing. The entire room was a glowing ember.

"You don't have to go home if you don't want, Lil," Will said. "You're safe here for the night."

It was only then his eyes rose to meet mine. They were wide and fathomless. All the bitterness I was accustomed to seeing there was gone. Instead, there was just frank understanding of someone who knew what it felt like to want to escape. And in that moment, I understood the offer for what it really was. Will had created a safe space for himself here—a sanctuary void of interaction with people. People whom, for whatever reason, he wanted to avoid. And now he was sharing that sanctuary with me.

Maybe I shouldn't have stayed. I hardly knew the man, and who was I to say this weirdo with a giant beard wasn't going to try to murder me in my sleep? But the house where I grew up was full of ghosts, alive and dead, just like the rest of this lake. I had fled one set of problems only to return to the old ones. But here, with this strange man, there was no judgment. No anger. With him, I was only me.

I swallowed and covered the hand at my waist with my own. Then slowly, I nodded. "Okay."

CHAPTER TEN

After a few hours of sleep on Will's giant couch (spent mostly, to be honest, thinking about the fact that he was lying on a bed somewhere underneath me), I woke up early the next morning to rays of sunlight shining through the trees. I pushed up and peered out the picture windows that looked out on the lake. Will's house was even nicer during the day than at night—the light glinted off the steel surfaces, refracting everywhere with peaceful brilliance.

Footsteps sounded, and few moments later Will strode into the kitchen, fully kitted out in a pair of athletic shorts, some sneakers that had seen better days, and a ratty tank top that did nothing to take away from his biceps.

Tying his hair into a messy knot on top of his head, he looked the same as every other time I'd seen him. Except for one thing.

I sat up fully. "You trimmed your beard."

Will froze halfway to the kitchen, hands still full of wayward locks and a rubber band sticking out of his mouth. For a second I found it hard to breathe myself. His beard now only consisted of a thick stubble, and the inch of dark blond that was left did nothing to hide what turned out to be a formidably square jaw, a neck that had the same tension-locked muscles as the rest of his lean body, and cheekbones that could cut glass.

I shouldn't have been surprised. I had seen the rest of him, after all. But nothing had prepared me for the beauty of Will Baker's face without a giant golden mess obscuring the lower half.

He finished tying up his hair. "Oh. Yeah, well, it was either that or carve a wizard's staff, I guess."

I flopped over the back of the couch, following him as he ducked into the kitchen. "You totally cut your beard off for me."

"I absolutely did not."

"You one hundred percent did." I pointed at him, wagging my finger around. "Yesterday, you were Nanook of the North. Today you look like a frickin' Abercrombie model. If I tease you some more, will you clean my house for me? Maybe help my mom get sober? What if I called you Fabio? Would you cut your hair too?"

I was pretty much lost in giggles at this point, but all I got in return was a dirty green look. I collapsed on the couch laughing.

A few seconds later, Will appeared over me, still glowering, but with one brow arched and humor clear in his eyes. For a half second, I imagined pulling him down on top of me, then smothering that face with kisses until he smiled. Maybe even laughed. Suddenly, the disturbing fact that I *really* wanted to kiss Will Baker mattered a lot less than the desire to make him laugh. I wanted to make Will Baker laugh so badly that my chest hurt.

"You done now, Lily pad?" he asked with a smirk.

I cleared my throat. "For now."

"Good. Let's have a bite, and then I owe you a run, if your ankle's healed up, that is."

I nodded, and he extended a hand. I allowed him to pull me back up to sitting before he abruptly returned to the kitchen.

"I like that sound," he said as I took a seat at the bar.

"What sound?"

"Your laughter. You should do it more." Will turned around and passed me a mug of tea that he'd miraculously conjured—this time, black. "Milk? Sugar? Honey?"

"Just a bit of milk, please."

He nodded, then retrieved the milk and started whipping up a batch of scrambled eggs and toast just as quickly and efficiently as he'd made tea the night before.

"Do you like your eggs wet or dry?" he asked as he whisked.

"Um…w-wet." My mouth was a little dry, and the way the movement was making his forearm flex was really distracting. "Really wet."

"You like your scrambled eggs really wet?"

I blinked. "Oh—um, no. In the middle is fine. However."

Will poured the eggs onto a heated pan and turned around to grab our toast, which allowed me to ogle him from behind. Yeah. The man filled out athletic shorts really, really well. A few minutes later, he slid two plates over and took a seat next to me at the bar.

"Thanks," I said, taking a bite. "This is good."

Will shrugged. "It's nothing."

We sat together for a bit, companionably chewing. The longer I spent with Will, the easier it was to be silent with him. I appreciated that. Silence had never been my strong suit.

"So, your mom," he said as he spread some jam on his toast. "Is her drinking really that much of a problem?"

"Oh," I said, taken by surprise. He really wasn't going to beat around the bush this morning. "Um, well. She likes a drink. Or five."

"And it's a problem?"

"She…sometimes it makes her a handful," I admitted. But I didn't say more than that. Instead, I took a big bite of eggs and shrugged, choosing to study the thick crust on my bread instead of looking at him. I knew he would see right through me, and I wasn't sure I wanted him to.

Will looked at me hard for a few more seconds, then turned back to his food. "It's none of my business," he said quietly.

For a second, I wanted to argue. I wanted to tell him that it could *all* be his business if he wanted it to be. But then I thought about the way he'd stood me up, or our first few interactions, where he had practically shoved me away from him. And of course, there was the minor fact that any time I asked him anything about himself, he completely and totally shut down.

So I kept quiet. Things like this made a person vulnerable. Everyone else liked to shove my mother's issues in my face. I didn't doubt that with one nasty snap, Will would do it too. And the problem with that was that I suspected it would hurt more from him than other people.

And just why was that?

I shook the question away while we ate in another round of silence.

"All right," Will said once we were finished. He cleared our plates and made quick work of the dishes before turning back to me. "We'll swing by your place so you can change before we run, and then grab some food after. Sound good?"

I nodded. "Fine by me."

Will paused, reaching back a moment to mess with his hair again. "Lil..." he started. "I...this is really hard to say."

I frowned, concerned. "What's up?"

"I...okay. I might still be an asshole sometimes, but I want you to know, it's not you."

I frowned, suddenly suspicious. "That's what assholes say before they do something dickish."

Will sighed and dropped his hands to the counter. "If I'm a dick, you can tell me to fuck off. But..."

He peered through the windows uneasily, lingering a moment on the few boats already buzzing around the water. There weren't many. It was seven in the morning on a Sunday, and most people in the area were either just waking up or getting ready to go to church.

"I don't really do well with a lot of people," he said. "Or any, really."

I cocked my head. "Yeah, I picked up on that."

Will drummed his fingers on the countertop. "Sometimes I might just need a break. If I...if we're ever hanging out, and I just need to take a walk or something, will you remember that? It's not because of you." He swallowed, and absently rubbed a hand over his newly shorn face, stopping a minute, as if he had just realized again that his beard was gone. He looked at me, green eyes glazed slightly with something that looked like fear.

And then there was a small smile. Barely visible, but both sides of his mouth turned up. It was so quick I almost missed it, but the effect it had on his face was undeniable.

"For some reason," he said quietly, "I don't seem to mind being around you."

His hand dropped on top of mine where it rested on the granite. He didn't move it, and neither did I—instead, we both just stared, transfixed by our sudden touch.

"I have an idea," I said, still looking at our hands.

"What's that?"

"A safe word." I dragged my gaze up and smiled at him. "If things get too much, you—or me too—can say the safe word, and the other will know it's not them. No harm, no foul."

Will licked his lips meditatively. It made it hard to focus, but somehow I managed it.

"What's the word?" he asked finally.

I sipped more of my tea. "Anything you want. But probably something you don't say a lot."

A hint of a smile spread across his face. "How about 'lily pad'?"

I rolled my eyes. "Really?"

The smile widened. It wasn't full, but it was more than before. I almost fell off my stool.

"No," Will replied. "You're right. I have a feeling I'm going to be saying that a lot."

Was it weird that I wondered when? And where? And immediately started thinking of some *very* dirty places? *Snap out of it, Maggie. This guy comes with a pickup truck full of issues.*

"How about 'pine cone'?" he suggested, pulling me out of my daze.

I shrugged. "Works for me. So, if you get overwhelmed, just say 'pine cone.' And I'll know you need a step back."

Will nodded. Our eyes locked again in mutual understanding, and the hand that was still over mine pressed down a little harder. Eventually, I started to pull away, but Will didn't let me. He weaved his fingers between mine, lingering his thumb over my knuckles for a second, before then and only then, letting it go.

I ventured another small smile. "You ready?"

Will sighed, full of reluctance I couldn't quite understand. It was just a run, right?

"Ready as I'll ever be," he muttered. "Let me grab the keys, and we'll go."

BUT THERE WERE no people to avoid on the trail that morning. Whether it was too early, or even too cold under the scattered clouds, the concrete path along the Spokane River was almost completely empty for the hour and a half it took us to jog close to ten miles toward the Idaho border and back.

The sun rose quickly, and by the time we returned to the truck, Will had been running for several miles with his shirt off, tucked in the waistband of his shorts. I had to keep my gaze strictly turned forward. One look at the thick blocks of abdominal muscles flexing with each step he took, and I was bound to trip over my feet right into the river.

When we reached the truck, Will unlocked the front so we could grab the water bottles he'd stashed under the front seat. I whipped off my sweat-soaked tank top and mopped my face off before pouring a bit of water on my head. I closed my eyes toward the sun, letting the water drip gloriously down my face and neck. The breeze coming off the river combined with the water felt amazing after the long run.

"Oh, for fuck's sake."

I opened my eyes. "What's wrong?"

Will just stood there, staring at me with one hand thrust into his hair, the other gripping his bottle hard enough that water had squeezed out of the top. His eyes grazed up and down my body, lingering slightly on the expanse of my bare legs and torso, then fixed completely on my breasts.

"Hey!" I snapped my fingers, breaking his daze. "Eyes up here! You live on a lake, Baker. I know you've seen women in way less than this before."

"Yeah, well, their swimsuits aren't white and transparent, Maggie," Will retorted as he slapped a hand over his eyes. "Lil, can you please cover the fuck up?"

"What? Why—"

I started to argue until I looked down and saw exactly what he was talking about. We had run for ten miles, and I'd sweat completely through my sports bra, as one does. But the problem was, the material was exactly as transparent as Will said, which meant my nipples, now erect from the cold water, were fully on display.

"*Oh my God*!" I screeched, jumping back to the truck to grab my sweaty shirt.

"That's what I was saying!" Will shouted, turning to the side to give me some privacy. "You dressed yet?"

"Yes, I am," I said, turning back around to find him standing in profile. "I'm—whoa!"

Now it was my turn to stare. Will's shorts were loose, but the thin material was relatively clingy, especially with sweat, and it definitely didn't leave much to the imagination when his, ah, equipment was on display. Which right now, it very much was. Apparently my nipples had quite the effect. You wouldn't know it from looking at him normally, but the man was seriously packing.

No joke. I practically had to pick my jaw up off the parking lot.

"Now what are *you* staring at—" he started when he opened his eyes before following my gaze down to his very prominent erection. "Oh, *Jesus*," he barked, scrambling behind the end of the truck when he realized what I was staring at.

I immediately collapsed into giggles against the car door. "I don't think Jesus is going to help with what you have going on there, buddy."

"What do you expect, flashing your headlights at me that way!" Will barked, now crouching by the fender. "Can you just get in the car, please? I'll, uh, just be a minute."

Still giggling like a middle-school girl, I climbed into the passenger seat, but immediately turned around and peered at him through the windows that opened to the truck bed. Will stood at the back of the truck, facing the sky with his eyes squeezed shut. His lips moved, and though I couldn't hear everything he whispered, a few phrases floated back to me.

"Golf scores…Grandma's underpants…Algae… God*damn*it."

"Everything all right back there?" I called through the window.

Will's eyes shot open, and he glared at me. "You'd like to know, wouldn't you?"

I grinned. "Sure would," I said without thinking, only afterward realizing how dirty that actually sounded.

Will rolled his eyes, but the glare was gone. "You're enjoying this *way* too much." He twisted his lips together, and I could have sworn it was to avoid smiling.

"I'm fine," he said as he came around to the driver's side. "If you're done torturing me, Lil, maybe we can grab something to eat." He slid into the driver's seat and started the car.

And then Will Baker, world-class misanthrope and grouchy mountain hermit, full-on winked at me. And it was my turn to repeat nonsensical phrases to myself all the way to the restaurant.

CHAPTER ELEVEN

Grabbing something to eat with Will turned out to be a little different than I imagined. We stopped at a diner on the way back to the lake for some breakfast sandwiches. But instead of waiting in line with me, Will took one look at the interior of Norm's Burger Barn, turned on his heel, and went straight back to the truck.

"What are you doing?" I demanded as he slouched into the front seat. "Something wrong with this place?"

He pulled a wad of cash out of the glove compartment and thrust it at me. "I just don't feel like waiting in line. Do you mind?"

I looked over my shoulder. "There are literally two other people in line to order, and one group of kids eating in the corner booth. It's not exactly hopping in there."

Will sighed. "Lily. I just don't want to stay in there. You saw the place. The owners are weirdos."

I frowned. The diner was decorated with a pretty standard mishmash of Hollywood paraphernalia and old car photos. Nothing to write home about. "Kate and Norman are super sweet," I said. "I've known them since I was a kid. Come on, I promise they won't be weird."

But Will just stared at the steering wheel, sticking his lip out like a toddler.

"Are you for real? Will. You're going to fry in here."

His truck didn't have air-conditioning, and he had refused to open his window while we drove. There was a bit of morning traffic circling the main road through Otis Orchards and Liberty Lake—the suburbanites making their way to the lakes for some Sunday fun. Will had glared at all of them.

He just set his jaw stubbornly. "Then you'll have to hurry, won't you?"

Seeing that I could either go without food or leave him in here to melt, I rolled my eyes and slid out of the car. Will clearly had major issues being around people, and this wasn't the time to fight them. But seriously? Sitting in a car in eighty degrees instead of waiting five minutes for a breakfast sandwich? It was a little nuts.

"Be serious," I tried again. "This is so dumb."

Instead, I just received a green-eyed glare. "I told you I don't like people, Lil."

"But, Will—"

"'Pine cone,' Lily."

I sighed. He had me there.

"All right, all right," I said, pushing off the truck. "What do you want?"

"Any kind of egg sandwich will do. Nothing with meat, thanks."

I nodded. "Coffee?"

Will shook his head. "I'll wait until I'm home."

"Okay."

I went inside grumbling to myself, and walked directly up to the counter to order.

"Heya, sweetie," Kate said from the till. "We heard you were back in town. We were wondering when you were going to pay us a visit."

She and Norman had owned the place since I could remember, and had made a name on their huckleberry shakes and endless baskets of fries. But I happened to know they made a kickass fried egg sandwich.

"Two breakfast sandwiches, please," I said. "Hi, Kate. How are you and Norm doing?"

"Good, good." She rang me up and took the cash with a smile. "Ellie in the car?" she asked knowingly.

I sighed. I couldn't count how many times I'd come in here on the way to school and bought breakfast while my mother nursed a nasty hangover in the car. Norm's was also one of the few diners anywhere in the Spokane-Coeur d'Alene area that had a twenty-four-hour drive-through. They were well acquainted with Ellie Sharp's late night munchies, as well as the assorted men who helped her satisfy them.

Kate didn't wait for my answer, just chortled away with a knowing smile to Norm, who was working the grill.

I loitered to the side, waiting for the sandwiches while Kate helped another customer. I tried to see just what about the restaurant Will found so objectionable. Red vinyl booths, all of them clean. Black-and-white photos of old cars, movie stars, Hollywood posters. Most of them were old, but some were new, too. They even had a row of signed headshots on one wall—"famous" people who had come into the diner. Most of them were bit actors, local politicians, etc., but there was even a photo of Dolly Parton.

I checked out the movie posters—Kate usually changed them out every few years to keep the place current, but they were still a fairly even mix of the last fifty years or so. There were classics, of course: *The Godfather, Titanic, Star Wars*. And there were newer ones that I didn't even recognize. It was funny—I didn't think I'd been to a movie in close to ten years. I never went in New York, where tickets cost close to twenty dollars a pop. In college, I had just been too busy with school (not to mention too poor), and when I left and tried to make a go of it with music, all of my attention had gone into that. Not to mention the tips I made waitressing went to my overpriced apartment. I knew absolutely nothing about the film industry other than what popped up here and there in the supermarket aisle or the news.

"Hey, Kate," I called out.

She moved down the counter. "Whatcha need, hon?"

"Have you seen any of these?" I asked, suddenly feeling the urge to stay in. Maybe binge a little on the pop culture I'd missed, ironically, trying to become a pop star.

"Oh yes, every one of 'em. I don't buy the posters for movies I don't see, y'know. And me and Norm, we're regular movie buffs. We watch 'em all." She sighed. "Now that one there was probably my favorite, a few years back. Did you ever see *The Dwelling*?"

"No," I said with sudden interest. "I haven't."

I squinted at the poster, which was a picture of a blond man, so gaunt you could see the vertebrae sticking out of his back, curled on the ground in a messy apartment. He looked over his shoulder at the camera, a searing green-eyed expression that seemed strangely familiar.

"So good," Kate sighed. "I tell you, Maggie, I didn't know anything about AIDS or alcoholism really at all, until I watched that movie. That actor, Fitz somethin' or other, isn't he dead now? Such a shame. He was so good."

I took a step closer. There was something about the poster. Maybe I had seen the movie. Something about it was intensely familiar.

Brrrrrinnnggg!

"Order's up, hon!" Kate called out.

I turned, my stomach growling, all thoughts of *The Dwelling* or any other movie gone. "Thanks, Kate. Say hi to Norm for me."

"Tell your mama to take it easy," she replied before turning to a new customer. I just nodded and went back to the truck.

"Thanks," Will said, looking appropriately sheepish when I handed him the sandwich. We both tore into them almost immediately, starved as we were after our run.

"Thank you," I said as I set his change in the center cupholder. "Thanks to your weirdness, you paid. But was it really a pine cone situation?"

There was a pause, and tin foil crinkled in place of conversation.

"It was," Will said a moment later, then started the car. "It just was."

We drove back to the lake as we ate our sandwiches and enjoyed the breeze through the window that Will had finally allowed me to open. But given his demonstrated phobia of people, I was surprised when he got out of the truck instead of just dropping me off at the stairs leading down to my house. He followed me to the top of the steps, then paused.

"Swim tomorrow morning?" he asked.

His hand fluttered out and almost touched mine again before he pulled it away. I wished he hadn't, but at the same time, the butterflies in my stomach after our run still hadn't died down, and I wasn't sure what I thought about that.

"Sure," I started to say, but was interrupted by Lucas's truck rumbling down the gravel. I could sense a new layer of tension radiating from Will as we watched the shiny blue Ford kick up dust and then roll to a stop next to us. Lucas stepped out carrying his toolbox and blinked between Will and me.

"Ah, hey, Mags," he said, rubbing the back of his neck. "Went for a run, huh?"

I glanced down at my shirt, and Will snorted, earning a dirty look from me. I turned back to Lucas and nodded.

"Yeah, we went early, up and down the Spokane," I said. "Lucas, this is my friend Will."

Lucas turned to Will, openly looking him up and down. "Will. Lucas. Nice to meet you."

He extended a hand, and Will stared at it for a moment before slowly returning the handshake. Lucas stepped back and stuck his hand in the back pocket of his jeans. "Thought I'd get started on the plumbing work on the bottom cabin," he said. "Your mom here? She wasn't at church this morning."

I blushed and gestured to the empty parking spot next to us. Lucas knew exactly why Mama didn't show up at church. "She's still at Barb's, but she'll probably be home by lunch. You know how she gets."

Will frowned, though Lucas nodded with understanding.

"All right," he said. "I'll just get started, then. We also have to move that wood pile before it rains again."

"It's nice of you to do all this work for free," Will said a little too quickly, before he clapped his mouth shut and glowered.

Lucas paused at the top of the stairs, looking between us again. "Just doing what needs to be done," he said with a darkened expression, though his eyes softened when they landed on me. "Mags, hey. About last night..."

"Already forgotten," I said, waving the memory away. I really didn't want to think about it, especially not right now.

Beside me, Will tensed, but thankfully he didn't say anything. Lucas nodded, and with another suspicious look at Will, walked down the steps.

I turned to Will. "Do you want to come down, have some iced tea or something? I have to start on the wood pile, like he said, but I have some time."

Will shook his head, though he wasn't looking at me—instead, his fierce gaze was still zeroed in on Lucas's broad back, now down by the water, closer to the house. "He comes here every day?"

I shrugged. "He has been. He has his own job and a business to run, so I doubt it will be every day. But Lucas is a good guy. He'll show up consistently until everything is finished."

Will turned back to me. "And you really think this is just out of the goodness of his heart?"

I pressed my lips together. "Maybe, maybe not. But this is what people do here, Will. They help each other out, no questions asked. Maybe they talk. Maybe they get all up in each other's lives. But when it really comes down to it, they are there for each other. That's just how it is."

Will chewed again on his upper lip, watching Lucas lugging his tools down to the bottom of the hill. Then he stepped back to his car with a mournful look.

"Rain check on the iced tea," he said, already getting back in. "I'll see you tomorrow, Lily pad."

I raised a hand. He started the engine. Though he hadn't said, "pine cone," I knew he was in a hurry to leave.

"See you," I said, but he was already pulling away.

SEVERAL HOURS LATER, I was in the front yard with Lucas, lugging freshly chopped logs to the wood piles while Lucas made quick work of a big heap of trees that had fallen during the winter storms. Mama was inside futzing around in the kitchen after slinking in sometime past eleven.

"I'm probably done for the day, Mags," Lucas said as he wiped his brow. "It's getting late."

He set the ax on the pile, then placed one last log on top of the two I was already carrying. The lake had calmed since the midday traffic had filtered out, with people returning home to get ready for the week.

I nodded. "Yeah, that's probably good. Thank you again."

Before Lucas could answer, a splash sounded at the end of the dock. Lucas and I turned to watch a man emerge from the ladder. It was Will, shining like a brilliant gold statue under the bright light of the sun and the dancing surface of the water. He emerged from the lake, his hair slicked back from his face, droplets of water clinging to his beard, sliding down his torso, falling from his abs. My mouth dropped. I couldn't help it. Lucas tensed.

Barefoot and clad in nothing but the clinging swim shorts now pasted to his long legs, Will walked the length of the dock directly toward me. He stopped in front of me, and without saying a word, took the logs I was holding.

"Where do these go?" he asked.

Unable to speak, I pointed toward the back of the house, and without waiting, Will immediately turned in that direction. Midway down the path, he stopped and turned.

"Also, I had your car towed to a mechanic in town," he said without moving his gaze from mine. "They said you can pick it up on Tuesday, probably."

"O-okay," I managed to stutter, still stunned that he was even here.

Will gave a curt nod and continued to the wood pile.

"Second thought, I could probably stay a little longer."

I turned around to find Lucas staring daggers at the spot where Will had just disappeared around the side of the house.

Lucas massaged his neck and scowled harder. "You okay with that?"

"Um, okay," I mumbled, still too lost in the long, lean form walking around the house to answer properly. "Thank you. I'm going to go check on Mama."

Inside, I found Mama watching Will and Lucas lugging firewood back and forth from one side of the house to the pile on the other like she was judging an Olympic sport.

"Maggie Mae," she asked, beckoning with one hand until I joined her. "Who in ever-lovin' Jesus is *that*?"

Like me just seconds before, she was also transfixed by the soaked column of muscle standing by the wood, looking like a dog about to shake itself off. Drops of water clung to every chiseled curve, with the light sparkling off the tiny prisms. Will looked around the property for a moment, and then found us at the window. His ever-stoic expression barely shifted, but he raised a brief hand in acknowledgement of our presence, then walked back to the other side of the yard for another armful of wood.

"That's…Will," I offered, barely able to get the words out myself as we watched him lift the large pieces of wood. The movement made the lean muscles in his back ripple while the sun flashed off the water drops still there. I swallowed, my tongue suddenly thick in my throat.

"Will?" Mama looked at me, her brown eyes uncharacteristically sharp as a knife. "That's all I get? 'That's Will'?"

I shrugged, even though I could feel my face turning red under her gaze. "That's all there is."

Mama studied me for a moment, then tapped her lips as she turned back to the show. "My, my, my," she muttered to herself. "Looks like I got some lemonade to make this afternoon."

CHAPTER TWELVE

The rest of the late afternoon passed quickly, with Lucas, Will, and me making efficient, if mostly wordless progress on a laundry list of tasks around the property. By six, we had gotten rid of ninety percent of the crap stored in the upper cabin, power-washed the walls and bathroom, and gotten a good start on clearing out the second cabin. It wasn't that talking didn't happen—it's just that every time one of them tried to strike up a conversation, it was always with me, and the other would immediately shut it down. It was subtle. Will, for instance, realized almost immediately that Lucas would button right up every time Will called me Lily pad or some variation. And Lucas caught on just as quickly to how much Will disliked answering any kind of questions about himself, to the point where he would usually find a way to move to another area of the property.

By the time Mama called us from the deck with a tray of lemonade and a warning that if we didn't stop soon, she'd come up and power-wash all of us herself, I was ready to jump in the lake to rid myself of grime. Not to mention the tension between the two men who had been working around me for the last few hours.

We all clambered onto the deck, a rather odd trio: Lucas in his completely appropriate work boots and jeans, me in my light summer shorts and t-shirt now stained beyond the capability of any cleanser, and Will, still barefoot and in nothing but his now dried swim trunks. Lucas and Will both eagerly took the glasses of fresh lemonade from Mama, but I shook my head when she offered it to me. If I knew my mother, that pitcher was about a quarter vodka.

"Thank you, Ms. Sharp," Will said before taking a drink. His eyes shot open at the taste, and I gave him a woeful smile. Yeah, definitely full of vodka. He took another long sip, though his eyes didn't leave mine the entire time.

Lucas accepted his and smiled after he downed the first half easily. "Thanks, Ellie. I forgot how good your lemonade is. You'll have to come teach my mom how to make it sometime. I bet the guests would like it."

"Well, then how would I be able to chase down my own guests, honey?" Mama called as she went back inside the house.

Lucas smiled, but didn't answer. Mama was joking, but the sharpness in her voice was audible. She knew, just as I did, that no one on the lake, including Lucas, ever thought she would be able to run a business. Ellie Sharp was the one you went to for fun. She was the one who poured your drinks and took an extra shot with you. She was not the one you trusted with a bank loan or any kind of ledger sheet.

But I was. I had to believe that. For her sake. For mine.

Beside me, Will cleared his throat. "What about you, Maggie?" he asked. "Do you have the magic lemonade recipe too?"

I snorted. "If only. But I would probably turn it green or something. I'm a totally shit cook."

Lucas's brows jumped a little at my profanity—he always knew me as a church-going girl growing up. A lot of things had changed since I went to New York. Beside him, Will held back a smile. Damn. So close.

"Oh. Well." Lucas perked up. "Hey, did you hear that Michael Grady's band is playing at Curly's on Friday?"

I shook my head. "No, I didn't even know they were still together. It's not the same garage band from high school, is it?"

Lucas chuckled. "Yeah. They got a real drummer, so now they can keep a beat, but everyone else is the same. They're actually pretty good. You should come by."

I turned to Will. "It could be fun, if you want to come. Get out of the house a little."

Will just folded one arm around his torso while taking a long drink of lemonade. His hand drifted to his face, as if looking for a beard to tug on.

"I don't know, man," Lucas joked. "There'll be people there. Not really your thing, right? After all, you've been here, what, four years now? And no one has ever seen you?"

It was barely visible, but Will cringed. He gripped his glass and said nothing, but it was obvious he wanted to leave.

"It'll be just me," I said to Lucas. "I doubt Will would be interested in Mike Grady's crappy banjo playing anyway."

Lucas nodded with a warm smile. "Cool. Well, if you want, I'll pick you up at—"

"I'll be there," Will interrupted suddenly.

Lucas and I both turned to him.

"Will," I started. There was absolutely no way he would be able to manage a crowded bar if he couldn't handle Norm's Burger Barn at nine in the morning. "You don't have to—"

"I'll be there," he repeated, this time staring darkly at Lucas. "I could use a copilot, though. I don't know how to get there. If you don't mind, *Lily*."

At the sound of the name, Lucas straightened up and swallowed down the other half of his glass. I bit my lip.

"Um, sure," I said, looking between them. "You can pick me up here, then."

"Great," said Will shortly. "I'm going to finish clearing off the porch so we can sand tomorrow. Would you mind putting that in the house for me, Lil?"

He handed his glass to me, which was still mostly full. I was strangely comforted by the fact he hadn't gulped it down like Lucas. When his gaze finally landed on me again, there was no darkness in his deep green eyes. Just warmth. Deep inside of me, something began to sing.

"S-sure," I replied.

Will left, and I turned to find Lucas watching me with a curious, if somewhat sad look on his face.

"What's with the 'Lily pad' thing, Mags?" he wondered.

I shrugged. "Just a nickname. Nothing major."

Lucas looked like he didn't believe it.

"I see," was all he said. "Well, I'll see you tomorrow."

I WAITED on the porch for a while for Will to come back, but he didn't. Not for several more hours, well after Mama had roasted a chicken on the grill, and we had set out a table to eat on the deck. He worked until the sun fell behind the hills, until the last glimmers off the water disappeared, turning to icy flashes of moonlight. The chicken dinner had been eaten and put away, a plate of leftovers wrapped up in the fridge.

"You better go up there," Mama said as she carried the last of the food inside. "It's past ten. Even if his feet aren't thick with splinters by this point, they're still going to hurt like the dickens tomorrow. Not to mention the skeeters must be eating him alive."

She pulled the glass door shut, and I made my way back up the hill. The thumps of furniture and yard debris stopped by the time I arrived at the topmost cabin to find Will standing on its rickety porch, hands perched on his head, holding his hair off his neck. At the sound of my footsteps, he turned. His green eyes glowed.

"How was dinner with Daniel Boone?" he bit out.

I frowned. "What are you talking about?"

Will wrinkled his long, straight nose. "I could smell it from here. You guys seemed to be laughing a lot."

I glanced down at the cabin, then up to the hill where the parking spots were empty except for Mama's.

"Will," I said. "Lucas left just after you came back up here. Didn't you see him drive off?"

Will's mouth opened, then closed as he glanced over my shoulder and saw the empty lot. "I…no. I was down at the other cabin."

I looked around. The porch was spotless, just like the one below. On top of that, it looked like Will had stacked and restacked the wood piles on either side. It was like he'd been looking for things to do to stay and stay away at the same time.

"I don't like that guy."

I turned back to him with a frown. "Okay…I guess that's fair. He doesn't seem to like you either."

"Why does he call you 'Mags' all the time? It's annoying. He sounds like a British tabloid."

My eyes narrowed. "He calls me that because it's my name."

"Your name is Maggie."

"You don't call me that either."

Will exhaled through his teeth. "He wants you."

"What of it?" My hands moved to rest on my hips.

Will glared through the wavy, dark blond ropes falling all over his face. Several strands stuck to his forehead from a combination of grime and sweat. He fished a rubber band out of his pocket and wound his hair into a knot. It only then occurred to me to wonder why he hadn't done it before now. It was close to ninety degrees this afternoon. All of us were sweating like crazy.

"Do you want him too?" Will asked as he yanked at his hair.

I blinked in surprise. "What?"

"I don't have to bring you to that bar on Friday," Will said. "I could let him be your date. Take you out. Show you around. If that's what you want, of course. So just tell me. Do. You. Want. Him?"

I pressed my lips together. I didn't like his tone. I didn't like the accusation in it, like I was some kind of two-timer just because someone else had asked me out. And who would I be two-timing, huh? *Will*? It was laughable.

"I don't think that's any of your business," I said.

"Just answer the question."

I pressed my lips shut and folded my arms across my chest. "No."

"Fuck!"

A solid block of wood went flying down the hill, bounced off a ledge and into the lake with a splash.

I turned back to Will. "That's our firewood, you know. And tossing it in the lake pollutes the water. Not to mention wastes the time that *Lucas* put into chopping it today."

Will crossed his arms too, and it was hard to ignore the way the motion made his muscles bulge. "I was mad."

"So was I. But I didn't throw shit like a child."

Will glowered at me, and our eyes locked—green eyes to brown. But the longer we stared, the more the anger started to fade, replaced by something unnamable. Something very, very potent.

"I don't like feeling like this," Will said.

I sucked a breath through my teeth. "Feeling like what?"

"Like *this*." He took a step toward me, and I fought not to step backward. Will had a quiet authority about him, and in the shadows of the moon, his shoulders seemed to broaden, his legs seemed to lengthen. He seemed larger than life.

When he had me backed up against the porch railing, he raised a hand, floating his fingers around my jaw, over my cheeks, but never actually touching me. I arched toward his hand. I couldn't help it. But he hovered, never making contact.

"You make me feel…" Will started. "Out of control."

I couldn't move. "Oh?"

"Like I actually have to *care* about what someone else thinks. Like I'm not alone anymore." He paused. His eyes opened wide, following the path of his fingers as they took hold of a strand of hair in my ponytail and twirled. "And for the first time in a very long time, I feel like I don't want to be."

He tugged lightly on the strand, and I felt the slight pinch like an arrow through my body, shooting down my arms and legs, and coming to throb in that place no man had been for so, so long. I bit my lip. Will's eyes dilated.

"Tell the truth, Lil. What do you want?"

You. The word echoed distantly, like a bell tolling from miles away. I didn't understand it. I was broken. A mess. What should I want with this man? We had a connection, sure, but overall, he was nothing but trouble. He was grouchy. A loner. Clearly had serious social and emotional control issues.

And yet. There was no denying that something was here. Since we met, it certainly felt at times as if the universe itself was tilting on its axis, trying to knock me into him. Breakdown after breakdown. Meeting after meeting. And now…

I tipped my chin up so I could look directly at him, drawn like one of the moths circling the porch light. Winging through the dark, ready to dive into his golden inferno.

"I don't want Lucas," I said quietly, drifting my gaze up and down his naked torso. A sheen of sweat glimmered in the moonlight, which also made the shadows of his muscles—the square pectorals, the solid rack of abs, the lickable V that dipped beneath his shorts—that much more evident.

Will followed my gaze, and his hand dropped. He stepped between my legs, and his unique scents engulfed me. Working all afternoon only made them that much stronger—the scent of pine trees, lake water, and *man* swallowed me with a heady rush that made me shake slightly. And it was then, only then, that he finally touched me. My waist was encircled by his wide palms, so broad that his fingers nearly touched on either side. It was relatively innocent, but the intent was clear. Just like last night, he held me still; I couldn't move unless he wanted me to. For that moment, I was his.

When I looked back up, his eyes were fixed on my lips. Unconsciously, I licked the lower one. His pupils dilated even more.

"Lil," he whispered as he leaned a little closer.

"What are you waiting for?" I murmured. Now I was the one staring at his mouth—so soft and full under his newly trimmed beard.

I panted. Will swore.

"Fuck it," he growled. "I don't fucking know."

Sometimes you don't know you wanted something until you have it. Sometimes you don't know you need something until it's there.

His mouth found mine in a fury, one that surprised me for about a half second before. The hands at my waist gripped so tightly, I almost couldn't breathe, and I felt like I was strangled—not for lack of oxygen, but for lack of *him*. Will's lips made me feel like I was breathing for the first time; like I'd been under water my entire life, and he was the air I'd never known I needed.

His tongue encircled mine with yearning and need, the kind that made me moan louder than the wind passing through the trees, louder than the osprey that gave a sudden cry from its nest above. Our bodies pressed together, and Will's chest, still slick from work, slipped against my palms pushing over his shoulders and into his hair while his hands grasped everywhere else: my waist, my thighs, my ass. He lifted me off the ground like I was nothing and urged my legs around his taut waist as he set me on the porch railing. We devoured each other completely, in a kiss that was both salty and sweet. That tasted like pine trees and fresh water and sweat and just a hint of fresh lemons.

"Will," I moaned as his lips found my neck.

He flicked his tongue in tight circles, then sucked hard enough that I knew there would be a spot there the following day. I groaned. I wanted more.

"Lily." His breath, hot and anxious, blew cool over the spot before he bit down on my earlobe, traced teeth across my cheek, and found my mouth again with fierce hunger.

He was more animalistic than ever, grunting into my mouth as I sucked on his lower lip, his hands kneading mercilessly at my thighs. The solid heat of his arousal—and by solid, I mean way more than anything I'd *thought* was there under his shorts—shoved between my legs. Will growled, and the soft prickle of his beard against my cheek sent ripples of want down my spine. *Animal,* I thought. It turned me on that much more.

"Ah!" I cried as he rocked into me.

I reached down for the elastic band of his swimsuit. There was so little between us. His shorts. My shorts. Two quick yanks, and we'd get what we both needed. It had been so long—*so* long. Only a few times had I tried to move past what Theo had done—more for the sake of moving on, a way of asserting my agency amidst a trial that swallowed my life. And every time had been a dismal failure. I'd run away, left my prospective partners in a wake of my fears, anger, thoughts of anything but them. Right now I could barely think of anything else. Will. He consumed me with just a kiss.

But as my fingertips followed the deep lines of his abdominals to just below his waistband, Will's hands wrapped around my wrist. His mouth, which was still devouring mine, was slower to stop, and when it did, pulled away from my lips with a light pop.

"No," I mewled, struggling against his grip. "Don't stop."

Will said nothing, just stared at me with his mouth half open. An expression that was half lust, half…fear.

"Fuck," he muttered, as he looked me up and down, taking in my heaving chest, my nipples poking through the light cotton, my thighs splayed open. Waiting for him. "Jesus *fuck*."

"Will." I wriggled again, but he held my hand on the railing. Then, slowly, he released it and backed away.

His large eyes, green and almost navy blue in the night, flashed bright and scared. He took another step backward, then one more.

"Will," I said again. I slid off the railing and took a step toward him.

"Pine cone," he whispered.

Then, without another word, he turned and strode into the trees, not bothering with the stairs that led down to the water, but instead scrambling as quickly as he could down the rocks and pine needles until he was at the bottom of the hill. I watched as he sprinted off the dock and into the water. The fury of his strokes tossed small waves into the night, visible until he was almost halfway back to his house on the other side of the lake.

CHAPTER THIRTEEN

"Have fun!" Mama said the following Friday as she pressed a kiss to my cheek, laced already with the sweet tinge of gin. "And don't drink and drive, y'hear? I'll be sitting by the phone. No more than one more gin and tonic for me in case you need a way to get home."

I pressed my lips together, holding back my comment. She knew I didn't drink in the first place, so if she was giving me the "don't drink and drive" spiel, it meant she'd already had at least two herself. I knew just as well as she did that there was no way Mama would keep herself to one gin and tonic. If she was staying home tonight, ten to one I would find her snoring in her bed when I got home, with an empty fifth on her bedside table.

"I'll be fine, Mom." I grabbed my keys off the counter. "Take it easy tonight. Don't forget, we have the septic guy coming in the morning, so you need to be up early."

"Now, who's the mama here, Maggie Mae?" Mama twirled around, spinning her finger through the air as she did. "I'll be just *fine*. You go have some fun for once. You and the boys have been working much too hard."

I shrugged. At least she was staying home. She'd already gone out the last two nights, and I was somewhat sure she'd had company on one of them. Whoever it was, they were gone by the time I'd gotten back from my morning run, but their car was in the driveway when I'd left.

"I won't be home too late, Mama," I said with a kiss on her cheek. "Be good."

"I'm the one who' supposed to be saying that!" she called. I just laughed as I shut the screen door behind me.

On the way up the stairs, my phone buzzed in my pocket. It was Calliope.

Please tell me you're doing something fun tonight. You're twenty-six, not eighty.

I smiled. My friend had been more insistent this week, sensing Will's rejection cut me more than I would admit out loud. I punched back a reply.

I'll have you know I'm on my way out to a show.

Her response was instantaneous.

Good. I hope you get laid. YOU NEED IT.

I rolled my eyes, but didn't answer. Sure, it had been a long time. I honestly wasn't sure I'd ever be able to open myself up to someone like that again. But it wasn't for lack of wanting.

My phone buzzed again. Apparently she wasn't going to take no for an answer.

"Christ, Cal," I muttered, taking it out again. But the message wasn't from her.

I miss you, Flower.

I stopped at the top of the stairs, stuck in place as I stared at the message, along with the three dots that said the person texting from the number, which I didn't recognize, was still typing.

If you don't find me, I'll have to come find you, bella.

I pressed a hand to my chest as the air suddenly deflated from it. It was just like him to use pathetic pet names, pretending fluency in a foreign language. Theo was all about the act.

I sank to my bottom, suddenly finding it difficult to stay on my feet. The wood steps seemed to sway. No. This wasn't him. Theo was in jail. I had been there, had stood in the courtroom while the bailiff had taken him into custody. While he had screamed at me that he would come after me, get me back, if it was the last thing he ever did.

My lawyer had told me not to worry about the threat. "They all say that," she assured me. And I chose to believe her.

I stared at the text. Then slowly, I typed out a question.

Who is this?

The response was almost immediate.

I'm offended. Who do you think it is, Flower?

It sounded just like him. It was just like Theo to answer a question with a question. Insinuate that my doubt, confusion, anything was somehow my fault. Not his.

With shaky fingers, I typed the only response I could think of. The only one I wanted to know.

Where are you?

But there was no answer. I waited thirty seconds. A minute. Five. Still nothing.

"Everything all right?"

I jumped so high that my phone fell into the dust under the stairs, and our heads cracked together when Will and I both scrambled to get it.

"Jesus!" I screamed. "For fuck's sake, Baker! Warn a girl, will you?"

Will chuckled, and for a second, a suppressed smile glimmered under his usually stolid mask.

It wasn't like we hadn't seen each other over the last several days. To my surprise, after our abrupt kiss in the moonlight, Will continued to show up wordlessly day after day, jogging down the stairs from his truck (instead of swimming) at 8 a.m., and meeting me even earlier on the others for a bike ride or a jog. But barely a word was said. Nothing about the kiss on the porch. Nothing about the heat that at least *I* continued to feel between us. He hadn't touched me, nor I him, and any attempt I made at conversation was generally met with curt, one-word responses.

But he was always there. Just...there.

So maybe I shouldn't have been startled when his voice broke through the pine trees. In fact, maybe I should have been mad, considering the icy treatment I'd gotten all week. But instead, as I clasped the phone to my thumping chest, I was so, so happy to see him.

"I'm just here to give you a ride," he said, obviously confused by my adoring look. "Who was that?"

Gradually, I let my hands fall, the phone with them, and I tucked it into my purse. "Oh...no one. You scared me."

Will looked like he didn't believe me, but he didn't press me on it. His hair was down, and his beard had been growing out all week again, much to my (odd) disappointment, but his green eyes still glowed with mischief. Although he was grooming, clearly avoiding the psycho yeti look, there was still a solid two inches of beard hiding his face.

He wasn't exactly dressed to impress—Will never was—but in the faded jeans and worn graphic t-shirt that molded against his lean swimmer's body just so, he looked nicer than I'd ever seen him. Better than nice, really. The man made wearing denim an art form.

"Sorry," he said as he came closer. "I didn't mean to scare you." He gestured toward the top of the hill. "I'm parked up there if you still want to ride together to the show."

"I can drive," I said, pointing to my newly repaired vehicle. It had been delivered today after the boys had gone, and to my surprise, was fully paid for. "Thank you for that, by the way. Please tell me how much the repairs were so I can reimburse you."

Will glanced at the Passat and frowned. "There's no need for that."

"Um...of course there is. You're not paying for a major car repair. It can't have been cheap."

"It was nothing," Will argued, but when he looked at me, his sharp gaze softened. "Call it...a favor. For putting up with me...pine coning... all week." He took a step closer and cocked his head. "Please."

Obviously there was no way I was going to accept this from him, but his expression was so open and adorable, I couldn't find it in me to say no.

"All right," I said. "And you can drive if you want to. But, wait! You're actually going out in public?"

I clapped a hand over my mouth. Immediately, two rows of lines appeared over Will's brow, and I felt terrible. I sounded like Lucas, who hadn't passed up excuses to goad Will about his monastic tendencies all week. It had gotten so bad that I had literally taken to sending them to different parts of the property altogether. More than once, Will had looked like he wanted to toss Lucas into the lake.

"Sorry," I said. "I'm just surprised, that's all. You haven't mentioned it since last weekend, so I figured it was part of the pine cone situation."

Will shrugged and rubbed the side of his face. The motion was so clearly self-conscious, it made me want to hug him. And not because I had been dying for that addictive scent of his all week. No, that wasn't it at all.

"Well, I'm mentioning it now," he said. "Unless you don't want me to come."

"No, no, no!" I surprised myself with how forcefully I objected.

Will looked up, his eyes hopeful. "Okay, then," he said gruffly. "Let's get going, then."

WE RODE in silence for a while, like usual, but it was chilly and as if Will knew just how long it had taken for me to make my hair behave, he kept the windows rolled up. He pushed a cassette tape into the ancient tape deck; it was the kind with a wire coming out that you could connect to the audio players of other devices. I watched with amazement as he connected it to a decrepit iPod—the old kind with the circular control in the center. The kind that had absolutely no internet access. There was only music.

"That's a pretty awesome setup, you have there, Hoss," I teased. "Very *2001: A Space Odyssey* of you."

Will arched a brow. "Oh? Do you remember 1999, Lil? These things were classic."

I blinked. "I remember some."

His eyes twinkled, and that wide mouth twitched. It reminded me that I still hadn't managed to make him laugh.

The sounds of The Head and The Heart floated through the speakers, haunting the air with poetry about "Rivers and Roads."

I smiled. "These guys are some of my favorites."

Will glanced at me. "Yeah? Mine too, actually."

I watched the lake glimmering through the trees. "I love the way they mourn in their songs."

It was a funny thing to say, of course. They weren't mourning, although the singer, Charity Rose, had a voice that reminded me of keening women I'd read about in an Irish poetry class I'd taken in college. She cried the way I had so many times when I'd found Mama passed out on the couch. When I'd felt alone in the world because she was too busy battling her own demons to help me manage mine.

I said as much to Will—the part about the poetry, anyway. I kept the part about Mama to myself.

He nodded. "She reminds me of some Yeats poetry. This one in particular, 'The Sorrow of Love.'"

"Oh, I *love* that poem!" I turned in my seat, excited. "It always reminded me of the lake. 'The brawling of a sparrow in the eaves, the brilliant moon and all the milky sky'..."

"'And all that famous harmony of leaves,'" Will continued, nodding his head. "'Had blotted out man's image and his cry.'"

I sighed. "So, so pretty."

"I didn't take you for a poetry person."

I shrugged. "I went to college, took a few literature classes. But really, poetry, lyrics. They're the same thing. It's all music."

"You're a music lover, huh?"

I opened my mouth, surprised by the pang in my chest at the question. That it should even exist. That anyone should even wonder.

"I was," I said, but didn't elaborate.

I could feel, rather than see, Will pull into himself, almost as a reflection of my own withdrawal. The "man's image" that Yeats spoke of in the poem seemed to apply directly to Will. Like he was that man from the Yeats poem, withdrawn behind the sounds and sights of the wilderness around him. Maybe that was the way he wanted it.

Except he couldn't. Not completely. I didn't know him well, but I knew that. Will exuded something magnetic, something bright that could never be hidden completely, no matter how plain or majestic his surroundings.

The volume of the song rose again, filling the car with tension and beauty. We listened quietly as the melancholic harmonies swirled around us. I closed my eyes. And for the first time in weeks, I felt that old yearning. The one that had made me take up my guitar at age seven. The one that had me singing ditties before I could even talk. An aching space inside me that yearned for the only thing that had ever filled it: music.

The song ended, and another came on, but the final melody of "Rivers and Roads" still haunted my mind like a ghost.

"God, I'd love her to sing my songs," I murmured.

It was what I'd always said. When I had first graduated with my music degree, my goal had been to sell my songs, not play them. I'd wanted to write and produce, and Calliope and my previous manager had assured me the best way to do that was to perform myself to make a case for my songs.

But I wasn't a natural performer. The butterflies in my belly had told me that ever since the first time I had gotten onto a stage. More often than not, I would vomit before a performance, and it wouldn't be until I was two or three songs into my set, fully immersed in my music, that I would be able to loosen up to sing my songs the way I meant them to be heard. Even then, it was never quite enough. I could play the guitar, of course, but my voice wasn't as strong as the melodies I heard in my head.

Will glanced at me curiously. "You write songs?"

I straightened up. "Um, yeah. Well, I used to. Did. I—I don't know."

Will watched me for a second before turning his eyes back to the road. I didn't say anything else, content to look out the window, and he didn't press me. We listened to the next few songs on the album as he drove across the border.

"Okay, I gotta ask," I said, turning to Will. "How can a guy like you afford a house like yours?"

Will spun the wheel with ease, turning the old truck along the twisting road. He gave me another one of his shy half smiles. "I used to work in...advertising, like I said. In New York and LA, mostly. I made enough that I could buy my place here and kind of disappear for a while. I wanted to keep things very simple, but...I couldn't really help myself with the house." His mouth twisted fondly, like he was remembering an errant child. "It's my baby."

"Why don't you ever have anyone over? It seems to be such a waste, just you living there."

Will sighed. "My life used to be very...complicated. I bought the house in a moment of weakness. I should get rid of it, but...I just haven't been able to do it yet." His mouth quirked at me. "Do you blame me?"

I grinned as one side of his mouth perked up a little wider. "Not at all. The house is amazing. Don't ever sell it."

"I'm glad I can impress you somehow, Lil."

"I'm more impressed that you're actually telling me something about yourself."

He rolled his eyes, but the half smile reappeared. "I don't know. You do something to me. You make me say things I shouldn't. Do things I shouldn't."

He steered the car onto Trent Avenue, the long highway that ran alongside the mountain foothills from Washington to Idaho. Besides farms and a railroad track running parallel, there wasn't much on it except for Curly's, the log cabin-shaped bar that straddled the border almost perfectly. We found a parking spot in the big gravel lot that was crowded with several pickups, much like his. Will turned off the engine, but didn't move, still holding both hands on the wheel and squeezing his eyes shut. I moved to get out, but before I could, Will grabbed my hand.

I jerked at the sudden contact—not because it felt bad, but because I wasn't prepared for the spark that came out of it. The memory of our kiss came flooding back. My lips ached for his—the way he had devoured me. Will had kissed me like a starving man, and I had been just as hungry. I wanted more. Even with the cold shoulder, the weirdness, the distance that always returned, I wanted more. But did he?

Will shuddered too, but kept my fingers firmly in his grasp.

"Will?" I asked. "What is it?"

"Lil, I..." His face screwed up tightly, and his breathing was audible, almost forced. His thumbs brushed over my knuckles, but his fingers weaved through mine even tighter than before.

"Oh, wow." I covered our intertwined fingers with my other hand, patting the top of his broad palm. His fear—or whatever he would call it—was palpable, shivering through his body like he was touching a live wire. "Will, you don't have to go in. I can get a ride home from someone else, easy."

"Someone else meaning Lucas?"

I shrugged. Several people in there would probably drive me home if I asked, but Lucas made the most sense, since he lived less than a quarter mile from my house.

Will scowled. He was jealous, and I would have been lying if I said a part of me didn't like it. In the back of my mind, another voice said he didn't have the right. He had kissed me and run off in the night like a bandit, like touching me physically hurt. Then he had returned, day after day, treating me like a stranger, like it hadn't happened. And I, in my stubbornness, had returned the silence with my own. This wasn't the start of a normal relationship. Whatever it was, it was dysfunctional.

But now here we were. Maybe I should continue to let him run, or even run myself. But instead, I felt inextricably drawn to this strange, curt, fearful man. His sadness seemed to understand my own. We were creatures alone by our own choices. A part of me wondered if we couldn't be alone together.

Will stared at our hands for a moment, chewing on his lip.

"Will you do me a favor?" he asked.

I cocked my head. "What's that?"

He exhaled. "If I need to leave quickly, can you be ready to go? No questions?"

"Sure. I wasn't planning on staying that long anyway. If you get freaked out, we'll jet, okay?"

Will nodded, still keeping his eyes fixed on our fingers, where his thumb continued to stroke over my hand. His touch was so unlike his personality. Light. Tender.

"I'll be fine," he said at last, more to himself than to me. When he looked up, his eyes were full of determination. "Just...don't let go, okay?"

I nodded solemnly. His penetrating gaze didn't waver. I wondered if he understood that every time he looked at me like this, he pinned me into place. That with every dark glance, every wide-eyed stare, Will was seeping into the depths of who I was. Places I wasn't sure I could even reach on my own.

"Okay," I promised. "I won't let go."

CHAPTER FOURTEEN

Curly's was full of people, most of them clustered around the bar and a few meandering around the dance floor while the band, a Tim McGraw knock-off, started their set. It was the usual crowd gathered from the neighboring lakes and Post Falls, the nearest proper town. The bar itself was nothing special—an old log cabin that had a permanent stage set up at one end and a long bar on the other, with worn vinyl booths rolling down the sides toward the stage while waitresses zigzagged between them.

I spotted Lucas and his group almost immediately crowded around a booth near the stage. A few people were familiar from the other night at the inn: Lucas's younger sister, Katie, and her boyfriend, as well as Lindsay, the blonde girl, who was already staring daggers at me. There were some I recognized from high school, along with other faces from the past.

Lucas found me and raised his hand, his eyes bright and warm until he caught sight of who was behind me.

"Looks like Ranger Rick spotted us," Will grumbled, and I chuckled in spite of myself. Between his buttoned-up polo and curved baseball hat, Lucas did kind of look like a Boy Scout.

"Be nice," I chided, but the joke faded when I looked over my shoulder. Will's face was tight as he glanced around the room, with two lines clear across his forehead. He had tied his hair up walking in, and as he examined the bar, he reached up automatically to tug it back down.

"Oh, please don't," I said without thinking.

He froze mid-pull, and his eyes unerringly found mine.

"I just…" I swallowed. Shit. "I like seeing your face, Will."

His eyes didn't waver, and for a second, the cacophony of the room faded slightly, almost as if we were the only ones in it. I swallowed again.

Finally, Will blinked, re-fixed the knot, and dropped his hand. "You win, Lily pad," he mumbled with a slight quirk of his mouth and immediately grabbed my hand. "Don't let go, remember?"

I kept my promise as I guided Will toward the booth, past a sea of flannel, cowboy boots, and a lot of whisker-faded jeans.

"Hey, guys." I greeted everyone with a weak wave. "We, um, made it. This is Will—he's a neighbor on Newman."

We listened as everyone announced their names—the girls openly perused Will, clearly noticing the way his shirt clung to his tall, lean form, and the way his legs filled out his jeans in just the right way. The guys were a bit cagier, checking out the stranger invading their turf. Will certainly cut an imposing form, with shoulders that filled out your average doorframe and a face with an immovable scowl.

Lucas's eyes latched onto our joined hands, but I didn't move. Instead, I tipped my chin up as Will squeezed my hand even tighter, though he remained firmly behind me.

"Hey," he said to everyone with a weak wave. "Nice to meet you."

"Sit down," Lucas said, gesturing at a few open seats at the end of the table. "Lindsay got us a pitcher."

"Do you want some?" Lindsay's kind tone was clearly pointed at Will, not me.

I sat down on the end of the booth while Will took a seat next to me.

"I waitress here sometimes," Lindsay added proudly, as if waiting tables at Curly's was a prize position. And to be honest, in some ways it was. She probably made good tips and got to listen to decent music. The way some of the guys at the table were eying the other waitresses circulating the room, it was clear that they had a bit of a reputation.

I shook my head at her offer just as Will nodded his assent.

"Do you mind?" he asked as he accepted a glass from Lindsay.

"Boooo," Lindsay jeered from her spot next to Lucas. She latched onto his arm and leaned her head on his shoulder. "Are you one of those teetotalers who glares at anyone who drinks? You're no fun."

I gave a tight smile. "It's just a personal preference. I don't mind if other people drink."

Lucas nodded. He knew that was my line. Though most of the old friends here knew who my mom was—to be honest, most of the people in this bar probably knew who Ellie Sharp was—Lucas was the only one who *really* knew what her choices meant for me. How often she had allowed her daughter to fend for herself, sometimes against the people she brought home.

Back then, Lucas wouldn't have drunk at all, but now I watched him eagerly refill his glass. Will examined his beer for a second, looking back and forth between it and me before leaving it on the coaster.

And for some reason, something inside me shifted at that decision.

"Hey," I whispered in his ear. "I really don't mind if you want to have a beer or two. Honest. Especially if it will help you relax a little."

He turned, and suddenly I was *very* aware of our close proximity. Shoved together by the crowded conditions of the booth, I could see clearly the way the long sweep of his eyelashes brushed golden across his cheekbones when he blinked, examine the tiny row of stress lines in between his strong brows, smell that unique scent of his, tinged with soap and deodorant. The memory of his taste flooded back. Without thinking, I licked my lower lip. His green eyes, flecked with gold, darkened and dilated.

"Relax," Will said hoarsely. "Okay."

With substantial effort, I turned back to the group, who were all merrily chatting with one another except for Lucas, who was watching me and Will with a stony face. He caught my eye, then deliberately lifted one arm up and set it around Lindsay's shoulders. She started at the surprise, but happily nuzzled into him. *How do you like that?* Lucas's expression clearly seemed to say. I shrugged. I honestly couldn't care less who he was involved with. I just didn't like Microaggressive Barbie period, whether or not she was dating Lucas.

"You know, you look kind of familiar," Lindsay said to Will, who immediately froze, beer glass at his mouth. "Have you been to the bar before?"

Will set his glass down at the table and stared fixedly at it. "Ah, no. I'm more of a homebody."

Lucas snorted. "More like a hermit," he said, earning a glare from me. Will said nothing.

"No, that's not it," Lindsay said. She tapped an acrylic nail on the tabletop. "It's something else. Hey, Kel, don't you think he looks familiar?"

She nudged the girl next to her, pulling her out of a conversation with the other two guys. Kelly looked over Will with Lindsay. In my lap, Will's hand squeezed mine so tightly I thought my circulation might cut off.

"You guys," I said. "Give the poor guy a rest. He just got here."

"See?" Lucas said. "He's nobody."

"I'm nobody," Will murmured and squeezed my fingers again when Lindsay and the girls started chatting about some celebrity gossip they had read that day.

"No, you're not," I said, so low that only he could hear me. "Not to me."

His eyes met mine once more and softened. "Thanks, Lil," he said softly, and again, there was that strange quirk of the mouth that seemed to be reserved only for me.

"What's Ellie up to tonight, Mags?" Lucas asked, pulling my attention back across the table after the waitress dropped off my water.

I took a long drink. "Um, she's at home tonight."

Lucas gave me a warm smile. "Quiet night in?" Understanding shone out of his open face—he knew what that would mean to me.

I nodded. "As quiet as it ever is with her, you know."

"Wait a minute, Ellie? Do you mean Ellie Sharp?"

I looked back at Lindsay, who had realization suddenly dawning over her vapid face. I should have known that eventually it would come to this. Mama was a regular at Curly's, and since Lindsay worked here, she would probably know her, just like the rest of the staff who would call me at closing time to pick her up.

"Oh my God!" Lindsay exclaimed. "*That's* your mom? You poor thing! No wonder you had to come back to Spokane. She needs help, Maggie, she really does."

I just studied my water glass. Lindsay had clearly had a few too many—she had that glazed-eyed look I knew so well. There was no reason to respond.

"What is she talking about?" Will asked quietly.

"Her mom is a fall-down drunk," Lindsay said sloppily, oblivious to the irony of her statement when she was already slurring her words herself.

"What?" Will said sharply, calling the attention of a few other people at the table.

"Lindsay," Lucas spoke up sharply, but she ignored him too.

"Hey, if it walks like a duck, you know?" The girl had no filter. The table had gone quiet, and I shrank, unable to escape. "Kel, remember the other night when we had to call a taxi for that lady, the one with the crazy brown hair? The one who kept falling off her bar stool? That's this girl's mom!"

Will pushed his beer away slightly and straightened beside me. Now I was the one squeezing his hand. I wanted to be literally anywhere else but here, reminded again of all the reasons why I had wanted to leave in the first place. But in the end, I had gone from being Ellie Sharp's daughter to Theo del Conte's girlfriend and back again, and neither had served me well.

A part of me wondered if there would ever be a point in my life when I didn't belong to someone else. When people would just see me as myself?

"Seriously, though," Lindsay was saying after she regaled the group with the latest embarrassing thing my mother had done. "How could you just leave her here? You must know she has a problem. What kind of daughter are you?"

"Lindsay!" Lucas's face was starting to turn red.

But I was done. "I guess that makes me a bad daughter," I said. "Just like calling you a bitch probably makes me a bad friend. Sorry, Lucas."

Lucas just shook his head while the rest of the group's mouths dropped. I rubbed my head, bracing myself for the utter onslaught that was about to come at me and trying to think of a reason to leave. This was a bad idea. Coming back here at all was a bad idea.

But before Lindsay could start her retort, there was a loud screech of the chair next to me. The booth silenced, all eyes on Will as he stood up tall and re-extended his hand to me.

"Lil," he called my nickname clearly, his green eyes bright in the dimly lit room. "Wanna dance?"

It was the same hand that had been holding mine since we left his truck. Across the table, Lindsay's jaw fell open, and Lucas frowned. But I barely noticed, captured instead by the strong, serious face of a man who had held me in his thrall since pretty much the moment I'd met him.

I smiled, the first one that night that felt genuine and true.

"I'd love to," I said as I let him pull me out of the booth and onto the dance floor where a few couples were already starting to sway back and forth to the slow country songs the band issued.

"Thanks," I said as he slipped a big hand around my waist.

Will pulled me to his torso, moving naturally, if slowly, in time with the sweet, easy rhythm the boys were playing. "Don't think about it," he said. "It was the least I could do. You don't need to listen to that shit."

I didn't respond, just pressed my nose into the soft cotton sleeve of his shirt and inhaled. He smelled so good. Enough to make me forget that I wasn't in any shape to be smelling a man to begin with. Enough to make me forget that most of what Lindsay had said wasn't shit—it was true.

"She does deserve better than me," I said quietly.

"Who? Lindsay?"

I shook my head, keeping my face pressed into the cotton. "My mom. I—I should have told you about her. Everything, I mean. So you'd know what you were really getting involved in. I'm sorry."

Will's finger slid under my chin and tipped my face up so that I was looking directly at him.

"You have *nothing* to be sorry for, Lily pad," he said. "Especially not to some sorry chick who has to shit all over someone else's life to make herself feel good."

"But—"

"Nothing." Will's hand fell away, but my chin stayed in place. His eyes dropped to my lips and back up. "You can't cure an addict, Lil. They can only cure themselves. I learned that the hard way."

Before I could open my mouth to ask just what he meant by that, another voice jolted the conversation.

"Can I cut in?"

Will and I both turned to find Lucas standing next to us, eying me remorsefully.

I raised an eyebrow. "Won't your date be a little jealous there?"

Will snorted.

Lucas rolled his eyes. "Lindsay's just a friend. And what she said was messed up. I'm here to make peace." He glanced at Will with more than a hint of disdain. "You all right if I steal 'your girl' for a second?" He sneered as he said it, like the idea of me being with Will was a huge joke.

But Will didn't argue. He just stepped back, his hands held out to the sides. "Be my guest. She's not my girl."

I swallowed and allowed Lucas to slip a familiar arm around me, burying the sharp, painful twinge of Will's quick dismissal. He was right, of course. I wasn't his girl—this wasn't even a real date, as much as it had felt like one up until now. But that didn't make it hurt any less.

Lucas turned me to face the other direction, pulling me a little closer as we moved around with the other couples. It was a familiar stance. One we'd taken many times at school dances and backyard barbecues, many years before. Familiar, but lifeless.

"I'm sorry about what Lindsay said tonight," he said. "When she gets a few drinks in her, she kind of runs off at the mouth."

I shrugged. I didn't know what to say about that. All it meant was that deep down, Lindsay was a bitch who just managed to hide it when she was sober.

"And I'm sorry about the other night too," Lucas continued. "I...I'd had a few myself. I just...well, I missed you, Mags. We all have. But I don't want to mess up our friendship. Not when we're just getting you back."

I looked up, worried I'd find that look in his eyes again—that desire, that entitlement to me that had sent me running. But there was nothing but hope and kindness—the same old Lucas I'd always known.

"I'll always be your friend," I told him with a smile. "I'm not that easy to get rid of."

He grinned, the movement shifting his broad face pleasantly. "Good," he said as he pulled me closer.

We continued dancing, and I tried to ignore it as Lucas kept me aligned with him, chest to chest. It was friendly, I supposed, but also intimate. Maybe too intimate, despite what he'd said. His hand stroked my lower back, and he turned us again. Over his shoulder, I caught Will sitting against the wall with his arms crossed tightly. He was ignoring the chatter at the table, facing mostly away from them while his beer sat untouched. His focus was entirely on me.

His eyes flared when Lucas's hand drifted a little lower to rest at the small of my back, and his fist clenched under his elbow. But when he realized I was watching him back, he softened. He blinked, then stood up.

"You okay?" he mouthed across the room, and even from this distance, I understood.

Lucas's hand drifted even lower, his palm curving over the top of my backside. Immediately, I had flashbacks from high school. The graze of fingers where they shouldn't quite be. The small, almost subconscious fear of what would happen if I encouraged it, even though part of me wanted to. The bigger fear if I didn't.

And this time, I didn't want it. Not at all. I didn't feel that way about Lucas anymore—hadn't for years. We were so young when we were together. We were different people now. At least, I was definitely different, and in ways he could never really understand.

My eyes widened at Will. *Help me,* I telegraphed. What else could I do? I'd already come close to burning bridges with Lucas once before, and he was one of my oldest friends. A scene in the middle of this bar, with all of his friends present, would probably set that fire all over again.

But before I could figure out how to extricate myself delicately, Will was already striding through the crowd, his tall form cutting an immediate path until he was able to interrupt us just as the song came to a close.

"I'd like to continue that dance now," he said. It wasn't a question. It wasn't even a request.

Lucas didn't bother hiding his irritation.

"Mags?" he asked. I wiggled, but the hand at my waist still hadn't moved.

"S-sure," I said stepping toward Will. "It would be rude not to, I think."

Lucas huffed, but finally released me. Will tugged me into his side. I shouldn't have, but I relaxed as his fresh, woodsy scent washed over me again. This grouchy, infuriating man shouldn't have felt this comfortable. This right. But he did.

Will began leading me through the dance, giving me space to lose myself a bit in the music and the laughter. He was a surprisingly good dancer. Not many men our age were, and he was actually able to lead in time with the music. Nothing Will did was particularly fancy, but his steps were confident, the pressure on my back and at my wrist sure.

Some things don't ever go away. The way I listened to the music was instinctual, testing the pitch or the pacing as natural as breathing. It was hard not to cringe as I noted a particular change the band made, or whether or not I thought they used the right picking pattern. I had even played a few songs with these guys back in high school, back when they were playing mostly in their garages and at backyard parties. I'd been relegated to backup singer most of the time because I didn't have the "right sound" for their band, though I had wondered if it was also because I had a tendency to correct their mistakes too often.

But in the end, my perfectionism hadn't gotten me anywhere. They were the ones on the stage, and I was the one in the audience. They were up there, playing with aplomb. I was the one with my tail between my legs, licking my wounds because I still couldn't stand to look at a guitar.

"You okay?"

Will's deep voice pulled me out of my gloom. I blinked and found him watching me. He continued to sway us in time to the music. His face was as stoic as ever, but those deep green eyes of his were open. Their usual hardness lessened somehow.

I gave a weak smile. "Shouldn't I be asking you that? I'm shocked you haven't bolted yet."

He didn't return the smile. Will, I was finding, wasn't one for social pretense.

He didn't answer my comment, just continued moving me around, though I noticed he kept his eyes securely trained on some part of me. My face, my neck, my collarbone. I was the absolute center of his focus.

I closed my eyes for a second. "It's just feeling a little crowded here at the moment." At that, one blond brow rose, and I chuckled. "Yeah, yeah, I get the joke. I just..." I shrugged. "I used to play with this band back in high school. I guess I was thinking about the irony. That they're up there, and I'm down here. And feeling a little disappointed with myself."

Will didn't hug me or tell me it was going to be okay. Instead, he continued to sway us back and forth, letting me digest my own emotions, though he did so without moving his gaze. His solid, immovable presence was an odd comfort. It was good to know that whatever melancholy I was feeling, he wasn't going anywhere.

"It's okay," I said a few moments later. "I'm okay."

I could feel my friends staring at me—Lucas most of all—but I didn't turn to look. I didn't want to see Lucas's disapproving stare, Lindsay's obnoxious scowl, or anyone else's reaction. I needed something else to focus on, and Will was providing it in spades.

The band launched into a lazy three-four meter, and on cue, Will's big hand slipped firmly up my back and pulled me closer as he launched into a waltz in time with the other couples on the floor. He even turned me a few times, although it was clear after a couple minutes that both of us would be more comfortable close, cocooned in our own small world, away from prying eyes.

"You're a good dancer," I remarked as Will led me through another turn. "Will Baker can waltz. I wouldn't have thought it."

Will rolled his eyes and smirked, and I was struck again how just a bit of lightness changed the entire landscape of his face.

"I had to learn once for—for a job," he said. "We, um, had an event."

His face shuttered with the recollection, but I grinned, trying to pull him out of it.

"Well, you've got some moves, Baker. You're no Fred Astaire, but I'm pleasantly surprised."

I was granted another delicious eye roll, but this close, I could see a dimple under his beard when that side quirked. *Smile,* I willed him, but after a second, the dimple disappeared. His head brushed my cheek as he hovered over my shoulder.

A shiver ran down my arm. Again, I wanted desperately to see what he looked like completely without the beard. Some men wore them naturally, a normal extension of their faces, their personalities. Will, on the other hand, wore his like a mask. As good as he looked in it, there was something about his facial hair that seemed unnatural on him.

"Will?" I asked. Suddenly, speaking was difficult.

"What, Lily pad?"

I pulled back so I could look at him. "Why did you run off the other night?"

His shoulders tensed for a moment, then dropped. "I don't know."

"Liar," I replied softly.

There it was again—that slight quirk of his mouth. His eyes dropped to my mouth, and another shiver flew down my spine. That moment at the top of the hill came flying back to me—the voraciousness of his mouth, his hands, his entire body pressed against me in the dark.

He sucked his upper lip between his teeth for a moment, gradually letting it go while he continued to stare at my lips.

"Will," I whispered.

We were barely moving at this point, oscillating in the smallest ways to the music.

"Lily," he replied, just as low.

"When are you going to kiss me again?"

There was another long pause. And then, just when I thought he wasn't going to answer:

"Is that what you really want?"

The sparks that always seemed to be flickering in his eyes flamed, but he didn't turn that deep gaze away. And for once, I found it hard to speak. But only because I realized I wanted it so badly, I could barely breathe.

"Y-yes," I stuttered, breathy and choked. Then, more assuredly: "*Yes.*"

"In the middle of this crowd? With all your friends watching? With Lucas watching?"

I swallowed, my tongue thick and my throat dry. My chest lifted. I couldn't find enough air.

Then I nodded. "Yes."

Will leaned forward, and for a moment, I thought he might do it. I closed my eyes and turned my face toward his, my lips parting naturally, waiting for the moment where his mouth would touch mine, where his beard would scratch softly as he consumed me. His hands encircled my waist again just like they had the other night, and my heart gave one loud thump.

"No," he whispered.

My heart dropped. And before I could help myself, I whimpered, a tiny, pitiful squeak that slipped out before I could stop it. It was a clear cry of desire, one that he heard just as well as I did.

"Lil," he started.

"No." I shook my head. "You, um, you don't need to say anything."

"Lily."

Two fingers tipped my chin up, forcing me to meet Will's penetrating gaze. I bit my lip. His pupils dilated.

"Maggie."

I cringed. For some reason the name sounded wrong coming from him.

"You didn't let me finish," he said. "I meant no, as in not here. Because if I kiss you right here, right now, I'm not going to be able to stop. Because I want you so badly right now I feel like I'm going to die if I don't kiss you. I'm not going to give a shit about what Lucas or his friends or any of these people think about it—all I want right now is *you*, Lil. And I'm not putting that on display for anyone's prying eyes."

My eyes opened as the music picked up again. It was obviously a well-known song in this crowd. Around us, people cheered, turning toward the band as they launched into a fast-paced jig that had people jumping up and down, hooting and hollering in a half second. But Will and I remained still, fully lost in each other.

"I'm going to ask you one more time, Lily," he called over the noise. "Do you really want this?"

This time I didn't speak. I only nodded. *Yes.*

Will's eyes flashed. "Follow me."

Suddenly, he was all action. I was yanked across the room, past my friends and plenty of other strangers who were probably more aware that I was "Ellie's girl" than I was of who they were. There was no time to say my goodbyes or mitigate the suspicious looks from Lucas or his sister. Will towed me out to the parking lot at breakneck speed, pulled me to the passenger side of the old orange Toyota, and summarily tossed me inside. He didn't wait for me to say anything, just slammed the door shut and jogged around to the other side before shutting the door behind him.

He turned to me with eyes like fire.

"Lily," he growled. "Come here."

Then he hauled me across the bench seat so I was straddling him, threaded his two big hands back into my hair, and dragged my mouth to his. My whole body sank into him, feeling the long, lean muscles pressed against me, the way his lips, full and insistent, molded perfectly to mine.

"Is this what you wanted?" Will growled as he nipped, sucked, pulled voraciously with every kiss.

The hands in my hair pulled slightly, and I cried out, sounds that were swallowed with more torrid kisses.

"Yes," I hissed as I bit down on his lower lip.

Will groaned. His hands moved to cup my chin, claim my neck, then down further to pull open my blouse. Buttons flew everywhere, and a moment later, he was pressing his face between my breasts while his hands circled my waist.

"I'm not good for you, Lily," he huffed even as his lips found my aching flesh, again and again.

"We're not good for anyone, Will." I threaded my fingers through his hair and pressed him closer, arching back when his teeth closed over one nipple, pointed and aroused through the lace of my bra.

"You are." His words were muffled by my flesh, hoarse. "Fuck, Lily. You are."

I shuddered, both at the slight bite and his words. "Then that's probably why we work."

"Do we work?"

Will spoke against that soft, sensitive spot directly between my breasts. He paused, inhaled deeply, audibly, and though I could feel him throbbing through his jeans, rubbing between my legs, the rest of him was suddenly perfectly still. His hair had fallen out of its knot, and I laid a kiss on top of his head. The fury of the moment had subsided with the question, though the desire still remained.

"Take me home, Will," I said softly as I rolled my hips against him. "Please."

He shuddered, his breath warm against my skin. The door to the bar opened across the parking lot, and we watched, still wrapped up in each other, as a few patrons left, arms wrapped easily about each other. Their laughter echoed in waves through the night air.

Will and I didn't laugh. We were too sad, too broken for that kind of joy, but we were broken together.

He sat up straight, and tugged my shirt back together. Then he laid a tender kiss on my lips, and I watched, enthralled, as his mouth quirked into a very, very faint smile.

"All right, Lil," he said. "Let's go."

CHAPTER FIFTEEN

We drove back to the lake in silence, Will keeping my hand clasped firmly in his lap, but it wasn't until he pulled up in front of my stairs that I fully realized the night wasn't over. Sure, I'd asked him to take me home. And yeah, I'd meant beyond just a drop-off. But he hadn't said anything else, hadn't made a move. I had assumed that in the twenty-minute drive from Curly's, he'd changed his mind, like he always did.

But then he turned off the engine and pulled the keys out of the ignition.

"I—you—what are you doing now?" I asked.

Will's fingers brushed over my knuckles, and we both watched the movement for a moment. I was the first to look up.

"Do you want to come down?" My voice was small, unsure. Hell, I was unsure. Was I ready for this? For what I was asking for? I didn't know. But I knew I wanted it. Will made me feel like a whole person, in a way I wasn't ever sure I would again. He kissed me like I was the key to his survival. Or maybe like he was the key to mine.

Will paused. I could understand it, sort of. He'd been through enough tonight. If the guy had a severe phobia of people and had forced himself into a crowded bar for my sake, I could understand if he was averse to sex too. He wanted it—clearly—but some things superseded desire. Sex made a person vulnerable, and I had a feeling that I'd never feel so vulnerable, so naked, than when I was alone with Will.

"The only person there will be my mom," I said. "And you already know her. And there's a good chance she's already out for the night, if she's had enough gin and tonics."

Will looked up. "Is it really that bad with her? You—and others—seem to bring it up a lot. But she doesn't seem like that during the day."

I shrugged. "She's very functional. Until she's not. The nights are the worst. She doesn't do well with being alone."

Will nodded, suddenly looking past me, like he was almost somewhere else. "Yeah," he replied. "I get that."

Before I could ask what he meant, he grabbed a fleece jacket off his seat and got out of the truck. I followed suit, and he met me around the other side, taking my hand again naturally after he finished zipping up his jacket.

"Do you think we could slow down?" he asked. "Maybe just go sit somewhere and...and talk?"

I nodded, slightly relieved. As much as I wanted to, I probably wasn't ready to dive into anything just yet. I wanted him so badly, but something inside me said it was better to wait. Being with Will made me feel like I was racing to jump off a cliff without knowing how far down I was going to fall.

"Sure," I said. "Why don't we go down and light a fire by the dock?"

Unfortunately, a fire was already lit. When we rounded the far corner of the property around the shack, we found Mama sitting there, semi-awake while she stared into the flames. She started as we arrived, then relaxed and smiled when she saw who was with me.

"Well, if it isn't William," she said, standing up with a wobble. A glass in her hand clinked—yes, the gin and tonics were definitely still going.

Will awkwardly accepted a hug, and I resisted the urge to hide my face in my hands. If Mama was past the point where she could read any kind of social cues, then she was at least three or four drinks in.

"Come, come," Mama urged us. "Sit down. Take a seat. I didn't expect you kids back for a long time yet, if ever." She winked. "I guess you're a gentleman, William. Can I get you anything?"

Will shook his head as he sank into one of the Adirondack chairs. "No, Ms. Sharp, I'm good, thanks."

"And how was the date?"

"Mama!" I chided her, suddenly even more embarrassed. Was that what this was? A date?

Will rubbed his lips together—lips that had been all over my collarbone, neck, the tops of my breasts, maybe fifteen minutes ago. Okay, maybe date qualified now. I flushed, and he quirked an eyebrow at me.

"It was good," he said to Mama. "Although the music wasn't really my style."

I blanched. "It was Mike Grady's band, Mama. You remember them."

"Ohhhh, yes!" Mama crowed. "My, my. No wonder you didn't care for it. Michael sounds like a vacuum cleaner when he sings. William, have you heard Maggie play yet? I swear, she really does sound like an angel."

"Mama."

"Margaret, hush." Mama stood back up. "I'll be right back. She hasn't played since she's been here. Let's see if we can get her to come out of her sad sack, shall we?"

"Mama," I protested again, but she waved her hand in the air as she tottered back to the house. I turned to Will. "Sorry," I said bashfully. "She, um, gets like this when she's had a few..."

"Lil." Will's voice called my attention. "Stop. I get it. And it's fine."

I shrugged. "It's not. But right now, all I can do is be here."

"That's all anyone could ask for."

We lapsed into silence, listening to the sound of the lake water lapping at the dock until Mama's footsteps crunched across pine needles. She rounded the shack carrying my nicest and most prized guitar like it was nothing more than a broom handle.

"Mama, be careful!" I cried when she stumbled over a rock and almost fell down. I jumped up and ran over to take the guitar from her hands, but she twisted away from me, then fell into her chair with a thump. I winced as the edge of my guitar bumped her knee. Better that than the chair arm, I guessed.

"Oh relax," she told me. "Here, play us something pretty."

I eyed the shiny black wood. "Mama, I really don't think—"

"Come on now, Maggie Mae. I didn't scrimp and save for all those years of lessons just so you could ignore your mama. You need to play. How long has it been?"

She thrust the guitar at me, until finally I had to take it, lest it fall to the ground.

"Christ, Mama," I muttered as I rescued it. "This is a Martin D-35, the same guitar Johnny Cash played on. You don't just toss that around."

"Well, let's hear you play it, then," Mama replied. She glanced at Will with a sly smile. "William, I bet you're the kind of man who likes a nice cold beer when he sits around a fire, aren't you? I'm gonna get one for myself. Would you like one?"

Will glanced at me, but I shrugged. I had meant what I said at the bar.

"That sounds great, Ms. Sharp." Will gave a friendly nod, and the uncharacteristic gesture practically lit up his face.

Mama practically melted right there, batting her eyes at him. I just rolled mine.

We sat there for a second while Mama went back to the house, letting the sounds of the night fall around us like a cloak.

"Why haven't you played in a while?" Will asked quietly.

I tried to ignore the natural way the wood felt, curved over my knee. I tried to ignore the easy feel of the neck resting in my palm. The way the strings seemed to call to my fingertips. I closed my eyes, wishing the feeling away. But it wouldn't go.

For a second I was back on that stage. I could see the reps my manager had brought for the night, mostly just shadows in the back of the room. I could feel the heat of the stage lights shining down on me, demanding that I be someone else again. That I ignore everything that had happened to me, put on a smiling face, pretend that I was okay when in reality, my insides were still thoroughly shattered.

I could feel, again, my fingers slipping on the strings. The squeal of the wrong chord. The hot rush of tears burning down my face as I ran off the stage. I blinked and shook my head, focusing again on the sound of the water tickling the banks, the light breeze through the pine trees, the crackle of the fire.

New York was a long way away.

"I just don't love it anymore," I said. "Not like I used to."

"I don't believe that."

I looked up. "Why would you say that?"

The firelight shone off Will's hair, turning the blond highlights on top a burnished bronze. His eyes, almost black in the night, were as deep, almost mournful, as ever. But the firelight danced in their depths.

"Because the second you took that guitar, your whole body lit up," he replied. He picked up a stick and started poking at the logs. "It was like that," he said as a thrill of embers flew up into the night air. "Sparks."

Our eyes met across the fire as the sparks disappeared into the black, and for a moment, I couldn't move. Will swallowed visibly, the movement causing the muscles in his neck to flex. It was easy sometimes to forget how handsome he really was. His beard covered most of his face, but the shadows cast from the fire still played up cheekbones and hinted at a jawline that looked like it belonged in a museum, not around a campfire. His eyes, I knew, were as green as the lake at twilight, but with gold flecks that looked exactly like the sparks he had just teased from the logs. I knew what his chest looked like without that fleece on—knew exactly how his sun-kissed skin pulled taut over the sleek, elegant lines of his torso, which looked particularly good when he had water dripping all over it.

But now I couldn't help wondering what the rest of him looked like. If his lower half was as well built as the top.

Then our eyes met again. As if he could see my illicit thoughts reflected on my face, Will's gaze reflected a different kind of fire—one I suddenly felt burning deeply within me as well. Slowly, his gaze dropped, pouring over my body with such intensity it was like he was actually touching me.

Sparks. Yeah.

He exhaled, and swallowed again.

"Play something," he said, his voice slightly hoarse.

I cleared my throat, suddenly aware again that I was still holding my guitar. I looked down at it. Once I knew this shape like I knew my own body. Now it was like holding a stranger. And somehow, I didn't think that was just because of how long it had been since I had played.

"What—what do you want to hear?"

"Um…" Will's voice sounded strained. "Just—just play something. Now. Please."

I opened my mouth to remark just how odd it was that he was saying please—I honestly wasn't sure I had heard Will say anything nice to anyone since I had met him. But before I could reply, we were interrupted.

"Margaret can play just about anything," Mama said as she stepped back into the clearing. She handed Will a beer and kept the other for herself.

Will accepted the mug with a brief nod, although something told me that the cheap beer Mama had poured into the frigid glass wasn't quite up to Will's standards. Based on his home, the tea he had served me, I already knew that he had a quiet preference for the finer things in life.

"Do you ever…?" he asked me.

I shook my head.

"Maggie doesn't drink," Mama confirmed. "Not like I haven't tried to get her to lighten up for years. But you can't move a mountain, I should say."

I looked down at the strings, strummed them lightly, and cringed. Well, I wasn't going to be playing a damn thing with that tuning.

"What's your favorite music, William?" Mama asked as she retook her seat, and I proceeded to tune the guitar.

Will shrugged.

"When Margaret was little, I didn't need a record player or a stereo. I'd put on the radio, and she would listen. Ten minutes later, she could play the song." She looked at me. "What'd they call it, honey? You have perfect pinch?"

Will chuckled into his glass, and I rolled my eyes. "Pitch, Mama. Perfect pitch."

"Pitch," Mama told Will. "Name any song. My baby can play it for you." She took another long sip of her beer, as if that covered everything.

Will looked at me curiously. "Really?"

I shrugged and focused on tuning the last string. "Yeah. Pretty much."

I didn't say that having perfect pitch had been as much of a hindrance as it had been a blessing. My dependence on my ear was the reason I didn't know how to read music, and so had failed just about every music class I'd taken at NYU. I had dreams of coming out of college a classically trained guitarist. So much for dreams.

"'Gimme Shelter,'" Will said. "Try that one."

Immediately I strummed the opening chords to the Rolling Stones' famous tune.

Will's eyes brightened considerably. "Wow. Okay, then. How about 'The Boxer'?"

I rolled my eyes. "Seriously." My fingers tickled the strings faster than I could think out the complicated opening pattern to Simon and Garfunkel's hit. "Come on, now. Challenge me."

Will smirked. "How about 'Stairway to Heaven'?"

"Sure, I know that. Me and every other eighth grade boy on the planet." I laughed while I teased out the famous opening pattern to the Led Zeppelin classic, but stopped a few bars in. "Satisfied? Someone's a classic rock junkie, I see."

"Just means he has good taste," Mama cut in with a nod to Will.

Will just nodded in agreement. "The classics never go out of style."

"Play one of yours, Margaret," Mama urged with her glass. "For me."

I froze. "I don't know, Mama. I haven't practiced in so long..."

"I'd like to hear one," Will said.

The open curiosity in his face was something I hadn't seen before. His voice was barely audible over the crackle of the fire, but his eyes were what really stilled me. Gone was the cold, harsh man who kept showing up on our dock like a wet stray dog. Gone were the guarded looks. The suspicion. The not-so-hidden anger. The hurt.

Now I only saw a face that was warm. Open. Hopeful.

And as much as it scared me, in that second, I knew. I knew I'd play anything he wanted, in front of anyone, if he would look at me like that again.

I gulped. "Um, okay. I guess...sure."

And so, for the first time since I had run off that stage and fled New York in both terror and shame, I picked out the melody of the song I had written once, long ago, as a way to voice those emotions that couldn't speak aloud by themselves.

It was a song about loneliness. A song about being saved. A song about staying with someone long after you should, and how it broke you to do it.

The last note hung in the air for what seemed like eons, and when I finished, even the fire seemed silent. I exhaled, enjoying for a moment the elation that always came when I played my own music, my own heart. There was a space that opened up where nothing else existed but those notes, those resonances. The sound of my voice, the unity of my fingers on the strings or the keys. Just me. Just music. Nothing else mattered.

I opened my eyes and looked to Mama and Will, hoping to see at least a bit of that same contentment on their faces, the same that I felt at the end.

"Oh, honey," Mama said as she wiped a tear from her eye. "You always do this to me when you play, sweetheart. Beautiful, just beautiful. Wasn't it beautiful, William?"

I looked to Will, ready for his more taciturn answer, but hoping for maybe a little more than usual. Music always made me open up more too. Maybe it would do the same for him.

But he said nothing. His face had shuttered, and the frown line over his brow had reappeared. His mouth was slightly open while he looked at me, an expression that quickly morphed into a glare.

"Will?" I ventured, my voice small. I tried to be light, to mask the way his reaction hurt. Why it should hurt so much, I didn't care to explore. "Will, what's wrong?"

He stood up in a sudden hurry.

"Thank you for the beer, Ms. Sharp," he said stiffly to my mother. "I should be going."

"William," she protested. "Sit back down and finish your drink. Don't be a rude guest to Maggie."

But the look on his face said he would rather do anything but that. He glanced between us, his eyes wide. Panicked.

"Will," I protested. "What's—"

"I have to go," he said, and before either of us could respond, practically ran out of the clearing. Mama and I listened to the sound of his steps tromping up the deck, and watched him a few moments later as he made his way up the rest of the stairs.

"Well," Mama said as she sat back into her chair. She shook her head and took another long drink of beer. "I don't know what crawled up his bum, but I think tomorrow you'd best find out."

I frowned. "What? Why?"

"Because," she said as she set her beer on the ground. Her speech was slowing, a sure sign that soon, she'd be asleep. "That's what friends do, Maggie."

"Mama, I really don't think he wants that."

"That's what friends do," she repeated as her head lolled to the side.

"Mama, come on," I said, rising from the chair and pulling her up. If she passed out here, she'd be impossible to move until morning, and I'd end up sleeping on the grass to make sure she didn't accidentally stumble into the lake.

After I helped her to bed and put away my guitar, I stood for a moment on the top deck, looking out at the lake. Across the calm waters, a light flashed through the trees—a car arriving, maybe, or a porch light turning on and off. And I knew my mother was right. I needed to be there. Now.

CHAPTER SIXTEEN

Thirty minutes later, I'd looped halfway around the lake, driven past Will's driveway at least four times trying to find the mostly hidden entrance in the dark, and was finally parking my car right behind his orange truck. The porch light of his house, a few yards down the hill, was actually on. I took it as a good sign.

Without pretense, I marched up the moss-covered walkway and banged on the door.

"Will," I called. "Baker. Seriously, I know you're in there. And unless you'd like your neighbors to figure out there is actually someone living here, you better open up before I start shouting."

At first there was nothing but the lapping of lake water and the occasional call of an owl. But I wasn't about to be deterred.

"Seriously, Will." I raised my voice. "I know you're awake. And since my mother's passed out on the couch, I've got nothing but time. I can do this all damn night."

I raised my fist to pound again, but a few thumps sounded from inside. I backed away, waiting. I felt strange, a little reckless, almost like I was drunk or high on something. My heart was beating inordinately fast like I had run all the way here instead of sitting in my car. *Adrenaline*, a small voice told me. *That's adrenaline.*

Then the door opened, and my heart stopped. Will stood there in nothing but a pair of black boxer briefs that showed off way more than they covered up, doing absolutely nothing to hide the acres of flat, muscular expanse that rippled over his chest, his abs, cutting in two diagonal lines below the waistband of his shorts. Sure, I'd seen it before, but not this close. Not this late at night. Not this…furious.

When I managed to drag my eyes back up, his expression was positively feral. His hair drifted around his shoulders in a glorious wavy mane, framing a face that could only be described as leonine. His eyes sparked.

"What. The fuck. Are you doing here?" he growled.

I almost flinched. Almost. But then I didn't. Because this was Will, and though there was still a lot I didn't know about him, I did know that gruff facade masked a much softer interior. He couldn't fake that with me anymore. Not now. Not ever.

So I shoved by him into the room, ignoring the pine and fresh water scent that called to me as I passed. He was still so warm, even at well past midnight, when the chill of the night air sweeping down the mountains took over the summer heat and cooled everything off.

"Get dressed, Baker," I said as I turned around, my arms crossed. "We need to talk."

"It's almost one o'clock in the morning, Maggie."

Maggie? I wanted to ask. *Since when do you call me Maggie*?

I shook my head. "You weren't asleep. In fact, I'd bet a hundred bucks you rarely sleep through the night. I'm right, aren't I?"

Will's fists opened and closed for a few moments, and he worried his jaw, pulling a little on his beard as he scowled. Then he sighed and rolled his eyes.

"You're a pain in the ass, you know that?" he said, though he was already moving toward the stairs. "Wait here."

Five minutes later, he re-emerged still pulling on a gray t-shirt over a pair of black sweatpants, giving me one last glimpse of tantalizing abdominals before covering them with cotton. He had tied his hair back up, revealing strong cheekbones and a muscled neck. I was tempted to tell him to put it back down. It was easier to be mad at him when he looked more like Sasquatch than a model.

"What do you want, Lil?" Will crossed his arms, causing his biceps to stretch the sleeves in a very distracting way.

I cleared my throat. "I want to know why you ran off. Why you *keep* running off."

Will wrapped a hand around his neck and looked away. "What does it matter?"

"Should I just ignore it?" I asked. "You kissed me, Baker. Twice. And after this last time, I'm pretty sure you were planning to do more, but instead you asked me to serenade you before you left me high and dry. So what gives?"

Will crossed his arms and stared fixedly at the gleaming wood floors. "Maybe I'm just an asshole, Maggie. Did you ever think of that?"

I scowled. "Stop calling me 'Maggie' like we just met and you haven't practically eaten me alive *twice* now. That's a cop-out, and you know it."

Will shrugged. "Or it's the truth. I tried being nice to you, but it didn't work."

His hands dropped to his waist, crossed again in front of his chest, grabbed at his hair, then went back to his hips, constantly moving like he didn't know what to do with them. His gaze was equally erratic, moving all over the place, landing everywhere but me.

"Fuck this," he muttered to himself. He grabbed some keys off a table by the door, and started out without even bothering to put on shoes. "I need to take care of something down by the dock. You can see yourself out."

"Will!" I called as I jogged down the steps after him. "Will, wait!"

"Go home, *Maggie*!" He waved a hand in the air, not even bothering to turn around.

"Will!"

Will's shoulders tensed like they were bearing some unseen load, but he kept going down the long staircase toward the water.

"I thought we were having fun," I called out as I followed, pushing errant branches of pine and alder out of my face. "I thought we were actually having a good time tonight. You picked me up. We went out for a show. Had a drink or two and danced, like normal people."

Will whirled around, four steps from the bottom. "Is that what you think tonight was? A normal date with a normal guy? Should I have brought you flowers? Opened your door for you? Bought you a drink instead of clinging to your hand like a fucking psycho?"

"I—I didn't say that," I said, with less strength than I wanted. I cleared my throat awkwardly. "Will, I didn't say anything like that!"

"I am *not* a normal guy, Lil. I'll *never* be that guy. I haven't been normal since I was seven years old, and now I'm more fucked up at my age than most people will ever be their entire lives. I'll never, ever be fucking *normal*, so you can drop-kick that idea out of your pretty little head."

He didn't wait for me to reply, just turned and practically ran the rest of the way down the hill, taking a sharp right into the trees. I followed, struggling to track him in the dim light.

"Stop following me, Lil," he called over his shoulder as he strode to a small boathouse close to the dock. It was shrouded in trees, but he moved about the property like he'd done this many times in the dark.

"Stop running away," I retorted as I ducked under a big pine tree branch, eventually coming to a stop behind him, just short of running into him.

Will pulled a set of keys out of his pocket and they jangled loudly as he struggled to unlock the door to the boathouse.

"You kissed me," I stated to his back. "Twice. *You* kissed *me*. And then you showed up to take me to that show even though I *never* said you had to go. You asked me to dance. *You* cut in. And then you kissed me. *Again*."

"And why do you think I did that?!" he exploded, smacking his hand hard against the door. "It's not healthy, the way I feel about you! Every time I see you, I want to pick you up, take you away from this place, these people—anyone who says the things they say to you. I want you for myself and no one else because I'm a selfish bastard. Does that sound like something a good person would think?"

"You would never do that," I said. "I know you, Will. You're not like that."

Will froze. He shoved his keys into his pocket, and his other hand braced the wall. His head fell.

"I'm not good for you," he said in a voice I almost couldn't hear, muffled as it was by his posture and the woods. "I don't know why you haven't run a mile away from me, Lily, but you should. I won't come by the house anymore. I won't help out or run or bike or swim with you. You walk away right now, and I'll do the same. We'll just leave each other alone."

The muscles of the arm braced against the door shook visibly, even in the scattered moonlight. I stared for a moment, feeling more than ever as if Will were some kind of wild animal, desperate to be tamed, but terrified of being trapped. With a light, careful touch, I placed my hands on his arms, and when he didn't move them—in fact, seemed to sag into my touch—I turned him around, guiding him in a circle so that he was leaning back against the door and watching me with wide, worried eyes.

"I don't want to leave you alone," I said softly as I stepped up onto my toes. "And I don't think you want me to either. I think you think about this, imagine this, *want* this just as much as I do."

Our lips weren't quite level, but it was close enough. Will stared down at me—at my lips—with his mouth slightly open, like a starving man looking at a row of pastries kept behind glass. I understood it because I felt the same way.

Well, I was tired of starving. I was tired of looking at a buffet when all I wanted to do was splurge. To hell with doing the right thing. If kissing Will Baker was wrong, then I was well on my way to hell and happy to be there.

I leaned in and closed my eyes. But just before our lips met for that ferocious yet sweet connection that I knew was waiting for me, Will spoke.

"Pine cone."

I blinked. "Wha-*what*?"

His eyes, which were currently glued to my lips, slowly dragged up to meet mine. They held them for a second or two before he opened his mouth and articulated the word loudly and clearly: "Pine. Cone."

I shook my head, but before I could ask him what the hell was going on, Will ducked away and started back the way we'd come, across the bank and up the stairs again.

"Where are you going?" I called as I scrambled after him. God, my thighs would be burning in the morning. I'd been up and down stairs all damn day. "Hey, I thought you had to take care of something down here."

"Pine cone, Lily," he called over his shoulder. "Go the fuck home!"

"What is this, Chutes and Ladders?" I yelped as I tramped up the stairs behind him, trying my best not to slip on the mounds of dried pine needles collected everywhere. "Stay in one place, Baker, and have a conversation like a grownup!"

He didn't respond, just ran back up the stairs two at a time, to the point where I couldn't keep up with him and shout at the same time.

"Will!" I cried as we finally reached the top of the stairs. "Will, *stop* and talk to me!"

He whirled around, shaking and red in the face.

"Pine cone!" he roared. "I said *pine cone*, Lily! Jesus *fucking* Christ, what good is a safe word if you're not going to use it!"

I took a step toward him, but as I did, my toe brushed something sharp and pointy. I looked down: it was, of course, a freaking pine cone. I stared at it, then picked it up, and with everything I had, hurled it at Will. It hit him square on the forehead, and he backed up a few steps, pressing a hand to his head.

"Hey!" he yelped. "What the hell was that?"

"Fuck the pine cone!" I cried back. "And fuck the safe word! I'm not hurting you here, and you're using it as a crutch. What is so triggering about my songs, my kiss, huh? You have to run off because I sang a song that *you* pressured me into playing in the first place! Was it really so bad you had to sprint up a goddamn hill?"

My voice trembled on the end of the sentence. I hadn't realized I'd felt that way until I said it. That maybe, deep down, my music wasn't that good. That maybe that's why I'd failed, why I'd never be anything more than a girl who was uncommonly good at mimicking others, but who couldn't create anything worth hearing on her own. Maybe that was why I'd let go, had found it so easy to allow a man to consume my life and push my dreams aside.

"Well, it's better than seeing you dance with Lucas Forster," he spat, like I hadn't just asked him a direct question. "Just looking at that ogre's hands on you, I felt *violent*, Maggie. I wanted to break both his fucking arms so he physically couldn't touch you anymore."

I shook my head and looked up. Where was this coming from? "You're kidding, right?"

"Believe me, I wish I were."

"You're *jealous*? *That's* what this is about? You came over there to *help* me!"

Will took a few steps toward me. "I didn't know. Maybe you liked it. Maybe you wanted him to grab your ass in the middle of the room like you were his cheap date. All I knew was that I couldn't fucking deal with it!"

"Stop it," I said, stepping backward.

"I don't know, Lil. Maybe it's familiar. Maybe you like the way he treats you like an old baseball glove he forgot in his basement. A toy he used to have, and now he wants to play with because some other kid wants it too."

"Be careful, Baker," I warned him with a pointed finger. "That's some sexist crap you're spouting right now. I'm no one's *toy*."

"No, you're not. You're amazing. Too good for him, and certainly too good for me." He bent over, like it physically hurt him to say all of this. "You loved him at some point. Once, Lucas Forster had something to offer, didn't he?" He pushed his hands through his hair and clenched his jaw so tightly, a vein popped out in his forehead.

"Stop it," I whispered, though my heart wasn't in this fight anymore. I just wanted to stop the pain I saw etched across Will's face.

"Tell me what it was," Will commanded as his gaze burned up and down my body.

I didn't know how he did it. I was absolutely furious with him, and at the same time, two seconds from yanking off my clothes and tackling him.

He stepped toward me, and I took another step back. It was like we were back on the floor at the tavern all over again, a fucked-up dance of intimidation that turned me on and made me want to run at the same time.

"Tell me what he has," Will ordered. "I want to know what a guy like that does to deserve someone like you."

This time neither of us moved. And one thought—only one—echoed through my head.

"Lucas Forster isn't scared of me," I said.

The wind rose through the trees, like it was whispering my words back to us.

Will cocked his head. "Is that so?"

I forced myself not to cower, straightening to my full five feet and five inches tall. "Y-yes," I managed, trying to sound stronger than I felt. "That's so."

"Lucas Forster," Will growled as he took another step, then another until he had me trapped against the long counter of an old outdoor kitchen wrapped around the house, "is absolutely *terrified* of you. Lucas Forster wouldn't know what to do with a woman like you if he had the fucking manual."

His eyes dropped to my lips. He took a deep breath. I couldn't breathe at all.

Then...*then* Will attacked. And to my surprise, I fought back. Our mouths, hands, limbs—everything—clawed, grappled with each other. Pushing away, yet trying to get closer. Will kissed me like he was engaging a battle for his life. His soul. Daring me to fight it, and fight it I did. I grabbed a handful of his thick hair—that erratic mane I both wanted to comb and cut, depending on my mood—and yanked, forcing him to look at me.

"Oh?" I panted, already breathless. "And you do?"

Will reached past my ass, and in one brusque move, scooped me up from the ground and set me on the counter. His broad hands pushed up the tops of my thighs, then wrenched them apart as he conquered my mouth with another vicious kiss that left me gasping for breath. He ground against me in slow, measured strokes, letting me feel just exactly what he had packing under those pants of his. And...yeah. Let's just say it took him some very nice, long movements to get from one end to the other. I squirmed against him, and he devoured me all over again.

He sucked hard on my lower lip. I moaned. Will grunted. "I knew how to do this before I met you, Lily pad. I was born knowing how to kiss you. How to touch you. How to fuck you."

His harsh words made me shiver. But still, I fought. "And is that all I'm worth to you?"

I bit his earlobe, and my fingernails dug into the curve of his shoulder. Will hissed, but didn't stop kissing me, back and back again, tongue dipping deeper inside, like he couldn't get enough.

"One fuck?" I gasped. "And then you're gone again, right? Isn't that what you do?"

Still squeezing my thighs hard enough that I thought he might leave bruises, Will froze. He stood back up, his full mouth half open, his green eyes intense and bright, and inhaled sharply, enough that his shoulders and chest rose and fell with the movement. My hand slid up his shirt, feeling his solid bones, smooth skin, the light sprinkle of hair over his impossibly hard chest. He caught it—over his heart—and trapped it there.

"You want to know why I ran away?" he asked.

I licked my lips, unable to help myself. Our mouths were maybe a half inch from each other, close enough that our breaths, our scents mingled, harbingers of what our bodies longed to do. I wanted more, wanted it so badly my chest hurt. I was panting, a sheen of sweat built across my brow from pure desire while my eyes were squeezed shut.

"Y-yes," I managed, trying and failing to ignore the way my lips throbbed with want. With need.

"Lily."

The anger in Will's voice was gone. Instead, all I heard, right on pitch, was a curious harmony of confusion. Resignation. Desire.

I opened my eyes and found Will staring, his mouth half open in that same pucker of want I knew was on mine. But his eyes, those deep green, gold-flecked pools of sadness that I couldn't quite reach, didn't waver or shutter. For once, it felt like he was wide open.

"I was scared, yeah," he said. "But your song…goddammit, it was stunning, Lil. It was so fucking beautiful, it scared the hell out of me. Just…just like you."

He shook his head and pushed a hand through his hair, yanking at the ends meditatively. But his gaze didn't move.

"You make me feel…like a dying man in the desert. And you're the fresh spring, the oasis. The water for my parched fucking soul." He shuddered, a movement that spread through his whole body. "But I'm terrified," he whispered, "absolutely fucking terrified…that you're just a mirage."

The wind rose again through the trees, blowing around us in a chorus that echoed through my soul. The lust I'd experienced just moments before wasn't gone, but it was second to whatever else this was that I was feeling. Like it or not, I was connected to this man. I didn't know why or how, or what it meant, but I knew that. And I wanted him to know it too.

"I'm not a mirage," I said softly as I framed his face with my hands, brushing his cheekbones with my thumbs. "I'm very real, Will. And I'm right here. For you."

Will's eyes closed, as if he were wincing, so I leaned in and delivered a soft kiss onto his lips. His mouth opened to me, welcoming me while he pressed closer, aligning our bodies at every point.

"Stay," he rumbled, low and fierce, into my mouth. He kissed me again, tasting my lips, savoring every bit of me. "Stay. And show me."

CHAPTER SEVENTEEN

He carried me effortlessly into the house and down the stairs. I wasn't a big person to start with, but I wasn't particularly tiny either. Still, Will's lean muscles kept me firmly wrapped around him as our lips remained fused, our eyes half shut with longing, so I barely registered the row of closed doors we passed on our way to his bedroom, and hardly noticed the open space with floor-to-ceiling windows that looked out into the darkness of forest and water, but which would be flooded with light come morning. Will laid me on the bed, his arms still firmly wrapped around my back while he drifted his lips around my jaw, down my neck, and just below the collar of my shirt.

His mouth was warm, almost sweet, and addictive to the point where it genuinely scared me that I wouldn't be able to stop kissing him when it came time. And it would. People like me and Will always had expiration dates. Our issues were too much to put on another person. But right now, I didn't care.

Then Will stood up. My eyes popped open at his sudden absence.

"Where are you going?"

"Wait here," he said, then disappeared, leaving me in darkness.

I stared up at the exposed rafters of the ceiling, trying to convince myself that this wasn't a bad idea. That getting involved with Will and his metric ton of intimacy problems didn't spell a load of trouble. That kissing him didn't feel like the best thing in the entire fucking world.

I failed. Miserably.

"Close your eyes, Lil."

Will's deep, sonorous voice broke through my doubts, and I did as he said, smiling as I covered my eyes with my hands. I heard the sound of shuffling, but kept my hands firmly in place, not wanting to spoil whatever surprise he was preparing.

"All right. You can open them now."

When I did, the first thing I saw was a balance of shadows and light dancing on the ceiling. Will had set up candles around several corners of his bedroom, and the effect illuminated the open space with a warm, yellow glow that cast every edge, every line under a softly moving haze. *Chiarascuro,* I thought to myself, remembering for a moment the paintings one of my Cultural Foundations professors had showed us in college, referencing the paintings of Caravaggio—a master of light. His use of light, the contrast between light and dark, had made his paintings of the body even more lifelike than so many of his contemporaries. He was known for making a painting seem like it was a person in the room with you. More than just paint and canvas. His work was raw. Real. Immediate.

But Caravaggio's work had nothing on the gleaming Adonis who stood in front of me. I had never met anyone more immediate than Will. More physical. More…present. When Will was around, I had a hard time sensing anything but him. Everything else seemed to fade away—the lake, the bar, my friends, my mother. And now, in this room, between four enclosed walls when it was only him and me, our lips still throbbing from the kisses we'd given and the kisses we had yet to give, he simply overwhelmed me.

I gasped. And then I did the only thing I could think of to ease the strange tension. I joked.

"Candles?" I giggled. "Really? What are we, in some cheesy romance movie?"

His hopeful expression faltered, and immediately, I regretted my words. Shit, he was trying to do something nice, and here I was making fun of him. Again. It was all right to do when he was being too serious for his own good, but this was my issue.

And just then, it occurred to me how long it had been—how long it had *really* been—since someone had tried to do anything nice. For me. Only me. No motives. No half-assed attempts. Just for me.

The thought erased any lingering humor as I burst into tears.

"Lil?"

I curled onto my side, mortified as I tried and failed to hide. *Fuck. Fuck*! What was wrong with me? I never cried. Sharp women didn't cry.

"Lil." Will lay down on the bed behind me, and the movement caused me to roll back into him. A tentative arm crept over my waist as he pulled me into his warmth. "Baby, what's with the tears?"

The sweet, common pet name only made me cry harder.

"Sh-shit." Viciously, I swiped under my eyes. I hadn't even realized I was about to cry until he'd said something. That was how lost I already was in him, and we hadn't really done anything else but kiss. How could I feel this way about someone I hardly knew?

Because he's yours. And you're his.

The thought came unbidden, and I wasn't sure from where. Will pulled me around, gently guiding me so I was turned toward him. We lay on our sides, facing each other, our heads pillowed on our arms. He reached out and wiped a tear from underneath my eye.

"Lil," he said quietly. "We don't have to…I mean, you can still change your mind…if you want to go to sleep, or just drive home… Whatever you want, all right? No pressure."

I bit my lip. *No*! Every particle in my body was paralyzed, but also seemed to scream with want. Will looked at me with a clenched jaw, unable to keep his gaze from slipping to my mouth. He wanted to kiss me again. Even with my tear-streaked face, he still wanted that connection I craved too. We were the definition of misery loving company. But then I wondered if the combination of our two miseries could make something beautiful. Maybe it could create joy.

I shook my head.

"No, it's not that," I managed. "I'm just—I'm scared too. It's been a long time."

Will frowned. He took my hand and started to toy with my fingers. His warm touch was soothing.

"I thought you had a boyfriend back in New York."

I shook my head. "I did. But we broke up a long time ago. I just meant it's been a long time since anyone's done…well, anything for me. Even something as small as candles."

I reached out, hovering my hand for a moment over his bicep before dropping it with relief and trailing a knuckle down his arm. Will watched its progress, rapt. The candlelight flickered in his big green eyes. When my hand reached his elbow and fell to the sheets, he looked up.

"It's been a long time for me too," he said softly. "I'm probably not supposed to admit that, but what the fuck? I'm doing a lot of things tonight that I shouldn't."

I nodded. "I know the feeling."

"But I don't want to stop."

"Me neither."

He leaned in. "I'm going to kiss you again, Lil."

I nodded again. "Okay."

"And when I start…that's it. You have no idea. *No idea* how badly I want you."

His hand traced the opposite path of mine up my arm, pausing on my elbow. Suddenly, my tears and worries had evaporated, and I was right back where I was ten minutes before—overcome with a pending tidal wave of lust that turned everything else to dust.

"Do it," I whispered. "And for God's sake. Don't stop."

Will had already snaked his hand around the nape of my neck and was pulling me close.

"Done," he growled before he kissed me again.

This time, he consumed me. I had thought he was a good kisser before, but in his movements, Will let go. His hands were suddenly everywhere, sliding over my back and around my ass, rolling us over so that I was on top of him, yet relinquishing absolutely none of the control as he pinned me over his body, keeping me captive to the onslaught of lips, tongue, breath, life.

He sat up, taking me with him, and allowed me to run my hands through his hair and over his bare shoulders while he kneaded my thighs, my ass through my jeans.

"We shouldn't do this," he said, even as he whipped off my shirt. His big hands slid over my shoulders and down my back, feeling everywhere with their broad expanse—palms, fingertips, all of them.

"Stop saying that." My words were just as breathless as I claimed kiss after crazy kiss. I didn't know why he was fighting this. The floodgates were open now. There was no point in trying to shut them.

I ran my hands up his torso, enjoying the way my fingers tripped over his abs while he tugged at the buttons of my jeans, managing to get the fly partially undone before giving up so he could kiss me again. Will sucked on my lips like they were candy, moaning softly as he did.

"I'm not good for you," he replied even as his hands slid up my back and started fiddling at the fasteners of my bra.

"That's my decision, not yours."

As his hands fumbled, I reached around to help him out—I was actually kind of charmed with the way he struggled. Will looked like the kind of guy who could get any woman he wanted, but if he kept people at arm's length the way he had with me, it had probably been months since he'd last gotten laid. Maybe even years.

No, I thought to myself. *There is no way.* Someone that good looking was probably jumped on a regular basis, hermit or not.

With a quick flick, the band released, and I pulled it off, baring myself to him completely.

"Jesus fucking Christ," Will breathed. His gaze was everywhere, casting a fiery net over my breasts, my darkened nipples, a color between brown and mauve that pebbled in the cool summer air, my skin that was always somewhere between milky tea and a latte, my hair, my face, and back to my lips.

"What?" I asked, growing a little self-conscious. I was getting back into decent shape again, but I wasn't anywhere close to Will's level of fit. The guy was seriously *GQ*-ready.

"You're just…" Keeping one hand firmly wrapped around my waist, he touched one finger to the tip of my breast, then, lightly, rolled the nub between his thumb and forefinger until it puckered and sent an ache directly between my legs. "Lily, you are the most beautiful woman I've ever seen." His gaze flickered back to mine and didn't move. "You are. You really are."

It was then, only then, that I was able to relax, tipping my head back, my entire body on display for him. Most of my life I'd felt like an oddity —men who slept with me thought of me as either too white or too… other. I was somewhere in between, a curiosity to be admired, enjoyed, shown off. Even with Lucas and his family, I'd felt that way—when Linda, for instance, would praise my "exotic" looks, Lucas would always agree. Or when I'd complain about my curly hair, he'd say he didn't care about it—that he loved me anyway. They were meant to be nice things. Meant to make me feel good. But instead, I'd felt excluded. Like an outsider.

But here, with Will, I wasn't other people's Maggie anymore. I was just me. I was *his* Lily pad. *His* pain in the ass. And it was just like he said: I had been waiting for this moment since long before I knew him.

The hand on my breast released its pinch, but when nothing else happened, I started to feel self-conscious again.

"What are you staring at, Baker?" I asked with a raised brow. I got up onto my knees so that we were chest to chest, though I still had to look up at him. "I thought you knew how to do this better than anyone before you were even born? Or was that all just talk?"

But instead of the sharp retort or distant look, I got something completely unexpected.

He smiled.

Will…smiled. And it was so much better than I ever thought it would be. Even in a room barely lit with candles, it was unbearably sweet, kind, dripping with charisma. The effect was blinding.

"Oh…God," I murmured, unable to speak properly. My heart was stuck in my throat. I was transfixed.

The smile broadened, and I couldn't move.

"Maggie," he said. "You okay?"

"You're beautiful," I whispered because it was the truth.

The smile faltered for a moment, then spread even further. Will cupped my cheeks, brushing thumbs over the bones for a moment.

"Not like you," he said, low and fierce. "Not even close."

And then he kissed me again, a kiss that was less lust, and more something else. Something deep, a little dark. Something that rocked me to my core, unsteadied me from the inside out. The more he did it, the less steady I felt. But the more he did it, the more I never wanted him to stop.

"Turn around," he murmured, urging me to obey even as he said it.

I did, looking out at the water and enjoying the feel of his fingertips and lips fluttering down my back. I had no idea that my spine was an erogenous zone until that moment, but apparently it was. His lips were feather-soft, lingering over each ridge, each curve. His nose hovered at the small of my back as he hooked his fingers over the waistband of my jeans and tugged them down my legs. Then he continued, pressing soft kisses over the curve of my ass, licking the cleft where my legs extended.

But I couldn't stay that way for long. I wanted to see him, not look away. When I did, I found he had removed his pants too. My mouth dropped. I couldn't help it. He was just so beautiful. Built like a statue, but with twice as much artistry, Will's body was a work of art in itself—a tall column of strength and golden muscle that radiated warmth.

I reached out a hand and touched him—the long rod of him that bounced slightly at even the slightest hint of my fingers. He was big—not insane, but fitting for a man his size. I licked my lips, and his eyes dilated.

"Is that what you want?" he murmured. He cocked his head. "It's just as well."

I blinked up at him in a daze. "What do you mean?"

A wicked curve captured Will's mouth, and involuntarily, I clenched my thighs together.

"You don't think I have contraceptives, do you?" He cocked his head, causing his hair to fall over one shoulder, then tipped my chin up so I had to look at him. "I wasn't exactly expecting you tonight. I want to, Lil." His hand captured mine, and he pressed it around his cock, moving our hands together slowly up and down his silky length. Will shuddered. "*Fuck*, you have no fucking clue how bad I want to. You're ready for me right now, baby. I can smell it."

I squirmed, but was unable to deny it. We had barely done anything, and already the room smelled like sex. I opened my mouth to tell him that I had an IUD. That it was fine, there was no need to worry about pregnancy, etc., so—

You don't know him, Maggie. And he doesn't know you.

My tongue felt thick in my throat as I continued to stroke him. I wanted to suggest that one of us could drive to the store, close to thirty minutes away. Bang on Cathy's door at 1 a.m. Go door to door until *someone* provided us with the one thing we needed to do what both of our bodies were clearly dying for.

But…no. It would have to wait. *Daaaaaaaaaammmmmmmmit.*

"Turn around." Will's voice was low—it wasn't a request.

The hands at my waist guided me back to face the bed.

"Now bend over."

I didn't move. Not because I didn't want to, but because his hands—those broad, strong hands, were still firmly at my waist, one of them sliding down to tickle under the elastic of my underwear, while the other slid up to cup one of my breasts. Will's mouth was hot at my ear, and he bit the upper edge of it lightly before growling. The long, steel length of him was pressed firmly to the cleft of my ass—I wanted to do nothing more than follow his orders and open to him. But he had me trapped.

"Lil," he growled. "Bend the fuck over."

I shuddered. "I can't."

I felt, rather than saw the smile behind me.

"That's right, beautiful. You can't. Not until I say."

I shivered as he toyed with my nipple, pulling lightly on the bud before sliding his hand up further to wrap his fingers around my neck.

"This is what you're going to do," he said, before sucking lightly at the skin just under my ear. I whimpered, and he kept talking. "You're going to bend over like I fucking told you. Then I'm going to bury my face between your legs and lick that pretty pussy until you're screaming my name so loud the entire fucking lake knows you're coming."

I shuddered again, more because of the way his other hand slipped into my underwear and started to stroke the particular body part he'd just mentioned.

"After that, I'm going to want to fuck you, Lil. But since I can't tonight, I'm going to have to settle for your mouth instead. That sweet, luscious mouth that I've wanted to fuck since the second I saw you on that hill."

His hips rocked into me, and his cock slid up the cleft of my ass. Will groaned lightly, and I did too, right along with him.

"One day I'm going to fuck you there too," he said throatily as he pulled back and then pressed himself between my curves again. "But for now, let's get back to the plan. Bend over."

He pressed on my back—and the slight movement caused me to fall forward onto the bed while my knees dropped to the floor. I was silent—words wouldn't come, I wanted him so badly. And it was a good thing, because Will had enough for both of us. He was so quiet and terse the rest of the time, it was like our connection—*my* body—released his voice. The idea was intoxicating.

"This ass has been killing me," he muttered against my skin as he knelt behind me. His mouth drifted over my flesh while both hands clenched it, one thumb drifting over the soft pucker at the top while the other parted my legs so he could press his face between them.

I moaned, long and low, into the comforter as his beard scratched the sensitive skin.

"I'm going to taste you now, beautiful," Will rumbled against my skin as he continued to drop kisses up and down the insides of my thighs. "I'm going to fuck you with my tongue while I play with your clit. You're going to want me so badly, you'll be begging for it. So what's it going to be, Lil? Rub it or pinch?"

"Fuck," I gasped as he licked one straight line up the middle of my legs. "I—I d-don't care!"

"Both it is," Will said, and then plunged his face between my thighs.

And the man knew his work. He devoured me like a man starved, his hands reaching around my legs to toy with my clit while he destroyed me with every lick, suck, and stroke.

"Will," I called into the pillow. "Oh, Jesus, *Will*!"

But he didn't stop. The man was relentless, not missing a beat, managing his pace to match the ebbs and flows of pleasure that washed through me. Because an orgasm doesn't happen in a straight line. It comes and goes unevenly like the tide, with waves of pleasure that build and build until eventually, one that's big enough comes crashing through you with enough force to break down your defenses. Some are just bigger than the others; some are tidal waves.

Most men didn't understand the process—they didn't understand the ebb and flow at all. But Will did. Will seemed to feel every single one, slipping deeper when I squirmed, pressing harder when I called out, and backing off slightly when my body fell from each miniature high.

"Oh my *God*, Will, *please*!" I shouted, my legs shaking around his face. I wasn't going to be able to keep my body propped up like this much longer. "Please! Please just *fuck* me!"

But he didn't. Will Baker might have been many things, but he was definitely a man of his word. Instead, he slipped a hand under my thigh and flipped me onto my back like I weighed nothing, then replaced his mouth with two long fingers and shoved them viciously inside me.

"Ah!" I cried at the sudden intrusion, though my hips were already moving in tandem with his fingers.

"I want to fuck you soooo bad, Lil," he groaned over my clit before he licked that as well, causing me to jerk against his mouth. "But I can't. Not there. Not yet. You're just going to have to come in my mouth instead."

The effect was immediate. His words, combined with the feel of him nestled between my thighs, the memory of where his face had been just moments before, and the idea of where I *wanted* him to be tossed me over the edge. That final, massive tidal wave came crashing down, and I started to shake.

"That's right," Will grumbled before he continued his onslaught, that delicate blend of licking, sucking, pinching. "Come for me, beautiful. Let me taste it."

"WILL!"

The name burst from me like some deep, primeval call and echoed through the room, past the window, out to the water, and beyond. I shook, feeling like the earth itself was causing the movements, and every muscle in my body seized and released with every long, heavy throb of my heart. Coming didn't cover it. Orgasm didn't cover it. This was an explosion.

"That's it." Will's voice broke through my cries as he pushed himself up in a frenzy, straddling my hips while he worked his cock over my body.

"Fuck, Maggie!" he shouted. His voice echoed into my bones as he released himself over my stomach and hips. His head tipped back, and his voice was hoarse, guttural, as he called my name twice more, his hand working furiously until eventually, it began to slow, and he had expended the last of himself all over me.

"Jesus," he muttered as he collapsed afterward, his breath gone as he heaved.

The sticky residue of both of our pleasure spread between us, seeping into our pores. Into each other. I knew we should get up, clean off, but I had absolutely no desire to move. I wanted it to seep inside me, in one way, if not the other.

"Your mom," Will whispered, just as sleep was about to capture us both.

I chuckled. "So not who I wanted to think about right now."

There was a light movement of his shoulders—laughter maybe?—before he rolled over onto his side next to me.

"That's not what I meant," he said with a small half smile. "Is she going to be okay if you're here tonight?"

I sighed as the levity disappeared. "She's never really okay."

Will nodded, managing the miracle of looking concerned without making me feel pitied. "Should we go back?"

That was always the question. It was the question I'd been wrestling with for six years, and I was grateful that Will didn't press me on it. Whatever his faults, he wasn't nosy. I'd give him that.

"I—I don't think so," I said finally. "She wasn't too bad tonight, all things considered. I helped her to bed, and she doesn't have to work in the morning. She probably won't even notice that I'm gone."

Will nodded, then got up. I watched as he disappeared into the hall and then returned shortly carrying a damp cloth.

"Here," he said, holding it out to me. "I'd suggest a shower, but it was hard enough holding myself together in the dark. You are so goddamn sexy when you come, you know that?"

"*That* was you holding yourself together?" I asked as I cleaned up. I handed it back to him, and Will tossed it across the room into a hamper.

"It was," he confirmed as he got back onto the bed and pulled a blanket over us. "Pretty sure if I had you in my shower, fully lit and wet, you'd get pregnant just from me looking at you. And I sure as fuck don't want that."

I rolled my eyes, ignoring the pinch of pain that came with his last statement. "You're such a man. Rut and impregnate, right? Beasts, all of you. What happened to my mouth, huh?"

Will chuckled again as he turned me toward the windows, fitting my back to his front.

"Tomorrow," he promised as he buried his face into my hair and tucked my body against his solidity. "Tomorrow I'll go back to being a beast and do the other half of what I promised. But now I need to sleep, Lil. And so do you."

His hair fell over my shoulder, and he pressed a kiss to the soft spot under my ear. Several candles had gone out by this point, and the last one, a small tea light, flickered in the corner, clearly on its last legs.

"Stay," he whispered as sleep fell over us. "For an hour. Forever. Just...stay."

CHAPTER EIGHTEEN

I woke up the next morning with light shining on my face. The sun was rising over the hill across the lake and glimmering off the water through the trees. I could barely make out the edges of the yellow house where I'd left my mother snoring last night.

A pang of guilt shot through me. I sat up.

Shit. Oh, shit, Mama. What kind of daughter was I? I had come home with the express purpose of helping my mother out of her rut, and instead I'd left her in yet another haze of alcohol and sleep. I knew better than that. I knew better…

There was a rustle in the sheets next to me, and a warm hand slid over my thigh.

"It's okay," Will said in a groggy voice. "She's okay, Lil."

I jumped slightly, then turned toward him, holding the sheets to my chest. I didn't even bother to ask how he possibly knew what I was thinking about before he answered.

"You practically bored a hole through the window, you were staring so hard. Your mom is fine, I promise."

"How do you know?"

I looked him over, taking note of our differences. I was still in my birthday suit, whereas Will was fully dressed in shorts and an old

Rolling Stones t-shirt. He stretched atop of the bed, causing the shirt to ride up above his navel.

"Where have you been?" I wondered, tearing my gaze away with difficulty.

His mouth quirked into a crooked smile. It was half-hidden, but just as heart-stopping as it had been the night before. "I—uh—might have gone to the store," he admitted shyly. "Sometimes I get up early. I needed something to do. I checked up on your mom on the way there."

I frowned, disregarding for the moment that he had just confirmed my previous assumption—that Will Baker generally did not sleep well. "How did you get in?"

Will shrugged. "She was making coffee. I let her know you were here and left for the store."

It took me a second to realize what he meant—or *why* he would have gone to the store this early. My eyes popped open, and immediately I swiveled around, looking for the shopping bag.

He chuckled and shook his head regretfully. "No luck, beautiful. Cathy—that's her name, right?—was pretty interested in why I was loitering around the personal hygiene shelf, though. 'No one is that interested in Pepto-Bismol,' she said." He shrugged, tucking his hands behind his head. "She's right."

I flopped back into the pillow and laughed, encouraged when Will chuckled again with me. I liked that sound. A lot. My thighs relaxed too —I hadn't even realized they were clenched at the idea of continuing what we'd started.

"Seriously, though, Maggie," he said as he turned onto his side to face me. He moved his hand up my waist and stroked the side of my arm. "Last night was…"

"If you say that was a mistake, I will slap you," I said. "No kidding, Baker. You don't get to hermit up on me now." I was holding onto enough of my own guilt over being here. I didn't need him to add to it.

Will's mouth dropped in surprise, and when it closed, that crooked smile returned. "I was going to say it was amazing," he said softly. "I'd like to do it again. Soon."

We lay there together for a few moments, just watching each other as his invitation sank in. I reached over and stroked his beard. Will remained still as I brushed the coarse hair down, then pulled at one side of the tangled dark blond waves hanging over his shoulder.

"Yeah," I agreed finally. "It was amazing. *You're* amazing."

Will blushed. As in full-on, head-to-toe, pink-nosed blushed. It was the most adorable thing I'd ever seen, and I immediately tackled him for it with a kiss.

But what started out as a barrage of joking smacks quickly morphed into something much deeper as a steel arm slid around my waist and another one took a larger handful of my flesh. I groaned into his mouth. Will grabbed harder.

When, to my disappointment, he finally broke away and released me, Will cleared his throat. "You should probably come over again tonight. Expected, this time."

I pushed back up on one elbow so I could look down at him clearly.

"Baker," I teased, reaching around to play with a strand of his hair. "Are you asking me out on a date? One where you're not jealous of my ex-boyfriend? Where it's going to be just you and just me? If I'm here, you can't run away again, you know."

An expression I didn't quite understand flashed across his face. A tightness. Maybe a little bit of fear. But the longer I looked, the more it fell away, replaced in the end by some measure of the relaxation he'd had before.

"Eight o'clock," he said as he pushed up, beckoning me to kiss him again. "I'm counting on it."

I DROVE BACK to my house some time later, lost slightly in the haze of the night before as I made my way down the long stairs. I felt lighter, like something had been lifted. For so long, I had always belonged to someone else. I was "Ellie Sharp's poor kid," and then I was "Lucas Forster's girl," and then "Theo del Conte's girlfriend" in New York. But with Will, even with his grouchy, misanthropic ways, I only felt like myself. Or maybe being *his* felt like the same thing as being *mine*. He didn't want to stifle me or judge me. He didn't want me to be anything other than what I was. And that feeling was amazing.

It was just an added benefit—a *major* added benefit—that the man happened to be that talented with his tongue. I mean, *damn*. A girl could get seriously addicted to that kind of treatment.

So I opened the door in an uncharacteristically sunny mood that was immediately clouded when I found Mama curled up on the couch, staring out the windows toward the lake. Crying.

My mother *never* cried.

"Mama?"

I crossed the open room to her quickly, dropping my purse on the counter. She jumped, held her coffee close, and quickly wiped away her tears.

"Oh, Maggie. I didn't know you were here. Don't worry 'bout me. I just have a case of the sniffles."

"Mama." I sat down next to her on the couch. "What's wrong?"

The question seemed to make her cry harder.

"It's that damn man," she whimpered, curling more into herself.

A photograph fell to the floor—a wrinkled picture of her and Alan, looking happy with their arms wrapped around each other. It was small, like something she might have carried around in her wallet.

"Oh, Mama," I whispered, picking it up. "Why did you keep this?"

She sniffed, but didn't take it back from me. "It's hard to let go sometimes. I know I shouldn't, but I do miss him. He took everything, but I still wake up in the mornings and wish he was here. I go to bed at night, and I stare at the little divot in the mattress he made."

I rubbed a hand on her back. I understood more than she knew. It was like there was something wrong with us, something that went deep. Something that made us love men who were bad for us, even when they were gone.

I used to feel that way about Theo. It was why, time and time again, I'd let him come back. Even if I had bruises on my face. Even before the blood was even dry.

"He didn't like it when I drank, did you know that?" Mama asked.

I kept staring at the picture. "No, I didn't know."

She nodded. "He—he said he liked me better without it. Said I was more beautiful without it."

It was the first thing I'd heard about the guy that made me like him. I looked back at her. "Well, it's the truth. I like you better that way too."

For a moment, the truth of what we were doing hit me. There was so much work still to do on the property to get it ready to be let out. But after that, what? Was it really reasonable to expect someone like Mama, who had a hard enough time holding down her part-time job as a hairdresser, to run a bed and breakfast? What was I going to do—run it with her?

"You could do it, Mama," I offered as hopefully as I could. "I could help you stop."

Mama cradled her head in her hands for a moment, sniffling back a few more tears.

"Oh, Maggie Mae," she murmured as she squeezed my hand. "Don't you think I've tried? Baby, you remember. I been to those AA meetings or church groups. They don't work. And besides, it's only a problem if you can't pick yourself up after. I can deal with a bitty headache from time to time. A few drinks never killed anyone, much less me."

I opened my mouth to tell her she was wrong. That her drinking had hurt me and alienated me most of my life. That a ten-year-old girl shouldn't know how to check her mother's pulse or to turn her on her side when she slept. That she shouldn't know the best way to remove vomit from upholstery or have an armory of excuses prepared every time her mother missed yet another parent-teacher meeting. She shouldn't go most of her life without sleeping through the night, knowing she needed to check on her mother to make sure she was still breathing. Or with the fear that one day again, her temper might turn worse than a quick slap on the cheek or a rough grab of the wrist.

I feared the kitchen implements for a long time, considering how often, under a haze of gin or vodka, they were yanked from their drawers and hurled across the room in my general direction.

"It just hurts," Mama whispered. "I had a man. I had a home. Everything was finally right, until he left and took damn near everything with him." Her eyes were wide, and her voice took on that crazed tone I recognized immediately—the one that made her reach for the bottle, even at 8 a.m. "Can you blame me for needing something to take the edge off, baby? All my life, I've been alone. No one, not even my own daughter, wants to stay around me."

I opened my mouth to argue. But she wasn't wrong. I hadn't stayed. I hadn't even been back since I was twenty, when I'd laid down the choice for her. Her drinking and the people that came with it, or me. She chose the drink.

And I couldn't promise I would stay either. While I was no closer to figuring out my own future, at least I was helping with hers. But that was all I could promise at this point. I had come home to lick my own wounds, figure out what was next for my life, and help Mama get hers together too. There was a reason I had yet to apply for a job, content to live off the very last of my savings and Glinda's eggs for as long as I could. A job meant I was here for good.

"He didn't take everything," I said as I rubbed her shoulder. "You have the property. And me. And…Lucas and W-Will." I shook away the stutter. I hadn't even started to process what had happened last night, and if she were in a better mood, Mama would have jumped on that like a bear on honey. "In a few more weeks," I continued, "everything will be up to code, and you'll be able to start running the place the way you want."

Mama leaned into me, still wiping tears from her eyes. I rocked her slowly, a perverse inversion of what mothers and daughters were supposed to do. But it was natural, because I had done it my whole life.

In my pocket, my phone buzzed. I pulled it out, one half of me hoping it was Calliope, calling to find out how my date went last night. But the other part knew who it was before I ever looked.

You might as well tell me, Flower. I'll find out where you are anyway.

I stared at the message for a long time before I tucked the phone away without answering. While my mother cried about her ghosts, I ignored one of my own. They were only as real as we allowed, I told myself. Only as powerful as we let them be.

"Shhhh," I said as I stroked her hair. "It's going to be okay. I promise."

And, God help us, she believed me.

CHAPTER NINETEEN

I spent the rest of the day working with Mama on the property, trying to cheer her up and make her forget about the photo that I "happened" to toss in the garbage. It was Saturday, so Lucas and Will were both absent—Lucas working at the inn and Will because he had said he was going for a hike today. But a giant delivery of drywall, enough to redo the walls in both outer cabins appeared sometime past noon, apparently having been ordered by a Mr. William Baker. I would have called him to protest the massive gift, or at least question how in the world he could pay for it (no matter what he said he had tucked away from his advertising business). But since he didn't have a phone, I just grinned the entire time I signed for it, and directed the men to leave it in the cabin at the top of the hill.

"My, my," Mama said as we watched them finish. "Well, if that's not sweet on you, I don't know what is."

"I know," I said. I felt strange, like jumping up and down for joy, but also like maybe I should run a mile.

"Be careful," Mama said. "It's the biggest gifts that always have the greatest costs."

Before I could ask her what she meant, she turned around to grab the gardening tools. Today we were cleaning up the front yard. Clearly there was no more time left for that kind of talk.

The summer days were heating up. We were well into June, and the triathlon was two weeks away, during the Fourth of July weekend. I was entered to do the Olympic, not having had enough time to train properly for the full marathon portion. The recent heat wave had meant training mostly in the early mornings or the evenings, and after skipping a few days, I was desperate for a swim and a run, with or without Will.

So it wasn't until a swim and a run that evening that I found myself in the bathroom getting ready for my second date with Will. One that was official. And at his house.

Mama was overjoyed for me, all traces of her earlier suspicions vanished with the help of a drink. She was going over to Barb's for dinner, so thankfully I didn't have to worry about her that night. She liked Will, which should have turned me in the opposite direction. She had always liked Lucas too, but it was a preference that had come slowly over the years, given the fact that the Forsters were powerful members of a community that had often berated the two of us. Will was like her—a bit of an outcast, with a bunch of demons he was battling. Of course, maybe that was why I liked him too. Darkness was all too familiar.

So it was somewhat fitting, as the sun was starting to set, that I drove to Will's house, parked my Passat behind his truck, and slipped. I had actually dressed up a little, much more than I normally would for anywhere else here. I had pulled out a short black dress I used to save for stage appearances, and tamed my hair into long waves down my back. My curls were returning again, more and more every day. Soon I wouldn't be able to brush it without going full Diana Ross, but for now, they were still manageable.

I caught myself just before hitting the ground and chuckled as I stood back upright. His porch light was off, of course. All I needed was for Will to come out and make some smart ass comment about me breaking down *again* in front of his house. I laughed louder. I would actually like that.

I approached the door, smoothing out my dress and balancing precariously in my heels, more from nerves than because I wasn't used to them. Butterflies stirred in my stomach. I hadn't felt this way in years.

I knocked on the door. No one answered. I knocked again. Still nothing. For a moment, I stood there on the dark, unlit porch, rubbing my arms through my cardigan sweater. That was the thing about Spokane—during the day, it could be as hot as a desert, and at night, the temperatures would drop to near freezing.

Where was Will? I tapped the toes of my patent-leather pumps on the scuffed wood porch. They looked so out of place here—no one in Spokane dressed like this unless they were going to one of the few clubs downtown, and even then, not really. Suddenly I felt silly. Ridiculous even.

I didn't know what to think. Twelve hours ago, he had asked me to come here. He knew I was planning to run around sunset to avoid the heat, and he had confirmed he would be gone today too. It was now a few minutes past eight, and his truck was in the lot. Was he not expecting me anymore?

But the house was dark. Maybe he had forgotten. A shiver traveled down my back; the butterflies turned heavy, iron wings of dread. Maybe last night hadn't meant as much as I thought.

I turned around to go, feeling like a fool. I'd have the house to myself. I could curl up in the shack and watch a movie on my tablet, forget about this night, maybe even forget about Will. Refocus myself on the important questions about my life and my mother's that still needed answering.

Go, I thought. *Just go.*

And that was when I heard it—a cry sounding from the bottom of a hill. It was a howl—visceral, piercing, almost primeval. I would have thought it was an animal—maybe a coyote or something like that—except just after the cry, I heard a choked string of profanity.

"Fuck!" cried Will, just before a loud crash. "*Fuck*!"

I sprang to action, jogging down the stairs to the water before I could stop to think. Will's pain echoed up the hill with every crash, every shout. All I could think was that I needed to be there. That *he* needed me.

"God*dammit*!"

Just as I reached the bottom of the stairs, Will came charging out of the trees, carrying a small wooden table, the kind that might have come with the big wooden chairs sitting on his deck. He wore a button-up shirt and a tie—a *tie*! I thought to myself, noting that at some point, he had thought to dress up too—but his hair was falling out of its knot, and his eyes were crazed, the visible part of his cheeks tear-stained.

"*Fuck*!" he shouted as he hurled the table at the side of the boathouse, hard enough that it splintered into multiple pieces upon contact. I froze. Breaking something solid like that was no small feat.

But it wasn't his only conquest. The small clearing was a mess. Two of the three wooden chairs had been completely wrecked, and an ax was lodged in the trunk of a nearby pine tree. He turned around, shoulders heaving like some kind of primordial monster, and stilled when he caught sight of me stepping into the clearing.

"Will?" I asked, my voice small, unsure. What was going on? "Are… are you okay?" He didn't say anything, and after a moment of silence, I took a few more steps toward him. "Will, what's wrong?"

He wilted, big body sagging toward the earth.

"Everything," he croaked, staggering toward me. "Every fucking thing."

In the glare of twilight, I could see clearly that his eyes were bloodshot—from pain, not substance. Before I could respond, ask why, try to offer some form of comfort, he attacked me with the same ferocity that he'd used on the chair. His mouth claimed mine, tongue diving deep, sucking my lips, almost like he was fighting with me instead of the furniture. Another loud groan emitted from deep in his chest, and suddenly, he bent down, grabbed under my knees, and pulled my legs around his waist as he walked us back into the trees. He took three more steps and slammed my back against the wall of the boathouse while his mouth continued its onslaught.

"Fuck," he whispered as his hands found my ass.

He tore at my underwear, ripping through the flimsy lace I'd chosen so carefully for the evening, then yanked down the elastic top of my dress and bra, not even pausing to look at my breasts, pale and almost white in the dim light, before he clamped his mouth around one nipple as viciously as he'd taken my mouth.

"Will," I gasped, banging my head against the wood, unable to keep up with what was happening. We needed to talk—he was clearly not in his right mind—but at the same time, his unfettered touch was doing things to me that, on some level, I'd been yearning for since we met. He was letting go, and it was unbelievably hot. The harder his mouth worked, pulling, biting, sucking, the more ready I got.

"Will!" I tried again.

He released the nipple with a pop.

"Shut up, Lily," he growled into my mouth once more as he ground into me.

He was big. I knew this, of course, but right now I could feel it through his pants, just as if we were both naked. He wasted no time in unzipping them, then fell against my thigh, a heavy weight of pure desire. My legs still wound tightly around him, urging him on as he continued kissing me in that way that was making it difficult to think at all. But it wasn't until I felt the head of him pressed against my slick entrance that I managed to tear my mouth away.

"Will!" I cried out, breathless. "C-condom. I—I want to. But, um, we need to use protection."

He panted into my neck, poised so painfully right where I yearned to take him. He would feel so good—I knew it. Perfect. Full.

But I hadn't completely lost my mind. Not yet.

My legs dropped to the ground, though Will kept me pressed to the wall as he inhaled deeply. Then he squatted, wrapped a strong arm around my knees, and toppled me over his shoulder.

"Will!" I screeched, only to receive a sharp smack on the ass as I was carted back through the trees and up the steps.

"Hush," Will snapped, now taking the steps two at a time. I watched the lake fall farther and farther away. Will was on a mission, robotic in his movement as he practically jogged me up the stairs. Moments later, he threw open the front door, grabbed at a small paper bag next to his key bowl, and tossed me on top of the counter before ripping a condom out of the bag. He tore through the flimsy foil with his teeth, rolled on the contraceptive with a slight hitch in his movements, then wrenched my legs apart and stepped between them.

He paused for a moment.

"Will," I whispered.

He swallowed; the wild look returned. Then his eyes opened wider, and he shoved inside with a howl.

"Ah!" My back arched with the sudden intrusion. He was big. Big enough that it hurt a little. Big enough that even with my slippery welcome, he still tested my ability to take him.

"Will!" I gasped, digging my nails into his shoulder, looking for something, anything that would keep me from toppling over onto the stovetop. But even through the pain, pleasure bloomed.

He started to move faster, his hands vises on my thighs, keeping me from moving away. I was trapped between him and the counter. Will buried his face into my neck, my hair, groaning and grunting like an animal as he took his fill.

But I took mine too. Because the more he moved, the better he felt. Once I adjusted, it was like the shape of him was made for me, touching places no one had ever reached before, causing a thrill of warmth to ripple from my core, through my middle, down my thighs, until every part of me was alive and glowing and pulsing in time to his vicious beat.

"Oh God," I found myself moaning much sooner than I would have thought. "Oh God, Will. I—I'm gonna come. Oh my *God*, I'm *so* close!"

His breathing was hoarse, full of grunts and shaky breaths as he continued his punishing movements, as if I hadn't spoken at all. But he released one hand from my thigh and slid it up a few inches, drifting over the place where our bodies met. I hummed in anticipation, my body tightening around him. A rumble of acknowledgment emerged from his throat.

All he had to do was touch it. Maybe a centimeter lower from the sensitive spot his thumb was teasing right now. I arched into him, willing his hand to move. And then...just a whisper of a touch. I was already primed, and as soon as his thumb brushed over my pulsing center, I exploded into a haze of cries and ecstasy.

"Will!" I cried as my head fell backward. Every muscle in my body shook as he pounded further.

"Hush," he snapped again before covering my cries with his mouth, absorbing them between his own harsh gasps.

"Please," I begged, unable to take much more of this punishing drive. There wasn't a hint of love in his movements, but I didn't care. I wanted whatever he had to offer. Whatever was going to push me straight over the edge of oblivion, just like this, again and again.

"I don't...I don't..." His words were stuttered, tripping over his movements.

I kissed the edge of his brow, the ridge of his cheek, his eyelids, nose, lips, chin—anything and everything he would allow me to touch. His entire body was pulled taut like a drum, while still he punished both of us—maybe himself more than me.

Then he paused, pulled his face back, and when he looked at me, I was shocked by the visible tracks of tears streaming down his cheeks into the thick dark blond around his mouth and chin. His green eyes shone, full of pain, sorrow, anger, and a host of other emotions I couldn't read.

"I don't—" he choked, barely able to get the words out. "I don't—"

"Will." I cupped his cheek, urging him back to me. "Will, talk to me. Will, I'm right here."

His forehead fell against mine. "I don't want to be alone anymore," he whispered with one last push. Then he shuddered, and with a loud, feral moan, collapsed on my shoulder as his orgasm and tears wracked through his body together.

I held him tight, as tightly as I could. My high was falling, and I was left with a man who was so visibly broken, I felt like his pain was cracking my heart in two, right along with him. I didn't know what was wrong. I didn't need to. All I needed to do was be here, with him.

"You're not," I murmured as I threaded my fingers into the thick hair at the nape of his neck and pressed him closer. "Will, you're not alone. I'm here."

He moaned into my shoulder, still pulsing slightly within me. But his long body finally relaxed slightly, released some of his tension as he exhaled long and low into my hair.

We stayed there for several minutes, lingering in the unity of our bodies while our breaths returned to normal. Finally, Will pulled back slightly, and I released his hair and laid my hands on his chest.

In his simple outfit of dark pants, a button-up white shirt, and a tie, Will really did look like a different man. I blinked. A tie on Will Baker was like seeing a tuxedo on a moose. His beard had also been trimmed again so that it was only slightly more than stubble at this point. He looked like the perfect mix of uncivilized and polished—a barbaric gentleman. I would have been ready to jump him all over again if he hadn't still been so clearly distraught.

Other things began to register. Like the fact that the dining table by the windows was set for two, complete with a lit candle, though a few plates of expensive-looking dinnerware were smashed on the floor. The distinct scents of different foods hung in the air over the scents of our joined bodies. Chicken that was maybe burned a little, and some kind of sautéed vegetable. Broccoli, I thought.

Under my fingertips, his heart still pounded. It wasn't until it had dropped to a more regular rate that I ventured to speak.

"Will?"

He didn't answer. His hands still rested on my thighs, but he refused to meet my gaze, instead keeping his eyes firmly fixed on the floor.

"Fuck," he murmured, clearly more to himself than to me. "*Fuck.*"

"Will," I tried again. "Talk to me, please. What's—what's *wrong*? What happened?"

But he only shook his head, then stepped away, pulling out and turning around to clean himself up. It was impossible not to notice the way the shirt, simple as it was, seemed like it had been tailored to his broad shoulders, or the way the man's ass was made to fill out those pants. But I was too worried about him now to say anything, or even to ogle for long.

"I'll—I'll be…" He shook his head, pushing a big hand over his brow while he looked me over with something approximating regret. I pulled down my dress and squeezed my legs together while he turned toward the stairwell, holding himself awkwardly. "I'll be right back."

I watched for a moment while he lumbered off, presumably to use the bathroom, then slid off the counter myself to put myself back together too. My hair was undoubtedly a wreck. But as I hopped down, a few pieces of paper fell to the floor—an envelope and a letter that apparently I'd been sitting on.

I didn't mean to snoop. But the words jumped off the page.

Baker—

I hope this letter finds you well. You seem to be doing all right, especially with your new friend. She sounds nice, man. Good for you.

Anyway, I'm so sorry to have to tell you this way, but the off-the-grid thing has some serious drawbacks, my friend. Better I just say it.

Mike's dead. There are probably nicer ways to get that out, but you know me—I can't beat around the bush. And I know you—you wouldn't want me to. So while I can't believe I'm typing this in black and white rather than calling you like a human being, there it is. Your dad is dead, F. I'm so sorry. Your mom called me last night to tell me. Shocked the hell out of me—you know Trish and I never got along. But she said we were family friends, and she thought I'd have wanted to know. Too true.

You were right. It was the blood pressure that got him. Heart attack, she said, but I don't know more than that. I wish I did, F. I'm so, so sorry.

Tricia is planning a memorial in about a month, to spread his ashes off the dock in Stamford. For what it's worth, I think you should go. I just don't think the shit between you and Trish matters anymore. She's your mom, F. I think she'd want to know you're all right. Especially now. And as for everyone else, well, you know I'll help you manage that. You're my brother, no matter what.

Call me when you can, even if it's collect, you cheap bastard.

Much love,

Benny

I returned to the third paragraph again and again, staring at the words that were typed there so bluntly: *your dad is dead.* It explained everything, of course. The ruined chairs. The burned food. The crazed, angry sex. Will's father was dead, and he had found out in a letter.

But quickly, other questions percolated too. Will really was off the grid completely. Why? And why did the writer—Benny, apparently—keep calling him F? What was going on between Will and his mother?

"What the fuck are you doing?"

I froze, letter and envelope in either hand, and practically jumped at the sound of his voice. "Oh, hey. Sorry, these um, fell to the floor."

Will strode across the room in a few long steps. "Where did you get that?" he demanded, snatching the letter out of my hand. He crushed it viciously between his hands and threw it into a trash bin. "Were you going through my shit?"

I backed up, trapped again between him and the countertop. "I—it fell off the counter, like I said. Will, I'm—God, I'm *so* sorry. Truly. What can I do—"

"You can start by staying the fuck out of my things, Maggie."

I recoiled. "What? Will, I wasn't snooping—I just picked it up when it fell, and the words, well they were there." I waved the envelope I was still holding. "Your dad, Will. I…I can't imagine."

And I couldn't. It was then it occurred to me—*really* occurred to me—just how little I knew Will. It never seemed to matter when we were together, because something innate just clicked between us. But really, I knew nothing about his past. Why he was here. What drove him to live so alone. For all the moments we had shared, he was still functionally a stranger.

I took a step toward him, like I was approaching a scared animal. "Will, please. You're obviously hurting—I can help. Please, just let me help."

"What are you going to help with, Maggie? Short skirts and broken bicycles don't fucking help when your parent is dead."

His words cut, like the weapons they were. But they were coming from a place of pain—anyone could see that, and I was willing to let them go.

"It says the memorial is in July." I glanced toward the trash bin at the crumpled letter. "Are you going to go?"

Will didn't answer, just crossed his arms and continued staring daggers at me.

I waited another moment, then looked back at the envelope I still held. The return address was printed professionally. "Who's Benny Amaya? That name sounds really familiar…" I frowned, then looked up. "Wait a second. Benny Amaya is a rep, isn't he? Calliope, my old manager, knows him. Will, why is a talent manager in New York sending you word of your father's death? Who's 'F'?"

The words were barely out of my mouth before Will snatched the envelope out of my hands fast enough that it gave me a nasty paper cut across my palm.

"Ow!" I cried, shaking my hand, then cradling it against my chest. "What the hell, Will?"

Will just glared at the paper, then crumpled it up and tossed it in the waste bin with the letter. "Let's get something straight. Even if I wanted to share *anything* about myself with you—which I fucking *don't*—I would do it myself. We're not together, Maggie. We're almost friends, and not even that, and the only difference now is that we've fucked. But I could have get off with a hundred other women, any night of the week, so don't think for a second that giving it up like free donuts after church makes you special to me. You got that, *Lily pad*?"

My mouth dropped, and I curled inward. For the first time, the name didn't sound like anything sweet. It sounded like the annoyance and anger Will had voiced when he'd found me caught up in the waterweeds to begin with. Contempt poured out of him as he stomped to the door. He opened it with a slam against the wall, then turned and glared at me.

"Time to go," he said, gesturing rudely into the blackness of the night. "Go take care of your drunk of a mother, and stay the fuck away from me."

My mouth gaped. "*What*?"

"Are you deaf?" he shouted. "I said get the fuck out!"

The harsh words boomeranged through me, and with the last one, I couldn't wait to get out.

I marched through the door and turned around.

"You're an *asshole*," I snapped, unable to think or say anything else.

"Glad that's finally getting through," Will shot back, and before I could get out another word, he slammed the door in my face.

CHAPTER TWENTY

"He's a dick."

Calliope had been saying this every few minutes for the last hour. I chuckled at my phone, which was lying on the bed, blasting my girl's voice while I finished painting my toenails.

After being kicked out of Will's house, I had driven back to my empty house and done what any sensible girl would do: called my best friend and given myself a pedicure while she listened to me bitch about my shitty date. It might have been midnight in New York when I called, but Calliope was a trooper. And a night owl.

And most of all, she understood. Not just that Will had been a dick (and he had). But also that it had been far too familiar. I had left New York to get away from that kind of behavior. The hot and cold thing was Theo's special brand of cruelty, the kind that always had me second-guessing my best intentions. If I was hurt by something he did, it was because ultimately, I had brought it on myself. And if he said or did something awful, it was because I had done something first to earn it.

It was the kind of sociopathic mood swings that escalated into shifts that were legitimately violent—the final one ending with me being treated in the hospital with stitches for a split lip, an ice pack over a black eye, and a rape kit for everything else. It had taken nearly a year of court appearances for my lawyer, an advocate from the YWCA, to help me put my ex behind bars, but in the end, I had been able to leave with a drained savings account and my dignity intact. A year of therapy with a women's advocacy group had certainly helped me to understand that what had happened to me wasn't my fault, not to mention helped me stay strong enough to endure a year-long trial at the same time. At least mostly.

But if I was going to repeat the process, I had no one to blame but myself.

"Seriously. Moody. Reclusive. Total asshole. You don't need him. Sure you don't want to join me for a glass of red?" Calliope teased through the phone, though she knew my response.

I sighed while I blew on my toes. "Don't think so, Cal. Hey, here's something weird for you. The letter—it was sent from Benny Amaya."

"The manager?"

I nodded, even though she couldn't see me. "Yeah. Weird, right?"

"What the hell would Benny Amaya be doing sending death notices to a dude in the middle of nowhere?"

"That's my question. Anything you can find out? I was pretty blown away, and it's just now occurring to me how crazy that is."

"Well, he did say he was from Connecticut, right? Maybe they were childhood friends or something like that. I don't know, but I'll ask around. Or…you could ask yourself if you're ready to come home now."

I rolled my eyes. "Cal, I just got here."

"Boooo. You've been there for almost three weeks. Isn't your mom's house fixed yet?"

I looked around the bare-bones interior of the shack. It was only one room, containing a double-sized bed, a small closet, a pullout loveseat, and a non-functioning sink. It was probably the most livable place on the property besides the main house, which was pathetic.

"Not even close," I said as I straightened my legs and admired the new red color on my toes. "I've got at least a few more months. Maybe more. And then I need to find a job, because that's when I won't be able to help with groceries anymore."

"Lady, you *have* a job. I can get you booked into clubs up and down the Eastern Seaboard like *that*. You know this. Come back."

"Callie, I had to come home. And not just for me!"

She sighed. "Worth a shot. Then you probably won't care then that Theo's out."

My bones froze. As in turned to ice inside my body. A chill rushed over me, and I almost dropped the nail polish as I was screwing the cap back on.

"Wh-what?" I asked.

"Maggie, relax. You knew he was only going to do two months tops—that's what the lawyer said. Slap on the wrist since you wouldn't settle. No one was ever going to keep Max del Conte's kid locked up for long."

In my lap, my hands shook. Out. He was out. I knew what she said was true, but I had been depending on having at least the summer to worry about what the world would feel like again with Theo free. After being locked up because of me.

It made sense now. The texts weren't from his friends at all. They were from him.

"Breathe, girl," Calliope's voice crooned. Like a good best friend, she knew exactly what I was feeling. "Just breathe. You're on the other side of the country. He's not coming anywhere near you."

I buried my face in my hands. "I know." I sat up again, ignoring the way the blood felt like it was rushing from my face. "I know. But you know there's not a chance in hell I'm coming back to New York now, right?"

Calliope sighed. "I know. But a girl has to try. You fought him once, babe. Chances are, he'll just want to put it all behind him and move on. It shouldn't stop you from pursuing your dreams."

"Maybe."

I got up and walked around the room, closing and locking all of the windows that had been left open to help it cool down. The shack heated up like a sauna during the day, so the circulating air was key to a good night's sleep. But tonight, I was happy to sweat in my dreams. I'd rather have locked windows and melt a little than be comfortable and open to attack. I wouldn't be sleeping tonight anyway.

When I was finished, I turned off the light, curling up on top of my bed with the phone in my hand while Calliope complained about one of her clients. She would talk until I told her to stop, knowing that I needed the extra company in order to fall asleep. No one haunted my dreams like Theo's angry face, and I had a feeling he'd be making an appearance tonight.

"Hey, Cal?" I said sleepily as I watched the moon rise over the lake.

"Yeah, babe?"

"Thanks for being here. I love you."

"Love you too, babe. Anytime."

Tap. Tap. Tap.

Tap. Tap. Tap.

The noise, insistent and strong, permeated my dream of running up the West Side Highway. All the cars had been cleared off, and it was just me, sprinting up the eight-lane thoroughfare.

Tap. Tap. Tap.

The noise came faster, waking me from my dream. I stared up at the rafters, listening for the sound again. But all I heard was the soothing ripples of the lake on the shore and the light call of a breeze in the pines.

Tap. Tap. Tap.

I sat up, my heart choking in my throat, and jerked toward the door. It was a knocking, not a tapping. And it was very, very real.

"W-who's there?" I called out. Dammit. Mama's gun was in the house, stowed in the safe in her closet. I knew better than to sleep out here alone, especially when my psychopathic ex was on the loose again. I knew better…didn't I?

"Maggie?"

It took me a solid five seconds to register the voice as someone who *wasn't* the person who haunted my dreams. It was a voice that, up until a few hours ago, I had still thrilled to hear, even when he was being a grouch. Someone who had only ever made me feel safe. Until he didn't.

"Will?" I asked. "Is—is that you?"

"Yeah," he said through the door. "Maggie, please. Can we talk?"

Perhaps against my better judgment, I slid off the bed and padded to the door. I opened it to find Will leaning against the frame, dripping wet in nothing but his underwear. The moon was high, shining bright through the trees, casting every muscle he had in full relief.

I gaped. "Did you *swim* here? At…" I checked my watch. "Three in the *morning*?"

It was hard not to be distracted by the rivulets of water running down his gleaming skin. But somehow I managed not to stare. After all, I was too angry.

"Where's your buoy?" I demanded. "Do you know how dangerous it is to swim openly in the dark?"

Will glanced over his shoulder to the empty lake. "There's no one out there."

"Except the bass fishermen," I said, gesturing outward to the water, where a few lights flashed at the far end. "They troll the edges, you know, late at night and early mornings when the fish are biting."

Suddenly, the fact of what he had done made me livid. I had been cast as an idiot. The daughter of a drunk. A slut. A klutz. And yet here he was, throwing caution to the wind like it meant nothing.

"What were you thinking?" I demanded. "You could have been turned to hamburger by someone's propeller. You think drunk people on the lake don't ever take their boats for joy rides? Trust me, I grew up here —I've been on enough of them. Fuck, and you call *me* reckless?!"

"Maggie."

I stopped my rant at the sound of his deep voice. He had that way—a quiet authority that always seemed to be able to cut through my chaos. And right now I hated him for it.

"*What*?" I gritted out.

The hand at the doorway gripped hard enough to turn his knuckles white, casting a long line of tension up his arm and through his torso. But his gaze remained straight, looking through me with honesty and intention.

"It was the quickest way to you," he said quietly, meaningfully. "I didn't care about anything else, Lil. I just needed to see you. I needed to apologize for what I did."

My mouth dropped. Whatever I thought he was going to say, it wasn't that.

"Can I come in?" Will asked.

He shivered as a breeze floated off the water. It was then that it occurred to me how uncomfortable he must be. The shack was still horrifically warm, but outside the temperature was hovering around fifty degrees. Will was in next to nothing, his wet hair lying in thick, dripping ropes over his shoulders, skin pebbled with the chill.

But the shack suddenly felt suffocating. And I wasn't interested in being trapped with a wet monster in a hundred and fifty square feet.

I grabbed a beach towel hanging behind the door and tossed it to him.

"Take this," I said as I slipped on some shoes and pulled a hoodie off the coat rack. I stepped outside and shut the door. "Follow me."

The moonlight was our only guide as I led Will around the shack, past the fire pit where he'd heard me play the guitar, up a steep, rocky hill, and back down a pile of boulders. I knew this route by heart. I'd been making this midnight trek since I was a kid, needing to escape my mother's chaos. I could hear Will struggling to find his footing on the dark, pine-needle-covered rocks, but he didn't complain—just followed me doggedly over the terrain until we wove through a few pine trees to reach a large, flat rock about the dimensions of a king-size mattress that stuck out over the lake.

"I called this 'Moon Rock' when I was little," I told him as I climbed out onto the stone. "It's a good place to think. And talk."

Will glanced nervously around at the dark water sloshing on both sides of us. "It seems very…exposed."

I plopped down on the granite. "You want to talk? This is where I'm comfortable. Take it or leave it, Baker."

His mouth twitched. "Fine. You win."

We sat there together for a while, looking up at the stars. The night was clear enough that the Milky Way was smeared across the sky's canvas, a whirling array of stars and blurred light that made me dizzy if I looked at it for too long. But I didn't close my eyes.

"I'm sorry, Lil," Will said quietly. "So fucking sorry about tonight. For all of it."

I didn't respond, just doggedly kept stargazing.

"There's nothing to excuse my behavior. I was a complete jackass. I shouted at you when I should have been thanking you. I fucked you when we should have been making love."

"Actually," I put in. "I thought the sex was pretty good. Unexpected, but good. I've never been opposed to a good, old-fashioned fucking under the right conditions."

Will glanced at me sideways, his mouth quirked to the side. "Good to know." His big shoulders relaxed, but just slightly. "Still…I didn't want it to be like that. Not our first time. Maybe not any time. I was using you to release all the rage and pain I was feeling. It's abusive, is what it is. And then I told you—*fuck*—I made it sound like you didn't matter, when the truth is…the truth is that these days, you're the *only* thing that matters."

My breath caught in my throat, and I stared at my hands, folded in my lap. What was I supposed to say to that? The words were exactly right, but he was…

"Wrong." Will was saying. "It was so crazy wrong I don't expect you to forgive me for it, but I needed you to know that I'm sorry. I was sorry the second I closed the door. I…" He drifted off, worrying the edges of the towel in his hands while he stared out at the lake. "It was killing me."

And then he turned to face me, and his eyes reflected the light shining off the lake. They were wide, open, and fierce.

"The thing is, Lil," he said. "You mean *everything* to me. No matter what happens, what we are or aren't, you are so much more to me than a…you know. When I'm with you, I feel like I'm breathing again, for the first time in years. You make me feel like the world is possible again. Like life is possible." He pushed both hands over his face, like he was trying to wipe away the tension cut into his features. "For a moment, I just couldn't handle it. But the second you were gone, it was like I'd cut off the air I needed to breathe. That's what you are to me, already. A necessity, like air, water, food. And like an idiot, I cut off my own supply. I suffocated myself with my own damn pillow."

He looked at me again, eyes shot with fear. His skin still glimmered, slightly damp, almost sparkling in the night.

"You're the best thing that ever happened to me, Lily pad," he said softly. "And I lost you tonight, didn't I?"

We held each other's gazes for a long time. Minutes, maybe, while the water ebbed and flowed around us. But eventually, I spoke. Not because I wanted to. Because I had to.

Was it wrong for me to say this? Would it be my fault if it happened again? Was I doomed to bring this kind of behavior onto myself, again and again?

I didn't know. I wasn't sure I cared.

"No," I said softly. "No, you didn't lose me."

Immediately, it was like a weight had been lifted from both of us. We sagged into each other, and Will's head dropped to my shoulder. He inhaled deeply, like a drowning man in need of a breath.

"Thank God," he murmured. "Thank fucking God."

"But, Will?" I asked.

He sat back up.

"Never again," I said as clearly as I could. "I'm not kidding. You *ever* treat me like that again, I'm gone. I don't care how much we n-need each other." I stumbled over the word, astounded by its truth. I didn't have to be weak. It *didn't* have to be my fault. He'd said what he needed to say. And now I was too. "I won't be with someone who treats me like nothing. Ever again."

His eyes narrowed at its implication of the word *again*. I hadn't told him much about Theo, but Will didn't miss a beat.

"Never again," he vowed, keeping his gaze pinned to mine. "On my life, Lil. I promise."

"One more thing," I said as we turned back to the lake.

"Anything," he murmured.

"I want to know why you were so angry," I said. "I…I deserve the truth, Will. All of it. No more hiding."

His shoulders tensed slightly, but eventually he nodded.

"Can I…do you mind if I hold you while I say it?" he asked.

I paused.

"Please," he said. "It's…easier to talk when you're close."

I sighed. But I couldn't deny it. As mad as I still was, a dam had broken between us over the last few days. My body yearned for him even if my rational mind was telling me to stop.

My body won.

"Okay," I said. "But no funny business, Baker. I'm still mad at you."

Will chuckled as he helped me settle back between his long legs. He pulled my back against his front, keeping the towel between us so that the wet of his boxers wouldn't seep through my pajamas.

I relaxed against him, enjoying the feel of his strong arms wrapped around my front, creating a sort of harness with his limbs. It was funny—when Theo held me like this, I always felt trapped. He would do it when we watched movies or something like that, and wouldn't let go for hours at a time. His touch was forceful, like he was holding me back from something. Will, on the other hand, kept his arms in a loose lock, more like he was warding the world away rather than keeping me from it. I didn't feel caged with him. I only felt secure.

"I saw you play once," he said quietly. "In New York."

I jerked. "What?" Every time he divulged something, the man continued to shock me.

"It was why I ran off that night when you played by the fire. You… fuck. I recognized your song, Maggie. I heard it when you opened for Gillian Keller."

I blinked. "You were at that show?"

That was the show that had opened up my career. I went from being a waitress and playing coffee shops to going on a small tour with one of alt-country's biggest names. I had come home to consistent bookings up and down the East Coast for over a year. The experience had allowed me to record an EP. Helped me gain access to better clubs, even do a few more small tours. It had made the entire showcase possible, even after my life had come crashing down.

Will nodded. "I lived in the city for a while. Benny was my—my coworker. But that life, the business, all of it…it wasn't good for me. I used to do a lot of stupid shit, and eventually it caught up with me. And my family."

He shifted slightly, then pulled me closer. I inhaled, enjoying the warmth of him, even in the chill of the night, and the clean smell of his body.

"You were amazing," he whispered. "Like a siren. You played that same song, and the entire crowd was transfixed. And I remember thinking…how badly I wanted to meet you in person. I actually tried to get backstage, but some bad stuff went down."

I nodded. It was a good night for me, but the concert itself had been a mess.

"It was such a weird night," I said. "I was insanely nervous. I honestly don't know if I would have been able to go on, but actually…oh my God, I almost forgot about this."

"Forgot about what?"

I frowned. "It's hard to remember, actually. But there was this weird guy who snuck into my dressing room before I went in. He was hiding out from some people. An addict, he said. He was kind of nuts. Hid behind the screen, but wouldn't let me see him at all." I turned around with a smile. "Kind of like you, actually."

Will chuffed almost forcefully. "Nuts, huh?"

I turned back to face the water. "Certifiably. Sweet, though. He talked to me for a full hour, and at one point, he actually reached around and held my hand until I calmed down."

"He sounds like a dick," Will said emphatically. "Weak and cowardly."

"That's a little harsh, I think. Actually, he promised to find me after the show, until everything went to hell during Gillian's set. Do you remember that? There was some kind of massive fight involving an actor." I paused. For some reason, all these memories were causing the hair on the back of my neck to stand up. I was missing something here. Something important. "Were you—you weren't a part of that, were you?"

There was a long pause. Then I felt Will nod on my shoulder. "I got kind of wrapped into it, yeah. Benny was there, remember? And I, um, worked with him."

I fingered the length of his forearm, stroking back the springy hair there. "So, what happened?"

Will sighed heavily and squeezed my arm. "Honestly, Lil, I couldn't really tell you. I was…I was high, if you want to know the truth. It was probably coke that night, but it could have been anything. I wasn't picky back then."

It was the last thing I had expected him to say. Other than a few sips of beer at the bar and at my mom's, I hadn't ever seen Will partake in anything that could be considered an illicit substance. His house was pristine—not even a lighter around. He lived an ascetic existence that was the next thing to being one with nature.

And yet. Someone who lived like Will was running from something. Addiction made sense. Especially if it had been bad enough to ruin others' lives.

I almost asked him then if it was him in the dressing room. That man had been an addict too, I thought. But Will's response stopped me. Why would he call himself a coward? It didn't make sense.

"Do you...do you hate me for it?"

I watched the water for a long time, still weighing his disclosures. Will waited, patient as ever.

"Do you still use?" I asked finally. My voice was sharper than I intended, and I twisted around. I needed to see the answer on his face. I didn't have room for more than one addict in my life. I barely had room for the one I lived with. "Tell me the truth."

Will didn't blink. "Absolutely not."

I swallowed. "You promise?"

"It was an escape," he said. "I used until the day I actually got out. But once I left that life...Maggie, I didn't need or want any of that shit anymore. Since I left New York, shortly after that show, actually, I've been clean. Completely. I promise you that on my life."

We stared at each other for a good long minute. In the back of my head, a voice spouting all of the things I knew from being Ellie Sharp's daughter started talking on repeat. Addicts do whatever they can to protect their escape. Addicts steal. Addicts hurt. And most of all, addicts lie.

But there was no trace of a lie on Will's earnest face. He was a dark person, but he'd never hidden that from me. And part of me, a part that spoke louder than every misgiving, insisted that I knew this man, deep down, on a cellular level that exceeded the limitations of mere words.

In the end, I relaxed. "Okay," I said as I settled back into his arms. "Okay."

"That was the last night I ever did anything," Will continued. "Because that night, I was arrested. And the sight of my face on a mug shot put my dad in the hospital. From a heart attack."

The gravity of that hit me, and my heart fell with dread. "Oh, Will..."

"It was the last of many, *many* fuckups of mine from those days," he said. "He recovered. But my mother and I…well, we hadn't gotten along for years, and she never forgave me for that night. And in the end…I had to leave. I had to get out. It took me a few weeks after the arrest to settle with the club and get everything out of the way, but once it was done, I packed up my shit and left. And I haven't looked back since."

"You just…took off?"

"I haven't talked to anyone in four years," he confirmed. "I told you, Maggie. I'm not good for anyone. If you…if you wanted to run a mile, I wouldn't blame you one bit."

I turned around completely, and automatically, Will pulled me onto his lap, wrapping my legs around his waist. I touched my nose to his, and we both closed our eyes.

"I don't want to run a mile," I admitted as our foreheads touched. "I want to stay right here."

Here we were, sitting together, eyes wide open. Our breaths mingling. Two separate beings, yet so close to being one.

And I wanted to be one. So, so badly.

So I kissed him. It wasn't like the other kisses we'd shared. This wasn't a torrent of passion that had been waiting to be let out—it was slower, more tentative, a slow unfurling of tension and forgiveness. Will moaned, long and low, but opened his mouth willingly to taste me deeper, working from my cues.

"I know I'm fucked up," he whispered against my lips. "So, so fucked up. And maybe it's selfish, but, Maggie, you make me feel like I could be better. I…I'm so sorry. For everything."

I just kissed him again as his words washed over me. The difference was striking. When Theo screwed up, apologies would come days, sometimes weeks later, and only after I berated them out of him. Not a few hours later. Not of his own accord. And Theo certainly wouldn't have swum across a freaking lake at 3 a.m. to get that apology off his chest.

I couldn't fight it anymore. And truthfully, I didn't want to. So I kissed him until we were both breathless, pushing the towel off his shoulders so I could feel the strong lines of his shoulders, his neck, the flat planes of his chest, the thick waves of his hair.

"Will," I murmured as his hands slipped up my shirt. "Will, please."

I reached between us to the stiff length of him outlined clearly through his still damp boxers. I pushed the fabric aside to pull him out, holding him briefly in my hand before I rocked onto my knees.

I didn't care that we shouldn't. I didn't care that there were still so many questions left unanswered. But it was like air, he'd said. Like food. Like water. It should have scared me how much I needed this man. But all I felt was instinct.

"Maggie, I—" Will closed his eyes as if in pain as the tip of him touched my entrance. "I don't have a condom."

I paused, tortured myself. "Have you been with anyone since you left New York?"

Will shook his head. His chest muscles quivered. "No one," he said. "I'm clean. There's been no one."

"Neither have I," I said. "Not—not for a year. It's okay. I—I have an IUD. I'm covered if you are."

Shaking slightly, Will nodded. "Please," he whispered. "Please, Lil."

I shook slightly. I was more nervous about this second coupling than I had been showing up to his house earlier. Because this was a meeting of the hearts as much as our bodies. Whether I was ready for it or not, I couldn't deny it any longer.

Slowly, I dropped down, taking him inside me. I was more than ready for him, even with his size. His eyes bulged with the sudden feeling. I shuddered against him. This was how it was meant to be between us. Nothing there. Only us. Nothing had ever felt more right in my life than joining with this man.

But there was still one more thing I needed to say.

"I'm not here to save you, Will." I stilled my movements, tipping his chin forward so he had to look at me. "Do you understand me?"

His eyes opened, deeper than the waters around us. One hand slipped up my body to cup my face, and then he kissed me with impossible tenderness as the other hand pressed my hips down, forcing me to take him fully. I arched my back as he filled me, all my lonely spaces, in ways that only he could.

"I know," he said against my lips, my throat, my cheeks, my eyes. His low voice touched some frequency that spoke to me and only me. "But you make me want to save myself."

CHAPTER TWENTY-ONE

I awoke the next morning much like I had the day before: content and bathed in light. But the warmth that spread through me had little to do with the sun that was already warming up my small shack, and more to do with the long, golden limbs wrapped around me like trees roots. For the first time—maybe in my life—I didn't feel like someone who was drifting. Will was becoming an anchor in my crazy life, and as the realization hit me, I released a long sigh.

This was what it felt like, I realized. Relief.

"Everything okay?" His voice rumbled against my cheek. "I can hear you thinking."

I hummed as his hand slid down my naked body, coming to rest on my hip. "Just realizing that I'm happy. Here with you. I kind of forgot what that felt like."

It was the truth. And maybe I had never really understood what it felt like to be happy *with* someone. I had spent most of my time in college running from a life I desperately wanted to escape, working to reinvent myself as Maggie Sharp, musician, rather than Ellie Sharp's poor daughter. Even years after, when I first met Theo, that feeling of running, that tension with myself, had never really disappeared. And in the end it had gotten worse the longer I'd been with him, too.

Here with Will, the tension was gone. Mama, Theo, everything about the world that hurt so consistently, seemed to disappear when I was with him. With him, I was simply Lil. And I had never felt more like myself.

Will's big body relaxed into mine. "Me too, Lil. Me too."

I turned onto my side to face him. "How did you sleep?"

He stretched, his mouth spreading into a lazy grin that made my toes tingle. He really needed to smile more. He had no idea the kind of effect it had on me.

"Probably better than I have in a really, really long time," he said as he pulled me close again. "Maybe I need to sell the house and live in a shack by the water too."

I giggled as his nose burrowed under my hair. The soft kisses he pressed into my neck caused goose bumps all over my body, and the hand on my thigh slid inward, brushing against the soft hair there, broad fingers teasing.

I arched against his light touch, but even as I did, my body reminded me that I was in absolutely no condition for a fourth round of Will-style loving. I was right: Will did not sleep very soundly at all, but it seemed that he had found a remedy for it. Twice more in the night, he had woken me up with deceptively soft kisses, teasing shapes from my body that I didn't know I could form, sounds I didn't know I could make. He was insatiable, and so, apparently, was I, meeting him kiss for kiss, yank for yank, until we collapsed each time in a glowing mess of sweat and satisfaction, only to do it again mere hours later.

"Ohhhh, no," I told him, pushing his hand as I rolled away. "I am way too sore for that this morning."

He popped up on his forearms, caging me against the bed. "Is that so?" he asked mischievously as he pressed himself between my legs.

His warm body fit to mine, reminding me once more of just how *good* it felt to have this man inside me. We matched like jigsaw pieces, my subtle curves to his hardened lines. I welcomed where he demanded, like our bodies were cut to match. At the feel of him, long, ready, and seeking entry, my thighs opened of their own accord. But while Will captured my mouth with another one of his kisses that made it hard to think, I pushed him away regretfully. I wasn't interested in living on ibuprofen for the rest of the day.

"Yes, that's so, Baker," I said, then gave him a quick peck and rolled out from underneath him. "A girl needs a little time to recuperate, unless you want me out of commission for more than a few hours."

Will lay on his side, letting the sheets fall down his body, tenting over the part of him that apparently did *not* need a rest at all. He caught me staring at it, and gave a crooked little grin that almost had me ready to jump him all over again, sore lady parts be damned.

So instead, I focused on the parts of him that were a little less tempting.

"You need a haircut, do you know that?" I said as I turned around to pull a swimsuit out of my dresser. "You look like the Abominable Snowman."

Going to sleep with wet hair had caused Will's locks to matt and stick out at hilariously bad angles all around his face. He was still disgustingly handsome, but this wasn't a good look.

Will snorted. "From the Claymation movies?" He watched appreciatively as I pulled on the spandex.

I nodded. "Minus the blue skin, pretty much. You scared the hell out of me when I first met you, you know."

He stroked his beard, which had been trimmed again. "I cleaned up since then."

"Not that hair. Babe, you're practically sporting dreadlocks back there. And not the kind that anyone should ever have."

Will pulled at one of the tangled strands on his shoulder. "Who's going to cut it? I don't want strangers touching my head, Maggie."

I rolled my eyes. "I didn't realize you were such a snob. But you know, I *am* the daughter of a hairdresser, dude. I'll do it. If you dare let me."

Will eyed me suspiciously. It made me want to smack him with a pillow and cover his face with kisses.

"I don't know..." he said. "I'm very protective of my look, you see." He mimed like he was fluffing his hair in the same way you might expect from an old-time movie actress. It was so antithetical to his unkempt looks I couldn't help but giggle.

"Yeah, you *are* a total prima donna," I replied. "It's something I've been meaning to discuss with you."

Will grinned. It lit up the room so bright, I stumbled, even though I was currently standing still.

"I thought you liked my hair," he argued. "You grab it whenever I kiss you. Or, you know, do other things to you."

I rolled my eyes, but laughed when he caught my hand and pulled me back on the bed with him, trapping me once more against a pillow.

"Mmmm," I moaned as his lips covered mine. "Will…*Will*!"

He tugged aside my suit and kissed down my neck.

"Don't make me stop," he said, the tip of him just barely sliding inside. Honestly, it was kind of hard *not* to take him once he was down there. That's how big he was. "Please, baby. You have no idea. No fucking *clue* how much I need you right now."

My mouth fell open as he pushed a little further, and my thighs opened without a thought. And of course my body, the traitorous thing, was totally ready for him, welcomed him deep in spite of the slight ache. He seated himself, setting his teeth on my neck as he did.

"Touch yourself," he said against my skin as he began. "Please, baby. I'm—*shit*—I'm not going to last long."

I had no choice but to obey, sliding a hand between us to feel that junction where our bodies met, where his skin slipped and skidded over my own. My fingers settled over the sensitive bundle of nerves that, together with Will's movements, would set me alight in no time. At the feel of my fingers finding their rhythm, Will moaned into my neck.

"That's it," he whispered, his voice hot and heavy. "Fuck, baby, I can feel you squeezing me. Lil, you're so…*uhhh*…you're so damn tight!"

"Please," I begged, though for what, I didn't know. My body arched up, already knowing its path, knowing the direction it was going. A warmth, a glow was already emanating directly from our joining. We were a star, about to reach its supernova. A few more thrusts, a few more pulls, and together we'd explode.

"I want to feel you come," Will said as he pushed slightly up to drive in harder. "I want to feel you squeeze my dick, baby."

He bent his head down to take one of my nipples between his teeth. But instead of licking or sucking lightly, with a gentle touch the way most men would, he bit, just a little harder than was strictly necessary. The shock of pain was exactly what I needed. My fingers doubled their speed. My body tightened, clenched. And then it burst open.

"WILL!" I cried out, my hands falling to the side as my body seized up.

"*Fuck*, yes, baby," Will shouted as he drilled further in. "That's it, beautiful. Oh my *God*, that feels good!"

His shoulders shook as he let go himself, shaking out the long release that seemed to take him several seconds, even a minute to complete. It allowed me to stretch mine out as long as I could until slowly, eventually, we both fell back to Earth together, safe once more in each other's arms.

"Goddamn," Will mumbled, his voice muffled in my hair. "You're going to be the death of me, you know that?"

His body flattened atop mine, fully relaxed despite the mess I knew I'd need to clean up when he moved.

But now the morning sun was streaming inside in hot rays. And the unopened windows seemed that much more stifling than last night.

"Off," I said, shoving at his side. "Hot."

"Spoilsport." Will sighed with regret, but finally rolled the other way off the bed and let the sheets drop from his naked body as he stood up. I practically had to wipe my chin.

"All right," he said, making no attempt to cover himself as he searched the room for his now dry briefs.

He located them, and spoke as he pulled them on. I curled into myself while I enjoyed the show.

"How's this for a plan: I swim with you across the lake, then you can maim me—I mean, cut my hair. But only in your suit, so I have something nice to look at. After that, we can come back and work on the property. If you think Lucas can handle it."

I nodded happily. I didn't really give a fig what Lucas would say about any of this. I was just thrilled that Will wanted to spend the day together as badly as I did.

When I said so, he stopped and grinned again, shining light through the cabin that was ten times brighter than any ray of sun.

"Haven't you figured it out, yet?" he asked as he rubbed his nose against mine. "I'll pretty much do whatever you want, Lily pad."

I smiled into his lips. "I'll keep that in mind."

ONE HOUR, one swim and a fairly naughty shower later (apparently I didn't care *that* much about my sore parts), Will was sitting on a chair in the middle of his kitchen with an adorable frown on his face while I draped a towel around his shoulders.

"Look at this," I admonished him as I combed out his thick mane. "When was the last time you brushed your hair? This is a rats' nest, sir. It's atrocious."

Will sniffed, but kept his gaze pointed obediently at the floor. "I've been going for the mysterious mountain man look. It helps me play hard-to-get with the ladies."

"I'm not sure your strategy is working," I replied. "Look at what happened last night."

He leered at me through the hair I'd combed flat on either side of his face. It was immensely unflattering, even for him.

"Maybe you should do it like this," I said. "It's brushed down, but with your hair in your face, you're totally unfuckable." It was a lie, but it was fun to rile him up.

Will sniffed and muttered something like, "More like unrecognizable." But that didn't make any sense.

"What's that?" I asked.

"Nothing," he replied quickly. "Look, I actually like it long, all right? If you have to do this, keep it long enough to pull back. Nothing too short."

I opened my mouth to argue that his cheekbones were dying to be shown off, and his hair kind of shrouded his good looks. But at the same time, I found that I agreed. Will's hair was sort of synonymous with his character. It was impossible to imagine him with the short, average cut that most men would have.

"Just a trim and some shape," I assured him as I continued combing out his waves, marveling at just how many shades of blond and brown there could be on one person's head. His hair really was beautiful. I didn't blame his vanity at all. "How about this?" I ran my hands over his beard, and Will hummed under my touch. "Would you ever let me shave this off?"

He twisted around, clearly appalled. "You don't like the beard either?"

I hid a smile and shook my head. "No, it's not that." And it wasn't. Though previously I'd never much liked men with facial hair, Will's fit him. "I just…I want to see what you look like. I want to see your whole face."

Slowly, Will and I were learning to bare ourselves to each other. I just wanted to see everything he was. I wanted to see his whole self, inside and out—whatever that was.

He blinked at me, then turned back around. "Maybe one day," he said, though his tone wasn't particularly optimistic. "But not today."

I decided not to press my luck.

We remained comfortably silent while I snipped away at his hair. I hadn't done it in years—not since college, when I used to cut boys' hair in my dorm for extra cash. It was one of the skills Mama had given me, and not something I would forget easily, working meditatively through the layers.

"You all right down there?" I asked at one point, realizing it had been a good fifteen minutes since either of us had said a word.

"Yeah," Will practically purred with a deep sigh. "Your touch just feels…good," he murmured with closed eyes. "It feels…right."

The word hovered in the air for a minute, but I was more shocked to discover how much I agreed with the sentiment than with the fact that he had said it. Will's eyes opened, their green piercing through my confusion.

Hastily, I nodded. "Good," I said, turning back to his hair. "Good."

I continued snipping, letting my mind wander as I did. Not for the first time, I noticed just how nice his house really was. The paintings that scattered the walls were real, not cheap prints, and the mid-century modern furnishings were the kind that looked comfortable, but cost an arm and a leg in real life. I was no interior design whiz, but everything in the place seemed to be top-of-the-line. Which led me back to wondering just how he was able to afford it.

"Will?" I asked as I combed out another lock to cut.

"Hmmm?" His voice was thick with hazy contentment. He was really enjoying this, and I almost hated to ruin it.

"What did you do in New York?"

"Mmmm what?"

"For Benny Amaya," I said as I snipped a few inches off the back. "You said you were a part of his team. What did you do for him?"

I couldn't see his face, but his shoulders tensed visibly. "I…I was his assistant."

I frowned. That made absolutely no sense. An assistant wouldn't just take off the way Will had—not without throwing away an entire career. And he wouldn't have had the means to live like this without a job for four years.

"Then how could you afford a place like this?" I pressed. "Why don't you have to work?"

Will opened his eyes and twisted toward me. "What's the likelihood that you're going to let me be completely vague about this?"

I tapped the closed tips of the scissors on the heel of my palm, like I was thinking. "Oh…slim to none."

I tried to keep it light, but the truth was, I needed him to be totally honest. Will shoved me out of his house last night because he couldn't deal with opening up to me. I needed to know that wouldn't happen again.

Will sighed and turned back around. "I helped Benny promote stuff. But the money for this place came from…a trust fund of sorts," he said. "I decided to put it to good use."

Oh. So…Will was rich. And his parents were rich. And his people were rich.

Well, it explained the nice furnishings, at least.

"So you took your trust fund and ran?" I asked before I could stop myself.

But really. It was one thing to hate your parents, enough even that you couldn't comfort your mother when her husband died. In my own way, I could kind of understand that. I had had plenty of moments with my own mother where enough was enough. But it was a total other thing to do it while accepting their money.

"I never said I was a good man, Maggie," said Will quietly. "In fact, I think I keep telling you the opposite."

I paused. He said it so matter-of-factly, it about broke my heart, especially since I knew the opposite to be true. Will was a good man—a very good man. If only he'd let himself acknowledge it.

"Then I know you better than you know yourself," I said, coming around to bend down in front of him. I pulled strands of his hair on both sides to compare their lengths. "Because I don't believe that for a minute."

He caught my hand and pulled it around to kiss the palm, keeping his face pressed into the sensitive skin for a moment longer than was necessarily. "And you have no idea how grateful I am for that."

He released me, and I went back to cutting his hair in silence. I didn't press him any more on his past, and he didn't offer anything else either. In the end, maybe it didn't matter anyway.

"All right," I said sometime later. "You're done."

I brushed off the remainder of hair still on his towel, then pulled it off his shoulders and shook it onto the floor with the other clippings.

"I'm going to shower," he said, shaking his head side to side like a dog. "How do I look?"

I perused his big body—the way his hair now fell in gentle layers just to his shoulders, making the clean lines of his collarbones stand out in high relief over the flat planes of muscle and stacked abdominals. Good Lord. What had I just done?

"You look good," I said, my voice suddenly thick.

Will's gaze traveled up and down my body, still clad in only my swimsuit. It was a typical sport one-piece—certainly nothing even close to the skimpy bikinis that would be out all over the lake by midday. But I knew without looking that everything I had was standing at attention, plain for him to see.

"You sure you don't want to join me, Lil?" he said. His gaze lingering over my breasts for a moment before dragging back up to my face. "The water's warm, remember?"

I should have laughed. That was a seriously corny line. But Will's expression, suddenly free of the heavy curtains of hair, carried absolutely no humor in it—only lust.

I cleared my throat. "I—I'm good, thanks."

His mouth curved in another half smile. One that brought out a shadow of a dimple under his thick scruff.

"Shame," he murmured as he turned toward the stairs. At the top, he stopped. "Before we go, I'll give you a tour, all right?"

I looked up from where I was still trying to cool my rising body temperature. "Really?"

Will shrugged. "It's the least I can do after kicking you out last night. I want you here, Lil. Everywhere."

"Sounds good."

I grinned, and when Will grinned back, I had to hold onto the counter to keep standing up straight. Maybe it was better the guy never smiled. He could do real damage with those pearly whites.

CHAPTER TWENTY-TWO

We meandered around the property for over an hour after Will loaned me a pair of old sweatpants and a t-shirt I could wear while my swimsuit dried on the deck. I needed to get back to the house. We had a lot of drywall to put up this week, and it wasn't fair to leave it all to Lucas, who had probably shown up just after Will and I started swimming. But Will was finally opening up a little, and I wasn't about to shut that down for a bit of home improvement. And maybe, if I was being honest, there was also a part of me that just didn't want to go home and face my mother. Or my future. Or the fact that somewhere in the back of my mind, I suspected they were one and the same.

The lot was much bigger than I'd thought, extending past the road up to the top of the mountain and running down to the water. Will basically owned an entire compound that allowed him to exist off the grid. He informed me that on the mountain side of the property, he had installed a well, a septic system, and a small solar array that powered his house most of the year. Down at the bottom, he showed me the boathouse, in which he kept a canoe and a kayak, as well as a bunch of exercise equipment that basically looked like a CrossFit gym. Well, that explained his exemplary physique.

But it was the rest of the house that I was the most interested in, since it said the most about him. The upstairs was the plush, loft-like space with a bathroom. But the downstairs had three other rooms besides the bedroom, all of them with an entire wall of windows that looked through the trees to the lake, each of them containing surprises.

The first shocked the hell out of me. I had been expecting a tame office, or maybe a guest room (though a reclusive misanthrope like Will having a guest room was probably less likely than discovering the Cave of Wonders inside his house). Instead, we walked into a real, miniature movie theater with two rows of seats facing a massive projector screen, and an entire wall of DVDs opposite the picture window, which Will assured me could be covered to darken the room for viewings.

I gaped. "Wow," I said as I perused the wall. "Bit of a movie buff, huh?"

Will shrugged, staying by the door. "A little. But there are some films you have to see on a big screen. It's just not the same otherwise."

"I guess. Wow, you must have every Cary Grant film ever made." I pulled out a copy of *His Girl Friday* and waved it at him. "This one's my favorite. Rosalind Russell is a badass."

Will chuckled. "For sure."

I continued perusing his collection, which was arranged alphabetically. "Whatever happened to 'Netflix and chill,' huh?"

Will didn't smile though, just sagged in the doorway as he watched me moving around the room. "I don't have internet access. Not to mention streaming quality on most films is shit. Come on. There's more."

We went to the next room, and I smiled, feeling a little like Goldilocks this time, trying out all the rooms. Will gestured into an office that was lined with built-in bookshelves, all of them stacked floor to ceiling with books.

"Holy smokes," I murmured as I took in the books. While his library was small compared to something like a university, it was comprehensive. I stared at the titles, seeing everything from Shakespeare to Chinua Achebe. He had a propensity for post-war fiction—there was a complete set of well-thumbed Kerouac books near the desk, and a first edition of *One Flew Over the Cuckoo's Nest* on one shelf.

The desk itself was piled high with papers—two stacks of crooked white packets that framed a laptop computer and a small printer on one side. It was a desk where someone spent a lot of time. The work was scattered, and there were a few old coffee cups in one corner.

I turned around. "I thought you said you didn't have internet access."

Will shook his head. "I don't. I did before, but even then, I mostly used it to type. The internet is...a distraction. I fucking hate it."

I put a pin in that. He spoke with a lot of vitriol for something that was so ordinary to most people our age. What was the point in hating the internet? It was everywhere.

"So...what did you type?" I asked instead, looking back at the stacks of papers.

"Well..." Will traced the edge of the desk with one finger. "I actually went to school for a while online and got my degree. And my MFA."

My eyes bugged even further. "*What*?" Up until now I had mostly just imagined Will roaming the countryside with an ax like some kind of demented woodsman. Not *studying*. Not reading *books*.

He grabbed his knot of hair meditatively, squeezing it like a stress ball before his hand drifted down to massage his neck. "I...had a bit of time on my hands since moving out here. I figured I'd do something productive for once in my life."

I looked back at the room. I didn't know why I assumed that Will had no intellectual education. He must have if he had gone into marketing, but I wasn't expecting such refined taste on his part. Maybe he had washboard abs and lived like an ascetic lumberjack, but he was also well spoken and intelligent, and as I looked around, clearly very well read.

For once in my life. What was he talking about? Drugs, maybe? Working in the entertainment industry? Advertising?

Something didn't quite match up.

"What was the MFA in?" I asked, looking sideways at the stacks of papers again.

Will worried his mouth a little. It made me want to kiss him. "Screenwriting, actually. It's, um, sort of a hobby now. In my spare time. Which is most of my time. So I have a lot of them."

He gestured shyly at the papers, which I then realize were clipped into separate files about a half inch thick.

"*Fletcher's Creek*," I read sideways. "'One man's journey through the heart of America.'"

"That one's junk," Will said quickly, swiping the screenplay off the desk and tossing it in the trash. "It's just a rip-off of *Into the Wild*. I've done much better since."

I glanced over at the others, but couldn't read any other titles as quickly. "Can I read one?"

Will frowned. "They're not any good. I don't really show them to anyone."

I tipped my head to the side, trying to make out the words on a screenplay on the other side of the desk. "You'll never know unless you put it out there."

He pressed his lips together and stared at his hands as a light flush ran up his neck. For some reason, the suggestion obviously made him very uncomfortable.

"Tell you what," he said finally. "I'll let you read one if you let me record you in the studio."

My head jerked up from the papers. "The *what* now?"

The sly half smile returned. "Come on, Lil. There's one more room down here."

He took my hand and guided me out of the office and down the hall to the final room at the end. When we entered, my eyes practically popped out of my head.

"What. Is. This?"

Next to me, Will chuckled. "You like it?"

I turned to him. "This is a recording studio. A real recording studio. Why in the world do you have a recording studio in your house?" A thought chilled me. No. It couldn't be. "You didn't…you didn't put this in here for me, did you?"

As soon as I said it, I realized how ridiculous it sounded. Will and I had known each other for a matter of weeks. It would have taken much longer to install something like this in his house, much less underneath my nose.

Will snorted. "Considering I didn't know you when I moved here four years ago, and it would be pretty impossible to do something like this in the time since we met, no, Lil. This isn't for you. But I'm flattered, you narcissist."

I socked him on the arm, and he chuckled more as he slung an arm over my shoulder and pulled me in for a kiss—the kind that made me stop thinking about mysterious screenplays and movie theaters. The wide smile on his face cheered. Even if it was at my expense, one day I was going to make Will Baker laugh for real. I could feel it.

He released me, and I turned back to the small room, walking around the calm, simple space. Unlike the previous two rooms, this one had no window, to keep the sound confined. The walls were padded with brown leather, and several instruments were set up on the rug beside the sound equipment: a bunch of guitars, a set of keys, and a drum set. All of them were pristine, top-of-the-line pieces. Through a small glass window I could see a tiny control room with space enough for maybe two people to sit comfortably behind the mixing console.

I fingered the cord hanging off a microphone. "So, why do you have all of this? Are you a musician too?"

For some reason—I couldn't tell you why—the idea hurt. Music was my thing, one of the only parts in my life that ever defined me in a good way. It started when I was little, playing on my friends' pianos. One of their parents had been a music teacher who had taken pity on me—the poor kid with a mess for a mother—and had given me lessons once a week. But it wasn't until I got my first guitar, the Yamaha Mama found without strings at a yard sale, that I really found my passion for it. I saved up for some strings and learned to play simple chords from YouTube tutorials on the school computers, but it didn't take long before I was sounding out songs by myself, and eventually writing my own. I wasn't well trained, as more than one professor at NYU had informed me, but I did have raw talent. This I'd always known.

So, I felt territorial about it—almost like it wasn't something I wanted to share, even if I wasn't exactly practicing right now. Will already had so much. He was rich, clearly, and talented enough that he could write stacks of screenplays in his spare time. Music was mine in this relationship. It was the only thing I brought to the table besides an empty savings account and a drunken mother. It was all I had to offer.

"It's stupid rich guy shit." Will touched a padded wall wistfully. "I never use it. I had this idea at one point that I could learn to be a rock star. But I have no rhythm, no pitch, no musical talent whatsoever. It's pathetic."

I tipped my head, ignoring the relief that coursed through me. "Well, you're talking to the girl who literally moved to New York for eight years trying to make that happen. I'm the queen of pathetic."

But he just shook his head, making the flyaway strands of blond that framed his face rustle back and forth. "You haven't heard me sing, Lil. I sound like a dying cow, and I play the guitar like a toddler. It's not pretty."

I couldn't help but chuckle. "Did you put anything down? Can I hear it?"

"Maybe one day..." he said. "When, I don't know, I lose a bet or something, I'll play you the few shitty recordings I made when I was bored. But since I'll probably lose you forever when that happens, I'm going to delay it as long as possible."

Sensing I wasn't going to get any more out of him on that point, I turned to the instruments. Will had a beautiful collection—there were a couple of Fenders, a very pretty Dobro, and even a bass next to the drum set and keyboard. The guitars were all mounted on the walls, waiting to be played, though I did notice the strings on a few were starting to rust. Will's house was immaculately clean, but a bit of dusting couldn't deter the effects of neglect and waterfront property.

I turned back to him. "This isn't just for you. You have an entire band's worth of equipment in here."

Will shrugged, but wouldn't meet my eyes. He shoved his hands deep into his pockets. "Well, I have a wicked guitarist now, don't I? Singer, too."

I ran a finger over the head of the acoustic Fender. It was a beautiful guitar, although not as nice as my Martin. I had saved for three years to buy that guitar. It was my prized possession.

"Would you ever let me record you?" Will asked behind me. "Maybe that song you played by the fire? Or...or whatever you want, really."

I hesitated, looking around. It was funny. For a long time, this would have been everything I'd ever wanted. I'd paid to have an EP done, of course, plus a few demos recorded my my own computer and some rented equipment. But I'd never been signed, was never able to finance a full album. Now I had access to a beautiful studio offered to me on a silver platter…and I didn't want it.

Didn't I?

For the last year I'd been a shadow, afraid of everything. Afraid of being on stage. Afraid of trying new things. Until I met this strange, mysterious man.

Being around Will made me feel stronger. Made me realize that maybe I didn't want to say goodbye to all my dreams by coming back here. That maybe I really did have more to offer the world than just being Ellie Sharp's pathetic bastard kid.

I took the guitar off the wall and turned to Will. "All right."

He glanced between me and the instrument, clearly surprised. "You want to do it right now?"

I weighed the neck in the curve of my palm. It felt good. Right. I inhaled, breathing the wood of the shiny floors, the slight metallic tinge that came from the equipment. "It's now or never, Baker. You want these pipes, you better press record."

Will pushed off the wall almost immediately, then moved about the room for a few minutes, unspooling cords, arranging the mics, and doing all the small things necessary to get ready to record. Then he went to the console, and I sat down on one of the stools, balancing precariously, trying to calm my heart pounding away in my chest. For some reason, this was scarier than playing in front of five thousand people at Irving Plaza.

"You ready?" he asked through the speakers.

I nodded, unable to speak. I just needed to calm my nerves. Close my eyes. Remember why, once upon a time, music had set my soul free.

"All right," Will said. "You're on."

A green light flashed on from the room, indicating that we were recording.

And I. Did. Nothing.

For nearly a minute. I sat there, frozen while I stared at the frets, looked at the way my left hand was poised over them, pressing so hard on a few. I knew how to start. A variation on a simple Travis pick, not much different than "Don't Think Twice, It's All Right." A strum on the bass E-string at the third measure. Hammer on the A-string twice, then sing.

But my other hand didn't move, and my mouth didn't open. I sat there like a statue. Completely paralyzed.

"Lil?"

Will's voice was muted, coming over a loudspeaker from the console room.

I closed my eyes. Suddenly, I was back on that stage. Back under those lights. A phantom terror watching me from the back of the room, there in spirit, though at the time he was still in jail.

Except now he wasn't anymore. My phone was at the house, but I already knew that when I got back, there would be another message or two waiting for me. Theo liked to play with his mice before he ate them. He loved to torment and tease.

"Maggie?"

I didn't even notice that Will had entered the studio until he was sitting on the seat next to me.

"I'm here," he said quietly. "You don't...just play for me, all right? There's no recording. It's just me and you."

I shook my head. "I...can't. I can't anymore."

"Lil." Will placed a wide hand on my knee and the warmth of his touch soothed my rapidly fraying nerves. "It's just me and you, Lil. Just us."

"I don't want to," I whispered.

It was a lie. I wanted to play right now more than I ever had. I had about a million emotions running around inside me, crashing into each other like pinballs. Music had been my release my entire life, providing an outlet for that energy that would have destroyed me otherwise. But I was stuck in place.

"Look at me, Lily pad."

Will's voice was barely more than a whisper, but I obeyed. I turned to him, and found his green eyes wide and open. Loving. Kind. He smiled, and my heart leapt and calmed at the same time. Slowly, my heartbeat fell back to normal.

"Let me hear you," he murmured, his voice so low I almost couldn't hear it.

He leaned over the guitar and pressed a light kiss to my lips. His scent surrounded me, blocking out the nerves, the awkwardness, the fear.

"Will you play for me now?" he asked, his breath still mingling with mine.

I blinked. He was so close that my eyelashes brushed the tops of his cheeks. Then he sat back, his expression warm and open.

Finally, I nodded.

And then I played.

CHAPTER TWENTY-THREE

I went back to your house for a funeral.
You showed me around.
Said I was beautiful.
But you didn't have to try so damn hard.

Wrote me a letter a little later that year.
Couldn't read it for a while.
Brought me to tears.
Should've known you'd be back here someday.
And that fallin' in love is bound to hurt anyway.

Finally someone to save me.
You can do what you want now that you forgave me.
And if forgetting's a little much to ask.
We can move on somehow with our heels in the past.

You showed up at my house around one.
Bags beneath your eyes,
Scraped knuckles and palms.
You wanted ice, a cold shower, a beer.

You said I asked you a little too much.
Have more questions than answers,
More vicious than just.
But what could I offer instead?
Was on my way out the door, when you grabbed me and said:

Can't you be someone to save me?
You can do what you want so long as you forgave me.
And if forgetting's a little much to ask.
We'll move on somehow, with our heels in the past...

In the morning I woke up alone.
Don't know why I was so surprised;
I was the one who sent you home, but
I miss your eyes...your smile...your brown hair.
And when I look to that goddamn door, I'm scared to death you'll be there...

Ain't there someone to save me?
You can do what you want, now that you forgave me.
And if forgetting's a little much to ask.
We'll move on somehow, try not to think about the past...

I finished out the last few chords, letting the song end on the fourth, in that drifting way it always had. It was a song I'd never figured out how to end properly, and every time I played it, I closed out in a different way. Maybe it was because the feeling of the song, that searching for someone, a savior, a rescue, even if they were bad for you, never quite ended either.

When the notes finally faded completely, I exhaled. That song always took it out of me.

"Jesus."

I turned and found Will staring at me, his green eyes shining brightly, as if they were deeper than the lake waters outside.

"Maggie, that song..." He swiped under his eyes, then blinked quickly, as if he were trying to chase something out of his vision. "When —how—where did that come from?"

"I wrote it the night my ex went to jail," I said quietly. "It's the last thing I wrote, actually."

"What did he go in for?"

I stood up and replaced the guitar on the wall, then paused, still facing the instruments. They were all so shiny and new. Completely unmarred.

"Rape."

I spoke clearly, trying and failing to control my voice when I said it. Instead, I warbled like a bird. It wasn't a word I ever said out loud, particularly since I'd had to say it so many times in the last year. In front of a judge. A jury. Lawyers. Theo. Again and again and again, while people tried to tear it apart, tell me I was fine, prove that the way my body had been violated was a figment of my imagination. "He was only sentenced for sexual m-misconduct, but that's what it was. R-rape, I mean."

I shook my head, trying to ward off that persistent stutter that had emerged ever since that night, a speech impediment that, among other things, had made it hard to perform like I used to. But Will needed to hear this. He carried his baggage around like a cross and still managed to open himself up to me. He deserved to know what he was getting into.

I took a deep breath and turned around.

Will stood stock-still. His eyes were still shining, dark, turquoise depths that carried an even mix of sympathy and anger. His hands were clenched into tights fists at his sides, but other than that he didn't look violent or poised to bolt. It was like he knew that in this moment, there was nothing else to do but listen. To bear our burdens together.

"Once?" he asked.

I looked at the ground. "More than once."

It had taken a long time to understand just what Theo had done, and I still wasn't sure it had totally sunk in. Over the course of two years together, he had wheedled and guilted and conned me into doing a lot of things I didn't want to do with my body. I had been little more than a trophy to him—something to conquer, something to dominate. And it was hard, really, to comprehend the fact that sex under any kind of duress, emotional or physical, was not done with my full consent, as the YWCA counselor had informed me every time I sat in her office. More than once, I'd shown up drenched in sweat after a particularly difficult day of the trial.

The worst had been the day I was deposed by Theo's gang of lawyers, all of whom had cross-examined me, made me out to be a hysterical, manipulative psycho while on camera. Why didn't you tell anyone until the end, they'd asked, working their hardest to prove that the last time, the time that was physically violent, which ended with me in the hospital, was really just a result of the kinds of attention I'd courted during our relationship.

Even now, months after the trial had ended and Theo had been served at least some justice for what he did to me, it was still hard not to feel guilty. Because after all, hadn't I said yes to him countless times before? And after, when curled in a hospital bed, as I'd recounted the events to a stolid officer in blue, hadn't my decisions ruined a man's life? Just like my own?

"When?" Will asked, breaking through that nasty cycle of thoughts that threatened to overtake me. Those spirals were fewer and farther between these days, but when they came, it was hard to get out of them.

I swallowed. "The last time was almost a year ago. He...well, that was the one that put me in the hospital. But it was also when it ended. I—I finally went to the police. I mean, I had to. The hospitals, they call the police when there is evidence of it. Of rape, I mean."

"Then what happened?"

I gritted my teeth. I didn't want to tell this story. I wanted to pretend that the last years hadn't even happened, and that was what I liked about Will. He didn't treat me like I was damaged goods. He made me feel, finally, like I could move forward.

"I found a lawyer," I said. "And I took him to trial. And it took a long time, but eventually, I won."

"He went to jail?"

I nodded wearily. I didn't mention that he was out now. I was tired, so tired of this story.

Will didn't speak for a long time. But when he did, it wasn't what I expected. "I'm not surprised," he said softly. "I wish I were, but I'm not."

I blinked. "What? Why?" Suddenly, I wanted to cry. Was it that obvious? Were my wounds, the ones inside that I couldn't stitch together, that transparent? Did I have "rape victim" etched so deeply into my soul that it appeared on the outside, like a tattoo?

Will took a step toward me, moving very slowly. "I used to…I used to work in a business where…that shit was everywhere, Maggie. Absolutely everywhere. So, yeah. I know the signs."

I nodded. If he had been Benny Amaya's assistant, he had been close enough to the entertainment industry to know how it worked. I'd been lucky to have Calliope as my manager. There were plenty of others who expected certain things of their clients, whether they said them or not. And plenty of other artists who offered it up on a platter to do what they needed to do.

Will pressed his nose to mine, and his warm, clean scent engulfed me. Immediately, my heart rate slowed as my body relaxed.

"I believe you."

Before I could stop it, a tear slipped out. I didn't know how much I had wanted to hear him say that until he had. Even though a jury and a judge had too. Even though after I had fought for a year to have my story validated, to have some kind of justice served, somehow it meant more that the person in this room understood it.

Will pressed a thumb to my cheek and wiped away the tear before he cupped my face, keeping me upright and facing him.

"In a way, it's g-good, isn't it?" I whispered. "If I hadn't lost everything because of him…I never would have come back here. I never would have met you."

Will sighed as he drifted his mouth over my forehead, eyelids, cheekbones, lips, chin. His fingers massaged gently around my ear and under my jaw, a slow, insistent motion that soothed my anxiety. My shame.

"I'll *never* be happy that happened to you, Maggie," he said quietly. "That's why you stopped playing?"

I glanced back at the instruments around me. Slowly, I nodded. "He—he was a big part of my career at the end. But he resented me for it. Guilted me for it. He said I loved my music more than I loved him. He—he was right, and he knew it. And punished me for it."

I squeezed my eyes shut, trying to shut out the memories of Theo's hand finding my face. The time he broke one of my guitars and smacked me with the jagged neck. It was only after he was locked away that I played again, forced back on stage in order to pay my bills. But the magic was gone, and my shows had never gotten the same kind of following they had before. The showcase had been my last shot at making it work. At recapturing that magic that used to overtake me.

But instead I'd failed. I'd looked out at that audience and only saw the eyes of a lover-turned-ghost. The music had escaped me. Until now.

"I'm a lucky bastard that you crashed on my property, though," Will said, pulling me back to the here and now. "I was a ghost until I met you." His other hand cupped the side of my face, and he tipped it up so I had to look at him. "You brought me back to life, Lily pad."

My hands slid around his taut waist, finding the skin of his strong, solid body under his t-shirt. Something coursed through me when we touched—a warmth, an energy, a new kind of strength.

I pulled him closer so our bodies were flush. "We brought each other back to life."

"Your music," he whispered, his lips hovering just over mine as I ran my hands up his chest. "It makes me feel."

"Feel what?" I murmured, my voice pouring out like water. This moment should have been hard, but it wasn't. Everything that had ever happened with Theo seemed very, very far away. All I could sense was Will.

"Everything," he replied hoarsely. "Anything. Anything at all."

He let me pull his shirt over his head before I removed my own. Though I was the one caged against the wall, Will moved with me, allowing me to do with his body what I wanted. He stepped easily out of his shorts and underwear, kicking them to the side, then tipped his head down obediently when I reached up to release his hair. When my hands slipped into the thickets of blond waves, he groaned, tipping his head back in ecstasy while I massaged his scalp.

"Mmmm," he hummed. "That feels really, *really* good."

My nipples tingled in response to the sound of his deep voice vibrating through his chest where they grazed his smooth skin. I licked his throat while his fingers slipped under the loose waistband of the sweatpants I'd borrowed. With barely a flick, they dropped to the floor, leaving nothing between us. He fell heavy against my thigh, but Will did nothing further. This was on my terms.

But my previously sore state had evaporated. It didn't matter that I had a day full of chores to get to. A mother I needed to check on. A life I needed to figure out.

The only thing that made sense in this moment was Will and me. And I needed him inside me. Now.

"It's too much," Will gasped in between kiss after hungry kiss. "You. Me. It's too fucking much."

I agreed, but that didn't mean I was going to stop. I wanted more. After years of not enough, I wanted too much.

I opened my legs and pulled his hands down my ribs to my ass. He didn't need to be directed further as he lifted me like I weighed next to nothing, keeping our mouths fused as the tip of him located my slick entrance.

"Maggie," he moaned into my mouth. "Maggie, *please*. Let me in."

"Come," I begged before welcoming his tongue again. "I need to feel you."

I didn't have to ask twice. There was no need to adjust as Will slid inside—I was ready for him, ready for this, maybe more ready than for anything else in my life.

I sighed as he sheathed himself fully. My body fit to his completely, like he was a key that unlocked something deep inside me.

"Fuck!" He pulled nearly all the way out, then pushed back in all over again, then tipped his head back and hissed aloud. "Jesus *God*, you feel good. Perfect. Just perfect."

"Again," I demanded, my nails digging into his back. "Fuck me, Will. Fuck me as hard as you can."

He straightened up as he slid partially out. "Are you—are you sure, Lil? I can—*fuck*, I can slow down. Or wait. I don't mind."

I wasn't sure I believed that. But I definitely didn't care. Instead, I reached up and grabbed a solid handful of streaked gold locks. "Just fuck me, Baker. Make love to me. Whatever. Sometimes they are the same, but I need it. Now."

"With fucking pleasure."

He slammed into me, causing my head to slam against the wall behind me. It hurt slightly, but I loved it, grappling at his shoulders and biting his neck as he repeated the action again and again. A long, low howl emerged from Will's chest.

"You turn me into an animal, you know that?" he growled as his hips pistoned away. "I fucking lose all control with you."

"Do it," I urged him on. "I want you to lose it. I want you to let it *all* go!"

I gripped his shoulder with one hand hard enough to leave crescent-shaped marks from my fingernails, while my other hand slipped down between us to massage the sensitive spot that would lead to both our releases. I didn't need much. I was already hyped, already halfway there when he started.

At the feel of my hand reaching that juncture where our bodies met, Will hissed again. He slowed his movements, looking down.

"That's right. Touch yourself, gorgeous," he murmured.

He kissed me again, then went back to watching. I found myself looking too, thoroughly entranced by the movements of his cock, my hand. My body clenched. I arched against the wall.

"Fuck," Will whispered as I squeezed involuntarily. "I can feel you getting close, baby."

His words only made me squeeze harder—not out of discomfort, but out of impending pleasure. That familiar wave was rising, and the sight of us joining, the ebb and flow of my fingers that moved in tandem with Will's harsh, steady movements, was quickly becoming too much to handle.

"Pinch your nipple," Will urged. "Don't worry. I got you. Just do what you need. I'm right behind you. You let go, and I will too."

His green eyes met mine, and in them, I saw the truth of what he said. That I *could* let go with this man. That I could be myself, take a leap, and he would be there to hold me up, catch me if I fell. Just like he was doing now.

My other hand released his shoulders, and drifted down his arm until I found my breast. I trapped my nipple lightly between my thumb and forefinger, enjoyed the surge that shot through my body at the light twinge of pain. All touches converged—Will's iron grip on my ass, the punishing rhythm of his cock, the pinch of my fingers at my nipple and clit. It *was* too much, in the best possible way. Two, three, four more pounds of Will's hips driving into me, filling me completely, and suddenly, I was lifted high on that crest of pleasure. My control evaporated. All pain was gone, replaced only with ecstasy.

"Will!" I shouted as my hands fell away. I didn't need them. My orgasm shook through me, matching Will's steady, unforgiving thrusts as he braced me against the wall.

"Fuuuuccckk!" he cried as he followed me. He shoved in deeply, so deep I could feel him at the limit of what I could take. It was almost painful, but I was so overcome by the pleasure of him, I could register nothing else. He was right. We *were* too much together. But too much was exactly what I needed in a world where until now, I couldn't manage to feel enough of anything.

It was only then, as we slid to the floor, still shaking out the remains of our pleasure, that the green light of the console caught my eye. The tapes had been rolling the entire time, capturing the sounds of our bodies joining right along with the sounds of the songs I had just played. Our cries mingled, creating harmonies I'd never heard, new rhythms I'd never forget. We were making our own kind of music after all.

CHAPTER TWENTY-FOUR

"Okay, you have to stop. Mama is going to think I dropped off the edge of the earth."

I twisted in Will's arms at the top of my stairs, but did nothing to disengage from the kisses he was feathering over my neck and bare shoulders.

We still couldn't stop touching, and it had been like this for almost two weeks. Instead of sating whatever appetites we both had for each other's bodies, a dam had been broken, and now a river of sexual tension was being released. The interlude in the studio had just been the start. Nearly every night, when Mama left or fell asleep, I'd either sneak over to his house or find him waiting for me at the shack. It was starting to turn into a game—how long could Maggie and Will last without having sex? So far our record was eight hours. Will had surprised me in the outdoor shower, in his boathouse, even the back of his pickup when he'd pulled to the side of the road halfway around the lake in order to shove his hand down my shorts and kiss me until I was practically unconscious. I was just as bad—I'd torn two separate t-shirts of his (granted, both had already had a few holes in them), and most of the time, his hair would have looked like it had been attacked by a wild animal if he didn't have it pulled back.

After yet another night and morning being occupied with each other, it was now well past noon, and I couldn't ignore the guilt blooming in my stomach at the fact that Lucas's truck was parked in the driveway, and probably had been since early that morning while I'd been getting plowed better than a cornfield since late last night. Will and I were acting like irresponsible teenagers, not two grown people of twenty-six and…

"How old are you?" I asked suddenly as his tongue flickered in a way that made my knees grow weak. I'd have a mark there in a minute, and I couldn't have cared less. "Thirty? Forty?"

Will broke away, looking adorably wounded. "I look fucking *forty*?"

I giggled, trying and failing to ignore the way his fingers had slipped under the waistband of my shorts. Again. "Honestly? I can't tell. With that pelt covering your face, you could pass for twenty or fifty. So I'd appreciate being told if I'm robbing the cradle or indulging in some daddy issues."

"You really hate my beard, don't you?"

I shrugged. "No. You're just so adamant about keeping it that it makes me want to see what's underneath that much more."

Will snorted, even though he stole another kiss that left me breathless before answering. "I'm twenty-fucking-nine, woman." His voice was practically a growl against my lips. "Fifty. Jesus Christ."

But I couldn't respond as he consumed me all over again, one hand twisting my t-shirt into a knot at the small of my back while the other took a solid handful of my ass and squeezed hard.

"Mmmmm," Will groaned just before his tongue twisted around with mine. "Fuck. Lil, I need you again. Where's that flat rock? You think anyone would notice if I fucked you there right now?"

"Well, considering it's broad daylight, I think they probably would," I said, even though my hands were already ruining his messy knot of hair all over again. The rubber band fell to the ground, and his newly trimmed locks fell about his shoulders in bedraggled waves.

Will bit his lip. "Damn. All right, plan b: a really big tree."

I giggled as he attacked my neck again, though somehow, I managed to press my hand against his shoulders.

"Will, we can't. Half the day is gone. I really do need to check on my mom, and poor Lucas is probably halfway done with the demolition today."

"Let's just demolition Lucas," Will grumbled before he worried my earlobe between his teeth.

I moaned lightly, and my hips pressed into his of their own accord. "Will." My voice was breathy and unstable as he squeezed my ass harder and ground into me. "*Will.*"

He groaned lightly. "Okay, okay, I'll stop."

Will released my waist and lifted his mouth from my neck. He chewed on his lower lip for a moment, looking like he wanted to take another bite out of me. I couldn't stop my blush.

"Damn," he murmured under his breath. "Tonight, then. I'll be coming for you, Lil, and you won't be able to run from me."

I swallowed. The words seemed meant as a joke, but his tone was fierce. "O-okay."

We tramped down to the house, Will holding my hand the entire way, like he wasn't totally ready to let go. Not now. Maybe not ever. From above, the harsh sounds of a sledgehammer slamming through the walls echoed from the topside cabin—Lucas, hard at work.

Guilt reappeared, like a bad penny.

"I just want to check on Mama," I said again. "Then we can go help Lucas."

But when I pulled open the sliding glass door, those plans were immediately smashed. The smell of toast snaked through the house, and as I stepped inside, I waved my hand through the light haze of smoke that filled the air. Something was burning.

"What the…" Will's dismay floated around me.

He jogged immediately into the kitchen while I scampered around the house, opening windows and turning on the ceiling fans. The smoke alarm hadn't gone off—which made me wonder if there were even batteries in the damn thing to begin with. I wouldn't have put it beyond Mama, in one of her 2 a.m. fits, to have robbed them to replace the ones in the TV remote or something equally mundane.

"Mama!" I called out. "Mama, where are you?"

"It was the stove and the toaster oven." Will returned from the kitchen. "She left bread in for too long, and there were some eggs burning in a pan."

I headed for the bedroom off the end of the living area, but she wasn't in there. "Dammit!"

"She's, um, in here, Lil."

I turned toward a sound I knew very well coming from the bathroom —the throttled chokes of my mother losing her breakfast and probably last night's dinner too.

"Shit," I muttered. "Will, maybe…maybe you should go up to help Lucas. I'll be up soon."

Will looked at me like I was crazy. "I'm not going anywhere."

I sighed. Apparently all of my secrets were being laid out on the table this morning. Sure, I had already told him my mother was an alcoholic, but most people didn't really get that until they saw it up close. If, of course, I let them at all.

"Maggie!" Mama yelled. "Where *are* you? Where did you *go*?"

I froze for a moment at the threshold. I hadn't heard it for several years, not since I had stopped accepting her phone calls at certain times of day, but I knew that voice. Torn with pain, like her vocal chords themselves had been tossed into a blender, that voice was the one that told me when I was a child that I needed to keep at least a five-foot radius away from her unless I wanted to get slapped, or worse. But it was the voice that also told me if I stayed away, my heart would be paying for it for days.

Maybe it was growing up in the church and being shunned by its members. Maybe it was never knowing if I was going to be my mother's greatest love or greatest disappointment. But I had always had a guilty conscience when it came to the people I loved. Nothing was ever good enough to fix her, and God knew I'd tried my damnedest for a very long time.

"Mama?" I pushed open the bathroom door.

She sat on the edge of the bathtub with her head hanging over the rim of the toilet. The bathroom was a mess—she hadn't quite made it in time, which meant I'd have a hell of a mess to clean up after she was done. Fuck.

She looked up. Her eyes were ringed with smeared makeup, and half her curly brown hair was matted down to one side of her face while the other side stuck up in haphazard tufts. Her skin was pale, sickly, but shone with the peculiar sweat of vomit and the slight redness of the blood still rushing out of her head.

"Who's that out there?" she demanded weakly. "Who did you bring here to embarrass me?"

"Will's here to help with the property, Mama," I said as I grabbed one of the faded washcloths stacked over the toilet. There was the audible sliding of the front door, and the sound of another pair of feet entering the house. "And Lucas."

"You want them to see me like this, don't you?" she bit out, swiping ineffectually at my leg before she turned back to the toilet and lurched as her stomach emptied itself of contents that it no longer had. "Why'd you bring them here, Margaret?" she moaned. "Why'd you let them see me like this?"

"I didn't pour the drinks down your throat, Mama," I argued before I could stop myself. "They are helping us. Getting the bed and breakfast ready to let, remember? So you and I can run it." Shit. She was clearly still drunk. At noon on a Sunday. Jesus.

"Oh, to hell with the bed and damn breakfast," she spat against the toilet seat as she set her cheek on it. Her eyes closed in relief. "You don't really believe we can do it, do you, Margaret? Not when the only good thing either of us has going is what we've got between our legs, huh? Ain't that where you were last night? Doin' what your mama taught you?"

I recoiled, taking longer than necessary to wet the cloth and wring it out in the sink.

"We *should* be opening a whorehouse," Mama continued, forcing herself back up. She turned, reached out with a shaky hand, and tapped me on the nose. "*You* could be my number one girl. All them boys been chasing my Maggie Mae since she was little. No different now, is it? Got two of 'em out there. Who do you think would be the highest bidder?"

"That's enough, Ellie."

I looked up to find Lucas's solid form filling the narrow bathroom doorway, watching us with a mixture of disgust and pity, while Will just stood behind him, looking confused.

Mama laboriously pushed herself up from the toilet, flushed the remains away, then grasped roughly at my arm while she wobbled like a newborn deer out of the tiny, stinking room.

"You think you're so high and mighty, Lucas Forster?" she sneered as we pushed past him and Will. She practically dragged me with her toward her bedroom. Her language was slurring now, like she was almost too tired to pronounce each word. "You think I don't know what you want from my daughter? And *you,* Mr. Mysterious? Don't *none of you* want *nothin'* more than what's in her pants."

"Mama, come on." I tugged her down to her room, but her feet dragged.

"And you," she said softly, turned to me. "My pretty little mini-me. Two little sluts, the both of us. One day, you're gonna feel it, just like I do. There are two types of women on this earth—Madonnas and whores. I'll give you one guess which one we are."

I didn't meet her eyes, and definitely didn't look back at Lucas and Will as I finished helping her to her bed. I had heard this before—heard some version of it my whole life, even when I was a child—but it had been years since I'd heard it in person. My heart fell, hating how familiar it still sounded, even after years of stepping away. How familiar...and *true*. I hated myself a little bit for *still* not being able to ignore the possibility that had sunk in when I was far too young to fight it. That maybe she was right.

Pretty little whore, Theo would say as he forced himself in. *That's what you are, aren't you? My pretty little slut. My pretty little flower. Pretty little whore.*

And I had never once suggested otherwise.

"You think they love you, Maggie Mae," Mama said as she crawled on top of her sheets. She collapsed into her pillow, her forehead still wrinkled, like she was engaged in some other battle. "But they don't. We don't deserve their love, baby. It's in our blood."

I EMERGED about ten minutes later, after she'd fallen asleep. I'd sat at the edge of her bed for a solid five minutes, my head buried in my hands, then took another five before I could get back up, clean the bathroom, shower again, and finally leave the house. I could sink myself in the hard work on the property before the time came for an evening run. By that point, Mama would be awake, hardly aware of what had happened. And if she was, she'd be mournfully apologetic, and we could at least try to put the episode behind us, like we always did.

Unfortunately, I didn't have the sweet bliss of manual labor waiting for me when I reached the topside cabin. The sanding was finished, and Will and Lucas were both sitting outside on the porch, drinking sodas in a tense detente while they watched my approach.

"She's all right," I said to Will's wordless question. I sat down on the porch beside him, and he rubbed my shoulder.

"Anything I can do?" he asked.

Lucas snorted.

Will looked up. "What?" The word suddenly had a sharp edge.

Lucas stood up, drained his soda, then crushed it under his heel. "You'll see, Bon Jovi. It takes more than a little pat on the back to deal with Ellie. Some of us have been doing it for a long, long time."

"Lucas, come on…" I started.

But he turned to me with a glare. "You left her here all night, didn't you? Maggie, you know better than that, even if you did leave the rest of us to deal with this shit for the last eight years."

I swallowed as guilt turned over in my stomach. "I—I was just across the lake, Lucas—"

"Right, and before that, you were just across the country. Skipped off to New York City while Barb and my mom had to hold her hair back for her."

"Give me a break," I said. "Barb, maybe, but Linda has never enjoyed anything more than gossiping about Mama's exploits with all those church bitches."

"Watch it," Lucas bit out, though the guilty look on his face told me I was right. "No matter. You should have been here. She's *your* responsibility now."

"Oh, come *off* it," I snapped, standing up. "And it's not like I went gallivanting off, hours away. I was a few miles away, for Christ's sake."

"With who?" Lucas's jaw tightened as he found Will. "With you?" He looked back at me with a gaze that could slice through granite. "Was it worth it?"

"That is none of your goddamn business," Will cut in, but Lucas didn't even spare him another glance.

I remained silent. My stomach felt like it was being eaten up. He was right, of course. I should have been here. Not just last night. But for the past eight years, instead of wasting my life on a failed music career.

"I know," was all I could whisper as I sank back to the step. "I know."

Finally, Lucas's shoulders relaxed, though Will's tensed instead.

"All right, Mags," Lucas said as he came back to sit on my other side. "So what are we going to do about it?"

I blinked. "What—what do you mean?"

"Mags, come on. You don't really think she can run a business like this, do you?"

My body stilled, prickled. "Are you—are you not going to help anymore?"

The property was half-finished. All our plans would be out the window without Lucas's generosity.

Lucas sighed. "No, I'm not going to bail. I made you a promise, and I don't back out on that. But to be honest, Mags, I figured you could probably just let out the houses permanently. You think Ellie's going to get up at the crack of dawn to make strangers breakfast every day? Are *you* going to do it?" He shook his head, not even waiting for me to answer the question. "She needs help, Maggie. Or are you going to wait for her to burn the entire house down before you get her what she needs?"

Suddenly, I was tired of being chastised, guilted for someone *else*'s mistakes that I had never been responsible for. This wasn't fair—the assumption that I needed to be chained to my mother, enabling her addiction with my presence. This right here, more than anything else, was the entire reason I had left. I was always, *always* going to be nothing more than Ellie Sharp's poor daughter or else her warden. A chip off the old sad, pathetic block. The only difference between now and eight years ago was that I now knew for sure that I wasn't good for anything else but picking up the pieces.

"And just how am I supposed to pay for that, even if by some miracle I could convince her to go?" I asked weakly. "Huh, Lucas? She filed bankruptcy last year. And everything I own came with me in my car. I could sell a guitar, but that wouldn't even come close to covering it, even a state-run program."

Lucas sighed and rubbed the back of his head. "I know. So maybe... maybe it's time to think about selling the property. She can't maintain it, and honestly, Mags...well, my folks would take it off your hands in a second. We've been thinking about expanding the inn, you know, and this would make a great addition..." He drifted off when he caught my look of horror, then held up his hands in surrender. "Okay, okay. Forget I mentioned it."

I just gaped. "Please tell me you haven't been helping because you were planning to buy my childhood home, Lucas. *Please* tell me that's not true."

"I... It's not true," he said, his big eyes were shot again with guilt. Clearly it *was* true.

"Fuck," I muttered into my hands. What was I going to do?

"I'll pay for it."

Lucas and I both jerked our heads up at the sound of Will's voice. He had been so quiet, I'd almost forgotten he was there.

"You'll pay?" Lucas's doubt was palpable. "How? Are you going to sell your little Toyota? Rehab costs more than five hundred bucks."

Will ignored him, turning his focus back to me. "I got this. Whatever she needs. Seriously, Lil."

"Why the hell does he call you *Lil*?" Lucas's voice was full of animosity. Contempt. "Did you get a new name when you were gone too? New life, new name?"

I stood up, suddenly feeling very overwhelmed. "I need to think."

Will stood too and watched me for a moment, clearly fighting not to do what we both craved. I wanted nothing more than to be wrapped up in his arms again, back in that sweet place where all the bitter disappointments of my life seemed to melt away.

But they always came back. I couldn't hide from them anymore. Not in New York, and certainly not here.

"I'm going to get started on the lower cabin demo," Will said with a dark look at Lucas. "Think about it. That's all I ask." He squeezed my hand once and walked down the stairs.

I turned to Lucas, who, now standing, was watching the doorway like he wanted to take his sledgehammer to it. Then he turned to me. "Who the hell is that guy? Why does he call you that?"

I sighed. This had been coming for a while, but I really didn't want to have this conversation right now.

"It's just a nickname," I said.

"A nickname," he repeated. He hissed through his teeth in clear frustration. "I don't like it. I don't like *him*."

"Lucas—"

"He's weird. He dresses like a hobo, not to mention he's lived on the lake for four years, and literally no one had met him until a few weeks ago. Who lives like that? And where the hell would he get the money to pay for something like rehab? Who does that without wanting something in return?"

"You're helping me out without wanting something in return."

Lucas looked like he wanted to argue with that statement, but didn't say anything.

I sighed. "We're friends, Lucas."

"Just friends?"

I didn't answer. Lucas huffed. For a moment, his hands opened and closed, the only indicator of a secret battle he seemed to be waging between maintaining the peace and starting a battle.

In the end, peace won. This time.

"Mom—Mom wants to know if you're going to come on Friday night," he said. "To the party."

I looked up in surprise. "What party?"

Lucas rolled his eyes. "Where've you been, Mags? You registered for the triathlon. It's the big Fourth barbecue bash at the inn, the one to start the festivities. Mom's doing an open house to welcome entrants. You can even invite Bon Jovi if you want."

I opened my mouth to protest the stupid nickname, but Lucas just smirked and kept talking.

"Bring Ellie too," he said. "Mom'll watch out for her. And then… maybe afterward will be a good time for…I don't know. An intervention or whatever. At least we can plan something."

I still didn't answer. I felt bad enough about what was going on with my mom. Was a party really the best idea?

But the reality was that Lucas's family had been nothing but generous to me since I was a kid. This was a small town. There was no excuse that was going to work for getting me out of supporting the Forsters' big night.

"Come on, Mags. Mom has been planning this for months. She'll be upset if you don't come."

I pushed some needles around on the ground with my foot and sighed. "Yeah. Sure. Of course I'll be there. I'll see if Will wants to come, although I doubt it. And…and Mama too."

Lucas smiled, though his eyes tightened at the sound of Will's name.

"Great," he said. "I'll let her know."

CHAPTER TWENTY-FIVE

"Charades!" Linda cried out. "Come on, everyone, it's my party, and *I* want to play charades."

It was the end of another successful event thrown by the Forsters, once again proving their status as the undisputed social royalty of Newman Lake. Their barbecue, which had consisted of a lake-wide potluck, four separate grills for burgers, ribs, and corn on the cob, and two kegs of Bud Light donated by Curly's, was a rousing success. It had started just past four and was still going strong at nearly ten at night.

After a week of suffering apologies from my mother, working my ass off helping the boys install the new drywall, sanding, priming, and painting the interiors of the cabins with Lucas and Will, and training for tomorrow's race, I was ready to go home and let the lake rock me to sleep in the comfort of my shack. Carb load, drink a gallon of water, and get a good night's sleep before I had to be up around five thirty to arrange my things at the Forsters' the next morning.

But there was no escaping Lucas's puppy dog eyes when, day after day, he continued asking me if I planned to come, disregarding Will's open glares or the way that Mama had been avoiding him all week. And really what choice did I have? The guy was single-handedly making a future possible for my mother. An appearance at a family barbecue wasn't going to hurt.

Mama, unsurprisingly, chose to stay home with a cocktail, muttering that she'd rather have her own party than deal with the catfights that inevitably happened whenever she spent time around Linda and her gaggle of friends.

Will had also declined to come, though the visual daggers he shot at Lucas on his way out that night told me he struggled with the decision, regardless of his phobia of crowds. The connection between us had just continued, despite Lucas's obvious disapproval. We spent every night together in my shack, more to assuage my guilt over what happened with Mama than because Will really felt more comfortable there. In the mornings, he almost always woke up frantic, as if startled by sleeping in a strange place. If he needed a little time on his own, I couldn't blame him. I did wish he had a phone, though. It felt a little mushy, but I wanted to hear his voice before I went to sleep that night before the race.

A chorus of half-hearted groans met an equally loud round of whoops and hollers around the fire pit at Linda's suggestion. The group that still lingered were the usual suspects: Linda's kids and their significant others, a few of their friends, plus some of the older crowd that made up the Forsters' circle of friends. Only a few guests of the inn were hanging around—most of the people who had come for the triathlon were safely in bed already.

Which was where I needed to be too.

"Mom, come on," Lucas put in, gesturing with the half-finished bottle of Bud Light in his hand. "No one likes charades."

"Lucas, what are you talking about?" Katie demanded. "You *love* charades. You never pass up an opportunity to be the center of attention."

Lucas shrugged, like that had absolutely no idea what they were talking about, and sank down on one of the big logs that circled the fire. Lindsay, of course, clung to his arm like a magnet, and he was responding in a way that made me think things had progressed beyond just friends for the two of them. I wouldn't have cared except for the way Lucas kept staring at me, as if to say *how do you like that*?

"Come on," Lindsay egged him on, her blue eyes twinkling. She cuddled up in his arms, and sent me a daring look. "I want to see your skills, Lukey."

Beside her, Katie rolled her eyes. I didn't even care about Lucas and Lindsay's whatever-it-was, but the name "Lukey" made me want to vomit.

"We can't," he protested more weakly this time. "We don't have even teams."

"We do if *he* plays."

Everyone turned to follow Lindsay's pointed finger. To my utter shock, Will came loping out of the shadows of the big yard, a dark, tall form in jeans and an unassuming navy blue hoodie that covered his hair and most of his face. He stopped short when he saw everyone looking at him, but when he found me, his shoulders relaxed.

I just grinned.

"Hey." I stood up and walked to him, ignoring Lucas's glare.

"Hey, beautiful," he said. The firelight danced in his eyes, and he revealed a small smile, only for me.

As much as I wanted to, I didn't kiss him in front of Lucas and his family. Will frowned at the lack, but relaxed more when I did take his hand. I turned to the rest of the group. "Everyone, you remember Will. Linda, Don, this is Will Baker. He lives just across the lake from us, over by Sutton Bay."

"Nice to meet you, hon." Linda shook his hand, followed by her husband. "Can I get you somethin' to drink?"

Will shook his head stiffly. "No, I'm all right. Thanks for having me. I'm sorry I'm a bit late to the party."

"You can have a beer if you want," I said. I worried sometimes he didn't drink at all because he thought it made me uncomfortable.

He just smiled at me. "It's fine. I don't need it."

"We're just getting going, so you came at the perfect time." Linda winked, then started writing down categories on a piece of paper. "Now then, Lucas. You and Lindsay need to divide up the teams, all right?"

Will followed me back around the fire where we could sit down next to each other on a big log. It was then he finally pushed the hoodie back, revealing his hair tied in its characteristic knot at the back of his neck and a face that was almost—not quite—clean-shaven. There was still a layer of scruff, but it was close enough that I could see the skin beneath it.

Everyone else was too busy chatting and arguing about teams to pay a newly beardless Will any attention. I, however, gasped.

"Oh. My. God!" I whispered. "You *shaved*!"

Will smirked, his eyes twinkling merrily, and I was a puddle.

"I didn't shave. I buzzed. And you better shut that pretty mouth of yours, Lily pad," he said in a low voice that made my skin tingle. "It kind of makes me want to stick something in it. Like my tongue. Or something a little bigger...like I did last night."

I shivered, but somehow I managed to press my lips shut temporarily, squeezing my thighs together. Because really, now that I could see Will's entire face, it was *really* hard to fight the bodily instincts to open whatever part of me this guy wanted. Will was so unassuming most of the time, but when he growled at me like that, it was hard to think about anything else than ripping his clothes off without a care where I was.

He smiled wider at my reaction, and the first thing I noticed was that he had *much* bigger dimples than I'd seen before. The more I stared, the more Will's shy smile grew, and two deep impressions appeared at the sides of his full mouth, now evident without the thick blond-brown pelt to cover them.

The second thing I noticed was that the guy seriously did have a jaw that could cut glass, and right now it was glittering in the fire, the light glinting over the stubble in a way that made him look like he'd been cast in gold. Holy shit. Will was one thousand percent *gorgeous*. And, I realized, he was *mine*.

He looked at me again, and his green eyes shone with pleasure. With a quick glance around the party, he leaned in and pressed a lightning-quick kiss on my mouth, which had somehow dropped open again, slipping in a bit of tongue for good measure before pulling back.

"Told you to shut your mouth. And don't get used to it," he said with a wink that practically made me faint. "After this I'm not cutting anything for six months."

I opened my mouth to argue, but found that, in a way, I didn't want to. Even as I looked around the firelight, just about every woman there was sneaking covert glances in Will's direction—even Lindsay, who did a double take when she caught sight of Will smiling at me. Hmmmm. Maybe I preferred being the only one who knew just what was hiding under that beard. Maybe I wanted him to save these moments for when it was just the two of us.

Feeling a strange possessiveness that was completely new for me, I realized I wanted to hide him away. Protect him from whatever demons he'd been running from.

"I like it shaved," I told him. "But I like the beard too. Do whatever you want. I like you just the way you are."

A layer of nerves fell away from Will's face, and he grinned, a smile that was brighter than the fire playing in front of us. My heart felt like it stopped for a split second, like the power in that smile was too much for it to handle. Seriously, it was like looking into the sun.

"Lil," he warned, though clearly he was enjoying this. "Shut. Your. Mouth."

I clapped a hand over it. Will chuckled hard—it was almost a full-throated laugh. Almost.

"All right," Lucas sharply interrupted my daze. "We got teams, and only because Mom wants to. Everyone has to play. That includes newcomers too." He quirked an eyebrow at Will, as if trying to dare him to back out.

Will just shrugged as he wrapped a long arm around my shoulders. "Sure, why not?"

Immediately I relaxed.

The game started out slow, then picked up as people jumped up to take turns. Linda tore up her list and put the crinkled papers into a bag, and several people started acting out things like catch phrases and film titles. Will, with his massive movie collection, was very good at guessing the film titles, though he would murmur them in my ear so I could call them out. I was pretty sure he was doing it to drive me crazy. The brush of his lips over the top of my ear every time he did it was unnerving, and half the time my voice would shake when I yelped the title aloud. But we were right, every time, and soon our team started to rack up points.

"Okay." Lucas jumped up for his turn, hopping from foot to foot like he was about to run a race. He held up two fingers.

"Two words!" called Lindsay.

Lucas nodded, and started acting out…something. He raised his thick arms over his head, then brought them down by his sides and started stepping from side to side before standing still.

"Soldier!"

"Rocket!"

"Jumping bean!"

The guesses from Lucas's team came furiously—mostly from Lindsay and Linda—but none of them were right. Lucas became more and more visibly frustrated, shaking his head vehemently as he continued his same strange dance with his arms occasionally held akimbo, but generally thrust down at his side.

"Telephone pole!"

"Pencil!"

"Ruler!"

"Penis!"

The group exploded with laughter, with even Will chuckling when Lucas fell onto the ground with disappointment as his dad, the official time keeper, called out time.

"It was *Forrest Gump*!" he shouted to the sky. "I was being a tree! Not my friggin' junk!"

"Ohhhhh!" His group all chanted their sudden awareness altogether, producing another round of laughter.

"Lucas, do your Forrest Gump impression," Lindsay said. She turned to her friends. "Have you guys seen him do this? He sounds *just* like him. Like, close your eyes when he does it."

Lucas didn't need more than that to start. He clambered back to his seat, and with a grin, turned to Lindsay.

"Life is like a box of chocolates…" he started to drone.

I rolled my eyes. I had heard this before. It wasn't actually that good of an impression—Lucas just effected a mild Southern accent and talked really slow, just like everyone else did when we were kids and our parents would put on that movie. It came out when I was about two, but every person I knew grew up with a DVD or even a VHS of that thing in their house. Everyone knew it.

Beside me, Will snorted.

Lucas looked up, irritated. "What?" he said. "You think you can do better, Bon Jovi? Good impressions are actually really hard."

Will shrugged, but the arm around me tightened. "It's all right."

Lucas smirked at Lindsay, as if to say, *Look at this fool.*

"But you got the accent all wrong," Will said like everyone else understood what he meant completely. "You sound like you're from Texas, not Alabama."

I turned and blinked at him. *What*? How would he know that?

"Oh, boys. Let's keep it civil, now," Linda warned.

Lucas crossed his arms. "Oh? What're you, some Southern accent specialist? Aren't you from somewhere back east or someplace like that?"

Will's jaw tensed, and I could practically feel the gears turning in his head. The hand over my shoulder clenched into a fist, and for a second, I thought he was going to get up and punch Lucas or something equally terrible. I was the only one here who had ever seen that temper, and though I *hoped* Will wasn't about to go throwing Linda's hand-carved camp tables into the lake, I wasn't completely sure he wouldn't. There was always that part of him that seemed completely unpredictable.

And he was. Just not in the way I ever expected. *Of course.*

All at once, Will removed his arm from my shoulder, scooted about a foot away from me down the log, and sat up. His entire body language and positioning shifted, though the changes were so subtle, it was difficult to tell what he had done. But in a second, he went from being closed-off Will Baker to being someone…else. Someone completely different.

Then he opened his mouth, and I knew *exactly* who he was: "Those must be comfortable shoes."

The whole group went silent. My mouth dropped, along with a few others'.

"I bet you could walk all day in shoes like that and not feel a thing," Will continued. "I wish I had shoes like that."

He stared at me, like he was waiting for me to say something. It took me a while, but eventually, I figured it out as the famous scene came back to me.

"M-my feet hurt," I said, and everyone laughed lightly, then dropped into silence again as Will continued.

For my part, I could do nothing but stare, enthralled, as he continued through the opening monologue to *Forrest Gump*. The messy blond hair, the muscles that bulged through his thin sweatshirt, the sculpted face and penetrating green eyes—all of it disappeared under the body language and absolutely pitch-*perfect* rendering of the Alabama accent Tom Hanks had used. Will Baker no longer existed. I was sitting right next to Forrest Gump, listening to him talk about shoes, people, all the things he could remember about them. I was on the set of the movie, watching him play with his nonexistent tie, shuffle his feet together, and there was practically a feather floating in the air next to him—that was how convincing he was.

By the time he got to the final line where the scene melts to a child in leg braces, Will turned to everyone else, and fairly shouted it, sounding exactly as it had in the movie: "Mama said they'd take me anywhere!"

As if on cue, everyone there, even Lindsay and Lucas, burst into sudden applause, whooping and hollering as Will scooted back to his place next to me, slipped his arm back around my shoulders, and pulled me into his side.

"Holy shit," I murmured as he glanced down. His cheeks were flushed, but it seemed to me to be as much from pleasure as from embarrassment. The dimples were out in force. "Where did that come from, Baker?"

He just shrugged and pressed an absent kiss to my shoulder. "Everyone has a few hidden talents, I guess."

"You should be acting or doing improv or something," I told him. "Seriously, you were amazing. You looked like you were a trained performer, Will."

He shrugged, visibly uncomfortable. "It's just a bit of fun. Let's drop it."

"Really, though," I continued. "Did you ever see any of those improv groups in New York? You were *way* better than those guys."

"Maggie, I said *drop it*."

His words cut through my excitement, and then I realized that he was shaking. Physically shaking. And immediately, I felt terrible. Will didn't like attention, and here I was, singling him out in front of everyone.

"Well, honey, I don't know how you're going to top that," Linda was telling Lucas, who was looking a bit put out. "I think you'd better stick to De Niro."

"Whatever," Lucas grumbled.

Will chuckled, but froze when he looked up and caught sight of Lindsay's phone pointed our way,

"Did you—did you record that?" he asked, a little too gruffly. I squeezed the hand resting on my knee, willing him to calm down a little.

Lindsay frowned. "What? No. Linda asked me to take some pictures of everyone to remember the night." She held her phone back up. "Want one?"

Will shook his head even as I leaned in to smile at the camera.

"No," he said. "I'm good."

I turned. "Why not? What's wrong?" He was afraid of pictures too?

"Come on, you grouch," Lindsay jeered as she held her phone up again. "It's just for memories, I promise. Don't you want a picture together as a *couple*?"

She was trying to rile up Lucas, and on the other side of the fire, I could see it was working. Lucas polished off the other half of his beer in one go while staring daggers at Will. His gaze flickered between us a few times, taking in the casual body language. He knew we were seeing each other, of course—he'd been around us all week, even after the blowup last weekend. But this was the first time either of us had been openly affectionate around him. Will was being territorial. And I was somewhat guiltily enjoying it.

Lindsay continued to prod. I didn't want to push Will, but I couldn't deny the appeal of having some kind of memory of the two of us. For whatever reason, this still didn't feel quite real. We could make all the proclamations we wanted to each other in private, but there was something about having a record of ourselves, something to show others, that made me feel more like this was real. That others could see it too.

"I'd kind of like one," I murmured into his chest. "If—if you don't mind."

Will looked down at me with softened eyes. Then he sighed. "I really can't say no to you, you know that?" he murmured. Then he turned back toward the camera, setting his chin on top of my head. "You sure you didn't record anything?"

"Yes!" Lindsay practically shouted. "Jeez. Paranoid much?" She held up her phone, swiping to the right app. "Man, it's really hard to get the lighting right. Maggie, you do kind of sink into the darkness, right? Must be hard."

I did my best to ignore her comments. Beside me, Will growled low.

"Okay, you guys, smile," Lindsay said after she was finished fiddling with the controls. "You too, mountain man. One, two, three—cheese!"

A flash went off, bright enough that I could see stars for a moment.

Beside me, Will had gone stock-still. As soon as I could see clearly again, I turned to him. He was still staring at Lindsay, who had since turned to snap photos of others.

"Hey." I tapped his cheek. "You okay?"

He blinked furiously. Every muscle in his body suddenly shifted, strung as tightly as one of my guitar strings. Like if I touched him, pulled him in any way, he'd shoot in the opposite direction.

"I have to go," he muttered, standing up so suddenly that I was practically tossed off his body. Without even saying goodbye or thank you to any of the guests or the Forsters, he practically jogged into the blackness.

"Here we go," Lucas remarked with a roll of his eyes.

But I was already jogging past him, preparing for another confrontation with the man I was dangerously close to falling in love with, if I hadn't already. I was confused. Embarrassed. Abandoned. And really, really pissed off.

Because this was ridiculous. I wasn't going to live my life walking on eggshells because of a man's neuroses. I was done with that, and this… whatever this was…was never going to work if Will ran away like a scared animal every time some random trigger set him off. If this was ever going to work, truths needed to be said. Cards needed to be laid. Things had to change. Starting now.

By the time I reached the parking lot, Will was already opening the door to his truck in quick, jerky movements that betrayed his panic.

"Hey!" I shouted, my voice echoing through the darkness. The joviality at the fire was behind us, only a faint echo swallowed in the night air.

Will froze at his car. "Let it go, Lil."

"What the hell?" I ignored him completely, reached around to slam the door shut, then pulled on the front of his hoodie so he had to face me completely. "Are we really doing this again? Is this going to be your M.O. every time someone does or says something that makes you the slightest bit uncomfortable?"

Will's face twisted in a dark frown. "I don't need to explain myself to you, Lily. I don't want my fucking picture taken."

I scoffed. "You don't have to *explain* yourself to me? You just left me stranded in front of all my friends, looking like an idiot. Are you mad about having a freaking picture? Or that I wanted to be there and you didn't? I never said you had to come, Baker."

"And I *didn't* want to be there!" Will burst out. "For a lot of reasons. But I sat there, twiddling my fucking thumbs in my office, and realized I'd be a dick if I let you sit here by yourself all night. I don't like your friends, Maggie. I don't like people making racist comments to your face and talking to you like you're nothing. You can't expect me to enjoy listening to these small-minded bitches degrading my girl! Lindsay. Lucas. Your own *mother*, for Christ's sake. I don't want to hear it, and neither should you."

I swallowed, my anger only slightly stifled by the idea that Will considered me his girl. I liked it. Too much. And I was just about to say it, but Will kept talking.

"I just don't know why we need to waste our time with these people," he continued. "I'm better than them. *You're* better than them, Maggie."

"No, I'm *not*!" I exploded, sending out a spray of gravel when I stomped my foot. "First of all, I'm *one* of them, Will. Maybe even less than them. I'm Ellie Sharp's daughter, half her crappy DNA and half some stranger who would screw a drunk woman in a bar without a second thought. I tried to get away from that sad fact for the last eight years, and you know what? I failed. I came back here because I needed to accept it."

Will opened his mouth, clearly ready to argue, but I held up a hand. I wasn't done.

"Those people over there? Most of them have done more for me and mine my entire life than you can possibly imagine. I broke Lucas's heart when I left town, and here he is, literally helping me put my home back together. Linda and Don? They were like second parents to me. So before you go thumbing your nose at the good people who live here, maybe consider your fucking audience, all right? We're not better than them. They're better than *us*."

"I didn't mean it like that," Will countered lamely. "But, Maggie...I hate hearing you talk about yourself like this. I hate the way you let them do it too. I look at you, and I don't see someone who should be stuck here taking care of her deadbeat mother. You should be back out there. Making music. Following your dreams."

He couldn't have known the way a statement like that would cut into me, but he should have known enough. After all, Will understood why I'd left New York. He knew, at least a little, about how hard I'd tried, for how long, giving everything I had to a career that, in the end, couldn't save me.

And that choice hadn't just cost me everything I had. It had cost Mama her life too.

"I *can't*," I said bitterly, now swiping tears off my cheeks. "My mom buried herself in the bottle for the last eight years because she thought I wasn't coming back, Will! I'm stuck in Newman Lake because I won't do that to her again. Ever."

He didn't say anything at first. From the fire pit, a few distant peals of laughter cut through the silence, but Will's eyes didn't move from mine. We were engaged in another one of his stare-offs, and I sure as hell wasn't going to break first, even though my stomach was completely tangled in knots. She was far across the lake, but from here, I could see Mama's body curled up on the bathroom floor, or maybe passed out on a deck chair. I wouldn't turn my back on these people ever again—not for my own stupid dreams, and certainly not to appease another man.

Will could take me if he wanted. But he had to take all of me. And that included them too.

"Look," I tried. "You can't let a few stupid comments determine how you think of an entire community. And you definitely can't just run away because of a camera flash or a song or whatever sets you off next. *I* can't deal with that."

Will opened his mouth, then shut it. He folded his arms over his chest and didn't speak.

I blinked. My eyes hurt. They welled a little at the thought of what I was going to say next. But I had to say it. I had to learn to put down limits. If I had learned one thing from my time with Theo, it was that.

"I want you to know me, Will. Know my life. And these are my people, whether you like it or not. You want to live your life alone, that's…well, it's your prerogative to do so. But it's not mine. So…maybe we need to think about this. What this *really* is. Whether it's really going to work."

Will's eyes closed, and my stomach dropped. That was resignation on his face—he was probably coming to the same conclusions I was. This… connection…or whatever it was between us might have the force of a tidal wave. But in the end, even that kind of power couldn't overcome fundamental personality differences. It couldn't overcome values.

Internally, I panicked. Being with Will over the last few weeks had made me feel more like myself than I had in a very, very long time. For the last…had it really only been a week?…I had gone to sleep in his arms, spent my days working alongside him. He had become more than a casual lover in such a short period of time—already, he was something of a rock. Was I really willing to throw that away for an alcoholic mother and a friend who sometimes couldn't take no for an answer?

The answer, of course, was yes. It could only ever be yes, because that's what family is, what my mother and the Forsters were to me. Will wasn't family. Not…not yet.

We stood there for a long time, me looking at Will, Will with his eyes shut tight. Laughter from the bonfire ebbed and flowed, but we were statues in the summer night breeze.

But still he said nothing. And slowly, eventually, that said as much as any single word.

"All right," I said finally, turning away so he couldn't see the next round of tears threatening to fall. I shouldn't have felt like this, but I did. It wasn't his fault that his paralyzing fears kept him from being around people. Just like it wasn't my fault that I had people in my life who needed my attention. After less than a month of knowing him, it shouldn't hurt so much, then, that we probably weren't going to work out.

But it did. It really, really did.

Will remained silent as I walked to my car, didn't call out or even try to stop me as I put the keys in the ignition and drove home.

CHAPTER TWENTY-SIX

I was too busy crying to notice the headlights that followed me right down Muzzy Drive instead of left. I was too busy feeling sorry for myself to notice that they followed me all the way around the lake, even down my gravel driveway. It wasn't actually until I had parked near the stairs, was bent over the steering wheel trying to suck in deep breaths, and a pair of knuckles were tapping lightly on my window, that I realized the old orange Toyota was parked next to me.

I jumped at the sound, swallowing back my tears and my pride as I caught sight of Will's face. Hurriedly, I rolled down the window while swiping under my eyes. Will leaned down, his face filling most of the window.

"Lil," he said quietly.

"Um. H-hi," I mumbled.

"Why did you leave?"

I sniffed. "Well…you didn't say anything. You were pretty clear."

"You didn't let me answer."

"I…I guess I thought *that* was your answer."

Minutely, so small it almost wasn't a movement at all, Will shook his head. "If I answer you, Maggie," he said. "You'll know it. I've got plenty to say. It was just more than I wanted anyone to overhear." He stepped away from the car, opening the door to let me out. "Can I come down and talk?"

I stepped out and nodded. "Oh—okay."

I strode down the hill, jogging the stairs one by one. Will was a silent shadow behind me, a wall of strength and fear that made me feel strangely protected and threatened at the same time. He waited patiently while I popped into the house to check on Mama, who was snoring lightly in her bed. Then he followed me over the deck, in front of the main house, and around the point to where the shack stood under a canopy of pine branches while the lake sloshed against the rocky shore.

And it was only when I reached toward the lock that he touched me again. A big hand closed around my wrist, and gently, he turned me around and trapped me against the door of the shack.

"I should stay away," he admitted as his gaze, hot and fierce, drifted over my face, my exposed collarbone, over my modest curves. "I should have always stayed away from you, Maggie. But we're here now, aren't we? I'm in way, way too deep, too tangled up…Lily pad." His voice tripped slightly over the nickname, the dimple appearing once more in the side of his face before disappearing again. "I couldn't stay away from you if I tried."

His palms wrapped around my upper arms, sliding up and down lightly before they cupped behind my neck and then my face. His thumb stroked lightly over one cheek. The shadows of the pines cut strong lines across his face and made his green eyes seem almost slanted in profile. He looked nothing like the warm, kind man I had woken up next to every day this week. Here, with his hands on me, he looked almost dangerous.

But that wasn't why I was scared.

His fingers threaded into my hair, which was almost as curly as it used to be. He pulled slightly at the roots, tipping my face up to his. And then, finally, he kissed me.

It started out gentle. Tentative. It was the kiss of someone who knew he'd fucked up on some level, someone who was testing his limits. His lips moved lightly, then more insistently, fitting our mouths together in that jigsaw fit I'd only ever experienced with him. Instinctually, I opened to him, allowed him to swipe his tongue inside, taste me completely, then hungrily until a loud, long groan erupted from deep in his chest.

He sounded in pain.

"Will!" I gasped as his lips traveled down my neck, licking and nipping at the hollow where the sensitive skin dipped under my collarbone. I shivered. "Will, we still need to talk."

He was always going to do this, I realized. Where words would never quite come quickly enough, our bodies spoke instinctually. I reacted to him as naturally as breathing, every nerve I had brightening with each insistent touch, every cell in my body perking toward him. His hands molded to my shape like he had made me himself. I couldn't think straight when he touched me, when he kissed me like this.

And maybe that was his goal.

"Stop," I said, summoning a bleak effort to push him off. "Sex isn't going to fix this, Will. This isn't going to work like this. *We* aren't going to work like this."

With visible effort, he raised his mouth. His full mouth that touched my skin for the first time without the tickle of a beard accompanying it. It took everything I had not to urge him back down.

But then he blinked. "Is that what you *really* want, Maggie?" he asked. "Do you want there to be a 'we'? An 'us'?"

"Yes!" I erupted, angry at him even as my body was angry at me for stopping. "Of *course* that's what I want. Why do you think I was crying all the way here, you idiot?"

Will remained still, bent over my shoulder, so close that I could see a muscle ticking in his jaw, but nothing else. Then, with a long, frustrated growl, he pushed off the wall and paced around the small clearing for a moment before turning back to me, his arms crossed in front of his chest.

"What do you remember about that concert at Irving Plaza?" he asked suddenly.

I frowned. Whatever I thought he was going to say, it wasn't this. "I... mostly just my own performance. I didn't stay until the end, as you know."

Will rubbed the back of his neck in that way I was starting to recognize. He did it when he didn't like what he was going to say. When he thought I wasn't going to like it either.

"I…it was my fault, what happened that night," he said. "I was fucked up back then."

I nodded. "Yeah, I know. You already told me this, Will. About your history with drugs and everything—"

He just shook his head. "It's not just that." He worried his jaw for a second, mulling. "Maggie, I used to—I just used to be in circles where—we used to get a lot of attention."

"Well, you worked for Benny Amaya," I replied. "That's not exactly surprising. The guy has some really famous clients."

Will's mouth pressed into a thin line. "Famous. Yeah. Well, anyway, that night, we were up in the VIP for the show. We had done…shit. I don't even know what we had done. We were up there, getting ready for the main show. I was high as a fucking cloud, just doing my best to drown out all the *noise*. My life back then…Maggie, it was so loud. Too many people. Talking. Shouting. Flashes and picture and—anyway, I could never make any sense of it. All the time, I was only ever looking for quiet."

I leaned against the shack as he started to pace around the clearing. I wanted to probe more, ask exactly what he meant by noise, why things had to be so crazy for him. But I knew enough to know that the entertainment industry was crazy for just about anyone truly immersed in it. Even if he had only been on the sidelines, it would have been enough to affect someone of his age, back then only twenty-four, twenty-five.

But instead, I waited for him to tell his story.

"We had just taken, I don't know, some fucked-up cocktail of molly and coke, and probably some other shit that should have killed me but somehow didn't. I just remember looking up at the ceiling and wishing I was dead. People always wanted things from me, to the point where I never knew who I could trust. My life was so empty. There was nothing in it. Nothing at all. So I left. I made my escape. To a room in the back. Where a nervous musician was trying to get up the guts to go on."

I couldn't speak, and for a moment, it seemed that neither could Will. We were so far from New York, from the noise and litter and crowds that made up a city that turned some dreams into reality and brutally crushed others.

"It was you," I whispered. "That night. You were the man who talked to me? Who held my hand?" I blinked, finding it hard to see straight. "I never would have made it on stage if it had been for you, do you know that?" I frowned. "You had pills in your hand. I remember hearing them."

Will leaned against the big boulder that faced the front door of the shack and watched me taking in his story.

"When you left, I tried to fight it. But I couldn't. I took the rest of the pills, and by the time I got back to my seat, I could barely remember your name, much less our conversation. But then…I heard you. Your voice was the purest, most beautiful thing I had ever heard in my sad, sorry life, Lily," he said softly, his words practically floating away over the water. "I felt it then, just like I did that night you played by the fire. For the first time, everything was clear to me. I knew what I had to do."

"What was that?" I whispered, reaching behind me to clasp the door handle. I needed something to hold me steady.

His eyes zeroed in on me. "Find you again."

He had spent the rest of the set away from his friends, watching me intently from the balcony of the VIP loft at the club. Irving Plaza wasn't a huge venue, but it regularly hosted major acts. That night I had been booked as a last-minute opener to Gillian Keller. It was the night that Calliope had officially become my manager. The night my entire career had started and ended at the same time. Because that was also the night Theo had first seen me too, although we didn't formally meet until months later.

"After you were done, I had to meet you," Will said. "For real. My friends thought I was crazy. We didn't leave the VIP area—ever—because of—of the people we worked with."

"Famous people?" I prompted.

His eyes flickered. "Um, yes. But I had to. You were this magnet. I could feel your strength, your goodness, your, I don't know, your *light* from across the room, Lily." He pushed his hands across his face and groaned. "Fuck, why is this is hard? I sound crazy, don't I?"

I blinked, not knowing what to say. *Was* he crazy? Maybe. I wasn't sure I cared.

"I *do* sound crazy," Will reiterated. "But when it comes to you, maybe I am."

I gulped. He continued.

"I left, fought my way through the crowd to get to the backstage entrance, but I was high with a certain amount of tunnel vision. To be honest, I'm not exactly sure what happened next. The guy at the club said I punched him first—I remember him pushing me. But I do remember feeling trapped. Like there was this sea of people determined to keep me from you. They *all* wanted to keep me away. And in the end…it was too much. I cracked."

He opened and closed his fists several times, as if they were recalling the memory of that terrible night along with him.

"I remember hearing about a fight after," I said when it seemed he couldn't speak. "I left pretty soon after my set, but Calliope—she was my manager—she told me about it. She said that actor and his posse were at the show, and they went to town on a bunch of people in the crowd during Gillian's set. So that really was you, wasn't it? You started the entire fight…just to get to me?"

Will nodded forcibly. His eye glimmered, like he was about to crack all over again. His breathing seemed strained. I knew mine was.

"They wouldn't let me get through," he said through clenched teeth, and I could practically see the intensity shimmering off him as he spoke. "I had everything. I had money, fa—fortune. I was the biggest fucking VIP in the place, but I couldn't get to the one person I wanted." He turned back, and his eyes caught mine. "You, Lil. It was always you."

I couldn't move. Couldn't breathe. I was like one of those heroines caught in the thrall of some supernatural creature. A sailor drowning in the song of its siren.

"Your client must have been really mad," I said. "That you got him into all that trouble."

Will frowned. "Who?"

"The actor. You were in his entourage, right?"

Will blinked and looked out at the water. "The actor. Oh. Yeah."

I tilted my head, waiting for him to tell me who it was. It could have been anyone. Zac Efron to Leonardo DiCaprio. But Will didn't reveal any names, and really, how would I know anyway, considering I'd been living in a music-made hole for so long?

Will sighed, long and low.

"That was the night that almost killed my dad," he said quietly. "He bailed us out after the arrest, and he was ashamed. So fucking ashamed at what a piece of shit son he'd raised. And that night, when I was lying in bed, still trying to figure out how I was going to get back to you, he had his first heart attack." He pushed his hands over his face, which was suddenly riddled with pain. "My mother blamed me for it. She had every right. I knew she'd never look at me the same. We never got along in the first place, so it didn't really matter to me what she thought. But my dad...I killed him. That life...all those people...the photographers, the studio-heads, the agents, the publicists...*all* of them turned me into a fucking worthless piece of shit. And that's what killed my father."

He slumped against the rock, folding his hands behind his neck in pain. I wanted to go to him, but I sensed he needed the space to decompress. Telling stories like this required some space for the catharsis, for the pain of purging pain. I had a feeling it had been a *very* long time since Will had told anyone his secrets.

"So I left," he said with a resignation that broke my heart. "I took everything I could with me...and I left. And came here."

"Why here?" I wondered. It was so far from New York. A tiny town that no one had ever heard of.

Will shrugged. "Why not? I just got in my car and kept driving. This was where I ended up."

"Was it worth it?" I asked, my voice small in the night.

Will looked up, his eyes full of sorrow. "I miss my dad," he admitted. "I never did say goodbye to him. But otherwise..." He trailed off, thinking, then set his jaw with a determined look. "Sometimes I think it was. Because all I wanted was to find you again. And then I found a place I knew no one would ever find me...and you appeared. I didn't know it was you until you played for me that one night, but when I did...holy shit. What are the fucking odds, you know?" He chuckled. "If that's not fate, Lil, I don't know what is."

I couldn't help but smile with him. When he said it like that, it *did* sort of seem like we were supposed to be together.

"But, Lil?" The somberness of Will's tone pulled me back. "I am *never* going back to that life. I might write for fun, but the screenplays just sit there. Because that world. That fucking *poisonous* world isn't worth any amount of money I could ever want. I'm done with it. Do you understand that?"

I swallowed. I wanted to ask why. Why was it he was so utterly against a world he had only been adjacent to? Or how, maybe, he had come to those conclusions? I understood the fear of crowds now—the man had practically been trampled at a nightclub, and that combined with the shock of it, in his perspective, had cost his father's health…sure. I understood.

But the look on Will's face told me it wasn't the time for those questions. He'd opened up enough for the night, had revealed more secrets in the past ten minutes than maybe he ever had. There was honesty between us now. And there would be time for more.

Will pushed off the boulder and approached me.

"So I have to ask you this," he said. "Do you still want to be with me, knowing I'm that kind of man? I didn't even know you back then, Maggie, and I was ready to kill about ten people who were trying to keep me from you. Now…" He shook his head, shaking off the memory. His green eyes were full and deep. "I'd kill a hundred," he said softly. "A thousand. I'd kill *anyone* who tried to keep us apart, Lil. Who tried to do you—*us*—harm."

I gasped lightly, my breath caught in my throat. I should have been scared by his words. But all I felt was lust, or something beyond that. Awareness. Acknowledgment. The terrifying realization that deep down, I wasn't scared of his feelings because…I felt the same.

"Now's your last chance," Will whispered, just inches from my face. "If you say go, I'll go. And you should, Lily pad. You really should."

I licked my lips. Will's pupils dilated visibly, and his breathing grew heavy.

"I won't go back to that life," he said as he caged me against the wall. He clasped my face between his hands and stroked one cheek with his thumb. "But being with you…Lil, I don't want to be alone anymore either. I want to live my life again. With you. If you'll…if you'll teach me how."

Even as he pressed his forehead to mine, his eye glimmered with that fear I was starting to recognize earlier and earlier. That fear to step out. To be vulnerable. Will still hadn't shared completely with me where his phobias came from—and maybe I didn't need to know, because in an odd way, we were the same. For years, well after the traumas that had occurred had supposedly been accounted for, but with one foot still in my nightmare.

Will woke me up.

"Me too," I whispered. "But, Will…you won't be alone. I'll be there with you. We'll have each other."

"Always?" His gaze was mournful. Hurt, even, for reasons I didn't understand.

I cupped his face too. He started, then leaned into the touch.

"Always," I said. I wasn't even sure what that meant…but somehow, I knew it was true.

Will looked at me for a long time, that deep, turquoise stare of his seeping through me just like water.

"All right," he said finally as he pulled me close. His lips sealed over mine, firm and warm, a hint of forever lingering in his kiss. "Prove it."

We kissed for what seemed like hours, pressing like one body instead of two against the cold wooden side of the shack. But eventually, Will snaked a hand around my back to open the door, and I allowed him to guide me inside, where he kicked it shut and made quick work of removing both of our clothes.

"Lie down," he commanded, pushing me gently backward onto the bed.

I fell lightly, a smile already playing over my lips, but instead of falling on top of me, Will knelt on the ground and tugged my legs forward so they dangled over his broad shoulders.

"I want you to come," he ordered, his breath hot and heavy on my skin. "I'm going to lick your pussy until you do, gorgeous. I want you to scream my fucking name."

It wasn't the first time he had done this, but it certainly felt like it. This time there was no beard scratching my thighs as he buried his face between them, nothing impeding his lips and tongue as they explored the most sensitive regions of my body. I fell onto the mattress, and his tongue proceeded to worship me for several minutes, driving me into a frenzy, bringing me close, and then letting me fall before starting the whole process over.

"Will," I gasped as he slipped one finger, then two inside me. His mouth was doing some kind of voodoo I'd never experienced before, and the combination of that with the insistent pressure of his curved fingers had me hurtling toward that familiar edge in no time.

"Hush," Will said before pressing kisses to my inner thighs. "Just take it."

He hummed as he worked, a low rumbling that I could feel through my entire body. The effect of the added vibration was instantaneous. I exploded.

"Oh *God*!" I shouted, my arms shooting over my head to brace myself against the wall. My body started to shake violently, but Will's other hand kept me pinned firmly to the mattress until he fulfilled his promise and made me scream his name.

"Will!" I cried, again and again. Loud, then softer, until finally, with one last flick of his tongue, it was only a whimper: "Will."

He sat up and wiped his mouth with the back of his hand with mischievous glee.

"You make me a fucking animal," Will said as he crawled over me, fitting himself between my legs. "I don't act like this with anyone else."

"That's because you're never around anyone else," I said in a half daze after he engulfed me with another ferocious kiss.

He pushed up and scowled, but the dimple that emerged in his right cheek told me he wasn't totally angry.

"Do you know what I thought when I first saw you, up on that stage?" he asked as he nosed around my neck, nipping my ear, my jaw—anything he could that drew breathy sighs from my chest.

"N-no," I whispered. "What?"

"*Mine*." His teeth bit down on my earlobe, with a delicious pinch of pain that made me squirm against him. His erection, heavy on my hip, quivered. "And again when I saw you in the woods. Scared the shit out of me, but that's what you are, you know. Fucking *mine*."

"Ahh!" I cried as his teeth closed over my neck. "You *are* an animal!"

"Only for you, baby," he growled as he nudged my thighs apart with his knee. "Only for you."

I tensed slightly as the tip of him found my entrance. I was used to it by now, but that first movement was always a shock. The sheer size of him always took a moment to get used to. But as he sucked on my lower lip, my thighs automatically relaxed, stretching to accommodate him slowly, steadily, as he pushed inside.

"Fucking *hell*, Lily," he breathed. His eyes closed in concentration, and then mine did too as we lay there together, getting used to the feel of our bodies joining.

"God, you look so beautiful," he whispered as he pushed in further. His eyes didn't leave mine as he threaded his fingers into my hair, palming my scalp for leverage.

"Oh *Goooooddddddd*," I moaned loudly, certain the neighbors could hear me from across the lake as he filled me completely. My back arched, and Will sat up on his knees, his hands slipping under my spine to support the movement. He bent down again and took one nipple into his mouth, sucking hard as he began to move.

"Fuck!" I shouted as he rammed in, again and again. He was so big; I was so full. I wouldn't be able to take much more like this, and by the way he slowed a bit, he wasn't going to be able to last long either.

"Maggie," he heaved as he pulled my hips up further. His thumb found that spot that he'd been worshipping with his mouth only moments before, and moved over the slick bundle of nerves with the sure practice of someone who was already learning my body better than I knew it.

"Ah!" My head fell back into the pillow, but Will's other hand, still splayed under my shoulder blades, lifted me easily so I sat atop his thighs

"That's it," he said, closing his eyes, almost as if in pain. "Feel it. Take me all. The way. In."

I couldn't speak anymore, could only moan and whimper against his lips while he ground into me from below, all the while pressing and flicking and squeezing as I came closer and closer to falling apart.

"*Fuck*," he hissed as I squeezed around him involuntarily. "*Jesus*, baby. I'm—fuck, Lil, I'm not going to be able to last much longer."

My head fell back as I ground down, taking him deeper than I ever had before. "Will!" I cried out. "Oh, God, I'm so close."

His teeth found the sensitive spot just under my ear and bit, like the animal he said he was. The hand around my back slipped down to grab my ass hard enough to leave bruises.

"Come with me, baby," he ordered as his hips moved mercilessly. "Let go, Lil. *Now.*"

The finger on my clit pressed down and rubbed furiously at the same time that Will rammed upward. He repeated the action, once, twice, and then on the third, I shattered.

"OhGodohGodohGodohGodohGodohGodI'mcomingWillplease-babypleaseIcan't*Oooooooohhhhhhhhhh*!"

The words flowed, a jumbled, alien song of deliverance and pleasure that had never sounded so beautiful or so harsh. Will groaned into my shoulder, biting hard enough that I was sure there would be marks as he pumped out his orgasm while he kept me in a vise-lock against his chest. He was big enough that I could feel him pulsing within me, a rhythm that matched my own heartbeat vibrating through my body.

And then finally, together, we came down from our beautiful incomprehension. Our breaths mingled as we both sought the kiss that would temper the ferocity of the moment before—a kiss that spoke not just of passion and desire, but also of the other, more potent emotion that neither of us had the guts to say. Not this soon. Not quite yet.

But it echoed through the back of my mind just the same while Will savored my mouth, my cheeks, my entire face. The word echoed, like it was a part of the primal rhythm we had just established, one that would never completely fade away.

The word was there, though I wasn't quite ready to hear it.

Wasn't I?

I closed my eyes and thought it to myself.

Love.

CHAPTER TWENTY-SEVEN

When I woke up, the light of the newly risen sun was glowing through a thick layer of fog still hovering over the lake's surface. Everything was socked in. I frowned. Although that meant it wouldn't be terribly hot for the race this morning, I wasn't too excited about swimming through fog so thick I couldn't see the person next to me.

The sheets stirred beside me, and I rolled over with a smile. Will had actually slept in (if you could say that five thirty was sleeping in), stretched out, long and tan beside me. Instead of curling against his lean muscle the way I had been getting dangerously used to for the past few weeks, I took a moment just to observe him.

He really was beautiful. His hair, long pulled from its typical knot at the top of his head, spilled over the pillowcase, an unruly mass of about five different shades of gold. Only a little bit of his scruff had regrown overnight, so I could still enjoy the clean lines of his jaw and cheekbones, razor-edged even in his sleep. His full lips pouted slightly while he slept, almost like he was still begging for the kisses he had taken again and again before we had both fallen into a dazed slumber.

But there wouldn't be any more of those today. I had a race. More than a race. A reclamation. It had been a simple goal, but one to work for until I could wrap my head around the larger questions, the ones that really mattered. And then there were a few more questions that needed to be answered: namely, what did the future hold for my mother and me?

Not wanting to wake him, I slid cautiously out of the bed and started putting on the gear I had set out the night before: the old triathlon suit I'd dragged out of storage and a pair of flip-flops. I'd packed everything else into the race day bag a week before.

"You're awake."

I zipped up the front of my suit and turned around. "Yeah. Call for the race is at six thirty. I doubt there will be big lines, but I want to get there first to get my stuff set up."

Will toppled out of bed, doing little to cover his naked body. He caught me ogling him and grinned. "You know, you don't *have* to do this race."

"Are you already trying to talk me into underperforming in my life to please you?" I joked after accepting his warm kiss.

Will frowned. "Of course not." He glanced behind me at the bag. "You look ready to go."

"I was just going to grab some breakfast at the house before I head back to the inn. You can stay here and sleep if you want."

Will just tugged on his jeans—without anything under them, as it was—and rolled his eyes when he caught me ogling. "Give me a second, Lil. I'll be right behind you."

We walked up to the main house and into the kitchen, where I went about making some coffee for Will (and Mama when she was up for the day) and grabbing a small breakfast for myself.

"That's all you're going to have?" Will asked, looking skeptically at the small bowl of oatmeal I set out.

I shrugged as I tucked in to my food. "I don't need much. Otherwise I'll feel sick later."

Will examined the oatmeal. "I'll make sure I have a couple of extra protein bars for you when we meet up for the run."

I swallowed my bite. "You don't really have to do the run with me, you know. That's where it will be really crowded, especially at the end when we get to the finish line. A lot of people will probably have friends and family race the last bit with them, not to mention the well-wishers. If you want to stay at your house, I can meet you there later."

"I'm coming, Maggie," Will said before taking a measured sip of his coffee. "Important to you?" He pointed at me. "Important to me." He pointed back to himself. "Enough said."

I opened my mouth to respond. I wasn't used to this—a man actually caring enough about me to put aside his own comforts. Show up. Be there. But before I could express my gratitude, a chime interrupted me—a text message from my phone.

Will flinched at the sound, like he'd never heard a basic text chime before. When I made no move to answer it, he just closed his eyes and exhaled.

"You'd better get that," he said as he pushed off his seat. "I need to use the bathroom anyway."

I nodded absently as he left. I unlocked my phone, opening up the message.

Good luck on the race today, Flower. I'll be rooting for you. And then we're going home.

I stared at the text for a very, very long time. The number was unknown, but only one person in the world had ever called me "Flower." And he had just been released from a minimum-security state penitentiary. With a potentially large grudge.

I shuddered and closed my eyes. *Relax, Maggie. It's going to be fine.*

"What's wrong?"

When I looked up, he must have seen something in my face, because immediately, Will returned to his stool at the counter and tugged me between his legs.

"Who was that, Lil?"

"N-no one," I said closing my eyes against the stutter that would *not* disappear completely. The phone lay innocuously on the countertop, but when I looked at him, Will was glaring at it.

"Maggie." He enunciated my name clearly. "You look like a ghost. Who the fuck was that?"

When I didn't answer, Will grabbed the phone off the counter and stood up as he tried to look at the screen. If I hadn't already been upset, I might have laughed. From the way he was using it, it seemed like Will hadn't used a cell phone for a very long time.

"Hey!" I yelped, jumping up. "That's my phone! Give it the fuck back!"

"How do you even open this thing?" Will demanded, turning his broad back on me while he swiped his thumb again and again across the screen.

"It's an iPhone, you goon. They've updated their technology since you threw yours off a pier."

I reached around and snatched it back, but there was no dissuading him.

"Maggie," Will said again. He opened his mouth like he wanted to argue, then shut it, apparently to try another tactic.

"It's nothing," I pleaded as I moved to the other side of the kitchen. I set the phone on the counter and made a big show of starting the dishes.

"Maggie."

"Please. Will, can you just let it go?"

There was a long silence while I ran a sink of soapy water. Then he said the last thing I expected.

"I love you, Lil."

I shut the water off and looked up. "What?"

Will smiled—not the kind of smile that was mischievous or vulnerable, but one that was open and, well, loving. A smile that was for me.

"I love you," he repeated. "Do you love me too?"

The question was so simple. So disarmingly direct. Since I'd met him, Will had been cagey and secretive, offering pieces of his past, of himself to me in crumbs that left me starving for more, and often frustrated when no more was offered.

But here he was, putting his trump card on the table, and asking for mine in return.

And, to my additional surprise, I found I had absolutely no problem giving it.

I loved him. Of course I loved him, though the thought, the word, caught me off guard. I'd loved him a long time before it had occurred to me that I could. It didn't matter that we still had so much to learn about each other. It didn't matter that we were both clearly damaged people with a mountain's worth of baggage. Will made me sing in ways I never thought would be possible again—both literally and metaphorically. He played my body like it was an instrument he'd studied his entire life, not because of the physical connection, but because when we were together, I didn't feel like I was Maggie Sharp or Lily pad or Margaret or anything else. With Will, I was my purest song, a voice that sang much more than a simple melody.

"Yes," I said without hesitation. "I love you too, Will."

Our eyes were glued to one another, locked in a tight bond that only comes from moments like these: moments where you truly bare your soul. Will leaned across the counter, set his big hands atop mine, over my phone, my bent fingers, and pulled me forward. His green eyes reflected the glassy surface of the lake outside—full of light and fathomlessly deep.

"So," he murmured as he bent close enough to kiss me. "Here we are."

His mouth hovered over mine, but didn't touch.

"Will," I murmured, transfixed. He smelled of coffee, sun, water. My Will. The message and the race seemed extremely unimportant. Forgettable, even.

"Maggie."

"You should kiss me now."

The smiled widened. "Okay, then."

When his lips touched mine, it didn't matter that it was almost six in the morning. That there was a mildly threatening text on my phone. Or any of the other myriad problems we still had to deal with.

All that mattered was this kiss, this love. This moment.

That was what Will did to me.

"Okay?" he asked a minute later after he pulled back, looking like he was anything but as he adjusted the front of his pants.

I sighed, fully content. My eyes clenched against the waves of emotions rocking through me. I felt solid and strong, yet also like I could crumble. It was intoxicating. Terrifying. Electrifying.

Slowly, my body came back to me.

"Yeah," I said. "I am."

"Good. Now open your phone and show me the text."

My eyes shot open. "What?"

Will smirked. "Do it, Maggie."

"You told me you loved me so I would show you my *phone*?!" I shrieked in a half whisper, not wanting to wake up Mama. "You asshole!"

Will quirked a blond brow. "Yeah, but I'm an asshole who loves you. And I deserve to know who the fuck is making my woman look like a goddamn sheet. Just show me."

I swallowed. "It's—it's nothing." But I was all out of excuses. I unlocked the phone and handed it to him, feeling like a guilty child while he read the message for what seemed like an hour.

At first he didn't say anything after he set the phone back on the counter, just rubbed his chin, which was still only lightly covered with gold stubble.

"Your ex?" he said finally.

I nodded. "I—I think so."

"I'm assuming his real name isn't 'Unknown.'"

I shook my head. "I wish I didn't know him. Theodore del Conte is what's on his birth certificate."

Will started at the name, and his eyes flew open. "Your ex-boyfriend is Theo del Conte? The producer's son?"

I frowned. "You know him?"

Will swallowed. "I worked in the entertainment industry in New York, Maggie. Max del Conte owns one of the largest conglomerates in the world, including a big studio. So yeah, I know who Theo del Conte is. He's a spoiled prick who treats everyone like shit. What was someone like *you* doing with him?"

He looked at me strangely, almost like he was trying to see something I was hiding.

I gulped. So many people had asked me that over the last year, since Theo and I had split so violently, and I'd never had a good answer for it. It was hard to explain—the way his attentions in the beginning had been so overt, almost naive in their over-the-topness, how addictive it had felt, for the first time in my life, to be the center of someone's life. To be told, without reservation, that I was beautiful. Adorable. Brilliant. Worth loving.

And then it was even harder to explain how that effusive praise had devolved, but gradually, slightly. First accompanied by minor criticisms that only undercut my sense of self so much to hurt, but never so much he couldn't deny the effects. I'd be even more beautiful if I got a nose job. I'd be close to perfect if my hair was straightened or if I just did a few more lunges. And all of it, *all* of it, was offered under the pretense of grooming me for my future music career, which he knew drove just about everything I did.

All I wanted in the world was to share my music, and while I wasn't dating Theo for his connections, I'd have been lying if I said the carrot of his father's influence wasn't attractive. But I wasn't ready, he always told me. He wanted to give my music to his father. He wanted to see me soar. And that was how he justified all of his insidious critiques for as long as he did—he was just getting me to a place where I'd be heard.

Finally, though, I began to see his bullshit for what it was. I'd speak out when he put me down, sometimes even in front of people. The first time I did that was also the first time he slapped me across the face, hard enough to see stars. I didn't stop, though, and neither did he, not until I gave him what he wanted: my obedience. My acquiescence. This continued for months, years, until finally, I refused completely. And that was the day I paid for it with nearly everything.

Will remained still and unwavering while I explained it all to him as best I could. His eyes showed none of the usual suspects that generally made me clam up when I had to do this: there was no pity. No disgust.

At the end, just like the last time I told the story, he looked like he wanted to punch someone—probably Theo—but I'd take that over pity any day.

"So he's the one who…"

"Raped me." There is was again. Maybe one day the word wouldn't cut quite so much, but I wasn't counting on it. I was already starting to understand that those traumas never completely die. "When I refused to marry him."

Will closed his eyes, like he was trying to get control of himself.

"Maggie," he said slowly. "You have to go to the police with this. It's a violation of his parole, isn't it?"

Miserably, I nodded. "It is. It's just…they haven't always been that much help."

Will frowned. "How so?"

Again, it was one of those things that was hard to explain. The way it had taken not once, twice, but at least five different reports of Theo's abuse until the NYPD would even file an official report about it. The way I was consistently questioned about whatever I had done to provoke his behavior. What had I worn? What had I said?

How was it my fault?

While I tried to recount those events to Will, I could see clearly how the next conversation with them would go.

I'll ask you again, ma'am. Are you sure *you didn't contact him in any way?*

Why would he be contacting you now? You must have done something.

Sure, sure. We'll look into it.

And nothing would happen.

Will listened patiently, again without any sign of judgment, until I finished. He placed his hands flat on the counter, like he was bracing himself against a strong wind, and then at the end, exhaled through his teeth for a long time.

"Do you think he's here?"

I folded my hands together. "I don't know. He may not even remember where I'm from, exactly. It's not like we ever came here to visit Mama, and he wouldn't have had a reason to have the address otherwise. I just…the race…how does he know?"

Will shook his head. "I don't know, Lil. But you're not alone. And he can't leave the state, even if he's just been released."

I exhaled. I hoped to God that was true.

"Okay, then. First," he said while he pulled at his hair. "You're going to do your race and kick ass. This fucker is three thousand miles away. He's not going to be here any time soon. And when you're done"—he bent down on the counter so he was eye to eye with me—"you're going to call the NYPD and report this shit. It's harassment, baby. He can't get away with it."

I stared at my hands. My heart was beating harder than it did when I ran, and I could feel sweat building in my palms. "I—I c-can't do this again with him. You don't understand. The last year of my life was..."

Just the thought was terrifying. My stutter emerged, as strong as ever, and I closed my eyes against the deluge of fear that threatened to wash over me.

For the last few months, I'd had a break, knowing that the biggest threat in my life was safely behind bars. And even when I'd discovered he was out, it had been easy to shove it aside for a few more weeks, ignore the texts, the warning signs. I was far away from New York, safe in Will's arms, in the house where I'd grown up.

But I couldn't ignore it anymore.

Will placed a hand over mine. His was so much bigger—his wide, warm palm almost more like a paw. His entire presence enveloped me, and my heart rate slowed. Until I looked up and saw the fear in his eyes.

"I'll be there with you," he said slowly. "You're not alone in this, Lil. I promise. But you need to call the police for another reason, too."

"What's that?"

"Because if he comes within fifty fucking feet of you, I'll kill him myself."

I watched, waited, while the fear and worry I saw in those green depths slowly receded. Receded, but never quite disappeared, and were replaced with a fierceness that I didn't quite know what to make of.

And suddenly, I couldn't stand having anything in between us. Will watched with amusement as I hopped up on the counter and scrambled across until I could sit in front of him, wrap my legs around his waist, and pull him flush to me.

"Thank you," I said as I buried my face in his strong, broad chest.

Clearly stunned, Will finally wrapped his arms around me, holding me to him. "For what?" he asked into my hair.

I laid my cheek against his heart, closing my eyes as the strong, steady beat of it thumped. "For being here. For being on my team. For being you."

Will was silent, breathing in through the curly mess that must have tickled his nose like crazy. Then he exhaled again. "I'm here," was all he said.

We stayed like that for a long time, until both of our heart rates returned to normal. Outside the windows, the waters of the lake lapped at its edges, as hypnotic and calming as Will's presence. And slowly, slowly, the facts of what I needed to do didn't seem scary. It was just something else to take care of. My life was still my own. And it was time to live it.

CHAPTER TWENTY-EIGHT

"You ready?" Will asked next to me.

We stood together at the water's edge, where the lake met the wide lawn that spread out from the Forster Inn.

The Forsters' campaign had been successful—there were at least a hundred people here to compete in the first ever Newman Lake Triathlon. Their inn, not to mention vacation houses all around the lake and adjoining areas, was filled to capacity with the competitors and their families. The public beach on Muzzy Cove was jammed with people, all milling about in anticipation of the race.

I'd gotten there early, set up my bike and running equipment at the designated transition points around the inn, and then found a quiet place by the water to wait with Will for the race to start. I pulled one foot against my butt, stretching out my quad muscle before switching to the other side.

"Ready as I'll ever be," I said. "It's just an Olympic-length. Iron Mans are way worse. I'll be fine."

"'Just an Olympic.' Yeah, that sounds completely tame, Lil."

"The swim isn't even a mile, the bike ride is less than a lap around the lake, and we ran ten miles last week together. The triathlon length is only six point two."

Will did not look convinced as he glanced covertly around the crowd. I was still amazed he had even come down to the start with me, considering how many people were huddled by the water. There was still a thin layer of fog settled over the lake, which was chilled through and gray. Will had his hoodie pulled up over a baseball cap, the brim shadowing a pair of aviator sunglasses. He was the only person in the crowd wearing sunglasses in this weather, but no matter how many times I teased him about them, he wouldn't take them off.

"You should go home and change into all black," I said. "Then we could be Spy vs. Spy."

Will pulled his sunglasses down briefly to give me a dirty look. "You're hilarious, you know that?"

I shrugged and grinned. "Not as hilarious as you, Inspector Gadget."

"Ha. Ha. Ha."

"Someone needs to give you a hard time, Columbo," I said, switching legs. "Or should I call you Iceman? Because of the aviators, get it?" I turned my face up to the sky and started singing "Highway to the Danger Zone."

Will just rolled his eyes and pretended to look annoyed. It only made me sing louder. He didn't protest, though, like he understood that half of this act was coming out of the nervous energy I had coursing through me. Nerves for the race, for which I'd only had a month to train and hadn't practiced at *all* for the transitions. Nerves because of Theo's messages and what they might mean. Nerves for whatever we were going to do about my mother after this was all over.

"Do you need help writing the number, hon?"

Will started and shoved the sunglasses back up his nose. Then he turned to Linda, who was holding out a permanent marker for me to write my number on my arm and leg.

"Upper right calf and right shoulder, they're saying, sweetie." She nodded at Will, though she was visibly cool. "Hello, there."

"I'll take care of it." Will took the proffered marker and squatted down to write on my leg. "What's her race number?"

"Eighty-eight," Linda said, folding her arms while she watched. "Ellie coming to the race today, Maggie?"

"N-no," I said, unable to stop the stutter when Will's broad hand wrapped around my ankle while he wrote with the other. I shivered. Even when I had a stomach full of nerves, his touch didn't fail to excite me. It was ridiculous I ever tried to fight it.

"It's a b-bit early for her schedule," I managed to get out.

Linda nodded knowingly. "Ah. Well, no surprise there."

Will's hand drifted up my leg, hip, and arm as he stood to write the number on my shoulder. I blushed.

"Something on your mind, Lil?" he murmured with a smirk.

"I take it back about Iceman in those stupid glasses," I retorted, though I couldn't shake the goose bumps his fingers left in their wake. "You look like Goose."

"Goose was the best one. Should I serenade you later?" Will grinned. "Have you lost that lovin' feeling?"

I rolled my eyes, then tossed the marker back to Linda, who was now watching us with a smile on her face as well.

"'You never close your eyes anymore when I kiss your lips…'" Will continued singing until Linda walked away chuckling. He wasn't lying when he said he was tone-deaf.

I tried to smack his shoulder, but he just pulled me close and laid a thick kiss on said lips.

"You closed your eyes for that one," he said when he was done.

"You're trouble," I said.

"It's your fault. You look hot in that damn cat suit. You wore white just to drive me crazy, didn't you?"

Immediately, I looked down, but my nipples were nowhere in sight—nor would they be. This thing was thick.

"You think you're *so* funny, Baker. Let's see what happens when I get you alone."

"Hey, I had to get one good dig in there."

I rolled my eyes. "Get out of here. I'll meet you on the road after the second transition."

But Will paused for a second. "Listen, I…" He pulled meditatively at his messy knot. "After the race, can we get out of here for a few hours? You think your mom would be all right by herself?"

I frowned. "Probably. Why?"

He nodded. "Yeah. I just…there are some things I want to talk to you about. I don't know…I think better when I'm not around people, you know? It's nothing bad. I just want to be honest with you. About my family. Some other things in my past. Cards on the table, all right?"

Slowly, I nodded. I had a few cards he should know about too. He had seen most of mine, but there were always a few others that probably needed to be shown.

Like the fact that you are fucking in love with the man and want to have his babies.

Well, he knew half of it, I supposed.

"Sure," I said. "We'll make it a date."

Will relaxed, then pulled me close one last time. I tipped my face up for a kiss. Will hummed against my lips while he stroked my face.

"So beautiful," he murmured. "So crazy fucking beautiful." His tongue twisted sweetly with mine for another second before he let me go with a resigned sigh. "All right. Finish your warm-up. I'll meet you here for the last leg, Lily pad. Don't get tangled."

I WAS NEVER GOING to win the race, but I was still surprised by how much it took out of me after not racing at all for close to eight years. Despite training for the last month, I was struggling to keep up with the group by the end of the swim, and by the end of the bike portion, I was completely dreading the six-mile loop I still had to run until it was finished.

The thought of quitting actually crossed my mind as I started jogging down the road from the transition site. I had changed into my running shoes and a baseball cap that protected me from the glare of the sun now that the cloud cover was starting to burn off. The sun was out in force, probably eighty degrees, which felt more like ninety on the pavement.

"Why am I doing this again?" I wondered as I started up the hill on the far side of Muzzy Cove.

"Because you need to."

I practically jumped at the sound of Will's voice, answering the question I hadn't realized I'd spoken aloud.

"Oh my God!" I cried, holding a hand to my heart. "Where did you come from?"

Will shrugged. "I figured I'd wait for you on the track instead of at the transition site. It was easier if I stayed out of the way. How're you doing, babe?"

I shook my head, unable to speak very well. I didn't have the breath to talk while I ran, and I still was hoping for a half-decent time.

So we just jogged quietly together, mile after mile until we rounded the hill and began the downward descent toward the inn.

Weird things happen at the end of a race. Exercise is strangely cathartic, even for the most intense athletes. It brings up emotions you didn't know you were feeling, makes you come to terms with issues you didn't know you had.

By the end of the swim, my muscles were burning. By the end of the bike ride, I was a mental mess. And now, coming to the end of the six-mile run, my imagination was definitely getting the better of me. Because somehow, in the last two and a half hours, I'd convinced myself that not only had my ex-boyfriend sent that text to mess with me, but that he was also here.

"Lily?" Will's voice managed to cut through the cloud of doubt and paranoia clouding my head. "What's wrong?"

"I just…"

Only one mile left in this stupid race, and I was already on the verge of tears. Theo was waiting for me at the inn. I just knew it. We were on the downhill trek that meandered around the cliffs that rose above Muzzy Cove. Through the trees here and there I could spot the inn below, with the masses of people that had gathered for the afternoon barbecue and to welcome back the competitors.

Will jogged ahead so he could turn around and face me, stepping lightly backwards. He had changed into running gear since I last saw him, though he still wore the baseball hat and the sunglasses, which no longer looked out of place because the sun was actually peeking through the clouds.

"You can do this, baby," he cheered me on. "Come on, you're almost there."

"No," I whimpered, my face in my hands. "I can't. Will—he's waiting for me. I need to go home."

"What?" Will asked. He looked around like he expected to see someone pop out of the trees. "Where is he?"

I didn't answer.

We rounded a corner, and I stopped. Several runners passed with curious looks at us, but none stopped. At the bottom of the hill, there was an even larger crowd than before. But I barely had time to wonder how the Forsters had managed to get this kind of press coverage for such a small event before I swore I saw something else that put the fear of God back in me. It was barely anything. A face.

Black hair that shone in the mid-morning sun like the polished marble of his floors. Bright blue eyes that twinkled, brilliant as the summer sky above, sharp as the knife I kept in my purse. A mouth pressed into a firm line except for a wicked curve on one side.

Theodore Scott del Conte. Out of prison. Flouting his parole. Waiting for me.

I wobbled on the side of the road, ignoring the way my muscles burned in response to the sudden shift.

"Hey. What's going on?"

Will stopped beside me, turned toward me and shielded me from the curious looks of the other runners who jogged by.

I pointed a shaky finger toward the crowd. "I s-saw him. Theo. I—in the back of the crowd. Will, he's *here*!"

I tried to keep my voice low, but there was no keeping the shakes away. Will stroked my shoulders, willing me to calm with his touch.

"Where?" he asked. "Point to where you see him. We'll go down there and tell the cops that are watching the crowd."

I looked over his shoulder, but now the face was gone. I scanned the crowd, which was far enough away that I couldn't actually make out each individual face. *Okay,* I thought to myself. *So maybe you imagined it.*

I shook my head. I was hungry. Tired. Between the swim, the ride, and now the end of a half marathon, I was about ready to drop. I was still worried about the texts I'd been getting. He wasn't here. He couldn't be here. It wasn't possible.

"It's...okay," I said as I gulped a few more breaths, leaning into Will's touch. I focused instead on his strong, solid presence. The way sweat gleamed over his smooth expanse of muscle. The gruff kindness that couldn't quite be masked, try as he might.

He took off his sunglasses so I could see him clearly.

"Listen," he said. "You're tired. I see it, Lil. But I'm here with you. We got this. Together."

Slowly, I nodded. I wanted nothing more than to stop. But he was right. I had to finish this, finish *something*. I'd been chasing more than just him all summer, had started this whole process to get back in touch with the parts of myself that Theo hadn't messed up during our time together. And if I stopped now for fear of his specter, all of that progress would be ruined.

Well. To hell with that.

"O-okay," I said after swallowing a bit of the water Will offered. "Let's go."

Will nodded, and we started jogging around the corner, following a stream of runners all making their way down the final half mile to the inn. Everyone was picking up their pace, cheered by the prospect of the end. Through the trees, I could hear the sound of the people waiting to greet the athletes, the beginning of Michael Grady's band starting a set to celebrate, the hum of people jumping back in the water to cool off.

"You got this, baby," Will said as I started to jog faster. "Half a mile to go. Get it."

I concentrated on my breathing, on putting one foot in front of the other. In through the nose, out through the mouth. Use my diaphragm, not my chest. Heel to toe, even steps. I was almost there.

There was a rustle in the crowd as we turned around the final corner, looking down the short stretch toward the gathering at the base of the hill.

But the crowd looked different now that it was in focus. It wasn't just the excitement of the end of the race that filled the air. There was a large pocket of the group, all bunched close to the finish line that was clearly filled with photographers. Their cameras weren't the kind that amateurs might purchase for taking pictures of sunsets and vacations. They were the big kind you might see in a press box at a football game, or in the paparazzi line at a movie premiere. Behind the jostling mass of lenses were several news vans, with cameramen and reporters speaking into microphones while kids made bunny ears behind them. There was a hum in the crowd that wasn't just about the end of the race. They were waiting for something. Something big.

All at once, the lenses turned our way, and while I couldn't see exactly who was moving whom, the sudden shift in the crowd toward us was noticeable. I frowned, but continued down the hill, realizing only a few steps later that I was alone.

I turned around to find Will frozen under a large pine tree. As the last few runners ran by, I walked back to him. When he pulled off his sunglasses, now he was the one who looked like he was about to pass out.

"Will? What's wrong?"

But for once, he couldn't look at me, his eyes instead trained directly ahead—at the odd mob of cameramen and reporters elbowing their way through the runners who had finished. Some of them were starting to jog toward us up the hill, huffing as they carried their heavy equipment. A few even pointed in our direction.

"Who—who are they?" I asked, unable to keep the warble out of my voice. My chest was pounding with something approximating dread—that same feeling you have when you know something terrible is about to happen. You just don't know what.

Maybe even then, I knew deep down just who Will Baker really was. There had always been something about him that seemed a little otherworldly and larger than life. He tried the best he could to mask it with overgrown hair, grungy clothes, and a beat-up car. But Will Baker couldn't hide his shine.

In that moment, all I felt was the pure, unadulterated panic coursing through the veins of the man I loved as he took a step backward, then another, up the hill.

"Will." I reached out, trying and failing to take his hand as he continued to back away.

Every muscle in his beautiful body was tensed, like an animal ready to bolt. His glance pinballed between the oncoming cameramen and me, flickering between us at breakneck speed.

"I...God...Maggie, I'm so sorry," he said with a voice cracked in fear.

"For what?"

Even from several feet away at this point, I could see the way his body vibrated from head to toe.

"So fucking sorry," he repeated, in a voice that was barely audible above the crowd closing in. And then, with one last sorrowful look, he turned and took off through the trees.

"What the hell..." I murmured as I turned back to the crowd. I couldn't have told you why, but everything in me screamed to turn around, go back the way I had come.

But my muscles ached. I wanted to lie down. I needed to finish the run, and then I could get a ride, or walk, if need be, back to my house to shower, change, and then check up on Will.

The cameras were closer now, but past them, I could see the table of water bottles they were handing out to participants. So instead of following my instincts and Will into the forest, I continued running toward the inn.

"Hey, that's her!" shouted one of the cameramen as I approached. "That's Maggie Sharp!"

"Maggie!"

"Margaret!"

My name was volleyed through the crowd, and suddenly I found myself swarmed with photographers and reporters.

"Hey!" I shouted, pushing them away when several reached out to touch my arms or grab my hands. "What the hell?!"

But there were no apologies, and definitely no space.

"Are you dating Fitz Baker?"

"Are you sleeping together?"

"When did you find him?"

"Have you known he was here the whole time?"

"When did you know he was alive?"

"Did you help him fake his death?"

"Where's Fitz, Maggie?"

"*What* are you talking about?!" I shrieked, shoving another photographer away. I looked around frantically for some kind of shelter. Where was Will? What was going on? *Who the hell was Fitz*?

But instead of the person I so desperately needed in that moment,

Lucas's solid form barreled through the crowd, cutting a path for his mother behind him.

"Move!" he barked at the photographers and pushed them aside as Linda wrapped an arm around my shoulders.

"Are you okay?" she asked as she ushered me into the inn and locked the door behind her.

I followed her past some of the guests milling in the living room; several looked up and pointed when I passed.

We went into the empty kitchen, where Linda locked the door, and Lucas rummaged for a bottle of water from the fridge.

"We're going to have to send everyone home," Linda said bitterly. "Maybe even cancel the banquet tonight! They are absolutely vicious, and it's not good for the guests. Oh, honey. Did you know this was going to happen?"

"Wha-what are you talking about?" I stuttered after I guzzled half the bottle of water. My entire body was shaking, full of terror I *still* didn't understand. "What in the hell is going on?"

"See, Mom?" Lucas said as he set his hat on the counter. "I told you she didn't know. He fooled her just like he fooled everyone else, the lying sack of shi—"

"Lucas, there's no need for that kind of talk," Linda admonished him.

She took a seat next to me at the counter and picked up the remote to the small TV mounted on one wall. The screen blared onto some sort of morning talk show. A picture of me and Will—the one taken at the barbecue just the other night—flashed across the screen.

"Here, honey," Linda said as she turned up the volume. "You should probably watch this."

I plopped onto one of the stools and fell forward onto the counter, transfixed as I listened to the overdone faces on the television talking to one another. About me. About Will. Except…it wasn't Will at all. Was it?

"It's the biggest news of the decade," the lady was saying. "This news is everywhere—absolutely everywhere. Fitz Baker, who was believed to have died off the coast of Maine only four years ago, has been discovered alive and well in a tiny town in Eastern Washington."

"If you're just tuning in, we've got four little words for you, ladies," the male host continued. "Fitz Baker is alive."

Another series of pictures flashed across the screen, and if I hadn't already been sitting down, I would have fallen over. They were of Will, but an incredibly different, un-Will-like Will that I wouldn't have recognized if they hadn't already said who he was.

He was still tall, of course, with the same tanned skin, penetrating green eyes, and broad shoulders I now knew intimately. But in one photo, that broad body was covered by an elegant tuxedo while he accepted some sort of award. In another, he wore a beautifully tailored suit while posing on what looked like a red carpet. The tangled blond hair that I had yanked so hard only last night was shorn and combed to the side. His face was clean, completely shaved, without even stubble, revealing an impossibly sharp jawline that was clenched hard enough to reveal a thin vein in the side of his neck and dimples so deep they looked like they'd been pressed in by two fingers. But though the man in the pictures was smiling in a way I had *never* seen Will smile—bright, incandescent—the rest of him was incredibly tense, and his eyes reflected clear misery.

"Apparently, he's been living out there, under the radar, for the past four years. No one even knew it was him!" said the blonde woman.

"How is that even possible?" asked the man with skin that was slightly orange. "How could someone as famous as Fitz Baker just fly under the radar for *four years* without being spotted? I don't believe it. I just don't believe it."

"You'll believe it when you take a look at this, Pat," said the woman. "He looks positively feral."

A picture flashed across the screen, and I sat up immediately when I caught a look at it.

It was Will. And me. Just last night, when we were snuggled together by the fire.

"Shit," Lucas muttered as he caught sight of the photo. We both knew who had taken it.

To me, Will didn't look feral at all. Compared to when I first met him, he looked positively dapper. His long hair was pulled back, and his beard, which he usually kept grown out to an inch or two below his chin, had been shorn also, close to his face. I recognized it now for the compromise it was—he knew I wanted to see him clean-shaven, while he preferred a full beard.

Now I knew why.

"Who do you think the girl is?" wondered Pat as he leered at a copy of the photo. "She's a looker, isn't she?"

"She's certainly...different," sniffed the woman. "I mean, poor Amelia, am I right?"

"Oh, Stacy, you're so *bad*," admonished Pat. "Clearly he's moved on from her by now."

"Well, wouldn't *you* want to know if your fiancé had disappeared into the woods?" Stacy asked. "The poor girl was absolutely devastated. I heard she paid for private search parties to sail up and down the coast-lines for weeks and weeks after they called it off."

"Yes, but we all know that relationship was on its way out, of course. They weren't engaged anymore at that point," Pat said. "If it were me, after what she did to him, I'd have said good riddance too."

Yet another picture flashed across the screen. One I stared at in horror as I realized it was a very young Will—or Fitz, or whatever his name was—walking down the street with a very, very beautiful woman whom I recognized as Amelia Craig, a well-known actress who, at least in this picture, had a very big diamond on her left ring finger. This picture had clearly been taken on the street, by photographers like the ones outside. The two of them were tense, unsmiling, and even under their sunglasses, you could see the anger and fear simmering just below his seemingly calm demeanor.

Still, miserable or not, he looked like a movie star. Which, I was slowly realizing, was exactly what he was.

Almost all the blood flowed out of my head at once. I slumped across the counter while Linda rubbed my back. *Oh, God*. What the hell was happening?

"So now the question is," Stacy was asking the simpering Pat. "What really happened? He clearly didn't die in that boating accident. So, what happened?

"What *really* happened to Fitz Baker?"

CHAPTER TWENTY-NINE

Splat.

My footsteps fell heavy on the ground, sending water in all directions as I jogged down the seventy-three steps that led down the hill to my mother's house. I felt like I was falling, lost in an avalanche, tumbling down the hill with no control.

The sudden summer storm had arrived moments before, opening with thunder and gushing torrents everywhere. It fit, really—in the space of a few minutes, my own life had felt like it was gushing open, full of talk, of people, of stares, of questions. Two seconds after the newscasters had uttered their questions, I had one of my own:

Who in the *fuck* was "Fitz Baker"?

Before leaving, I had sat in the Forsters' kitchen, slowly numbing, turning the question over in my mind again and again, until Lucas forced me to drink some orange juice before I passed out. Then he stayed with me, not saying a word, just keeping me company while I continued to process. Continued to figure out…what next?

There was a bang at the entrance. A nasty knock, followed by a dozen more, and incomprehensible shouting. The guests in the lobby were silent, their glances ricocheting between me and the knocking. But before anyone could answer them, the big double doors of the inn flew open, and at least twenty different people carrying cameras, microphones, and notepads toppled inside, filling the tiny lobby with chaos.

They found me almost immediately. One tripped and had to roll to the side to avoid being trampled by the others.

"Maggie!" they shouted. "Maggie, did you know? Maggie, where's Fitz? Come on, Maggie, give us a smile!"

"Will." I turned to the Forsters. I couldn't feel my knees. I couldn't feel anything. "Where's Will?"

But Lucas just shook his head, his eyes wide, stunned in the litter of flashes, and Don, who had come in for a coffee refill, had basically the same expression as his son.

"Lucas! Don!" Linda's sharp voice jerked the men out of their daze. "Get the poor girl out of here!"

With remarkable presence of mind, Linda sprang to the front door and locked it, while Don barred the entrance to the kitchen as Lucas shepherded me out the back and into his truck.

"I'm guessing you've got a five-minute head start," he said as he started it up. "Maybe ten if we can get out early enough that no one follows. You're lucky—Ellie's place is kind of hard to find."

And so, for the second time in just over a month, I was on the run. It was the last thing I ever thought I'd be running from, but here I was, scrambling down the side of the hill while Lucas waited in the truck up top. I'd pack up whatever I could as quickly as I could, and he'd take me away from the madness until his parents gave word that the cameras and reporters—whoever they were—had left. Then I could retrieve my car and go…somewhere.

It wasn't much of a plan, but it was the only one we had to get away from the chaos. For now.

For eight years, I'd chased this kind of attention, the kind that had swarmed me at the Forsters' house. I'd moved to New York with dreams of making it big. Hopes that one day, I'd catch my break and be allowed to play my music in front of the world, and they'd all sing along with me.

What a fool I was.

Flower. The word echoed through my mind, reminding me in my misery of my tormenter, the man who had ruined my chances at that future. The man whom I thought had ruined me.

And then I'd met Will.

Intense.

Evasive.

Just as damaged as me.

His combination of strength and vulnerability had captivated me from the start, even when I was furious at him (which happened a lot). Little by little—or maybe it was all at once—we had fallen for each other, until just a month after I arrived back in this place, I found something resembling hope that my future might belong to me after all.

Now my brain was fogged over with the deception. The knowledge that for four weeks, I hadn't been falling in love with a hermit, a self-banished recluse who simply preferred to be away from others because of some strange phobia of crowds. It all made sense now. Every time he ran away. Every time he shouted "pine cone." Unbeknownst to me, I'd been falling in love with one of the most famous faces in the world, hidden from me and everyone else behind a thick beard and a wild riot of blond hair.

Not just a writer.

Not just a neighbor.

A secret freaking movie star who had faked his death to escape the trappings of fame.

And idiot that I was, I hadn't sensed a thing.

I still couldn't see straight. The flashes from the wall of cameras that had been waiting for me when I finished the triathlon still made me see stars, even in this horrific weather. I practically had to feel my way down the last steep flight, terrified that with one misstep, I might go toppling down the deck and break my arm.

"Maggie!" my mother's voice croaked from another night of alcohol-fueled dreams through the open screen door as I dashed by. "Maggie Mae, are you all right?"

I ignored her, beelining for the outdoor shower on the other side of the house. I didn't want to see her. I didn't want to see anyone right now. I had just had my heart split open in front of a hoard of cameras, had my heartbreak and gullibility broadcast across the entire world.

I could still see them—Lucas, Jenna, Katie, and their parents, Linda and Don, circled around me in the kitchen of their inn while guests peeked through the swinging doors. Everyone watching me while I watched the vapid, surgically enhanced faces on the television screen gossip about the fact that the man I had been seeing, the man I had fallen desperately in love with within the span of only a few weeks…wasn't that man at all.

There was no Will. There was only Fitz Baker. Playboy. Actor. Drug Addict. Fiancé.

Once in the shower, I unzipped the front of my triathlon suit and yanked the straps over my arms, eager to shed the evidence of the morning. Five minutes. Maybe ten. But I had to get clean before I went anyway. The exhaustion I should have felt after running six miles, biking twenty-four, and swimming one that morning hadn't hit me yet—I was still reeling on adrenaline. Though my stomach was growling like a beast, demanding replenishment after hours without, I knew that if I tried to eat a thing, it would all come up. Nerves will kill you.

Hurry, Maggie. Go. The photographers, the tabloids, the news people—it was only starting to dawn on me what Lucas had already figured out when we left. That they all knew my name, so it would only be a matter of time before they figured out where I lived. Found out my story too. That I was a failed musician. The daughter of an alcoholic hairdresser. A bastard child without a known father. Frankly, I was surprised they weren't already here, knocking at the sliding glass door of the main house, or on the flimsy particleboard entrance of the outer shack I'd claimed as my own. I scrubbed frantically at my skin. If I didn't finish up, there would be naked pictures of me in every supermarket across the country within an hour.

"Maggie?"

Mama's voice was creaky, like she'd been shouting all night long, though I recognized it for what it was: battling the remnants of a hangover while she had come out in the rain to make sure I was all right.

I closed my eyes and scrubbed a little too hard at my hair. "What, Mama?"

"Linda called. She wanted to know if you got down all right. She told me all about what happened. Baby, I'm so sorry. What can I do—"

"Pack," I said abruptly, staring at the wet wood while the shower rained over my scalp.

"Pack?"

I finished rinsing, then yanked the curtain aside enough to see her. "You're going to have to go stay at Barb's for at least a few days, Mama, unless you'd like to have about twenty cameramen chasing you all over the property. And I have to get out of here."

Her tired face screwed up with confusion. "But I—"

"You saw the news?"

Reluctantly, she nodded.

I yanked the curtain back into place, not wanting to see the pity already blooming on her face. It was the same way the Forsters had all looked when I'd turned around in their kitchen. Poor Maggie. Poor sad, pathetic, duped Maggie.

"So you know, then," I said a little too sharply as I grabbed the soap and a loofa. "We called Calliope on the way here. She says the news broke early this morning. Everyone knows. The inn was absolutely swarmed with paparazzi and reporters, who will probably be here any minute. So we need to get off the property until things die down a little. Or at least until I can get out of town and make sure they'll leave you alone."

I shook my head. The idea of leaving all over again was terrifying. I really didn't know what I was going to do.

"All right," Mama was saying quietly. "All—all right. I'll go put some things in a suitcase."

"Mama?"

"Yes?"

"Lock the door and draw the shades. If they come…don't let them see you."

There was a long pause as I supposed what was happening really started to sink in.

"All right," she said again. "I'll wait for you up there."

Her footsteps faded into the rain, and I turned my face up to it, listening instead to the sound of it falling harder onto the lake water, cold water that complemented the hot cascading over my aching limbs.

I love you, he'd said to me earlier that morning. *Let's put the cards on the table.*

"Fucking *joke*!" I shouted, suddenly hurling the soap against the opposite wood shower wall with a terrific thwack. "Aaaaahhh!" I screamed again, letting the noise echo off the boulders and trees that shaded the property.

The sound was quickly swallowed by the downpour. It was the Fourth of July, one of the busiest days of the year, when families and weekenders basically took over the lake with speed boats and jet skis. Later on, when the storm passed and the sun was back, they would be out, and so I was betting, would the press. Who would also quickly realize it might be easier to approach this property from the water than by land.

But for now, Mother Nature was buying me some time. And I was grateful.

A massive clap of thunder sounded over the water. It was a little early in the season for a storm like this but they weren't unheard of in July. The combination of the hot air greeting the cold in the center of the sky. A violent meeting of opposites. The sky opened, and water flooded through the clouds, pounding through the trees, onto the lake, dock, and pine-soaked earth with the fury I felt inside.

Boom! The thunder sounded again, and in the distance, a cord of lightning lit up the sky. The wind was picking up now. The storm would blow through harsh and heavy, would be over in a matter of minutes, and then the skies would turn blue again. But the rage would be left behind, always threatening just below the idyllic surface.

That rage was just what I wanted.

I stayed like that for another full five minutes, letting the brief bout of thunder and lightning clap through me until even I felt foolish standing outside in the shower while an all-out storm howled around me. I grabbed the now soaked towel off the hook and wrapped it around my body before shutting off the shower and scampering across the lawn to the shack.

I stumbled into the hundred-and-fifty-square-foot space I currently called home, my footsteps squelching into the carpet as I moved around trying to find something to wear. I tossed half my wardrobe onto the threadbare carpet before finally settling on a pair of pajama shorts and a tank top. Everything else seemed suffocating. Like I could barely breathe.

Because it wasn't just learning that the person I'd trusted with my whole self, the person I'd given my heart to, had turned out to be a complete and total liar. It was also that just moments before, I could have sworn I'd seen the other man I'd once given myself to that way. The man who had taken everything from me that a man could take, including my body, against my will. The man who had made me a shadow of myself for years, whom my lawyer and I had finally vanquished to jail for his crimes. And though I hadn't seen him since, I could have sworn his face had been in the crowd of people waiting at the finish line. Angry. Vengeful. Theo.

Another clap of thunder sounded, and at the same time, there was a loud, thundering bang at the front door. I jumped about three feet, suddenly wishing I had just stayed in the main house with my mother and borrowed some of her clothes instead of coming out here. I wasn't safe here.

I grabbed a pillow and held it to my chest reflexively. There was another loud bang on the door.

"Lily!"

I froze. His deep voice practically blended with the thunder, but there was only one person in the world who called me that. And the last time I'd seen him, he'd been hightailing it through the woods as far away from me as he could get.

He'd promised not to run anymore. But then again, who was he to promise anything when he had done nothing but lie to me for weeks? When he had never even told me who he was in the first place?

This time, the flimsy door shook with each loud bang.

"Lily, I know you're in there! Open the goddamn door before I break it down!"

I swallowed heavily. I knew him. He would do it. I chucked the pillow onto the bed, crossed the room, and flung the door open.

Will stood in the rain, palms braced heavily on either side of the doorframe while water streamed down his face in twisting torrents. He still wore the same set of running clothes from before. Shorts, t-shirt, sneakers, plus a baseball cap over the mass of blond knotted at the base of his neck. All of it soaked through. Yet another clap of thunder sounded, and behind him, lightning flashed through the sky, but he didn't move, didn't even blink through the merciless pellets of rain. His green eyes drilled into me while he gasped through the water.

"Did you know?" he shouted through the storm, his voice hoarse, yet still demanding. He sounded like he'd run a marathon himself.

"What?" I shouted back. "Did I know *what*?"

"Did. You. Know?!" he cried out. "Who I was! Tell me, Maggie, I have a right to know. I have a right to know if the one person in this fucked-up, piece-of-shit, godforsaken world I finally learned to trust again sold me out to those vultures! Was it you who told them where I was? Who I am? *Did. You. Know?!*"

He was practically shrieking at this point, his face reddened and eyes bulging. He looked like a man straddling the line of sanity, like with one small push, he might topple to the other side, and there was no telling what he might do then.

But I couldn't focus on that. All I could feel was the pain punching holes through my poor, cut-up heart. The revelations of the morning had shoved the knife in deep, so deep I couldn't breathe. But this new accusation twisted it further. And oh, but I hated him for it.

"No!" I finally replied, having to shout myself to be heard over the rattle of raindrops pelting the roof. Another clap of thunder sounded, and the sky flashed white before turning a deep, nasty gray. "No, I didn't know!"

He relaxed, but only slightly. The hands on the doorframe still gripped it so tightly his knuckles were white.

"But, Will?"

Like we were in the middle of one of the cheesy movies he must have starred in at some point in his stupid career, the thunder quieted, and the rain lightened a bit. Not completely, but just enough for Will to raise his head, his green eyes searching. Enough where we could speak without shouting.

Suddenly even the lowest whisper seemed like it might be too loud. I felt like one word from him could knock me over.

How could one person feel so many warring things at once? I wanted to pull him to me, assure myself he was real. I wanted to shove him away and slap him across the face. I wanted to know the last four weeks weren't a dream. I wanted to know that *he* wasn't a dream a dream.

"What?" Will asked, his broken voice cutting through my confusion. He sounded wary. Unsure.

Well. At least we still had *that* in common.

"*I* didn't know," I repeated, keeping my warbling voice louder than necessary, surer than I felt. "But you did—*Will. You* did. And you never said a goddamn thing."

And then, before he could answer, I slammed the door shut on *Will* Baker. Because, in all truth, that man never existed.

All that was left was some stranger named Fitz, and I didn't want to know him at all.

To Be Continued...in Hollywood Chase.

**Read Hollywood Chase now: www.
nicolefrenchromance.com/hollywoodchase**

Be sure to sign up for Nicole's mailing list to **receive a FREE book** and get first alerts about Nicole's upcoming work: www.
nicolefrenchromance.com

ACKNOWLEDGMENTS

First up: To my family. My husband, who lets me call him The Dude even though he kind of hates it. Our kids, all three, who understand when I'm too lost in my world to answer their questions with less than a five-second delay. My aunt, Trish, who is in *no way* like her namesake in Discreet. My mom, who cheerleads me every step of the way. Family is everything, and I'm so grateful for mine.

Secondly, to my incredible editorial support team. My amazing alpha readers, Patricia and Danielle, who fell in love with Will immediately and urged me to meet my deadlines, reading as I wrote, chapter by chapter. You ladies are amazing. This book is for you. Also, to Shauna and Erika, who offered lovely beta notes on the finished manuscript, thank you. And, of course, to my editor, the ever-diligent Emily Hainsworth, whose eagle-eye and flexibility with my shifty schedule are both indispensable. Last (but not least), to Judy Zweifel, who catches ALL the tiny things that no one else notices.

Thirdly, to the author support network that convinces me daily that this grind is worth it. We all love to write. It's the selling of books that is hard. I would absolutely despise social media if it weren't for Jane

Anthony, Harloe Rae, Ava Alise, Kim Loraine, Maya Hughes, Jessica Wayne, and CL Stacey, among many others. You guys are always willing to let me complain, ask advice, send weird photos, and basically just demand your attention at all hours of the night. Thank you ALWAYS.

Last but not least, to my other ARC reviewers, reader group members, newsletter subscribers, and basically every reader who has been asking for this story since I dropped the first "Goldilocks" tidbit: Thank you. You are the lifeline to my work, it's absolutely reason for being. Your excitement to read feeds my desire to write more stories for you. I would not be able to do this at all if it were not for you.

ABOUT THE AUTHOR

Nicole French is a hopeless romantic, low-key fashion addict, and complete and total bookworm. When not writing fiction, she is hanging out with her family, playing soccer with the rest of the thirty-plus crowd in Seattle, or going on dates with her husband. In her spare time, she likes to go running or practice the piano, but never seems to do either one of these things as much as she should.

You can find me on all of the following social media and communication platforms:

- Email: nfrench@nicolefrenchromance.com
- Website: http://www.nicolefrenchromance.com/

ALSO BY NICOLE FRENCH

The Rose Gold Series

Months. I had been looking for Nina Astor for months.

Ever since she gave me one red-hot night and disappeared into the city.

The woman was a phantom, and I was obsessed.

Now she's back in my life, as real as ever.

And completely unattainable.

Because Nina Astor is beyond off-limits.

Daughter of a dynasty.

Cousin of New York's most notorious billionaire.

Married to the scum of the earth—the subject of my next investigation.

As a criminal prosecutor, I'm supposed to be on the right side of the law.

But when it comes to Nina Astor,

I'm a very bad man.

I'll do anything to claim this woman as my own.

And to save her from this monster, I'd sell my soul to the devil himself.

Truth be told…

Maybe I already have.

Start FREE: www.nicolefrenchromance.com/theotherman

The Spitfire Series

I had a plan.

Finish law school. Start a job. Stay away from men like Brandon Sterling. Cocky, overbearing, and richer than the earth, he thinks the world belongs to him, and that includes me.

Yeah, no. Think again.

It doesn't matter that his blue eyes look straight into my soul, or that his touch melts my icy reserve. It doesn't even matter that past all that swagger, there's a beautiful, damaged man who has so much to offer beyond private planes and jewelry boxes.

But I had a plan: no falling in love.

I just have to convince myself.

Start FREE: www.nicolefrenchromance.com/legallyyours

The Quicksilver Series

Eric de Vries.

Looks like millions.

Worth billions.

A body like the David with a mind to match.

Unfortunately for this wayward heir, to keep his money, he needs a wife. And of all the women in the world, he chooses me.

Too bad I've hated him for five years, since he took all my tears and tossed me away.

The guy slept his way through half of New England and discarded women like hotel toiletries. Been there. Done that.

Still...what would you do for twenty million dollars? Would you wear the dress? Fake a smile for the man who broke your heart? Or would you run far, far away?

Yeah, that's what I thought.

I'll see you at the church.

Read The Hate Vow here: www.nicolefrenchromance.com/thehatevow

The Bad Idea series

Repeat after me: stay away from the hot girl. The beautiful girl. The f**king ray of sunshine in the middle of your delivery route.

Layla Barros is everything I never knew I wanted. Everything I'll never have.

She's an innocent young student.

I'm a convicted felon.

She's rich girl from a nice family.

I've got nothing but a broken home.

But if I'm an addict, she's my drug. I can't stay away, even though I know I'll ruin her in the end.

She might be the girl of my dreams, but I was always a bad idea.

Read Bad Idea here: www.nicolefrenchromance.com/bad-idea

Keep reading for a taste of The Other Man and Legally Yours.

Printed in Great Britain
by Amazon

17453751R00180